Dragon Dojo Brotherhood

Reign of Dragons

Fate of Dragons

Blood of Dragons

Age of Dragons

Fall of Dragons

Death of Dragons

Queen of Dragons

A Legend Among Dragons

The Nighthelm Guardian Series

City of the Sleeping Gods

City of Fractured Souls

City of the Enchanted Queen

Demon Queen Saga

Princes of the Underworld

Wars of the Underworld

Blackbriar Academy

The Trials of Blackbriar Academy

The Shadows of Blackbriar Academy

The Hex of Blackbriar Academy

The Blood Oath of Blackbriar Academy

The Battle of Blackbriar Academy

Sentinel Saga

By Dahlia Leigh and Olivia Ash

The Shadow Shifter

STAY CONNECTED

Join the exclusive group where all the cool kids hang out… Olivia's secret club for cool ladies! Consider this your formal invitation to a world of hot guys, fun people, and your fellow book lovers. Olivia hangs out in this group all the time. She made the group specifically for readers like you to come together and share their lives and interests, especially regarding the hot guys from her novels.

Check it out! Everyone in there is amazing, and you'll fit right in.

https://www.facebook.com/groups/LilaJeanOliviaAsh/

Sign up for email alerts of new releases AND an exclusive bonus novella from the Nighthelm Guardian series, *City of the Rebel Runes*, the prequel to *City of Sleeping Gods* only available to subscribers.

https://wispvine.com/newsletter/olivia-ash-email-signup/

Enjoying the series? Awesome! Help others discover the Dragon Dojo Brotherhood by leaving a review at Amazon.

AGE OF DRAGONS

Book Four of the Dragon Dojo Brotherhood

OLIVIA ASH

BOOK DESCRIPTION

All my life, I was trained to be the perfect killer.

An assassin. A ghost in the night. The sort of phantom that gives grown men nightmares.

But the woman who raised me to hunt dragon shifters made a mistake, and that blunder left me marked. Magical.

Determined to undo all of this, Zurie is now at war.

With me.

My mentor won't stop until I'm dead, but we know each other too well. Moves. Tactics. Fears. Strengths. Weaknesses.

This will be a gruesome end for one of us—and I don't care if she's the best assassin in the world.

No one tries to kill me and survives.

Because I'm not the same little girl she trained to murder and steal from dragons.

I'm a warrior, something neither human nor dragon. There's more power brewing within me than even I realize, and it's about to break free.

Age of Dragons is a full-length novel with a badass heroine, a riveting storyline, and an alternative relationship dynamic. Get ready for a heart-pounding story filled with a dragon shifter romance unlike anything you've read before.

Buckle in for heart-pounding action, breathtaking magic, deadly assassins, four drop-dead gorgeous leading men, lots of toned muscles, **and most** importantly—a young woman's journey of justice, self-discovery, and freedom.

READ THE WHOLE SERIES

The Dragon Dojo Brotherhood: a riveting and addictive dragon shifter fantasy romance series.

Book 1: Reign of Dragons

Book 2: Fate of Dragons

Book 3: Blood of Dragons

Book 4: Age of Dragons

Publisher's Note: *The Dragon Dojo Brotherhood is an adult urban fantasy series with explicit scenes and is meant for mature readers who enjoy spellbinding stories with a few fan-your-face moments in their fantasy fiction.*

CONTENTS

IMPORTANT CHARACTERS & TERMS

CHARACTERS

Rory Quinn: a former Spectre and the current Dragon Vessel. Rory was raised as a brutal assassin by her mentor Zurie. After her first taste of freedom, Rory never wants to go back to the life Zurie forced upon her... even though she knows Zurie will never let her live in peace. Rory's newfound magic has developed a growing dragon within her, and even though her dragon keeps trying, she hasn't been able to shift yet. As the only human to ever grow a dragon, no one knows what kind of dragon she will be—or if she will ever shift at all.

Andrew Darrington (Drew): a fire dragon shifter. Drew is one of the heirs to the Darrington dragon family. With no real regard for rules or the law in general, Drew tends to know things he shouldn't and isn't fond of sharing that intel with just anyone. Though he originally intended to kidnap Rory and use her power for his own means, her tenacity and strength enchanted him. They have a pact: if he doesn't try to control her, she won't try to control him. Drew sees her as an equal in a world where he's stronger, smarter, and faster than nearly everyone else.

Tucker Chase: a weapons expert and former Knight. Tucker's a loveable goofball who treats every day like it's his last—because it very well might be. His father is William Chase, current General of the Knights anti-dragon terrorist organization. Tucker was originally assigned to hunt Rory down and turn her in to his father, but as he spent more time with her, she became the true family he'd never had. To protect her, Tucker fed his father false intel about her abilities. When the Knights found out, his father tried to drag him back and reprogram the insubordination out of him in a failed attempt that ultimately destroyed one of the Knights' primary fortresses. It's now unclear what the

General's stance on Tucker is, and whether or not the Knights have a kill-order out on him.

Levi Sloane: an ice dragon shifter and former Vaer soldier who went feral when his commander killed his very ill little sister. When he was feral, Rory saved him from a snare trap on the edge of the Vaer lands, and he has been by her side ever since. Feral dragons slowly lose touch with their human selves, but Rory helped bring him back from the brink. Though all dragons can communicate telepathically when they touch, Levi and Rory can also communicate this way in human form. He's still healing his relationship with his dragon after being feral for so long, so he hasn't tried to shift yet.

Jace Goodwin: a thunderbird dragon shifter and Master of the Fairfax Dragon Dojo. Jace grew up in high society and has the vast network to prove it. A warrior, he operates as the General of the Fairfax army—and his only soft spot is for Rory. His dragon marked her as its mate and will accept no substitute. Unfortunately, Rory and Jace butt heads more than they get along. If she dies, his dragon will go feral, so he has quite a bit at stake if one of Rory's many enemies comes after her.

Irena Quinn: Rory's sister and former heir to the Spectre organization. She betrayed Zurie when she discovered her former mentor wanted to sell Rory as an assassin-for-hire, which would mean they would never see each other again. A brutal fighter, Irena's only purpose in life is to keep her sister safe. A powerful bio-weapon created by the Vaer gave her strange super-strength and bright green eyes that are eerily similar to Kinsley Vaer. Irena might develop magic or even a dragon of her own, though no one knows for sure what Kinsley's experiments have done to her.

Zurie Bronwen: current leader of the Spectres and former mentor to Rory and Irena. Zurie is a brutal assassin and holds the title of the Ghost. Cold-hearted, calculating, and clever, Zurie considers both Rory and Irena as failed experiments—and she's determined to kill them both.

Diesel Richards: a former Knight turned Spectre. With Rory out of the picture and Irena excommunicated for her betrayal, Diesel will become the Ghost if Zurie dies. His incentive is to get rid of all three of them. He's helped Rory once and tried to kill her on other occasions, so Rory isn't sure what Diesel really wants or what game he's playing with her life.

Harper Fairfax: a thunderbird, the Boss of the Fairfax dragon family, and Jace's cousin. Harper is friendly and bubbly, full of life and joy, but Rory knows a fighter when she sees one. The young woman is smart and cunning. Rory is slowly opening up to the idea of having a friend, but she's also not sure of Harper's real intentions.

Guy Durand: an ice dragon and former second-in-command to Jace Goodwin at the dragon dojo. Guy has always wanted power. When he lost the challenge to Jace for control of the dojo, he joined the Vaer and gave over top-secret intel about Rory and the dojo itself. The last time he and Jace met, each man swore to kill the other.

Ian Rixer (deceased): a fire dragon, Kinsley Vaer's half-brother, and a master manipulator. Ian was smarmy, elitist, and arrogant. He was often referred to as honey-coated evil for his ability to speak so calmly and kindly, even while torturing his prey. He treated everything like a game, and playing that game with Rory cost him his life. He tried to control her and

Jace's magic with specially designed iron cuffs to block their power, but Rory's magic can't be contained. She destroyed the cuffs—and him.

Mason Greene (deceased): a fire dragon and sadistic Vaer lord tasked with dismantling the Spectre organization. Irena gave him access to their sensitive Spectre intel in exchange for giving her and Rory a fresh start, but he betrayed them both. His attempt to kill Rory backfired massively and ultimately cost him his life.

Kinsley Vaer: an ice dragon shifter and the Boss of the Vaer family. Her power and cruelty make most grown men tremble in fear. She's utterly ruthless, cruel, vindictive, and vengeful... the sort to kill the messenger just because she's angry. She's increasingly frustrated that Rory has slipped through her fingers so often, and she's giving her minions one more chance to come through before she gets directly involved.

Jett Darrington: a fire dragon, the Boss of the Darrington family, and Drew's father. He wants Rory for reasons not even Drew fully knows, but everyone's certain it can't be good. He disowned his son when Drew wouldn't hand Rory over, but he promised

Drew everything he could ever dream of—including ruling the Darrington family—if he betrays her.

Milo Darrington: a fire dragon, Drew's brother, and current heir to the Darrington family line purely because he's older than Drew. Not much of a fighter, but an excellent politician and master manipulator. He's been growing increasingly resentful of his younger brother's skill and charm.

Isaac Palarne: a fire dragon and the Boss of the Palarne family. A skilled warrior and empowering speaker, Isaac can rally almost anyone to his cause. He's a deeply noble man, but there's something unnerving about his eagerness to get Rory to come to the Palarne capital.

OTHER TERMS

The Dragon Gods: the origin of all dragon power. The three Dragon Gods are mostly just lore, nowadays. No one even remembers their names. But with the Dragon Vessel showing up in the world, everyone is beginning to wonder if perhaps they're a bit more than legend...

Dragon Vessel: According to legend, the Dragon Vessel is the one living creature powerful and worthy enough to possess the magic of the Dragon Gods. Rory Quinn was kicked into an ancient ceremony pit —the one Mason Greene didn't know was used to judge the worthiness of those who entered. With that ritual, Rory unknowingly brought the immense power of legend back to the world.

Castle Ashgrave: the legendary home of the dragon gods, said to be nothing more than ruin and myth. Drew believes he's found the location, but he's not yet sure.

Mate-bond: The connection only thunderbirds can share that connects two souls. The mate-bond is not finalized until the pair make love for the first time. Even before it's finalized, however, the mate-bond is powerful. The duo can vaguely feel each other's whereabouts and, if one should die, the other would go feral.

Spectres: a cruel and heartless organization that raises brutal assassins and hates dragonkind. The Spectres specialize in killing dragons and are known as some of the fiercest murderers on the planet, in part thanks to their highly advanced tech that no one else has yet to duplicate. They're a spider web network that spans the globe, all run by the Ghost. Often, Spectres are raised from birth within the organization and are never given the choice to join. Once a Spectre, always a Spectre—quitting comes with a death sentence.

Override Device: Spectre tech. Very frail and easy to break, it fits into USB ports and can grant access to sensitive files. Though imperfect and obscenely expensive to create, it *usually* works.

Voids: Spectre tech. Fired from a gun with special attachments, a void can force a camera to loop the last 10 seconds and allow for unseen access to secured locations.

The Knights: an international anti-dragon terrorist organization bent on eradicating dragons from the world. Run by General William Chase, they'll do anything and kill anyone it takes to further their mission. There are some rebel Knights organizations that think the current General is too soft, despite his brutal rampage against dragons and his willingness to kill his own family should the need arise.

Fire Dragons: the most common type of dragon shifter. Fire dragons breathe fire and smoke in their dragon forms. They're found in a wide array of colors.

Ice Dragons: uncommon dragons that can freeze others on contact and breathe icy blasts. Usually, ice dragons are white, pale blue, or royal blue. The only known black ice dragons belong to the Vaer family.

Thunderbirds: dragon shifters that glow in their dragon forms and possess the magic of electricity and lightning in both their dragon and human forms. They're the most feared dragons in the world, and also the rarest.

Seven Dragon Families: the seven dragon organizations that are run like the mob. Each family values different things, from wealth to power to adrenaline. Usually, a dragon is born into a dragon family and never leaves, but there are some who betray their family of origin for the promise of a better life.

Andusk Family: sun dragons who prefer warm climates, almost all of which are golden or orange fire dragons. They're notoriously vain, focused on beauty and being adored. Somewhat materialistic, the Andusk dragons hoard wealth and gems and exploit those in less favorable positions.

Bane Family: ambitious fire dragons who deal mainly in illegal activities. They view laws as guidelines that hold others back, while they aren't stupid enough to follow others' rules. They like to see what they can get away with and push the limits.

Darrington Family: the oldest and most powerful family. Darringtons are mostly fire dragons, and angering them is considered a death sentence. They're well situated financially, with a vast network of natural resources, governments, and businesses across the globe. They're notorious for thinking they're above the rules and can get away with anything... because they usually do.

Fairfax Family: a magical family known as the only one to have thunderbird dragons. They have innate magic and talent, but sometimes lack the drive it takes to use those abilities to obtain greater power. They prefer to think of life as a game, and the only winners are those who have fun. To the Fairfax dragons, adrenaline is more important than money, but protecting each other is most important of all.

Nabal Family: wealthy fire and ice dragons. Money and information are most important to the Nabal, and they have an eerie ability to get access to even the most secured intel. Calculating and cunning, the Nabal weigh every risk before taking any action.

Palarne Family: noble fire and ice dragons known for their honor and war skill. Ruled by their ancient dragon code of ethics, the Palarne family operate as a cohesive military unit. Their skills in war are unparalleled by any other family.

Vaer Family: a secretive family of fire and ice dragons, they're known to be behind many conspiracies and dirty dealings in the world. Some see them as brutal savages, but most fear them because they have no ethics or morals, even among themselves.

CHAPTER ONE

This is about *honor*.

I duck as Irena swings her staff at my face, the solid wooden handle missing my jaw by an inch. A gust of air hits my face instead. I roll out of reach as she slams the butt of the staff into the stone at my feet, where I stood moments before.

She's stronger, now, after Kinsley's bio-weapon screwed with her blood. To me, however, that only makes sparring with her more fun.

Irena watches me with those piercing green eyes that practically glow, and it's eerie how similar they look to Kinsley's. To the dragon shifter who has tried to kill me and destroy everything I love.

Several times.

As Irena circles me in the dojo's center courtyard,

she smirks. "You've gotten better, baby sister. Think you can duck my blows forever?"

"Oh, that's cute." I grin as I swing my staff over my head, aiming at her face. She ducks, and the wooden weapon dives through her thick black curls. "You don't know what you've gotten yourself into, Irena."

Oh, how I've *missed* this.

The sparring.

The banter.

The adrenaline.

"Kick her ass, babe!" Tucker shouts from the stairs nearby.

"You got it, honey." I grin at my goofy weapons expert, lazily spinning my staff as Irena and I circle each other once again.

"Thanks for the support, cheerleading squad," Irena says dryly with a fleeting glance at Tucker.

"You're fine," he mutters dismissively. "Besides, I have a clear bias, here."

I steal another peek at him. He lounges on the stairs, equal parts gorgeous muscle and devilish charm as he winks at me.

Beside him, my sweet Levi chuckles and bites into a chunk of bread. His brooding, ice blue eyes meet mine, and butterflies shoot through my chest as he smiles at me.

Drew sits a few steps higher than the two of them, his elbows on his knees as he leans forward, intently watching the match. Those brilliantly sharp eyes narrow, studying every movement Irena and I make.

Learning, probably. Seeing how Spectres move.

Well, *former* Spectres.

Jace is off running his dojo, though I suspect he will stop by before our match ends.

As Irena swings her staff once more at my face, I notice a small huddle of dojo soldiers against the far wall, arms crossed as they watch me and Irena spar.

I don't love having an audience, but Irena wanted to practice on the infamous black stone of the dragon dojo's courtyard. It's a different terrain than either of us is used to fighting on, what with the uneven tiles and unique texture of the ancient black rock, and she wants to learn every inch of this place.

Can't blame her. I did the same thing when I first got here.

Irena takes a cautious step back, a wry smile on her face as we circle each other. I spin my staff absently, the wood whistling as it breezes by my ear at break-neck speed.

I'm tense and ready to spring at a moment's notice. With my other hand raised for balance, I never take my eyes off of her.

Until, that is, I notice the soft glow of my skin in my periphery.

It's like a hiccup—sudden and violent—and just like that, I'm distracted. The soft outline of golden chains climbs up my arm as my sleeve slides up, and my playful grin fades.

I try to focus on Irena, on the match, but I hate that the glowing, magical chains are there.

Mainly because I have no idea what they mean, or if I'm stuck with them forever. Given the choice, I wouldn't have picked chains as my first tattoo, but I didn't have much in the way of choices when I was down in that ritual pit.

Down in the hole where Mason Greene left me to die.

Deep within my chest, my baby dragon stirs. She's growing stronger every day, brighter and more powerful with every moment, and I wonder if the chains have something to do with her.

With doing the impossible—for a human to not only grow a dragon, but *shift*.

"Pay *attention*!" Irena snaps.

Instantly, I'm yanked back into the present moment.

At the staff barreling toward my face.

Running purely on instinct, I launch backward and

flip through the air as the weapon passes inches above me. The hiss of the staff whizzing by reminds me of a construction truck racing down the highway, and I figure that would've left me dazed if it had hit.

I roll onto my feet, crouching as my staff slams against the ground to give me added support.

"I *was* paying attention," I lie.

Irena huffs impatiently. "I know that face. You were brooding over something."

On the stairs behind us, Drew just laughs.

I playfully glare at the dragon shifter who so often likes to make fun of the moments where I lose myself in deep thought. "Quiet, you."

He shakes his head, flashing that devilish grin of his.

That adorable asshole.

Irena attacks again, brutal and fierce, the staff sailing through the air like lightning. I block and parry, ducking out of the way always a mere second or two before she can hit me.

I grimace in frustration as I avoid blow after blow. This is a familiar technique, one she's used on me many times before.

She's trying to end the fight, and she wants to do it quickly.

There was a time not long ago when an attack like

this would always knock me down. Even before her freaky Vaer-powers, Irena was wickedly fast and deadly accurate. I could never, for the life of me, last very long.

But I'm faster, now, and I have brilliant magic of my own.

I duck a powerful blow and shove my staff into her gut. It hits. She doubles over, the wind knocked out of her. I move with the staff's momentum, spinning briefly before I attack once more.

She lifts her own staff seconds before I can take her down, and the ear-splitting crack of the weapons colliding echoes through the courtyard.

In a three-part attack, I knock her staff out of her hands and raise the butt of my staff to her throat. I pause, the end pressed against her jugular, and she stiffens on impulse at the silent demand for her to forfeit.

In a real battle, she would be as good as dead, struggling to breathe as I crushed her throat.

Irena groans and squeezes her eyes shut, chest and shoulders heaving as she tries to catch her breath.

I grin.

I won.

I won against *Irena*.

My dragon curls within me, both in victory and

delightful warning. Jace is nearby, and it wants me to get closer to him, to go share our victory with our mate.

Whoa, slow down girl, I chide my dragon. *He's not my mate yet.*

He would have to stop being a sexy jerk for more than five minutes to get a commitment like that out of me.

"You really are incredible." Irena grins, her words a little shaky as she tries to catch her breath. "I'm so impressed. Who trained you since, uh—" Her jaw tenses as she briefly looks around us. "You know."

Since Zurie.

Since Irena went into a coma.

Since all hell broke loose on us both.

"Jace," I admit with a nod back to the embassy. "He's not a bad teacher."

"Thanks for that glowing endorsement," Jace says dryly.

I tilt my head toward the stairs, and sure enough, he stands at the top with his arms crossed and a cocky smirk on his face. My heart skips beats as our eyes meet, and my dragon aches for him.

She's getting tired of waiting for us to complete our strange mate-bond. She chose him. His dragon chose me. The longer Jace and I butt heads, the more I suspect both dragons are getting highly impatient.

"Hey," I say simply.

His shoulders relax a little as he watches me, his eyes lingering a second too long. "Hey."

"Oh, get a room," Tucker says loudly.

Levi grins, but Drew's smile fades completely. He glares at the dojo master, his body practically radiating anger. Jace seems to notice, and the two have a brief glaring match.

Frustrated, I lean on my staff and shake my head in disappointment. For a time, I really thought they were getting along. Maybe, in some way, learning to hate each other less.

Guess I was wrong.

Irena nudges my arm and leans briefly toward me. "Meet me on the tower roof," she mutters under her breath, her lips barely moving as she speaks. "Ten minutes."

"So bossy," I whisper back.

She rolls her eyes and jogs off without another word, and I give her a few moments' head start since she seems to want this little meeting to be secret.

Levi jumps up and grabs the staff from me, his fingers gently trailing up my arm as he leans in. The moment his skin touches mine, our strange connection opens—the baffling link that lingers only between us, even when he's in human form.

You did great, he says through the magical connection, smiling at me.

I smile back, unable to rein in the burst of pride that flutters through me at the compliment. *Thanks.*

We'll have to spar sometime, too, he adds with a roguish wink. *I might be a little more fun to play with.*

I lift my eyebrow in surprise at his sex-charged playfulness, but Tucker interjects before I can answer.

The weapons expert wraps his hand around my waist and plants a big kiss on my cheek. "You guys are way more brutal than I expected."

I laugh. "I'll take that as a compliment."

"Duh," Tucker says with a playful shrug. "How did you think I meant it?"

Drew stands, shoulders squaring as Jace walks down the stairs toward us. The two of them glare darkly at each other as they pass. Bodies stiffen. Hands curl into fists. Eyes narrow.

It looks like they could start throwing punches at each other at any moment.

"What the hell has gotten into you two?" I ask, frowning at the newfound depths of their hatred for each other.

That seems to snap both men out of it. Drew shakes his head and looks silently away.

Jace runs a hand through his hair, grimacing. "Disagreements. Nothing new," he answers.

In unison, Levi, Tucker, and I all groan in frustration at the blatant lie.

The sudden instant-rage that makes them both bristle at the mere sight of each other *definitely* suggests these "disagreements" are new.

And, if I had to guess, it probably involves me. I seem to be their favorite topic to argue over.

This ought to be fun.

CHAPTER TWO

As I hoist myself onto the tower roof, a strong gust of wind whips at my hair. A late summer breeze carries the scent of grass and gunpowder, and I wonder if Tucker's managed to get into trouble in the five minutes it took me to get up here.

That man sure loves his guns—especially the ones he "borrows" from Jace.

Irena sits on the edge of the roof, staring out at the forest that surrounds the dojo, her dark hair dancing in the wind. As I sit beside her, she doesn't move. She doesn't even look over.

She just watches the sky.

"It's beautiful here," she admits.

I nod. "It really is."

A green dragon soars past, casting a wary eye at us

as he makes his rounds. He banks to the left, his powerful wings lazily flapping against the air as he coasts along the wind currents.

Irena groans. "But the *dragons*…"

"It is a dragon embassy, girl," I point out with a chuckle. "There be dragons."

She scoffs and lays on the roof tiles, eyes closed as she sucks in a steadying breath. "How are you not in a constant state of anxiety?"

"You didn't see me when I first got here." I point out with a laugh. "I barely slept. I was too busy breaking into Jace's command center and trying to swipe intel on where I could find you."

Irena sits upright, her brilliant green eyes staring at me intently. Eagerly. "Command center?"

"Irena, *no*," I chide, waggling my finger at her. "Bad assassin. *Bad*."

She rolls her eyes and lays back down, pouting.

"We don't have to sneak around anymore," I continue with a relaxed gesture at the brilliant dojo around us. "Jace basically gave me free rein. If we want to go somewhere, we just walk there. If we have questions, we just *ask*."

"This is so weird," Irena mumbles under her breath. "Excuse me, dragon master sir, can I have all your chatter on Spectre movements?"

I chuckle. "Might want to keep that name under wraps there, sis."

She shrugs. "You and I both know it's secure up here. No one can hear us. That's why you come up here."

"Yeah," I admit. "But it's better to be safe than sorry."

Irena doesn't answer, and when I peek over at her, her eyes are closed. With her hands behind her head, she looks utterly at home on a roof several hundred feet in the sky, and I wonder if that's what I looked like any time Jace or Drew met me up here.

Cool.

Calm.

In control.

I don't know how true it is, but it's a fun thought.

I lean back, resting my weight on my palms as I let my mind wander. It's a hell of a thing, letting my guard down, and the dojo is the only place I feel as though I can even consider doing it.

Irena has a point, though. Zurie's out for blood, and we're at the top of her hit-list. I killed the one man she could even hope to consider good enough to become her heir, and both Irena and I refused to accept the role.

We made a true enemy of our former mentor, and

there will be no redemption. There will be no negotiation or peace agreements, not with that woman.

The next time Zurie and I meet, one of us will die.

It will be *bloody.* With Zurie out for my head on a platter, I may as well accept that hell itself is after me.

Not to mention the Knights. I screwed up the General's one chance to brainwash his son into submission, and I don't regret that at *all.* If the General comes for Tucker again, I'll do a hell of a lot worse than blow up a building on him.

If he's even still alive, of course. A very large part of me hopes that cruel, vindictive man died in the rubble.

More than that, though, is the growing dissent in the anti-dragon communities. I'm pretty sure they all hate me at this point, even though I'm still technically human.

With both the Knights and the Spectres, there probably won't be any more requests to capture me. From now on, it'll be a kill order.

"You've really made a life for yourself," Irena says softly.

I tilt my head toward her, wondering where this is coming from. "What do you mean? I'm fairly certain the whole world wants me *dead,* Irena. How's that making a life for myself?"

She shrugs. "As much of a life as someone like us

can have, I mean." Irena pauses, her eyes opening even though she won't look at me. "A family."

Oh.

I smile.

She's right, of course.

My men. My team.

My family.

"You trust them?" Irena prods.

"With my life," I admit.

Irena softly whistles. "That's certainly saying something."

It really is. It took a lot for me to get to this point, and I never want to go back to the way things were.

"You missed a lot, Irena," I say softly. "When... you know..."

"The coma," she finishes for me. "I'm sorry I missed this. I'm sorry I wasn't there for you."

"It's not your fault."

"I'm glad you trust them, Rory, but I just... I *can't.*" She groans and rubs her eyes. "They're dragons."

I hesitate, staring at the lines in my palm as I carefully choose my next words. "So am I, Irena." I hesitate, trying to find the words. "In a way, I mean. I haven't shifted yet, but I'm the dragon vessel. I carry the magic of dragons in me, now. I have a *dragon* in me."

Her glowing eyes dart toward me, and for once, I

can't read her expression. Her face is calm. Emotion-less. But her eyes narrow, ever so slightly—like I said something wrong.

As she studies my face in the tense silence, I want to add what we're both thinking.

You're a dragon, too, Irena.

But we don't know that for sure, yet.

That's what this is really about. She doesn't know how to deal with this new world. This new reality. She and I were supposed to ride off into the sunset once the Vaer destroyed the Spectres, and then we would've been forever free.

But that's a pipe dream, now. It'll never, *ever* happen.

People like Irena—people like me—we can't be normal. We can't integrate with society or be content with the status quo.

We'll always want more.

Deep down, she knows that.

"That Levi fellow," Irena says casually. "He was feral, wasn't he?"

I nod.

"And you brought him back?"

"We did it together," I correct. "We—"

Irena laughs. "Oh, shove your modesty off the roof,

Rory. You love him, and you fought for him—same as you fought for me. You love all four of them."

"Love is a strong word." I look away, but I can't hide the sly smile on my face that confirms everything she just said.

My sister sits up, watching me intently. "Tell me about them."

"You're so damn *bossy*." I chuckle, rubbing my hands together absently as I stall for time. I don't really want to talk about this—feelings just aren't really my thing.

She shrugs and playfully gestures for me to get the hell on with it.

Ugh.

Fine.

At first, I don't say anything. I'm so protective of my men that my impulse is to simply remain silent. To not share a thing.

But Irena isn't asking me for a bit of giggly girl talk. She wants to know who they are—and if she can trust them, too.

"Levi is quiet," I begin. "He doesn't say anything unless it adds to the conversation. Serious, observant, always on guard. I don't think he sleeps," I add with a small smile. "I don't know how he does it, but he manages to sneak up on even me. The man has ridiculous stealth."

"Damn," Irena says, clearly impressed. "Noted."

I examine my nails, trying to find the words worthy of describing my ice dragon. "Levi makes me… I don't know. Feel. He pushes me to be a better person. He makes me feel safe. Untouchable. Protected."

Irena raises a skeptical eyebrow. "You're a Spectre. You *are* untouchable."

"I *was*," I correct, and after that, all I can do is shrug. "That's who he is. That's how he's changed me."

"Hmm." Irena sits upright and leans her elbows on her knees, her eyes slipping out of focus as she processes all of that. "What about Tucker? The Knight?"

"*Former* Knight," I correct her once again.

"Fine," she admits with an exaggerated wave of her hand. "Former Knight. Former Spectres. Former whatever."

"Charming. Funny. Horny as hell." I laugh. "Guns and weapons expert. There isn't a weapon on this planet he doesn't know how to operate."

"I assume that's the General's doing."

My smile falls at the mention of Tucker's brutal father. "Yeah. The General treated Tucker like an investment, not a person. Back when he and I first met, Tucker lied to them to protect me. Fed them false intel until they figured him out."

"He *lied* to the *General*?" Irena balks. "For *you*?"

I sarcastically huff, lifting one eyebrow as I study her baffled expression. "I'll have you know I'm quite a catch, dear sister of mine."

"That's not what I meant." Irena chuckles, studying her palms as she pauses to sift through this new information. "He risked his life for you. He risked *everything*."

"Several times," I agree. "He taught me how to trust, Irena. How to open up. He makes me laugh, relax, and take life less seriously. I just feel so—I don't know—happy and carefree around him." I pause, grinning. "He's also a *beast* in bed."

"Gah!" Irena covers her ears and laughs. "My innocent baby sister is having *sex*?"

I roll my eyes. "Oh, shut up."

"So this Drew character," Irena prods, gesturing for me to continue. "He's obviously a high-ranking official."

"Darrington heir," I correct. "Well, former. Jett says he can only lead if he turns me in."

The look of utter shock on Irena's face is almost funny, but all shreds of humor dissolve from her eyes.

Her pupils dilate, and I can almost detect a hint of panic.

"We have to get you out of here." Irena leans forward, tense and ready for war. "We have to find another—"

"He's safe," I say softly. Calmly.

"He's a *Darrington*—"

"He had his chance to turn me over," I admit, none too proud that he had the upper hand down there in the tunnels. "He had a moment where he could have gotten everything he ever wanted—money, prestige, fame, power. And he gave it all up." I pause. "For me."

As silence settles between us, I can only imagine what's going on in Irena's head. The doubts. The plans. She will probably want to have a little talk with Drew, and even then, I doubt she's going to trust him.

"Irena." My voice is quiet. Intense. "He's almost superhuman. Incredibly strong. A natural leader. I blasted him at point-blank range with my magic, and all he did was *wince*."

"And you *trust* him?"

"Completely," I admit, marveling a little at how far I've come. "He doesn't really do feelings, either. He isn't one for the touchy-feely mushy stuff, but he has put his life and reputation on the line again and again to keep me safe. Sometimes when I'm around him, I have to surrender and give up power, to compromise and not try to control every little thing. He's dominating, muscular, and commanding—and he is devoted to me entirely. He makes me feel…" I trail off, sucking in a deep breath as I debate how to finish that sentence. "*Powerful.*"

Irena sighs, jaw tensing as she stares out at the forest. "You're so forgiving. It's hard for me to see past what his family has done."

"Forgiving isn't a word I would've used to describe myself before I came here," I admit with a shrug. "But they've changed me, Irena. For the better, I think."

"And Jace?" She nods toward the courtyard. "This mate-bond thing you two have?"

I huff, not entirely sure where to start with him.

Jace.

The Dojo Master.

The controlling, commanding badass who is one of the only fighters I've ever met who can match me.

"He makes my dragon happy," I admit. "When I'm around him, it's like I'm home. I don't understand it." I groan. "I don't understand *him,* but I can say he's done more than his fair share to watch over me."

"But you're a *Spectre,*" Irena says again with an annoyed groan. "What does he think you are, a delicate flower in need of a vase?"

I shrug. "I can't deny what he and I have, Irena, but I don't know what's going to happen with us. He has all these female soldiers, so it's not a girls-can't-fight thing. He's just protective over me because of the mate-bond." I pause, frustrated. "Because of what it would mean if one of us died."

"Feral," Irena finishes for me, nodding. "I'm surprised you haven't tried locking *him* in a tower to keep *yourself* safe. He seems a little too willing to jump into the fray."

I laugh. "That's a *damn* good idea."

Irena chuckles. She opens her mouth to speak, but her bright green eyes dart toward the forest as the canopy rustles in the distance. Seconds later, a brilliant green dragon soars upward through the canopy, breaking through the branches as his stunning emerald wings spread open. With a powerful stroke, he barrels toward us.

I haven't seen this guy before. Even though I don't know all of Jace's soldiers, I don't like the direct path he's taking toward our roof.

Toward *us*.

Wary, I ball my hand into a fist and stand as the wind whips my hair across my face. He gets ever closer, and I call on the magic in my core should the need arise. White light dances across my skin, ready to fire at a moment's notice.

Irena, however, just groans in annoyance.

He banks around the tower as he nears, his sharp black eyes locked on her. With a charming wink, he banks toward the ocean and flies off.

That dragon never even *looked* at me.

"Well *that's* a nice change," I mutter, more to myself than my sister.

For a moment, I'm not sure what to make of what just happened. My eyes dart between Irena and the quickly disappearing shifter, a puzzled expression on my face.

Irena shakes her head. "He's been flirting with me ever since I got here."

Oh.

Oh!

"You found a boyfriend already?" I grin. "You hussy!"

She laughs and grabs my arm, yanking me back down so that I sit beside her. Once I'm settled again, she punches me in the arm.

"Ow," I say, cradling the impact site with an exaggerated flourish.

I totally deserved it, though.

"What's his name?" I ask with a nod toward the shifter.

"Eric." She watches him disappear into the misty ravine on the other side of the castle. "He's certainly… *persistent.*"

I watch her for a moment, noticing the way her gaze lingers after the dragon shifter, noticing the tension in her neck and shoulders as she subtly leans toward him.

Irena's fighting her attraction to this guy—hard— but I can see through the lies she's telling herself.

With a grin, I simply shake my head. "Poor man doesn't know what he's getting himself into."

"I know, right?" she says with a wry smile. "Poor fool."

CHAPTER THREE

As a full moon shines above me, I slip through the shadows of the forest. The occasional silvery ribbon of light filters through the canopy, but I sidestep each one.

I have no intention of being seen.

The darkness engulfs me as I move along the leaf-strewn paths through the woods. As I slide from shadow to shadow, from trunk to trunk, I have to confess I'm looking for trouble.

Well, for Levi, mainly.

I can't sleep, no matter how hard I try. Each time I close my eyes, my mind wanders to Zurie. To Kinsley. To the Bosses. To the General. To the Knights. To the dozens of organizations that are hunting me right this moment.

They all want something from me. Something I refuse to give.

I figure if I can't sleep, I can at least take Levi up on his offer to spar. A good match usually helps me burn off excess energy and get to sleep faster.

Of course, this is Levi I'm hunting, so finding him has been a chore in and of itself.

If I'm being honest, that's part of the fun.

Something in the air shifts, and my intuition pangs in warning before I can even consciously understand what the threat could be.

I pause, careful to keep to the shadows of a nearby tree, and I listen. At first, there's nothing but the soft howl of air through the leaves above me and the occasional peep of a frog nearby.

But the longer I pause and listen, the more prominent the sound of breathing becomes. It's steady and quiet, soft and still, but it's there.

I kneel to get my bearings, as well as an understanding of where the breathing might be coming from. As I scan the world around me, I eventually spot a silhouette on the edge of a cliff nearby. I pause, narrowing my eyes, trying to get a better view of it in the distance, and that's when I make out the familiar form of a man reclining against a tree trunk.

Levi.

I almost don't believe it. The thought that I could sneak up on Levi is practically impossible to consider, and I wonder if this is a game. If he's toying with me in some way.

If he is, I'll indulge him.

Carefully—as silent as the night around us—I steal through the forest toward him. I don't make a sound. I barely breathe. My entire focus is on him, on the form reclined against the tree.

As I get closer, the details of his face come slowly into view. The dark hair. The square jaw. The broad shoulders. The thick and muscled chest stretching against the fabric of his shirt.

But his eyes are closed.

Everything about this scenario strikes me as impossible, and I hesitate to consider what might really be happening. I still don't quite believe that he would take a nap beneath a tree, where he's exposed and vulnerable.

Even if he's comfortable here at the dojo—even if he feels like he can let his guard down around these dragons—I should never be able to get this close to him. I never have before. No matter how hard I tried, I could never get the leg up on him. He always knew I was coming.

Every. Time.

So either this is a trick, or he's unconscious and possibly hurt.

A flicker of worry snakes through my chest, and I suppress the impulse to crash through the woods to get to him more quickly. It's never a good idea to charge in to any situation, no matter the stakes.

Rule 42 of the Spectres—assess all risk first. Act second.

My eyes scan his shoulders, and they lifts with the gentle flow of his breath. His chest rises ever so slightly, and I can even hear the soft exhale of his powerful lungs. He's not in pain. His face isn't scrunched up in agony.

It truly seems as though he's just sleeping—even though I know it couldn't possibly be that simple.

All right.

I'll bite.

Time to see what kind of game my stoic ice dragon is playing.

Without so much as a whisper to give me away, I creep through the woods until I can kneel in front of him. With each step, my full and entire focus is trained on him. I pause now and then to scan the woods—a girl has to be aware of her surroundings, after all—but out here, tonight, it's just him, me, and the silence.

As my knees press into the dirt mere feet away

from his gorgeous and toned body, he doesn't flinch. There's not even a twitch in his eyebrow to suggest he knows I'm here.

For the briefest moment, I triumphantly wonder if I have truly somehow snuck up on Levi Sloane.

With him at my mercy like this, I wonder how I want to play with him. Kiss him on the nose, maybe, or playfully pull him into a headlock.

Equally romantic options, all things considered.

In the end, however, I decide to take it easy on him. If I was able to sneak up on my silent protector, something must be deeply bothering him. I don't want to make it worse.

Gently, I reach my hand toward his face to brush aside a lock of hair from over his eye.

Like a flash of lightning, he grabs my wrist before my fingers can so much as touch his face.

His eyes snap open, and he glares at me with murderous rage. The fire and fury in his gaze catches me off guard, and in that brief moment, I'm speechless.

Even though he's in human form, his eyes look almost feral.

This must be what it's like to face him as an enemy. That anger, that intent to kill—it's overpowering.

My training kicks in, and my immediate impulse is

to counter. To twist my wrist free, pin him, and diffuse the threat.

In the seconds that follow, however, his expression softens. I see a glimmer of recognition, and his features relax. He loosens his grip on my wrist and smiles.

"You shouldn't sneak up on people like that," he says.

I let out a slow breath to calm my nerves. "Now you know how it feels."

Grateful he's all right, I lean back on my heels. I figure he might need to talk before we spar, so I simply wait for him to speak.

He has other ideas.

With his hand still around my wrist, he gives me a soft tug and pulls me into his lap. I laugh and fall into him, letting him have his way with me as he holds me tight. He adjusts me, controlling every movement, and my back falls flush against his hard chest. He weaves his arms around my body, holding me close as he props his legs on either side of me. To tease him, I wiggle my ass just a little, grinding against his cock. He laughs and holds me tighter, pressing me against his hardening dick, teasing me right back.

So ruthless.

As we settle into this new position, he sighs happily

into my hair and kisses my ear. I keep expecting him to say something, to start the conversation and air out whatever was bothering him, but that's not his way.

He only speaks when he truly has something to say —but I can tell there's something boiling beneath the surface. Whatever is going on with him, he needs to get this out.

"What were you doing?" I ask.

He sighs, burrowing his face into my neck and pausing a moment before he answers. "Talking to my dragon."

"Ah," I say with a small nod. "I take it the conversation didn't go well?"

"You could say that," he says with a shrug. "We're still trying to make peace. There's still some fallout from being feral for so long. The connection isn't shattered anymore, but we still don't fully trust each other. It could break again if I'm not careful." He sighs, leaning his forehead against my hair. "Honestly, Rory, I'm not sure if I'll ever shift again."

"Don't say that," I chide softly. "Of course you will. You're a man that does the impossible, Levi. It's just how you operate."

He chuckles, taking a deep breath as he holds me a little tighter. It's weird to be cradled like this, to be held and comforted and soothed.

But I have to admit, I kind of like it.

For a while, we sit there in the silence, listening to the night and the wind, and it's a pleasure to simply enjoy each other's company. To enjoy the quiet. To not need to be anywhere or have anything expected of us.

Tenderly, Levi brushes his thumb across the back of my hand, his skin igniting shivers of delight and pleasure that run through the lengths of my arms and into my core.

Deep within me, my dragon stirs at his touch, responding to him, curling with delight and joy as he gently caresses me.

I close my eyes, reaching toward her, wondering what it will take for her to come out. For us to shift. For her to be more than just a baby dragon deep within me.

"How did you first shift? I ask Levi, shattering the silence.

"You don't want to hear that story," he answers simply. There's a hardness to his tone, a stiff formality I'm not used to hearing.

I crane my neck until I can see him, and he's staring off over the cliff. His eyes slip slowly out of focus as my question tugs on an old memory he's trying actively not to recall.

His eyes dart suddenly toward me, clear and

focused on my face, and he smirks. "You're going to make me tell you anyway, aren't you?"

In the past, I would have said yes. The old me would have been relentless. I would've prodded and poked until I got my answer, but I know Levi better, now, and I would never want to cause him pain.

"No," I say simply. "It's okay."

His smile broadens, and he tenderly kisses my cheek. "You want to shift, and you want to know how it happens the first time. I understand. If you want to hear this story, I'll tell you."

"Your call," I say, shrugging.

It's weird—giving up a bit of power. To not press for information that would benefit me. It goes against all my Spectre training, goes against everything Zurie ever taught me about life and self-preservation.

But this is a new life, and I've changed.

I like to think it's for the better.

"I don't want pity," he says. "But this isn't a pretty story. The Vaer are cruel and heartless," he adds, his shoulders stiffening as he holds me ever so subtly tighter.

I rub my thumb across his knuckles to comfort him, letting the silence be my answer.

"I used to train with my commander every day for six hours," Levi says, setting his forehead once again against the back of my skull. His warm touch shoots ribbons of comfort and delight through me, and I impulsively lean into him as he continues. "My commander never told me what the training sessions were for, or what the goal was, or what he was trying to accomplish. I was only eight, and I didn't understand why he was pushing me so hard. Breaking my bones and asking me to do the impossible." Levi gritted his teeth, his jaw flexing as he lost himself in the memory. "Looking back, it's obvious. He was trying to get me to shift as early as possible, trying to push me to tap my dragon and do more than I should have been able to do for that age. And when I didn't shift fast enough, one day he pushed me to the absolute brink. It wasn't a sparring session. It was an attack, a full-on brutal, near-death experience." Without moving the rest of his body, Levi grabs my waist tightly, his fingers pressing hard against my skin for comfort. "He forced my first shift because at that point, my choices were to shift or die."

For a moment, I don't know what to say.

Grown men don't treat kids that way. They shouldn't try to break a child, much less bruise and shatter his soul.

But the Vaer operate differently than the rest of the world, with unusual morals and ethics.

And by *unusual*, I mean next to none.

I want to say so much. I want to apologize for the cruelty he experienced in his life, for the brutality and for the hate he should have never seen.

But everything that comes to mind feels empty. Hollow. Like nothing but words.

With my hand on his, I open our connection—the strange line we have between each other even in human form. A tangled web of emotions bleed through the open channel, and I can feel him trying to rein them in out of either shame or a desire to save me from them.

Instead of saying a thing, however, I just listen. I open up to him completely, and I feel his pain. I feel the horrors he has been through. I share them, letting him know he's not alone—and never will be again.

We sit there in silence, feeling and being, simply sitting with the grief.

Levi breaks our connection, lifting his hand to grab my waist. Effortlessly, he turns me around to face him, spreading my legs on either side of his as he sets me on his lap. I lean my forearms against his solid chest, leaning in to him as his eyes wander across my face.

After a moment more of silence, Levi winds his arms around me and holds me tightly to his chest.

"It's not fair, Levi," I say quietly. "You've had such a

hard life that it seems almost impossible that you turned out as good as you are."

He laughs and runs his hand through my hair, leaning back slightly so that he can see my face. "That's a kind thing to say, Rory."

"Well, it's the truth."

It gives me hope. It makes me think there might be more like him, other Vaer dragons who aren't evil, who aren't merciless, who aren't cruel and brutal at all. Other Vaer who are just good people forced to do vile things.

My dragon stirs, aching for more of this man, and I'm not about to deny her the pleasure.

Without giving it any further thought, I lift my chin and kiss him deeply. Flurries of delight snake through me as his warm mouth moves against mine. His hands hold me tightly, like I'm a precious thing he fears losing, and he tenderly cradles the back of my head.

His touch is both strong and tender, like he's almost afraid I'm not real.

Through the kiss, our connection opens once again. The surge of emotions flooding from him into me are almost more than I can handle.

Devotion.

Gratitude.

Love.

I gasp as the emotion burns through me, hot and fierce, dedicated and unyielding. I break the kiss to catch my breath, a little dazed as I try to get my bearings once again.

Everything with Levi is so intense, so full and fierce and completely *wild*, that sometimes I can't handle it.

His icy blue eyes study me, waiting for me to say something. No doubt wanting to know what I'll do next.

Hell, even I don't know.

To escape his intense gaze, my eyes trail down his torso, past the tight pecs straining against his shirt. I run my fingers along his hard chest and down his abdomen. A long, thick line runs underneath my fingertips, and I pause.

The scar.

It seems like ages ago that I met him in the forest and saved him from the snare. Even back then, there was this huge scar across his abdomen, but he never told me how he got it.

"Kinsley," Levi answers as my fingers hover over the wound. He didn't have to read my mind to know what I was thinking.

"What's she like?" I ask, not entirely sure I want to know.

Levi shrugs. "I never knew her personally. I just had that one fight with her when she came to end me —the feral dragon who killed her lover." He scoffs and shakes his head. "She's brutal, Rory. Absolutely merciless. She doesn't tolerate surrender, and she doesn't show pity. The only reason I survived is because she knocked me off a waterfall. I'm pretty sure she thought the drop into the sharp rocks killed me—and they nearly did."

I tense at the thought of the Vaer Boss fighting Levi, of her digging her claws across his abdomen and ripping him open. Of her tossing him off a cliff and leaving him for dead.

It makes me hate her all the more.

Eventually, I know it will come to a head between me and her, and I won't leave her to die. I won't assume, and I won't make mistakes.

When the time comes—as I'm increasingly sure it will—I will watch the light fade from her eyes.

Kinsley Vaer won't survive *me*.

The strained grunts of two people fighting catch my attention, and I sit upright on instinct as I listen closely to it. My ears strain in the silent night, trying to catch another hint of the fight.

For a moment, I can't hear anything, and I look at Levi quizzically. He frowns, eyes narrowing in focus. His ear twitches as he, too, listens for the noise again.

There, in the distance—the clear thud of knuckles breaking over skin.

Urgent and silent, we stand and steal through the night toward the confrontation. As we stalk through the shadows, it takes everything in me not to let myself simply watch Levi move.

He's distractingly stunning as he steals through the darkness.

His striking eyes narrow, clear and focused on the world ahead of him. His muscles flex, his body crouched and coiled. Every motion, every step, every breath is concentrated and alert.

No wonder he can sneak up on even me. It's almost like he becomes one with the shadows, one with the darkness and silence.

It's hypnotizing.

The smack of skin hitting skin and the grunts of pain that follow get louder as we near the confrontation.

Before long, we come to a clearing in the woods. Through the trees, two figures duck and weave, nothing but silhouettes darting through the silvery beams of moonlight at breakneck speed.

It's not until I kneel beside the nearest trunk and lean around it to get a better view that I recognize one of them.

Irena.

Her bright green eyes briefly sweep the forest as she circles a handsome man about our age. His dark eyes are narrowed with focus and intention, his hands raised as he waits for her to attack again.

But Irena's no fool. She frowns, scanning his body. Her gaze lands on his left shoulder, and I figure she's trying to guess what he will do next.

Rips and tears in her clothes reveal the flurry of cuts across her body, the blood hidden by the dark colors of the shirt and loose pants the dojo gave her.

Beside me, Levi stiffens and takes a step toward the clearing, probably to interject. To stop this before it gets truly ugly.

I set a hand across his chest and silently shake my head.

He catches my eye, frowning—but I know what this is.

I run my fingers along his forearm, opening our connection so that we can speak unheard.

They're sparring, I tell him.

He quietly scoffs, scanning the two fighters that circle each other in the clearing. Blood drips down

Irena's fingers from a gash in her bicep, and the skin along the man's neck is black and blue. *That's one hell of a brutal sparring match, Rory.*

Well, yeah, I say with a shrug. *It's an audition.*

Levi quirks one eyebrow in surprise, his grip on my hand tightening slightly. *An audition?*

Most Spectres do this, I confess with a nod, even though it was never my thing. *She wants to know if this guy can handle her. Irena only dates men who can at least match her skill.*

Levi smirks as a flurry of emotion snakes through our connection—equal parts astonishment and respect. The connection dissolves as he leans his elbow on his knee, watching the two fighters go at it.

"I could just shift and fly off with you, you know," the guy says, smirking as he rolls out his shoulders, ready for her next blow. "Maybe drop you a few times to knock some sense into you."

Irena laughs. "Try me, Eric."

Eric grins and charges her, grabbing her arm and flipping her over his back. Irena's faster, however, and she hooks her arm under his. With a soft grunt of effort, she uses his own momentum against him as she throws him onto the ground. He hits the dirt with a hard smack, groaning briefly in pain and surprise.

Beside me, Levi winces.

That's got to hurt.

Hell, I *know* it does. I've been there before, sparring with my ruthless sister in the ring, and I don't envy that man at all.

But if he wants Irena, he needs to be able to handle her.

Irena is going to notice me sooner or later, so I decide to cut to the chase and make myself known. I step into the clearing and lean against a tree, crossing my arms as I watch them fight.

Irena's gaze darts instantly toward me, and she just rolls her eyes.

Eric, however, grins. "Come to watch the show?"

"Something like that," I answer.

Irena sighs and lowers her hands, relaxing her shoulders as she steps back from the fight. "No, I think we're done."

"Oh, don't let me kill your fun," I say, grinning.

"You're not," Irena says with a smug glance toward the stranger. "I've got all the information I need."

"So," Eric asks with a playful smirk. "How did I do?"

Irena shrugs. "I've seen worse."

With that, and nothing else, she walks off into the woods.

The shifter frowns, tilting his head toward me with

a quizzical expression on his face, clearly asking me to decipher that for him.

I grin. "You passed."

He smiles, practically beaming as he jogs off after Irena. He puts his arm around her shoulders, and just to be difficult, Irena counters. She grabs his wrist and twists it, bending his arm behind his back.

Eric, however, seems to expect her to put up a bit of a fight. Without so much as a moment's hesitation, he twists in her grip and breaks free, only to put his arm around her shoulder yet again. Exasperated, she allows it this time.

I chuckle. It seems as though Irena has finally met her match.

Just as Eric did with Irena, Levi puts his arm around my shoulders. I, however, lean toward him, setting my head on his shoulder as I smile. Irena is going to fight it, but I can already tell that she's found someone worth keeping.

It's about damn time.

CHAPTER FOUR

The next morning, I take a deep breath as sweat rolls down my back.

Today is beautiful—the kind of day where you need to stay outside and soak up the sun, to enjoy the breeze and the fresh air and do nothing but relax.

But I can't remember the last time I relaxed.

Jace attacks me with a broadsword, the blade coming down over my head. In my life as a Spectre, I wouldn't have even been able to lift a sword that big—but now, my body is enhanced with the power and strength of *dragons*.

I lift my own broadsword just in time to hear the clang of metal as the two collide.

Even with my enhanced strength, he's a force to be reckoned with. As I grit my teeth to fight his blade from coming down on my head, I slowly begin to lose ground. The edge of his blade looms nearer as his jaw tenses from the strain of our battle, and I know I can't hold this for long.

I have no choice but to roll out of the way.

With a grunt of effort, I twist my sword and let his blade slide off. The razor-sharp steel digs into the dirt by my foot with a heavy thud.

Quick to regain the upper hand, I dart out of the way and put distance between me and the dojo master my dragon has chosen as her mate.

I regain my footing and stand, the two of us slowly circling as we glare at each other, each trying to figure out what the other's next move will be. The canopy above us sways, the treetops bending in a gentle breeze, but I don't give myself the luxury of focusing on the world around me. I pay only enough attention to the forest around us to listen in case someone unwelcome decides to join in our match.

Sparring with Jace takes my full and undivided attention.

He attacks again, the blade swirling almost too fast to see, but I'm just a hair faster. I duck out of the way, rolling again as I give myself a bit of distance. He doesn't even pause to breathe. He swings his sword behind him, nearly catching me off guard, and I'm barely able to block the blow in time.

The clang of steel echoes through the forest as our blades meet again.

There's something different about today. Usually when we spar, he's focused and attentive, so that part isn't new.

It's the grim expression on his face right now that startles me—the way his eyes narrow, as if he needs to make sure I understand something. As if he's trying to teach me a lesson that he hasn't yet put into words. One that could save my life, if only he can impress the importance of it.

He's hiding something.

"Rory, *focus*," he chides.

What the hell does he *think* I'm doing?

Jace attacks yet again, never one to give me space or a moment to breathe, but this time I'm ready. I duck under the blow and ram my shoulder into his chest, knocking him backward and onto his ass. He lets out a huff of air, a little groan as he hits the ground *hard*. The muscled thunderbird pauses for a moment to regain his composure, his face scrunched in pain.

"That was good," he admits through clenched teeth.

I chuckle. "How's that for *focus*, Sensei?"

He doesn't laugh. Normally, he would, and that just seals it for me—something is definitely wrong.

Instead, he stands and twirls his sword, eyes roving my body as he searches for a weak point to attack. Despite being knocked on his ass a moment ago, he's already preparing his next assault.

I frown, my grip tightening on the hilt of my blade as I slowly circle him, trying to buy time to catch my breath. "What's going on with you, Jace?"

"Nothing," he says, his eyes focused on my shoulders—no doubt in an effort to predict my next move.

The shoulders always give it away.

"Liar," I say, calling him out.

I know him by now. He's worried. I don't know what he's worried *about*, though. Whatever it is, he wants to make sure I'm ready for it.

It would seem as though Jace is, yet again, hiding things from me.

The man never freaking *learns*.

This time, I attack first, mostly out of anger and frustration. He's ready, parrying instantly. Like lightning and thunder, we land blow after blow. For several minutes, we simply dance a deadly waltz of steel and sparks.

I have a couple of choices here.

Either I can ignore him and let him come to me

when he's ready to talk, or I can prod him and force the information out of him through sheer, stubborn tenacity.

Option two sounds like more fun.

"I know something's wrong," I press as I duck his blade. The steel cuts through the air above me and nearly slices off a lock of my hair. "You may as well tell me what it is."

"I don't know what you're talking about," he lies.

As I bring my sword down over his head with a furious growl, he blocks it. His biceps flex, bulging with the effort of his attack. The clang of clashing metal reverberates up my blade and into my arms, ringing clear to my teeth.

I step away, shaking out my hands as I take a moment to recover from the blow. "If you won't tell me what it is, maybe I'll have to take a peek through your secured files."

He scoffs. "You don't even know where they are."

"Don't I?" I smirk.

I don't.

It's totally a bluff, but he doesn't need to know that.

"I've been playing nice," I say, still smirking. "We had our truce, and I've been honoring it. But if you're hiding stuff from me, well..."

I trail off, letting him fill in the blanks and hopefully take the bait.

He doesn't.

Instead of answering, he swings his blade furiously at my face. I duck, my sword catching his, and the momentum of our blades hitting throws me off balance. I lean in, twisting my heel into the dirt, but it's not enough to keep my footing.

He circles me as I fall backward, his body a blur in my periphery. I expect to fall to the ground. To hit the dirt hard, to look up and find him smirking down at me.

Instead, I fall against his hard chest as he catches me. Our swords lock, the hilt of his intertwined with mine.

I'm instantly pinned.

Damn it.

In the past, he would have knocked me on my ass, held the sword blade to my throat and declared himself the winner of our little match. But for whatever reason, we simply stand there. I crane my neck to see what he's up to, to try to figure out what he's doing, and those stormy eyes of his snare me.

Just like that, I'm lost—in him.

My mind goes fuzzy, and inwardly, my treasonous body aches to be somehow closer. I instinctively lean into him, and his powerful arms subtly tighten around me. It's a possessive motion, more than anything else —a silent way of saying, *mine.*

I debate wriggling out of his grip, but I'm curious. He doesn't usually pause in a sparring match. It's not his style. His style is brutal and fierce. Forceful. He doesn't hesitate, and he never gives his opponent a chance to catch their breath or recover.

With a deep sigh, he buries his face in my neck. His sword drops to the ground, and his muscled arms engulf me. He holds me tightly to his chest, my back to his body as he holds me tenderly in place.

"Fine," he says quietly.

His touch is electric. It burns through me like lightning, like desire and joy, and I impulsively wrap my fingers around his wrists as my body reacts to his presence. Our connection only bristles with more power as I quietly give in, the fiery sensation of our magic bubbling beneath my fingertips.

Deep within me, my dragon reaches for him, *aching* for him, somehow needing to be even closer to him than this.

"You have fourteen active bounties on your head," he says quietly. "Three of those were added just this morning, and those are just the ones that want you dead." He presses his jaw against my ear, roughly sucking in a deep breath as if he's trying to calm himself. "Nine more bounties placed in the last few weeks want you brought in alive."

My chest tightens, and for a moment, I can't breathe. Throughout my life, I've had a bounty on me here or there—but nearly two dozen, all at once?

"Hit squads have been after you since you arrived here," he continues. "I've intercepted all of them, but they're becoming more frequent. Every time a hit comes, they bring more men. They're getting brazen. Desperate, even."

I elbow him hard in the stomach and wriggle out of his grip as he chuckles in surprise, holding his stomach where I hit him.

"Jace, why didn't you tell me?" I snap. "This has been going on from the *beginning*? I thought we had a deal!"

He gestures vaguely to the forest around us. "What good would it do? You needed to focus on your training and not be distracted. Besides, I'm protecting you. You're fine."

I grimace in annoyance. "I'm not some stupid kid! I need to know things like who wants to *kill* me, Jace!"

He groans in aggravation, like I'm being entirely unreasonable.

Me. For wanting to know who's trying to off me.

I shake my head, stabbing the blade of my sword into the dirt as I process what he's saying. "Even after everything we've been through, you don't see me as an equal. I'm just something that needs constant safeguarding."

"That's not true," he says quietly.

I wait. I want him to continue. I want him to finish that sentence.

But he doesn't.

I cross my arms, pacing the small clearing we'd been sparring in as I try to reconcile what he's saying with what he's done. His actions and his words don't match.

And I'm running out of patience.

I *want* him on my team. I *want* to trust him. I want this back and forth of ours to end. But he is so goddamn stubborn.

He doesn't see my strength at all.

Jace slowly closes the gap between us, and I'm tempted to simply walk away. To be done with this conversation and with him, at least until I can think about it all without this simmering anger in my chest.

But I let him get close.

I let him take my hand.

I let him pull me near, and I let him set his forehead against mine. As our skin touches, the electrifying connection we share coils through me once again, and a little bit more of my anger fades away.

It's like he knows what he does to me, and I freaking *hate* that.

I try to hold on to my rage and remind myself of why I'm furious, of why this isn't okay. But I can't.

"I want to," he says quietly, his hands holding either side of my face.

His tone is intimate and soft, unlike I've ever heard it before. With the tender undercurrent in his voice, I'm speechless. I simply watch his face, waiting for more.

Waiting to understand.

"I want to let go of this," he confesses, his eyes darting back and forth between mine. "To give in to you, to tell you everything. But every bit of my training says I can't. Every time I tell you something, know that I had to fight my very nature to do it. Every time I tell you something that could put you in danger, it violates my dragon's need to protect its mate. To protect you."

He swallows hard, his eyes squeezing shut like he's being tortured. "I want you so badly," he says, practically growling with lust. "To give you everything you desire. I just don't know *how*."

"All I want is your trust," I say quietly. "To be seen as your equal."

He opens his eyes, staring into mine with an intensity that I've never seen on his face. It's like he wants to tell me everything, like he wants to let his inner world pour out of him and into me.

He opens his mouth to speak, but the crash of footsteps interrupts us.

We both flinch, turning our heads toward the sound even though they're still a long way off. Whoever it is, they're running toward us quickly, and they'll be here soon.

"Jace—" I start to say.

He shakes his head. "We'll continue this conversation later."

I frown, rolling my eyes. Of course.

A soldier crashes into the clearing, his chest heaving as he tries to catch his breath. "Sir," he says breathlessly, "Harper is on the way, along with—."

"Already?" Jace cusses under his breath, interrupting the soldier before he can finish.

I frown, confused by his tone. He had clearly been expecting them, but that wasn't as surprising as the subtle hint of anxiety that laced his words. Whatever they were going to discuss, he wanted to put it off a little longer.

"What are they here to talk about?" I ask.

He hesitates, his gaze settling on me as if he's debating answering the question.

In the end, he apparently decides not to.

"We'll continue our training tomorrow, Rory," he says with a shake of his head.

With that, he jogs after the soldier toward the dojo.

Sighing in annoyance and frustration, I grab our swords off the ground. Before long, I can't even hear their footsteps anymore, and all I can feel is the faint tug on my navel as he moves through the woods, our connection hot and burning as I sense him move farther away.

There's a shift in the air, like I'm not alone anymore. Carefully, I tilt my head so that I can see behind me—only to find Drew leaning against a tree trunk nearby.

Huh. He managed to sneak up on me—I must be more distracted than I realized. Not good.

The fire dragon's arms are crossed, one leg propped against the tree, and he leans back against the trunk with a smirk. "What were you two talking about?"

I debate telling him, but I figure messing with him is more fun. "I have secrets, too, you know."

He chuckles, running a hand through his hair as he rolls his eyes. "Fine. Be difficult."

"I will, thank you."

"Are you going to follow him?"

"Duh," I say with a grin, returning my attention to the path the dojo master had taken. "It's like you don't know me at all, Drew."

CHAPTER FIVE

Drew and I steal through the dark tunnels beneath the dojo, the only light coming from the occasional lone bulb hanging from the ceiling. We slip through the shadows, silent as ghosts.

The fact is I don't know how far my access will get me, or if I can even eavesdrop on Jace's conversation with Harper at all. Jace gave me the codes to these tunnels as a sign of peace. It was a truce, an act of goodwill to make me feel more at home here.

But he said himself that even my access had limits. I haven't yet had a chance to fully test my newfound freedom through the dojo.

Time to see what I can get away with after all.

The path splits, and both of the new paths lead downward. I hesitate, my eyes darting between the two, uncertain of which to take. The way these tunnels are designed seems to be intentionally confusing, like an orchestrated attempt to sink you deeper through the maze and get lost in the labyrinth.

I, however, have a secret weapon.

"Drew, which way?" I ask.

He stands beside me, his thick and muscled body towering over me as he gets his bearings. His eyes narrow ever so slightly as he looks in each direction, studying each path.

For a moment, he doesn't say anything. He simply stands there, thinking, and I give him the space that he needs.

"Left," he finally says. "I'm pretty sure."

"Pretty sure will have to be good enough." I run my hand along his arm in thanks. As my fingers graze his skin, a fiery current shoots through me, one of lust and desire.

But most of all, *gratitude*.

Out of the corner of my eye, he smirks. It's brief, but happy. His gaze lingers on me for a moment, and I pretend I don't notice as I lead the way into the darkness.

As we continue to steal through the shadows, I wonder what this could possibly be about—this meeting between Jace and Harper. The way his expression shifted in the forest struck me as so odd. Like he knew this was coming and still wanted to avoid it.

I have the sinking feeling it's about me.

We pause at a corner in the tunnel, and I carefully peek around the edge only to find a steel door barring any further movement through the passageway. A camera in the corner monitors the hall, and I freeze at the prospect of getting caught. It's an instinctive hit of adrenaline stemming from my years as a Spectre— when getting caught meant death.

Thankfully, the stakes aren't quite as high this time.

Grateful for the stealth training, my mind buzzes with ideas on how we can avoid detection. But after a moment, I notice a small, silver device implanted in the wiring on the camera, and that's when I realize there's no red light.

That's one of my voids.

Without a word, I shoot an accusing glare at Drew because I know exactly who put it there.

He grins sheepishly. "Thanks for letting me borrow one, I guess?"

I shake my head in exasperation. "You've been down here before, then?"

"Of course, I have," he says with a mischievous grin. "But I can never get past that door."

"Why not?"

"No code I ever had let me through." He shrugs, shaking his head. "Any time I tried, it alerted some-body. I nearly got caught about half a dozen times."

"You're getting rusty then," I say with a smirk.

He chuckles. "Well, let's see you get through it."

"Maybe I can."

Since the camera is taken care of, I step into the hallway, knowing no one can see me as the last ten recorded seconds of the camera feed loop indefinitely.

I walk up to the steel door, gently running my fingers along the cold metal as I eye the pad in the corner. I hesitate, almost not wanting to know if Jace gave me access to this area or not.

If he didn't give me access down here, it means he doesn't trust me. It means he doesn't want me to truly move through this place like it's a home.

Part of me doesn't want to know the truth, but I can't live in denial.

Not with him.

I take a soft breath and hold it, tapping the keypad and entering the code he originally gave me.

The day we met.

The one sentimental thing I've ever seen him do.

My finger hovers over the submit key, but I need to do this.

I hit it.

The door rumbles to life, swinging open and letting us through.

I grin, simply watching in awe for a moment, grateful and amazed. Dazed and a little disbelieving.

Maybe Jace is coming around after all.

Drew pats me on the back as he passes into the new hallway with an excited expression on his face, like a kid at Christmas. "Good job, Rory."

"Oh, yes, thank you," I say with a sarcastic nod as I walk through. "Entering the keys into the keypad was a very difficult task, after all. It's nice that my contribution is being acknowledged."

He laughs.

"Drew," I add, crossing my arms as I point toward the camera. "Aren't you forgetting something?"

The fire dragon pauses in the hallway, his gaze drifting from me to the camera and back. "You're really going to ask me to remove the void?"

"You promised," I remind him.

Any vulnerabilities in the dojo's security compromises us all.

He knows that.

He just doesn't like having to follow the rules.

Grumbling to himself, he rolls out the shoulders,

and I can practically hear the gears turning in his head as he tries to weasel out of this.

"Fine," he mumbles, reaching up to pluck the little silver device from the wiring.

I grin.

So grumpy.

He pockets the device in a motion so smooth I wonder if he thinks I didn't notice—but honestly, I don't care if he has the voids, especially a spent one.

Time to find Jace.

My first impulse is to scope for cameras as we walk through the doors, and thankfully, there's none in this stretch of the hallway. It's something we're going to have to be careful of, though. I get the feeling we're not supposed to be down here.

Well, I am. Drew's not. And technically, Jace didn't say I *couldn't* bring Drew. So, if we get caught, it's not the end of the world.

Much to my disappointment, there's nothing in the way of directions or navigation down here. It's just endless tunnels with the occasional vent near the floor, and I wonder how on earth we're going to find him.

Drew jogs over to a nearby vent and leans toward the ground, peering through the gaps and into whatever room lays beyond. "Interrogation room," he says calmly. "Empty."

I nod, hands on my hips as I try to come up with a plan. "We saw them come down here. We just need to figure out where they went. They're here *somewhere*."

As he jogs to the next vent, I close my eyes, mind buzzing with possibilities that I consider and just as quickly discard—until one becomes perfectly, astoundingly clear.

Jace and I can feel each other, and the sensation has been getting stronger lately. More powerful.

More than that, it's *clearer*. Recently, I've begun to sense what direction he's in—like after my sparring match with Irena, when I knew he was standing at the top of the stairs.

It's imperfect, of course. Just bits and pieces here and there. Sometimes it's fuzzier than others, but maybe I can use this.

I take a deep breath, trying to center myself and clear my mind. My dragon stirs within, grateful for the attention.

And I listen.

The pull is sudden and fierce. It's almost overpowering, but it only lasts for a second. I feel tugged to the left, away from where Drew is headed. It's like somebody stuck a hook in my chest and is yanking me, pulling me, almost *dragging* me away.

Jace.

"They're over here," I say quietly, my eyes still closed as I follow the connection Jace and I share.

Drew doesn't say anything. Almost instantly, I feel his presence beside me—his warmth, his towering body. He hovers nearby, his hand on the small of my back, and it's comforting to know he's close.

With every step, the sensation in my chest gets stronger, more powerful, more undeniable. This is the longest it's ever consistently burned for me, but I don't deny it. I don't fight it.

I just let it be, and I pay attention.

As we take the turns and corridors, the sensation pulling me toward Jace occasionally waivers and flickers like a bad Wi-Fi signal. I frown as our connection fades away yet again, and this time it fizzles out. I reach for it, almost trying to force it to come back, but it won't cooperate.

I pause, biting my lip as I try to feel for the sensation again.

I've lost it.

My eyes open, and I find Drew standing in front of me with a frown on his face and his arms crossed.

"What?" I ask.

He shakes his head, looking away without a word.

But I know.

He's jealous.

He's jealous the mate-bond is stronger than it's ever been.

Jealous and afraid he might lose me.

"Drew," I say softly, running my hand along his bicep to comfort him.

He holds up a hand to interrupt me. "I know you, Rory," he says simply. "I trust you, and I know."

"Know what?"

"You're my woman, too," he says with simple, utter confidence.

"Exactly." I smile, and in that moment, I know we're good.

A powerful burst through my chest catches my attention, and I gasp in surprise as the tug leads me down another corridor. I follow, and finally, I feel as though Jace is near. I can practically sense him on the other side of the wall. I lean my palms against the stone impulsively, my dragon aching to be closer.

Before I can speak, Drew nudges my shoulder and nods to the floor.

A vent.

I kneel, peering through. From this vantage near the ground, I can see Harper sitting in a chair against the far wall. She's frowning, rubbing her temples with her eyes closed. A man walks past the vent, his legs casting shadows across my face, and he sighs.

Jace.

"Is he coming or not?" Jace barks.

"Just be patient," Harper chides.

"Patient?" Jace snaps back. "You're the ones that ushered me into this emergency meeting when I was in the middle of—" He cuts himself off with a groan, and I suspect he doesn't even know what he and I do out in the woods anymore.

Tease each other, mostly.

And bicker.

"Why isn't he here yet?" the dojo master demands.

"He's *coming*," Harper promises.

"I don't even see why he has to be here," Jace snaps, his voice tense and irritated. "I don't even know why we *have* a priest, Harper."

She chuckles. "It's ceremonial, Jace. You may not care about ceremony, but most dragons *do*."

Drew leans his back against the wall beside me, his eyes shifting out of focus as he listens.

The creak of a door opening catches my attention, though I can't see the door from this angle. Moments later, footsteps thud across the floor, and Harper turns to look as someone enters.

"So glad you could join us," Jace says sarcastically, his voice dripping with annoyance.

"Apologies," says a man I don't recognize. "Your hallways are a little confusing. I got lost."

"Now that we're all here and accounted for," Harper says, "there's an important matter we need to discuss."

"Don't do this, Harper," Jace says quietly, his tone almost pleading.

She sighs, eyes closing as her shoulders droop. "I have to, Jace."

He groans, and I can imagine him rubbing his jawline like he often does when he's frustrated.

Harper leans back in her chair. "We've been putting this off, but we can't anymore. This is important."

"I'm afraid so," the priest interjects. "The master of the dojo can have no conflicts of interest. The mate-bond you have with the dragon vessel puts you and everything here at risk."

"I know the law!" Jace snaps.

Harper stands, her attention focused a little ways off to my left, and I figure that's where Jace must be standing. "You have to choose, Jace. Rory, or your dojo."

For a moment, no one speaks. No one moves. It almost seems as if no one even breathes.

I know I don't—because I can't believe what I just heard.

My heart twists in agony at the impossible choice Harper just demanded of him. An ache thuds through my chest. My palms begin to sweat, and for a moment, my dragon writhes in panic.

"I can't deny the mate-bond," Jace says, breaking the silence. "You're not giving me a choice, Harper. You're asking me to step down."

"I'm not," Harper insists with a quick shake of her head. "That's the real reason you and I aren't having this conversation solo."

"If I may interject?" The priest's voice is apprehensive and a little shaky, which I assume means he's more than a little afraid of Jace. "There *are* ways to break the bond. It leaves a void in both parties, but it does work. As long as the two of you haven't mated—"

Jace scoffs contemptuously, cutting the man off, and I can practically feel his jealousy seeping through the wall.

I know he hates it—the fact that I've slept with Drew, Tucker, and Levi, but not with him. That must burn him clear to the bone, but he knows why it hasn't happened.

The *only* reason it hasn't happened.

He and I want each other. *Badly*. But just one night of passion means he and I are bound for life.

For me and Jace, it's not just sex. It's eternity.

Before I can give in to him, I have to know without a doubt that we're not going to destroy each other in the end. To give each other that much power over the other—it could be catastrophic.

"I need more time," Jace says, ignoring the priest's offer.

"I can't give it to you," Harper admits quietly.

"Even just one month, Harper," Jace says. "Please."

"With everyone hunting her, I can't let you wait," Harper says. "You have a week, and that's the best I can do."

"A *week*?" Jace asks incredulously. "Harper—"

"I'm sorry," she interrupts, walking toward him. There's a rustle of clothing, and I wonder if she set her hand on his arm to comfort him.

I wish I could do the same.

Jace groans. "This is an impossible decision, Harper."

"I'm making you choose between the two things you love most," she says, her tone gentle and understanding. "I know."

"I'll think about it," Jace begrudgingly concedes.

"You already know what you want to do," Harper

says. "You just don't want to admit it to yourself, to me, or to *her*."

There's a tense and eerie silence, and I wonder what the expression on his face must be. I have a feeling it's probably one of disgust, or disappointment, or even an incredulous disbelief that she would dare say such a thing.

Or maybe those are just the expressions on my face. At this point, I'm not entirely sure.

"If that's all?" Jace asks tensely, and I know him well enough by now that he probably nodded toward the door for emphasis.

"That's all," Harper replies softly, almost wounded.

Without another word, she walks past the vent, and I hear the creak of a door opening. More footsteps follow, and it sounds like the priest has also left the room, leaving only Jace behind. He sighs deeply, hesitating for a moment before he too walks past the vent and into the hallway.

When the room is empty, I still don't move. My shoulders are tense, and I can feel pain radiating down my spine. I can barely breathe, and my mind is astonishingly blank.

It's almost as though I can't let myself feel for fear of what might come up if I seriously debate the choice Jace is going to have to make.

Silently, Drew sets a strong hand on the back of my neck. It's huge and warm—and, I confess, soothing. With him near, I can breathe a little bit better, and his fiery touch slowly melts my frozen muscles.

It lets me think.

My chest aches. It's a hollow kind of hurt, the sort of emptiness that comes with losing something you'll never get back. Even though Jace has been an ass half the time I've known him, my dragon chose him for a reason.

Jace Goodwin soothes my magic in ways no one else can. He sparks a life deep within me that makes me feel full. Content. *Happy.* He pushes me to my limits, breaks them, and builds me into something *more.* He has a connection to my power and my dragon that not even I have.

After all this time in his dojo, he's finally coming around. The two of us, we're—well, I don't know. I'm not sure what we are, not really. But it's changing. It's growing. It's becoming *something.* Becoming *better.*

The question is, will it happen in time?

I don't know what's best for us. I don't know what the correct choice is.

Jace was right about one thing—this is an impossible decision. Either way, he loses something dear to him, and I wonder where I could possibly rank compared to the dojo that has given him purpose and drive for so much of his life.

His role as the general of the Fairfax Army has been a part of his identity. It has been a lifelong goal for him, one he accomplished at an almost impossibly young age. He will be immortalized in Fairfax history —he's a living legend to them, all because of what he's done while he's ruled here.

Finding a mate was never even on his top ten list. He's never wanted that life—not even once. How could he, when he had everything else he could ever dream of?

I sit back on my heels, staring at the dark floor as I lose myself in thought. As impossible as this decision is, I have to confess that I selfishly know which choice I *want* him to make.

I just doubt he will *make* it.

CHAPTER SIX

Harper and I need to talk.

I don't bother to mask my movements as I stalk through the hallways on my way to her room.

I may have snuck around just a *little* bit to get information on where she was staying. I probably could have just asked, but I don't want her to know I'm coming. I don't want to give her time to come up with answers or prepare for the questions I have to ask her.

I want honesty. I want the truth.

When I reach the door to Harper's room, I impulsively kneel to pick the lock. My hands hesitate over the doorknob, and I pause.

For a moment, I simply sit there, debating what I want to do.

On the plus side, picking the lock and kicking open

the door is one hell of a dramatic entrance, and in the past, the right entrance alone has won me valuable intel without me ever having to break a single nose. It would show Harper that I mean business, and the old me would have done it in a heartbeat.

It's a power move that lets others know exactly what I'm capable of—and exactly why they shouldn't lie to me.

But Harper and I have been through enough at this point that I should at least grant her the decency to knock.

Despite my training screaming for me to do otherwise, I stand and rap my knuckles against the wood.

For a brief moment, nothing happens. There's a rustle of clothing inside, and a few footsteps heading toward the door. The doorknob rattles, and seconds later, the door opens to a rather surprised Boss of the Fairfax family—the one person in this world to hold some amount of control and sway over Jace's life.

As our eyes meet, her eyebrows shoot up, and she briefly scans my face. "Rory. What a surprise!"

"Do you have a second?" I ask.

She nods and steps aside, gesturing for me to come in.

How surreal. Me, a former Spectre, being invited into a dragon Boss's room.

I indulge her, stepping into the parlor and giving the suite a quick scan. No cameras on the elegant, ornate walls and very little in the way of effects across the massive marble fireplace and mantle. A cup of coffee steams on an end table beside an overstuffed chair, and a book about political theory lays open on the armrest.

I narrow my eyes skeptically.

Interesting reading material, Harper.

"Sorry to interrupt," I say, more out of courtesy than anything else. My shoulders are tense with everything I'm about to ask her, and part of me wishes I was somewhere else.

I really hate this *feelings* stuff, but I know in my bones that I need to do this. I need to clear the air.

Knocking on a dragon Boss's door, only to be invited in. I never once thought I would see the day when this was my life.

But my life has changed, and this is my world now —as uncomfortable as it sometimes can be.

"To what do I owe the honor?" Harper asks as she shuts the door behind me.

"Which choice do you want Jace to make?" I ask, not bothering with pretense now that we're alone and no one can overhear us. I train my gaze on her and stand a little taller, more for emphasis than anything else.

I want her to know I'm serious. That this is a question she must absolutely answer before I leave this room.

Harper lets out a slow breath, her eyes drifting to the floor as her shoulders droop slightly. "Jace told you."

"No," I say simply. "He didn't."

At that, Harper laughs. Her eyes dart toward me as her smile lingers. Clearly impressed I found this out, she crosses her arms as she studies my face.

Without answering, she begins to circle me slowly, taking her time with each step as she inquisitively tilts her head. "I've always wondered what training you had," Harper admits, the smirk still on her face. "The way you move. The things you know. You're not just a normal girl. You never were, were you?"

The deceptively powerful thunderbird pauses and lets the silence settle in the room, clearly expecting me to answer. I figure at this point, she assumes she's gained my trust. She must figure I'll just jump into a conversation about this and not question the change in topic.

I don't answer.

The silence stretches on to the point where it's

clear this is a tactic we're both using against each other.

Many people are afraid of silence. They ache to fill it even if they share things that aren't in their best interest to share. It's a technique salespeople use to get their prey talking—in the quiet, most people will do anything at all to keep the conversation rolling. It's like wringing a towel, only answers pour out instead of water.

But Harper and I both know the tricks, and they don't work on us anymore.

The Fairfax Boss absently rubs the back of her head and walks toward a mini bar in the corner. She lifts one of the crystal decanters and pours brown liquid into an equally ornate glass. When the cup is half full, she raises it toward me, gesturing for me to take it.

I shake my head.

Harper shrugs, setting down the decanter and sitting on the plush sofa nearby as she takes a sip.

"I don't know where to start, Rory," she admits, finally breaking the silence.

Good.

I won.

"How about you begin with an explanation?" I say tensely, not bothering to mask the accusation dripping from every word. "How about you tell me how you could *possibly* force Jace to make a choice like that?"

With the glass inches from her lips, Harper pauses, staring at me with a tortured expression. "It's out of my control. I don't want to do this anymore than he wants to make the choice, but facts are facts. The master of the dojo can have only one love."

With that, Harper takes a sip of her whiskey, all the while watching me with a knowing look on her face.

Love.

The word makes me uncomfortable, and I impulsively shake out my shoulders to loosen up the tension building in my back. I briefly look away from her, not quite able to stand the intensity of her gaze.

Like she knows what neither Jace nor I will admit.

"You asked what choice I want him to make," Harper says. "Do you really want to know?"

"Yes," I say without hesitation.

"Before I tell you, answer me this. Why does it matter?" Harper counters. There's a genuine curiosity in her voice. It's not accusation, not resentment. There isn't a hint of defensiveness or irritation—nothing but quiet and calm interest.

"He listens to you," I admit. "You're his Boss, so he has to. If you give him an order, he has to obey it."

"Have I ever given him an order?" she asks, though it's clearly rhetorical.

I tilt my head in annoyance at the bait she just dangled in front of me, wishing she would just get to the damn point already.

"This is not a choice I get to make," Harper continues, leaving the previous question hanging in the air. "This isn't something I can choose for him, Rory, not even if I wanted to."

"I suppose," I admit. "But he will still listen to what you have to say."

"Maybe," she says with a smirk, taking another sip of her whiskey. "Most of the time, he just talks over me."

I chuckle, but the laughter quickly dies in my throat. I set my hands on my hips, staring off down the hallway of her suite toward the rooms farther down. "Just tell me, Harper," I say quietly. "I need to know."

Harper pauses. I can tell she's struggling with this, probably debating whether or not she even wants to confess it at all. If there's any reason or point to all this. After all, this isn't a decision either of us gets to make.

I hate that—not having control. To have something so powerfully affect me, and yet to not have any say.

Maybe that's why I'm restless.

Harper sets her whiskey on the coffee table and tucks her legs beneath her. "As his Boss, I want my general. I know how he operates. I trust him. It's going to be a nearly impossible task to find a replacement for him, and even then, I'll have to spend another decade getting to know and trust the person who comes next. Ideally, he would have a second in command we could simply promote, but, well..."

Right. Guy Durand.

I grimace in disgust at the memory of a traitor I would rather just forget.

Harper shrugs. "No second has officially been named for the dojo since Guy was banished, as that's a long and tedious process. We do have a top contender, so there's that at least. Russell—I believe you remember him?"

I nod. He was a chauffeur who got us out of the neutral zone back when we had to meet with all the Bosses. He's good at what he does, but I don't know him well enough to predict whether or not he would be a good general.

The fact is I hate her answer. It's the one I was expecting, but not the one I wanted.

My shoulders are so tense they ache. They hurt so badly that they almost *burn* with the strain of all these unknowns. I can feel the pain radiating up my neck into my head, where the dull throb of a headache is beginning to brew.

This must be what denial feels like.

"However," Harper continues, her voice softening, "as his cousin, I feel differently. As his family and his friend, I want him to be happy." She pauses, looking briefly at the rug beneath the coffee table. "I want him to get his head out of his ass and marry you already."

I sputter and cough involuntarily. I can't help it because I wasn't expecting that answer at all. "Let's take baby steps there, Harper."

"A baby is good, too." Harper laughs. "And no, absolutely not—there are no small steps with thunderbirds. That's not how our kind operate, Rory. That's not how mate-bonds work. The only two things holding him back from throwing you over his shoulder and making you his—the only things stopping him from fulfilling this mate-bond you two share —are his jealousy and his need to control everything around him."

"Thunderbirds don't share." I recite Jace's words, my jaw tensing in irritation.

"He's full of shit," Harper says curtly, rolling her eyes.

I lift one eyebrow in surprise.

"You heard me," she says as she reaches for her

whiskey once again. "The fact is mated bonds *can* share. I've seen it before. Since this poly thing is important to you, it's something that will become important to him, if he chooses you."

That's just it though.

If.

"If you had to choose," I prod, "which side of you wins—the cousin, or the Boss?"

Harper shakes her head, holding my gaze as she tries to drive her point home. "Neither, Rory. I'm not making this choice. Jace is, and as much as you may think you don't have control in this situation, this is your choice, too."

I pause, letting the silence once again settle over the room as I simmer on everything Harper just said.

As young as she is, I have to admit she's pretty damn smart.

"So, now that I've answered your question, do I get mine answered, too?" Harper asks, taking another swig of her whiskey.

I quirk an eyebrow. "Which one?"

"Your training." Harper pauses, giving me a brief once-over. "What you are—or, rather what you were before you came here."

I impulsively stiffen. "Are you sure you want to know?"

The question is as much for me as her.

Am I sure I want to tell her?

I pause, holding her gaze as I simmer on the question. In the end, I know the answer.

Yes.

What she and I have—it has the makings of true friendship. However, given what she and I are, it would be too easy for us to become enemies.

We need to trust each other—and I need to test that now, with something big, before I find myself in need of her help. Before I can really rely on her.

I need to know this is a real friendship. That everything we have is real. It's time for the final test, and if I can truly trust Harper Fairfax.

An interesting expression crosses her face as she gently smirks. It's a blend of mischievousness and curiosity. "Tell me."

I calmly pace the length of the room, my eyes intently focused on her. "Once you know, there's no going back," I point out, hating how dramatic it sounds even if it *is* the truth. "Once you know where I came from, everything changes."

Her smirk broadens into a full grin, and she looks almost excited. Hopeful, even. "Are we really going to do this?"

I nod. "First, I want you to piece together what you know. Tell me your theories."

It's kind of fun ordering a dragon Boss around.

Harper gets comfortable, stretching out across the couch as she bites her lip, thinking deeply. She sets her hands behind her head and looks at the ceiling. "You're polyamorous," she starts off. "That doesn't narrow it down a ton, but it does help a little. You have advanced training that's brutal, and you know how to take a hit as well as give one. You have skill and knowledge of dragon culture that doesn't make sense for a normal human," she adds with a brief glance toward me. "And you had access to the pits. Not many do."

I grit my teeth at the mention of the pit Mason Greene threw me into. He left me to die a horrible death, but I refused to go quietly. The pits were where I acquired not just my magic, but my dragon and my new life. So, even though Mason was an absolute dick I enjoyed killing, I have to admit I'm still a little grateful for his sadistic attempt to murder me.

Just a little.

"I've been debating this," Harper admits, interrupting my thoughts. "With everything I've seen and everything I know—which I admit isn't much—I have a couple of theories."

"And they are?"

"A Vaer prisoner of war," she starts, listing her theories off on her fingers. "American elite military. Maybe a Knight," she adds with a suspicious sidelong glare toward me.

I try not to give away anything on my face as I wait for her to finish. "Is that all?"

"No," she admits, the lingering smile on her face dissolving. "There's one more, but I was hoping you would've stopped me by now."

I just watch her, silently urging her to finish.

I need to know.

Her jaw tenses, and she swallows hard. "Or…"

"Or?" I ask calmly.

"A Spectre." She freezes at the last word as if she was afraid to say it. As if that's the one theory she desperately hopes is wrong.

From her tone, it almost sounds as if even mentioning the name will speak a Spectre into being. Like we're the bogeymen.

Well, in all fairness, that was always kind of the point. To drive fear into the hearts of even dragons.

We did it well.

I was worried about that—the fear—because this could change everything. If she fears Spectres this much, that could change the way she feels about me. It could shift our entire friendship or outright destroy it.

If she can't accept what I am, everything that I've built so far in this new life of mine is at risk.

After all, this is her dojo.

But that's the point of doing this—even if she calls the soldiers, even if she tries to kill me, I can get out of here in one piece. It's better to test her now than when my life truly depends on it.

Because I get the feeling that, at some point, it absolutely will.

I debate shutting down. I briefly consider stopping this before it goes any further. Hell, Zurie would have never let it get this far at all. But Zurie doesn't trust anyone, and in the end, that's going to be what destroys her.

This isn't just about confession. This isn't just a test. This is a moment of truth, a moment of change, and I have to show up for it just as much as she is.

I can go back to the way things were if I want. I can go back to lying and hiding what I am. Hiding what I was.

Or I can step into what I am now. I can shake off the shame and let myself be more than Zurie ever dreamt I could be. More than even I used to dare let myself dream.

"If you had to choose just one?" I ask quietly. "What would you choose?"

Harper leans slightly forward, her eyes fixed on me as she answers. "I would hope for elite American military," she confesses. "But," she adds after a pause, "I would have to say I suspect you were a Spectre."

My chest tightens, but I don't show anything on my face. I simply stand there watching her, and I never give anything away.

"I'm right, aren't I?" A look of concern—almost horror, but not quite—crosses her face. "You were a Spectre."

And here it is.

The moment of truth.

Slowly, Harper gets to her feet, her gaze never leaving my face. She studies me with almost a breathless expression.

The longer the silence wears on, the more the disbelief settles into her features. She slowly walks toward me, and I impulsively prepare myself for war. My instinct is to draw my gun from the holster on my hip, to put it between her and me, to keep her at bay because a dragon Boss that knows what you are is a deadly, dangerous thing.

But I let her get close—because this is Harper.

This is my friend.

When Harper's standing right in front of me, her eyes darting back and forth between mine, she pulls me into a tight hug. She buries her face in my shoulder, her hands wrapping around my back and holding me close.

For a moment, I just stand there, letting her hold me, utterly and completely in shock. I was expecting an attack, perhaps a weapon to come out of nowhere or for her to just shift and try to eat me.

I was prepared for pretty much anything but this.

Eventually, I return the hug, holding her tightly as I confess to myself that this feels rather nice.

"So, does this mean you're not calling the guards to whisk me off to the dungeons?" I ask.

Harper laughs and lets me go. "If you were a monster once, Rory, you're not anymore," she says. "You're my friend, and your secret is safe with me."

I smile, and I can't deny the flurry of gratitude burning through me.

A friend—a real one. One I can rely on and—gods forbid—*trust*.

I never thought I'd see the day.

CHAPTER SEVEN

As Harper and I hug each other in her living room, a flash of intuition snaps me from the moment.

Danger.

I tense, my arms impulsively tightening around Harper. It's a protective movement, something I'm not used to doing for anyone but my men.

As I listen to the intuition, to the little flare of warning, I let go of her and gently push her behind me, putting myself between the dragon Boss and the door. My attention sharpens, my eyes focused on the door handle, and I'm still not sure why.

"Rory, what—"

My eyes dart to her, and I lift my finger to my lips.

Her mouth audibly clicks as she closes it abruptly,

nodding in the silence. Her eyes narrow as her attention is diverted toward the exit.

Good. At least she can listen.

Over by the door, there's the slightest scrape along the wood. Anyone else would have ignored it, but my training kicks in. Anything out of the ordinary is worthy of attention, and this little noise has mine.

Without even a breath, I steal silently toward the door, my eye on the handle as my senses kick into overdrive. I listen for any hint that someone's there, for the slightest indication that someone doesn't want to be heard or seen.

As I stare at it, the handle twitches ever so slightly.

Someone's on the other side, and they don't want us to know they're trying to get in.

I draw my gun, aiming it toward the door, toward where a head would be if they were kneeling and trying to pick the lock. My left hand hovers over the knob, and I prepare for whatever is about to happen.

In a dojo, nothing like this should *ever* happen.

This should be a safe place. A refuge. The embassy should be a place of peace, where nothing can get in or out without Jace knowing.

And he would never let anyone in that would hurt me or Harper.

Behind me, I hear the click of metal.

A gun.

I instinctively pivot, caught between the person trying to get in and the sound of a gun being drawn—only to find Harper lifting a handgun toward the exit. Her eyes narrow as she trains her attention down the barrel, and she nods once at me to signal that she's ready.

I smirk, impressed. I hadn't even seen a gun under her clothes—they must be specially designed to hide weapons.

Harper is a dragon Boss, after all. She must have all sorts of humans and dragons alike trying to kill her. Like me, she always has to be prepared.

Tensed and ready for a battle, I throw open the door. There, kneeling, is a woman with dark hair and bright green eyes, her pistol raised and aimed at my face.

Irena.

The moment our eyes meet, we both relax, the barrels of our handguns lowering toward the ground.

I shake my head. "Irena, we talked about this. You don't have to sneak around here."

My sister stands and holsters her gun, her shoulders tense as she glances between me and Harper without answering.

I step aside to let my sister in, and only then do I

catch the expression on Harper's face. Her frown has become a scowl, and there's a clear recognition in her eye.

It's almost as if they've met before.

Even as Irena and I stow our weapons, Harper doesn't lower *hers*.

"Harper," Irena says with a slight nod toward the Boss. Her tone is dry and humorless, without a hint of welcome or joy. She's still standing in the hallway with the door open, as if she can't decide whether or not she wants to come in.

"Well, isn't this a small world?" Harper says with a hint of humor in her voice that isn't apparent on her face.

These two have history, and that can't be good.

"You two know each other?" I ask, glancing between them.

"You could say that," Irena says matter-of-factly.

"She was sent to kill me once," Harper answers, gun still raised. "Two years ago, is it?"

"Three," Irena corrects.

"Huh." Harper smirks, her eyes narrowing. "Time flies."

I groan, pinching the bridge of my nose.

"That's why I'm here actually," Irena admits as she

takes a step into the room and closes the door behind her.

"To finish the job?" Harper asks, her finger hovering over the trigger. She's surprisingly calm despite facing her assassin for the second time.

The Fairfax dragon looks like she's ready to spring, and at any moment, this entire room could erupt in blood and bullets.

"Only if I have to," Irena answers. "I came to make sure Rory was safe with you here. It seems like you and I need to have a little talk, *Boss*." Irena doesn't mask the sarcasm in her voice, and I frown at the direction this conversation is quickly heading.

A tense moment of silence follows, and I have to confess I have no idea what's about to happen.

I *hate* that—the not knowing. I usually do everything in my power to retain—or at least *regain*—control.

I don't know if either of the women in the room is about to start a torrent of bullets, or if I'm going to have to hurt one of them to get them to stop.

To her credit, Harper laughs. It's big and full and hardy and real, and for the first time since the doorknob rattled, she seems a little bit more at ease.

She lowers her weapon and rolls out her shoulders, as if she finally feels safe letting out the tension she's been holding there since I first told her to be wary. "You have some serious balls, girl. You want some whiskey?"

Irena frowns, a hint of confusion on her face as the Boss walks calmly toward the whiskey cabinet and pours another glass out of the decanter.

I let out a slow breath of relief. For the moment, at least, it seems like no one's about to die.

Probably.

"Do you have a drinking problem I need to know about?" I ask Harper, feigning disappointment as I lean against the nearest wall.

The Fairfax Boss shakes her head and chuckles. "It's just been one hell of a week."

Harper lifts her glass off the table and examines it for a moment while she waits for Irena's answer. When Irena doesn't say anything, Harper swirls the brown liquid around in the crystal glass and throws it all back in one fell swoop. She grimaces as the whiskey burns down her throat, and the glass makes an audible *clink* as she sets it back down.

Irena's hand tightens into a fist, and I know her well enough to see the warning signs of a fight about to break out.

I glare at my sister. "Irena, if you try to kill her—"

"Will you be *quiet?*" Irena snaps, narrowing her

eyes as she glares at me. She tilts her head slightly, and I know that look.

I'm trying to help you, it says.

Ah.

Now, it all makes sense.

On her previous mission, when she tried and failed to kill Harper, Irena's cover was blown. And now that it's apparent Irena is my sister, it's a short leap to connect the dots and say I'm one, too.

I shake my head, nodding to the Boss and rolling my eyes. *She already knows,* the look says.

For once, someone knowing our secret isn't a horrible disaster.

I have to confess, that's a nice change of pace.

Irena's eyebrows shoot up her forehead. An incredulous fury crosses her face. "You actually told a Boss that you're—"

She cuts herself off and can't even finish the sentence. Instead, she rubs her face in frustration and paces in a slow circle, like she can't believe I would be so stupid.

But this is my world, and Irena isn't comfortable here yet. She doesn't understand that it can be safe. That we can trust people, at least some of them.

She will. I know it in my bones. It's just a matter of

time and faith, neither of which come easy to a Spectre.

"Consider yourself forgiven, Irena," Harper says, leaning her shoulder against the wall as she pours herself another glass of whiskey. "Considering what we learned about you when you came to kill me, I figure you were acting on orders and don't have some lifelong vendetta against us. Besides," Harper adds with the smirk, "I kicked your ass once, and I can do it again."

The Boss winks at Irena, who practically growls in irritation.

I grin broadly. "Low blow, Harper."

The Fairfax Boss shrugs.

Irena shakes her head, still furious. "Well, if you two are such great friends, I assume you told Rory about everyone after her," she snaps, not enjoying this in the least. "Or do the Fairfax dragons prefer to keep their secrets?"

"Everyone keeps secrets," Harper calmly says as she takes another sip of whiskey.

Irena scoffs. "The secrets you keep tell me every-thing I need to know about your ethics, and Rory isn't safe here if you haven't told her the truth."

"And what truth might that be?" Harper asks, her eyes glinting with a deadly focus as she studies Irena's face.

I tense, my gaze flitting between the two of them, not quite sure what to make of this—or where Irena's going with it.

"The *facts*," Irena snaps. "The kidnapping attempts. The blackmailing. The bounties. The Spectres. The Knights. The other families. How everyone wants her. Some dead, some alive."

"And how do you know?" I ask wryly, crossing my arms. "This is the first *you've* told me of it, you damn hypocrite."

"One of my contacts is active again," Irena says simply. "Communications expert—and I've only *just* reconnected with him, thank you very much," she adds with a snippy glance toward me.

Oh, nice.

I suspect that man will come in handy down the road.

"That's good," Harper says with a nod. "I'm impressed, Irena. Rory needs allies like you, considering all that's coming her way."

I tilt my head in suspicion. "What do you mean?"

Harper pauses, and her gaze slowly drifts toward me. Only, she's not looking at me—she's looking *through* me. At something else.

It's like she can see clear into my soul.

My skin crawls ever so slightly, and the whole thing feels a little... well, vulnerable. Violating, even. Something in her expression makes me feel bare, and not in the fun way.

As Harper looks clear into me, her brows slowly twist with worry and dread. "Your magic is shifting," she says wistfully. "Your dragon is nearly grown. I can see it. There's a huge change within you, and that means your dragon is becoming real. But it can still die if you don't protect it."

My heart flutters in my chest at the thought, at the possibility of really shifting. At the thought of flying.

But the fear follows soon after at the thought of losing it all. Of losing my dragon.

"Even if your dragon does survive," Harper adds, "you may never shift, Rory. I've never seen a late bloomer. But there's something... well, *other* to your magic."

"What the hell does that mean?" Irena asks.

Harper shakes her head as if she's just as confused as we are. "It's just... *different.* I've never seen anything like it. I've never..." She trails off as if she can't even find the words. "If you do shift, Rory, your dragon will be extraordinarily powerful."

"Like a thunderbird?" I ask.

At that, Harper's gaze sharpens, the foggy haze to

her eyes quickly dissolving. "No, Rory," she says quietly. "Something far more powerful than even that."

"What could possibly be more powerful than a thunderbird?" I ask, not quite believing her.

"I have no idea," Harper confesses.

I frown. There are still so many unknowns about my magic—where it comes from, what the limits are, what the voices in the mist really wanted of me.

I briefly debate telling Harper about them, but I'm not sure that would be productive at the moment. It's not like I'm going to go chasing off through ethereal fog anytime soon.

An uncomfortable silence settles on the room, the sort that makes me feel like they're both trying to get me to leave. It's like everyone has something to say, but they have no idea how to say it.

Usually, I'm fine with the silence, but this is different. Seeing as my sister tried to kill arguably my only friend at some point in the past, I don't want to leave these two alone.

"What's it like to shift?" I ask. Yeah, it's useful info I need to know—but I also just want to break the silence.

Harper smiles, her eyes wrinkling slightly with joy. "The first few times are exhausting," she says. "You can never hold it for very long, but you *can* fly almost right away. Dragon instinct is incredibly powerful. In the beginning, you and your dragon are still learning each other, and you're learning how to operate and navigate in a new body. You're in the driver's seat, after all, in a shift. You control your dragon, and she—well, it's hard to describe."

The Fairfax Boss trails off, biting her lip as she thinks through her answer. "Your dragon, she speaks to you, in a way, through intuition. When you first shift, it's awkward and wobbly because you're just not used to it yet. The access to your magic is limited, and it takes a lot of training to reach it in your dragon body."

I frown. I'm honestly not sure what I was expecting, but I have to confess I thought it would be more instant. More intuitive, right from the start.

"I know you'll get it quickly," Harper adds with a small smile. "After your first shift, it gets a little easier every time you do it. Sometimes a shift can come when you can't even control it though, right at the beginning. I've destroyed a few buildings in my youth while I was figuring it all out," she adds with a laugh.

I smile, imagining Harper's beautiful dragon head breaking through a roof and roaring into the sky.

Out of the corner of my eye, I catch Irena watching

Harper with a distrustful glare. Harper must see it, but to her credit, she doesn't appear to care.

It will take a while for Irena to let down her guard here, surrounded by all these dragons. Hell, I wouldn't be surprised if some of the shifters here were other failed assassination attempts in her past.

I wasn't exactly at ease when I first got here, and I can't expect her to acclimate just because I'm comfortable in the dragon den now.

"I should get ready to leave," Harper says. She walks toward me and sets her hand on my shoulder. "I promise you that all of this will work out."

I'm not sure if she's talking about Irena, my shift, Jace's choice, or everyone who's coming after me.

Despite myself and everything I've learned about trust, I smile. I have to confess, I'm grateful to have a friend.

"Have a safe trip," I say, returning the gesture and patting her lightly on the back as I head toward the door. "Irena, you coming?"

Irena hesitates, and it's clear she wanted to stay to have that chat with Harper in private, but Harper just smiles and nods toward the door.

I hope this isn't going to become a problem.

Irena joins me and walks into the hallway as I take one last glance at Harper over my shoulder. The dragon Boss downs the last of her whiskey and sets the crystal glass on a nearby table with a soft thunk before the door closes behind me.

As Irena and I walk through the hallways back to our rooms, I can tell there's something wrong with her. The frown that's practically a scowl. The subtle shaking of her head, as if she's having a conversation with herself and is disgusted by the entire thing.

Irena is a good person at heart. She loves and protects me so fiercely that I know she would do anything for me.

But when she feels like she has to put on a front to terrify or threaten people, she does a *really* good job of it.

"Will you chill out?" I ask, not bothering to mask my annoyance. "She's not going to kill us, damn it."

"It's not that," Irena says with a small shake of her head. "I didn't even hear you walk to the door until it was too late. You were both in that room probably having a conversation, and I didn't hear any of it. I wasn't even sure she was in there." Irena grimaces, absolutely disgusted with all the ways she just failed herself. "What is *wrong* with me?"

"You were in a coma," I say tenderly, shifting gears and trying to be as compassionate as I can. "We don't even know what you *are* anymore. You have dragon blood in your veins, now. You have abilities—enhanced strength, glowing green eyes, and who knows what else," I add with a shrug. "You're getting used to your new body, to your new skill. That takes time.

"Yeah, but—"

"Besides," I interrupt, not letting her pity party continue. "When you come out of a coma, I would imagine you don't get to just jump right back up and be perfectly fine again."

Irena shrugs. "It's still frustrating. I don't feel as in tune with my body anymore. Everything feels harder, and I don't know why."

"Because you're fighting it," I say without really thinking about my answer. It's like the truth just poured out of me, unconscious and unwilling to go ignored any longer.

I sit with it for a second, that intuitive little answer.

I think it's true.

"What do you mean, *fighting* it?" she snaps. "Fighting *what*, exactly?"

"You don't want to be part dragon," I point out. "We were raised our whole lives to hate them. I know for a *fact* that if you were the dragon vessel, you would think it was a curse," I admit. "You don't see these new abilities as a gift yet, but I hope someday you do."

I let the quiet settle between us, hoping my words were hitting home with her even if it was just in a small way. She frowns, slipping her hands into her pockets as we walk, and she doesn't say anything.

"I know it's hard to accept the truth," I admit. "You're not wholly human, anymore. Everyone who was once your ally will now actively try to kill you, if only because of what you are. Of what Kinsley did to you." I grit my teeth with hatred, trying to quell my rising fury with the Vaer Boss and stay in the moment with my sister. "Irena, the more you fight what you are, the more you're going to overlook. The more you'll miss. The weaker you'll be. Because the more you fight what you are, the more you reject every skill and ability you have and try to make things like they were..." I trail off, not even sure what the full consequences of that could be.

She could die in battle.

She can miss something in a fight, something that could otherwise save her life.

Or, even worse, she could kill the dragon that I'm starting to suspect is growing within her, too.

I pause in the hallway, grabbing her hand so that she has to swing around and face me. Our eyes lock, and I do everything my power to drive this next point home. "You're a fighter, Irena. You always have been, and you always will be. You're powerful, you're strong, and you're fierce. But this is one fight you don't want to win." I tap my finger on her chest, hitting the same spot on her as where I feel the dragon within me. "There's something growing in there, something powerful. Something that can save your life. But you have to let it grow. You have to listen to it. You have to *trust* it. And until you face what you are now, you'll never find out what you can be."

For a moment, she simply watches me, and I'm grateful she at least heard me out. The odd expression on her face leaves me a little bit uncomfortable, however, and I'm not entirely sure how she's going to take everything I just said.

Eventually, the corner of her mouth curls slightly, and she studies my face as if she's truly seeing me for the first time. "I go into one little coma, and suddenly, my baby sister knows everything," she says, her grin widening. "When did you get so damn smart?"

I laugh. "It's all a front, I promise."

She chuckles and cracks her neck with a weary sigh. "I don't know about this whole dragon thing," she admits, gesturing in the air as if she's addressing every dragon all around us and the concept of dragons in general. "But I'll try, Rory. It's all I can do right now."

"Then that's enough," I concede. "Harper could train you, you know."

Irena snorts. "Yeah, let me ask the person I tried to kill once for help. That's not weird."

I laugh and lead her back down the hallway, toward our rooms. "Considering where we came from and who trained us—and comparing that to where we are now—I'd say our lives are pretty weird already." I gesture out the nearest window as a dragon races by. "What's one more thing?"

CHAPTER EIGHT

I want answers, but Jace isn't in his suite.

Shocker.

I sit in the private war room adjacent to Jace's master suite, tapping my finger on the table as I lose myself in thought.

The access code Jace gave me didn't technically let me in here. I had to break in the old-fashioned way, with a bit of elbow grease and my trusty lock pick. I'm a bit disappointed, to be honest, that I was able to get in—but I figure that's by design.

Jace doesn't *want* to keep me out of here, and he's probably just playing games with me at this point.

I lean forward in my chair and rest my elbows against the table with my chin on my fists. I want to know who's after me, what the bounties are, and who set them. I've exhausted the resources I have access to, and I came here as a last-ditch effort even though I knew I wouldn't find a damn thing.

Irena didn't have as much information as I thought she would, since apparently her contact is still sifting through the data. It's hard to keep up with the sheer volume of people who want me dead.

The joys of being popular.

Yay me.

Short of asking nicely, I don't know how to get the information—and let's be real, asking nicely won't get me anywhere.

Not with Jace.

I'm not entirely sure where to look next, since I don't know the tunnels as well as Jace does. I know I can probably find something down there, if I hunt long enough.

With a sigh, I lean back in the chair, wondering why this all feels so off—so *wrong*—but deep down, I already know.

Jace should just tell me these things, pure and simple. I shouldn't *have* to hunt them down, and the old way doesn't work for me anymore. The secrets. The half-truths. The running around in the shadows, stealing what intel I can find.

That's not my life anymore.

I hear footsteps by the door, and the doorknob jostles. On impulse, I reach for my gun—and, with immense effort, I resist the urge to draw it.

Seconds later, the door opens and a gorgeous, brawny fire dragon enters.

Drew.

As our eyes meet, he stiffens.

Caught in the act—he's not supposed to be here, either.

A second later, we both burst into laughter.

"It looks like we had the same idea," he admits.

I relax my shoulders and set my hands on the table once again. "What are you looking for?"

"Information on that crystal," he says as he closes the door behind him. "Whatever Zurie had that drained your power is a serious threat, and it's even more alarming because I can't find any information on it at all. I don't know what it is or where Zurie got it." He hesitates before reluctantly adding, "I was hoping Jace had better luck."

"That must hurt your pride," I say with a smirk. "Coming to Jace for help."

"I was not asking for help," Drew says sternly, pointing his finger at me for emphasis. "I fully planned on stealing the intel, *thank you.*"

I laugh.

We're so messed up.

But he has a point—the crystal *is* still a threat. One I haven't given much thought to in all the chaos.

That's the kind of mistake I can't allow. It's the kind of mistake that can get me killed, or worse.

To be fair, I destroyed the thing. In my mind, I suppose I felt like that was that—but Drew's right. There could be more, and we need to know what it was. Between being reunited with my sister, testing my newfound friendship with Harper, and getting to know the dragon growing in my chest, there's just so much going on.

I'm grateful that Drew is following up on this—it's comforting to know the men I adore will always have my back.

A shiver snakes down my back at the thought of the crystal or whatever dark magic Zurie had gotten her hands on that had slowly drained the life and magic from me. I can still see the crystal in my mind, the memory sharp and clear as the otherwise beautiful stone sat on the black satin in that little box.

Destroying it was the right thing to do, but every-thing about it struck me as just... *wrong*. It shouldn't have existed in the first place, and the scream I heard when I destroyed it still haunts me.

I have no idea who screamed. At the time, I thought it might have been Zurie—but the more I think about it, the more I relive the memory, the less certain I am. It didn't sound like her, and besides—Zurie doesn't scream.

"I'll keep looking," Drew says, interrupting my thoughts. "I'll find out what it is one way or another."

I smile. "I know."

He flashes a cocky grin at the confidence I have in him. "I should probably leave. Jace would be furious if he knew I was here."

My smile falls. "I was really hoping you guys were starting to get along."

Drew shakes his head. "We've always hated each other, Rory. A few months crammed together in an embassy aren't going to change a lifetime of hate. We've never known another way. It'll get bloody before it gets better."

I stand, my chair scraping along the wood as my calves push against it. "It doesn't have to be that way," I point out. "Jace nearly shot Tucker in the head, and now they're best friends," I add with a gesture toward the door.

Drew runs a hand through his hair, letting out a slow sigh as he tries to find the right words. "You don't understand, Rory. With the history Jace and I have, there won't be anything like that. No clean break. No easy shift."

"But he doesn't know the truth," I point out, closing the distance between us as I try to make him see reason. "If you just told him—"

"Rory, don't," Drew interrupts, looking at me with his intense dark eyes. "I know you want us both. I know you want us to get along. You want the entire team to get along." He gestures out the window. "But it's just never going to happen. Not with me and Jace."

"You don't know that," I say quietly. "You haven't even tried."

I expect him to grimace in annoyance or wrinkle his nose in outright disgust at my accusation, but instead, he just watches me calmly. After a moment, he takes another step, closing the last gap between us, and lifts my chin until my lips are inches from his.

He watches me carefully, no doubt waiting for me to close the gap between us.

This man is so damn transparent. He's just trying to distract me and change the subject by getting me all hot and bothered.

Well, two can play at *that* game. I smirk playfully and wait.

Drew leans in, his warm lips brushing lightly across mine, and I can't stop my eyes from fluttering closed in delight. Warmth and joy snake through me, the utter delight of his touch almost overwhelming.

The things this shifter does to me—it's just not fair.

"I should leave," he says again. "But my bed is open tonight if you're interested," he adds with a flirty wink.

"Oh, good. You were able to pencil me in?" I lift one eyebrow, grinning as I toy with him.

He laughs. "Maybe. If no one else beats you to it."

It's a bluff. He's mine, and I'm his. He's just messing with me, but a little surge of jealousy rises in my chest regardless.

I chuckle, playfully nudging his shoulder. "What? Am I going to have to fight Tucker for the honor?"

Drew laughs, and I'm absolutely ensnared by the happiness on his face. It's addictive, the kind of joy that makes the rest of the world melt away.

"I don't know," Drew says, shrugging mischievously. "I think you can take him."

My lips part, ready to dive in and launch off another retort, when I hear the thud of familiar foot-steps approaching the door.

Drew cusses under his breath, and we both know who that is.

The confident gate.

The urgent step.

It confirms the fluttery burst of joy that charges through me as my dragon stirs, its mate near.

Jace.

The doorknob turns, and Drew leans against the wall, his arms crossed, a familiar stoic expression on his handsome features as he watches the entrance with his game face on.

If he's going to get caught, it would seem as though he's not going to apologize for it.

The door swings open, and Jace enters. His eyes drift briefly between me and Drew, but there isn't a hint of surprise on his face like I expected.

"What did I not tell you *this* time, Rory?" he asks, slamming the door behind him.

I smirk. As difficult as this man is, as much as he and I butt heads, at least he's starting to figure me out.

"I want to finish the conversation we started in the forest," I admit, leaning my hands on the back of one of the chairs. "I want to know—"

Jace lifts a hand, interrupting me. "No, Rory."

I quirk an eyebrow. "Excuse me?"

"No," he says again, his voice even more firm than before. "I've thought it over, and I shouldn't have told you that in the first place. It was a moment of weakness, Rory. I want you to trust me on this. It's better if you just focus on your training. Focus on *shifting,*

Rory. Connect with your dragon, and for *once* in your life, let *me* handle this."

I frown. My impulse is to tell him off, to dig in and just be an obstinate ass until he gives me the information I want. The intel I freaking *need* to keep myself safe.

But I don't.

There's something about his tone that makes me stop. It's authoritative and controlling, but beneath it all is a hint of pleading. Like there's just a *little* bit of a request hiding beneath his dominant, *do-what-I-say* personality.

I push off the chair in annoyance, pacing as I try to figure out how I want to handle this. What I want to do.

"You act like it's easy, Jace," I say. "Just shift," I add with a mocking gesture toward the window at the dragons outside. "Harper says it might not even *happen.*"

"Ignore her. You just need to train," he says, willfully ignoring Drew's existence at this point. "You just need to build that connection to her and open the line of communication. Make sure she trusts you."

I shake my head in irritation, pacing the room with my back turned to him. "What do you think I'm doing?

What do you think we've *been* doing? All this time? All this training?"

"I know," he says quietly.

It's tender almost. Comforting.

Before I can help myself, I look at him to find him standing still by the door, his full attention and focus on me and his shoulders tense. There's an imploring twist to his eyebrows, as if he wants to say something but hasn't figured out the words yet.

He's not going to tell me, but that won't stop me from figuring it all out.

Fine. As much as I hate to admit it, I'm going to have to dig the old fashioned way—and I figure Irena will be more than happy to help me find everything I need.

With a slow breath, I release the simmering anger that's burning in the back of my shoulder blades. It won't do any good to yell or argue. I still need to know everything about the bounties, and with time, I know I will. But for the moment, he's raised a very good point.

Shifting.

It's something I need to master, and soon.

"Tell me about your shifts," I say, my gaze darting between the two men before me. "Please," I add a little begrudgingly as my anger slowly dissolves. "It'll help me figure out how to do it."

"My first shift was during a sparring match with Jett when I was just a boy," Drew says, his gaze on the floor and his arms still crossed.

I do a double take as Drew calls his father by his name.

The man truly has no sway over my fire dragon— to Drew, he and his father are equals. I smirk with pride.

Jace, however, briefly glares at the fire dragon as if his mere presence is a grave annoyance. I try to ignore the feud that seems to be raging, ever stronger, between them.

"It was brutal and unfair," Drew continues. "But it dragged my dragon out of me, exactly as Jett wanted. The man always gets his way."

The fire dragon is calm and collected, even as he shares a horrible truth about his past. But that's Drew —never show emotion, never let anyone know that something gets to you. Never appear weak.

He's not weak. Even now, all these years later, that memory scars him.

My impulse is to go over and hold him, to comfort him, but I know Drew wouldn't want me to do that in front of Jace or anyone else, for that matter. When Drew has feelings, he prefers to have them in private.

In the silence that follows, I don't really know what to say—I didn't realize so many shifters use stress and near-death experiences to spark the shift.

"Is that the best way to do it?" I ask. "To force it like that?"

"Absolutely *not!*" Both Drew and Jace say in unison, glaring at me.

I lean back slightly in surprise at their tone. After their outburst, they both glare at each other and look away just as quickly, but the urgency in both their voices says everything I need to know.

That's a last-ditch effort.

"Okay. Fine," I say, leaning my fists against the table. "Jace, what about you?"

Jace's gaze flickers to the windows, and he smiles. It's the barest hint of a grin, like he's remembering something nostalgic. "It was during a race back when I was just a kid. A few of the other competitors shifted and were cheating. And Harper was no better," he adds with a sideways glance toward me. "She used to cheat all the time when she was little."

I chuckle.

"There I was trailing the pack, furious and angry, and I just..." he paused, trailing off and shaking his head. "I just let the dragon take over because I knew in that moment that he could help me win."

"Did you?" I ask.

A cocky grin spreads across Jace's face. "You know we did."

I laugh.

We.

It really sinks in for me, in that moment. Me and my dragon—we're a team. An *us*. She has a life, and it's my duty to protect her.

"The point is," Drew interjects, "it's all about a moment of heightened emotion and alignment with your dragon. It's all about learning to trust each other and work together." He pauses. "When both of you are ready, all you have to do is let go. You'll shift the moment you give in."

I frown, not entirely sure what that would even feel like. What it would mean. I figure it's one of those things that only makes sense in the moment, when everything aligns perfectly, and all you have to do is relax into it.

Like Drew said—give in.

Truth be told, I'm not very good at that.

Besides, there's no way I'll shift before I have to face Zurie again. It's a bitter pill to swallow, since it would be easier to just dig my talons into her than fight her as a human.

Zurie is coming. It's just a matter of when, how, and where she will attack. I need to find a way to intercept her, but I don't even know where to start.

"Any word on Zurie?" I ask.

"No chatter," Drew admits.

Jace frowns, shooting another irritated glare toward Drew like he's exasperated the man even exists. "None for us either."

I wait for a moment, watching Jace's expression for signs of a lie. Any twitch, any tell at all that will give him away.

There's nothing. He's telling the truth.

"I *have* heard from the Darringtons, however," Jace adds, his intense glare fixed on Drew. "I know all about your father's promise, Drew. Hand over Rory, and you get everything you could ever dream of. You'll become the Boss. Money, power, women—you'll get it all."

Drew stiffens, his eyes narrowing as he stares down the thunderbird, silently daring him to continue.

Jace squares his shoulders like he's aching for a fight. "Is that what you're waiting for? The moment you can steal her away to hand her in?"

Drew's nose wrinkles in disgust. "I would never."

"I find that hard to believe," Jace admits, his jaw tensing as he prepares to draw blood.

"I don't need his money *or* his power," Drew says, sneering. "I have everything I could ever need already," he adds, pointing at me.

I can't help myself—I cover my mouth with my hand to hide my flattered smile.

Aw.

"You're a *Darrington*," Jace says, taking a few menacing steps closer. "All you *want* is power."

All right, this is going too far. At this point, they're just looking for an excuse to rip each other's throats out.

"Guys," I say tensely, my tone warning them to stop.

They ignore me.

"And your kind are so innocent?" Drew snaps. "Every Boss wants her, and somehow the Fairfax are the only ones with no intel leaked to the chatter? They're the only ones who don't want her dragged off to their Capital?" Drew scoffs. "Everything about you is suspicious. The Fairfax have their secrets too."

"Stop it!" I snap.

Primed and aching for a fight, both men freeze and tilt their heads to look at me. Jace is leaning forward, ready to throw a punch the moment Drew says the wrong thing—and Drew is no damn better. I catch his fingers curl into a fist, like he's ready to land a blow of his own on Jace's nose.

I put myself between them, forcing them to back away from each other as my glare darts between both of them. "Spectres don't live long if they trust too easily, and I'm no idiot. I know who I trust and who I don't, so you both need to back off."

My gaze shifts toward Jace, and for a moment, we share a tense look.

The fact is I'm not a Spectre anymore. I have three men and a sister I trust with my life. Harper is on my side, and Jace—well, I want him. I want to trust him. To have him. To feel his hands along my body. To feel them—

Hey, I snap inwardly at my dragon. *Stop being horny.*

She curls around herself in irritation, as if she can't believe how obstinate I can be.

Oh, baby girl, we're *just* getting started.

I shut my eyes, squeezing them as tightly as I can as I try to quell the tide of desire and lust that races through my traitorous body as it reacts to him once again. To him being so close. To my dragon's need for us to finally mate and finalize our bond, at any cost.

But there's tension too. Uncertainty. Dread.

Before I can say anything else, there are footsteps once again outside, and the door swings open once more.

This time Harper walks in, and her gaze falls instantly toward me.

"Oh, good, you're here," she says as she shuts the door behind her. "I figured you wouldn't be far. Find anything good?"

Jace groans, exasperated. "Can't you women give me a moment of peace in my own damn suite?"

Drew scoffs. "Did you just call me a woman?"

I try and fail to hide a small smile at the jibe, admittedly grateful for the interruption and not at all surprised Harper is here.

"Look, I don't have long before the chopper leaves," Harper says. "But I ran into Irena."

I impulsively stiffen with concern, and the only thing that moves is my gaze as I look at her. "Yeah?"

Harper hesitates, her mouth parted, as if she can't quite form the words or isn't sure what to say. "I see incredible magic lying dormant within her," the Fairfax Boss eventually says. "It's alarmingly similar to Kinsley Vaer."

"How similar?" I ask, tense.

Harper pauses, frowning in the silence. "Identical."

Her words sit on the quiet room as we all process what she just said.

Identical.

"Through a fluke in both the bio-weapon and the vaccine, it would appear that Kinsley inadvertently gave Irena all of her power," Harper says quietly, letting it sink in. "Kinsley gave Irena an *exact copy* of her abilities."

"What does that mean?" I ask.

"I don't know," Harper admits. "But it would seem you both have incredible power that you haven't yet accessed."

"Wait," Drew interjects, lifting his hand to slow down the conversation. "How do you know any of this?"

"I'm a thunderbird," Harper says dryly, with an annoyed glance at Drew, and I figure there isn't a Fairfax dragon alive who actually likes him. "Part of my training and trials to even become the Boss forced me to learn how to read dragons—especially the gifted ones. I have to be able to see a dragon's magic. A dragon's ability and potential," she adds, gesturing toward me. "I have to be able to see what other people can't, and my thunderbird lets me do that."

"And Kinsley's magic?" I press. "How are you so familiar with it?"

Harper frowns, her nose wrinkling slightly as a grim expression crosses her face. She gently lifts her shirt, revealing a long scar across her side that trails down beneath her pants, and I wonder how far down her leg it goes.

"Kinsley and I have met," Harper says simply.

I grit my teeth as a blast of rage shoots through me. I tighten my fists to keep my anger at bay, but white light flutters along my skin as I think of the pain Harper must have gone through.

It makes me want to rip out Kinsley's throat even *more*, and I didn't think that was even possible.

That woman—she's just *evil*.

Harper lowers her shirt and nods toward the door. "I offered Irena training, but—well, I'm sure you know how that went."

My shoulders slump a little in disappointment, and I set my hands on my hips as I try to figure out what the hell I'm going to do with my sister.

She can't fight what she is. She's running out of time to face it, but instead, she just keeps running *away*.

"Rory, look," Harper continues. "You need to push Irena to train with me. And if not me, then Jace. With *someone* who is at least *mildly* capable. Either an ice dragon or thunderbird."

She pauses and briefly looks at Drew, the only fire dragon in the room, but he doesn't seem to care about her unspoken jab.

"Irena's dragon is stifled," Harper continues. "If she doesn't give it room to breathe, it may not survive."

I take a deep breath, rubbing my temples as I try to figure out how on earth I'm going to do that. "I'll try, Harper."

"Good," says the Fairfax Boss with a nod. "Now—"

"Nope, we're done," Jace interjects, pointing toward the door. "Everyone out! Just go."

"I'm not finished talking," Harper says with an indignant look at the dojo master.

"You are," Jace says, lifting his eyebrows skeptically, as if he's astonished she would challenge him here in his domain.

The Fairfax Boss rolls her eyes and indulges him by walking out the door, leaving it open for the rest to follow. Drew stalks past Jace, the two of them glaring at each other until Drew disappears into the hallway. I go to join them, but Jace gently grabs my arm and pulls me back, closing the door so that only the two of us are in the war room.

Surprised, I wait to see what he wants.

He holds my arms, my forearms resting on his as he gently grabs my elbows and pulls me closer.

He presses his forehead against mine, and the electric current of our connection burns through me.

In that instant, he becomes tender, softening at my touch as he breathes me in.

But that's Jace—an asshole to everyone else, and tender toward me.

I have to admit, I kind of like it.

I relax my shoulders, leaning into him and giving him at least this moment of truce. There's so much I want to say, and I have absolutely no idea how to say any of it. I want to ask him about this choice Harper's forcing him to make. I want to tell him I was listening. I want to know what he's going to do and what he's thinking.

But I don't.

"Why won't you tell me about the bounties?" I ask instead to distract myself from the sensation burning through my traitorous body. I can't manage to pull away.

He doesn't answer at first. Instead, he gently runs his knuckle across my cheek as his gaze wanders my face.

"It's not weak to let someone protect you," he eventually says.

I smirk, looking up at him in playful challenge.

"Then maybe I should lock you in a tower and out of trouble, just to see how *you* like it."

He grins, and instead of answering, kisses me lightly on the nose. It's a feathery brush of his lips against my skin, and it leaves the lingering sensation of fluttery joy. Of love and devotion, all shared without a word.

It's his way of asking me to drop it. By indulging what my dragon wants, maybe he can distract me from what *I* want.

It won't work.

"You can stay," he says quietly with a nod toward his bedroom. "If you want."

Of course I *want* to.

But I won't.

"Goodnight, Jace Goodwin," I say instead.

I'm tempted to brush my lips across his, but I don't want to torture either of us any further.

As I walk into the hallway, I feel his eyes on my shoulder blades. It takes everything in me to not look back at him, to not give in to the burning desire that practically controls me every time he's near.

I'm just not sure what to make of him anymore, but that's kind of how it's always been. Jace Goodwin—the sexy, frustrating enigma.

And, for the time being, my mate.

CHAPTER NINE

As I lay in the wrinkled sheets of my bed, staring at the ceiling, I just can't sleep.

All I can think about is Zurie's next move. I'm trying to figure out what she will do. Where she will go. How she will try to draw me out—and then how she will try to kill me.

And, more importantly, how I could possibly kill *her*.

It's hard to stay ahead of the person who trained me.

There are just too many options. The one that makes the most sense is for her to try to lure me out of our secure location, but Irena and my men are the only bait I'll take. They're all safe here—for the moment. Irena's clearly cooped up. She's the risk, and probably the bait Zurie's counting on manipulating to her advantage.

But Irena's no idiot. She won't play into Zurie's hands.

That said, it's inevitable that Irena will eventually try to leave. She's cooped up and surrounded by the enemy—well, at least as far as she thinks. She's still not used to dragons, and even though she knows this is the safest place to be, it's only a matter of time before I catch her trying to sneak out.

Briefly, I debate putting a tracker on her. It would help me keep an eye on her, as well as let me know where she is if she gets into trouble.

Right. Because *that* won't backfire.

I chuckle quietly to myself. I'm such a damn hypocrite. This must be what Jace feels like all the time.

I close my eyes, trying to force myself to sleep. Irena isn't some helpless girl. She knows her limits, and that's one of the reasons she hasn't left yet. After the coma, Irena isn't at full strength. Her senses are off. Her body feels weirdly *new.* She has all these unfamiliar skills she doesn't understand, and she misses things.

She's re-learning everything she ever knew about herself—and that takes time.

Besides, I know she wants to watch over me, too. Maybe I can use that to my advantage to keep her here a little longer.

I groan, pressing my head further back into the pillow and give up on trying to sleep.

Surrendering to the insomnia, I roll out of bed, my hair a tangled mess as I yank on some clothes and strap my gun to my hip. If I can't sleep, I'll go visit Tucker. It'll be a treat to see my weapons expert, and I might as well see if he knows anything about the Knights' plans or movements.

Without so much as a creak of the hinge, I peek into the hallway and scan the empty corridor. The closed doors of the suites in this section of the castle stretch down the hallway—Tucker's, Irena's and then Levi's, all in a row. Everyone's up here except for Drew, who Jace still has on lockdown in a less glamorous part of the embassy.

I frown as I walk toward Tucker's door, hoping Jace and Drew get the hell over whatever argument they're having now. It seems like there's a new one every day, and it's only getting worse.

I'm sick of it.

I twist the knob of Tucker's door, fully expecting it to be locked. To my surprise, the door opens.

Huh.

I hesitate for a moment, simply staring at the now-open door, and it's difficult to believe that Tucker would leave his suite unlocked.

My impulse is to worry. To be on guard.

Something about this isn't right.

Why would a former Knight leave his door unlocked in a dragon embassy?

My hand impulsively goes to the gun at my hip, and I lean into the parlor, trying to get a sense of what might be going on. Nothing feels off. Nothing's out of place. The soft rumble of Tucker snoring filters through his open bedroom door to the left, and for a moment, I just stand there, listening.

No footsteps.

No creaks in the floor.

There's no one else here.

I relax my shoulders and shut the door behind me, still careful to scope the room even though it doesn't seem like there's any danger.

When I reach his doorway, I lean against the frame and simply watch him for a second. He's sprawled across his bed, half tucked into his blankets as they drape over the side of his mattress.

For a moment, I just admire him. The hard muscle of his chest that peeks out from beneath the sheets. His handsome face. The stubble along his jaw.

My Tucker.

I set my gun on the nightstand and crawl into bed beside him, wrapping my arms around his waist as I burrow my head against his neck. He mumbles in his sleep, and I can't quite make out what he's saying as he wraps his arms around me, pulling me close.

"Hey, Rory," he says groggily, his eyes still closed.

"Hey," I say quietly, watching his face to see if he's waking up.

If he needs to sleep, I really shouldn't wake him— but I can't stop thinking about Zurie. About the Knights. About everyone who's coming after us, and all the ways we need to prepare.

"Is there any chatter from your father?" I ask softly. "From the Knights?"

With his eyes still closed, he chuckles. "Do you ever sleep, woman?"

I laugh. "Sleep is for the weak."

"Then I'm a frail old lady because I need some shut-eye." He grins, his eyes still closed. "Stop thinking and start snoring, will you?"

"I can't. I just—"

He interrupts me by putting his strong hand across my face, chuckling to himself as he wordlessly shushes me and snores at a comically loud volume to get his point across.

I laugh and pull his palm off my face. "Tucker, this is serious."

Yet again, he interrupts me—though this time, he takes one of the pillows off the bed and gently sets it over my mouth. The soft fluff covers most of my face, and I'm barely able to peek over the edge to teasingly glare at him.

Ass.

I sit up, poking him playfully on his cheek. At first, he doesn't do anything, so I do it again. As my fingertip presses against his skin, he grabs my hand. With a lighthearted tug, he pulls me onto his chest. His eyes finally open as he watches me, his strong grip pinning me against him.

"Fine. You win," he says with a sexy smile. "But you have to help me clean my guns if we're going to be talking about work."

A mischievous little grin spreads across my face as I playfully look down at his crotch. I wiggle my ass just a little, teasing him.

He laughs. "No, my real guns," he says with a nod toward the closet. "Pervert."

I laugh as Tucker releases me and stands. His well-defined muscles accentuate his gorgeous body, and with only pajama pants on, he gives me a full view of his beautiful back. The muscle along his spine trails toward his ass, and I'm tempted to just rip off what little clothes he's wearing.

Sexy and shirtless—this man knows *exactly* what he does to me.

Tucker runs a hand through his hair as he walks toward the closet, and my eyes linger on his stunning body as he disappears into the closet.

I have to confess, I'm a little disappointed that he's actually going to put me to work—and not in the fun way.

He returns a moment later with a half dozen rifles in his arms and sets them on the bed before tossing me a rag. I briefly scan the weapons—various short-range dragon killers, as well as a more traditional rifle of a lesser caliber.

The kind of rifle you reserve for killing humans, rather than dragons.

My smile falls as he hands me that one to clean. It's a subtle reminder that he knows everything's at stake. That he's been preparing. That he's doing everything in his power to keep us—both me *and* himself—safe.

I quietly begin to disassemble the gun, not entirely sure what to say now that I have him awake. There was so much I wanted to ask—so much I wanted to debate and discuss—but now the room feels somber.

In the silence, all I can do is get to work, to keep

my hands busy and to let my mind wander about what's coming for us.

"There's no chatter from the Knights," Tucker says, interrupting the silence after a while. He disassembles one of the dragon killers, checking the barrel as he wipes it down. "I suppose that's to be expected, since they think I'm a traitor to the cause."

I pause, watching him as he works. "How are you doing, Tucker?"

He briefly looks at me, a bit of a confused expression on his face before he returns to the gun. "Fine. Why?"

"They were your family," I remind him, setting down the gun I was cleaning. "They were everything to you before—well, before *me*."

He shakes his head. "You're wrong, Rory. They're just killers. They always have been, and even when I wanted them to be more, they could never step up. They didn't want to." He pauses, looking at me with a small smile. "*You're* my family."

I grin, flattered as hell and equally as honored by the compliment. "When did you become such a softie?"

He laughs and nods to the rifle I've set on the bed. "I believe you have a gun over there to clean, babe."

I chuckle. "A bossy softie, but still a softie."

As we return to our work, the room once more settles into a solemn stillness. Every now and then, I check on him, glancing over to the former Knight as he becomes a bit too invested in his cleaning. He polishes the same spot on one of the barrels four times, his eyes slipping in and out of focus, and I know he's concerned. He has to be. He's lost himself in some kind of memory—or worse, some kind of dread.

It's not like him to keep things from me. Aside from Irena, he was the first person I ever trusted. For him to be this silent for this long means whatever he's about to say is going to be dark—far darker than I'm used to hearing from him.

My shoulders tense impulsively, my back arching as I wait for him to speak. The waiting is agonizing, but I need to give him space to work through what he wants to say. I need to bite my tongue and let him speak when he's ready.

"Knights aren't as sophisticated as Spectres," he admits, his eyes still on his weapon. "But they *are* deadly and smart. They're not to be underestimated, and I think that's what a lot of people do wrong. They think the Knights are just a bunch of stupid terrorists who don't know better and make mistakes." He hesitates, shaking his head. "They're wrong."

With a few loud clicks and a grunt of effort, he

reassembles the largest dragon killer, snapping the barrel into place as he examines it. "The nearest Knights facility is ten hours away by car. They'll guess I've told you about it, and they'll leave it abandoned, maybe stage some activity to throw us off their scent."

"What will they do instead?" I ask as I snap my rifle together, finally done cleaning it.

"Easy." His voice is deep and dark, his mouth a grim line as he grabs the next gun to clean. "They'll assemble at the second-nearest encampment, a facility Father was never fond of using because of its isolated nature, far from supply lines." His biceps flex as he disassembles the new rifle. "Seeing as you and I are enemy number one for them, they won't wait long to mobilize against us. They'll be getting recon and coming up with a possible plan of attack—one they'll act on quickly. For the moment, none of the other missions will matter as much as either capturing or killing us both."

I square my shoulders, ready for whatever they try. "What are they going to do, Tucker?"

He shrugs. "They're going to try to switch things up. To surprise me," he says, staring off out the window. "They're going to pull out old techniques, old strategies. Ones they think I haven't studied. If I had to guess, they'll probably pull a terrorist event and blame dragons, frame them in some way." He grimaces and checks the scope on his rifle. "They're going to try to stir up some dissent, to make the humans hate the dragons all the more. It'll be an attempt to get Jace and Harper to kick us out, which makes any and every Fairfax dragon the Knights' prime target."

"By terrorist event, you mean they're going to blow up human-run buildings?" I ask, disgusted as it all clicks for me, making perfect—albeit absolutely *deranged*—sense. "They're going to hurt people, all to make their attack seem like some pro-dragon assault?"

He nods. "Anything to stir up trouble. They have all kinds of propaganda stored all over the world in every language. Pamphlets, banners, signs—you name it. If they can make it seem like the dragons are trying to orchestrate a hostile takeover and overthrow human governments worldwide, they can undermine any dragon alliances with human militaries." He pauses, shaking his head. "It's been on my father's list for a while, something he's always talked about but never quite had the resources to pull off."

I balk. "You think he's found a way to secure the resources he needs to orchestrate something as monumental as this?"

"I don't know," Tucker admits. "But he's desperate enough to try even if he doesn't."

With a deep and discouraged frown I have to admit
—Tucker has a *very* good point.

"The Knights have tens of thousands of troops
worldwide," Tucker says. "They get more every day,
every time the dragons do something short-sighted or
outright cruel. But it's still not enough. So, as long as
they can't outright attack dragons, they'll try to
villainize them instead."

"As awful as it is, it makes sense," I admit.

"They've done it before." Tucker cleans the barrel
of his dragon killer and clicks it back into place. "Here
and there—small trials, just to see if it'll work. They…"
Tucker grinds his teeth, trailing off as he shakes his
head in disgust. "They've destroyed small towns, Rory.
Killed everyone there. Man, woman, and child.
Humans. Fellow *humans*," he says, his voice nearly
breaking. "All to make the dragons look worse."

My chest tightens with horror. With revulsion. I
don't even know what to say. There aren't words for
that kind of evil.

Tucker's gorgeous green eyes settle on me, slipping
briefly out of focus as he relives something horrible.
He pinches the bridge of his nose to distract himself
from the memory and shakes his head. "Nothing's
beneath my father."

I lean forward, kneeling on the mattress as I

tenderly brush my thumb across his jaw. He looks at me again, those gorgeous eyes stealing my breath away, and something in him relaxes. It's a subtle movement, but it's there—knowing he's not alone. Knowing I'm always here for him, no matter what his father has done—or forced *him* to do—in the past.

Tucker grabs my wrist and gently kisses the heel of my palm. "We have to be careful, Rory. In fact, all Fairfax dragons have to be careful right now because they're protecting us. They're at the greatest risk. The Knights will probably find and torture anyone who's even remotely connected to the Fairfax family."

I frown, swallowing hard as my gaze drifts down toward the gun beside me. A familiar rage starts to brew within my core, smoldering and simmering as it flickers to life.

I know this feeling all too well—it's the kind of hate that burns me alive anytime I see injustice. It sparks and fizzes, growing more powerful with every passing second I think about the General.

The longer I stay here, the more Fairfax dragons I put at risk.

The more I put Harper at risk.

"The things he's made me do, Rory," Tucker says quietly, his voice cracking with anguish. He sighs and sits on the bed, his back to me with his head tilted to look out the window.

I hug Tucker from behind, my arms wrapping around his hard body as I hold him to my chest. He sighs and grabs my wrists, pulling my arms tighter around him, like he's afraid I'll let go.

"I've always hated him for that," Tucker admits. "Every torture session he forced me to join or lead made me hate the man more. The screams, the begging for mercy, the begging for *death...*" Tucker trails off, his body rigid as he remembers things I'm sure he doesn't want to recall.

He's lost in it.

In the grief. In the pain. In the memory of all he's had to do to stay alive. Of all the ways he's had to compromise his morals and who he is, just to *survive.*

Tenderly, I kiss his neck. I hold him tightly, letting him know I'm there without having to say a word.

Together, we share the silence.

I lose track of how long it goes on because it doesn't matter. All that matters is that we're here for each other, always and forever.

His pain is eerily familiar, and I know exactly what he went through. What he's going through now. Zurie forced me to do unspeakable things, often to people and dragons who didn't deserve that kind of brutal agony. I've assassinated. Hunted. Stolen. Tortured. I've been her executioner while she simply sat there and watched, all to prove a point.

To *punish* me, she tried to strip me of the things that made me human—my values, my decency, my sense of right and wrong.

She failed, of course, but not for a lack of trying.

From a young age, I was nothing but a tool to her. Nothing but a weapon. Nothing but something to sell or be used as she saw fit.

"We found another way, Tucker," I say tenderly. "We escaped that life."

He shakes his head and looks at me over his shoulder. "You *gave* me another way."

Our eyes meet, and for once, he's not grinning or joking. He simply sits there, uncharacteristically serious, and I can feel the gratitude radiating off of him. It's breathless, and just like that, I get it.

I get *him*.

"You're so *gooey*," I joke, grinning.

He laughs and turns around, kneeling on the bed as he pulls me into a tight hug. His hands cradle the back of my head, his fingers weaving through my hair as he holds me tightly.

"The Knights and the Spectres are coming for us

both," he says quietly. "They're not going to stop until we're dead. You know that, right?"

"Then we kill them first," I say, weaving my hands around his waist. "Or better yet, we destroy them all and stop them from ever hurting anyone else."

He chuckles. "You're such a sweet talker."

I laugh, setting my head against his chest—and, deep down, I think he suspects I'm joking.

But I'm not.

Not even a *little*.

CHAPTER TEN

Naked and wrapped in Tucker's sheets, I awake to the patter of stealthy footsteps creeping through the living room toward me.

Toward *us.*

The warmth from Tucker's naked body seeps through the sheets beside me, so it's not him slipping through the shadows.

Whoever's coming toward us, they shouldn't be here.

With my left hand pinning the sheets to my chest, I grab my gun off the nightstand and sit up. In one fluid and deadly motion, the barrel of my gun is aimed at the door and ready to take a life.

Silent and still, I wait as a silhouette steals through the darkness outside the bedroom. My thumb presses against the cold metal as I cock the gun, the subtle click of the mechanism almost inaudible in the cold, silent night.

The shadow nears, stepping into a beam of moon-light cutting through a gap in the curtains.

Irena.

I sigh, releasing the tension in my shoulders as I lower my gun and glare at her. She holds a phone in her hand and frowns as she watches me, stern and utterly unsurprised that I'm naked in Tucker's bed.

I open my mouth to speak, to demand that I get some privacy now that I've *finally* gotten to sleep—mostly thanks to Tucker wearing me out with some exercise between his sheets.

A familiar voice pipes through the phone in her hand, interrupting my thoughts and killing the words in my throat.

"I know you're there, Irena," Zurie says. "Answer me, damn it."

I impulsively tense, my gaze locked on the phone as my eyes narrow with hatred. My heart skips a beat, mostly in surprise, and I quickly sift through all the ways this can benefit us.

There aren't many.

At the sound of a strange woman's voice in his room, Tucker bolts upright and lifts his own gun from beneath his pillow. His aim isn't as sharp as mine, as he still has a groggy fog in his eye, but he angles his weapon in Irena's general vicinity. He's poised and coiled, ready to spring and ready to fire at a moment's notice, even as he's not fully awake.

Thankfully, he doesn't shoot anything.

It takes a moment for him to recognize Irena, and when he does, he groans and lowers the barrel of his gun. He rubs his face, trying to clear the sleep from his eyes. "You Quinn girls sure know how to make a man jumpy."

"Are you muted?" I ask, nodding toward the phone.

Irena nods. "I don't even know how she got this number. This is the phone Jace gave me."

I raise an eyebrow in surprise, impressed and grateful that Jace would do such a thing, considering what Irena and I once were. He really is doing everything he can to make her feel at home, and he's doing it all for me.

"She's trying to rile you up," I point out. "Zurie wants you to leave this place and expose yourself."

"Obviously," Irena says curtly. "She wants to isolate us."

"I have to confess, I'm disgusted," Zurie interjects, her dark voice piping through the phone once again even though she can't hear us. "Keeping company with dragons. I thought even *you* were better than that."

Irena frowns, momentarily glaring daggers at the phone. I watch my sister's face, concerned that such a mild jab could get such a reaction.

Even though Irena knows what Zurie's doing, it seems as though our former mentor found a way to pick at some very old wounds.

Beside me, Tucker reaches toward his nightstand, and I hear the quiet beeps of his phone as he texts someone. "The guys are on their way."

"Great. Sure," I say, shrugging as I wave my hand over my naked body. "We can do this without clothes. That's not weird at all."

Tucker grins and stands, holding a sheet over his lower half as he reaches for his pajama pants off the floor. "Fine. If I absolutely must let you dress, I'll get you a shirt. But that's all, you hear me?"

"You're such a gentleman," I say, rolling my eyes.

In the living room beyond the bedroom suite, the door to the hallway is thrown open. Levi charges in, furious and fierce, scanning the room as if he's ready to kill whoever was stupid enough to enter and threaten us.

Seconds later, his eyes land on me, and he closes

the gap between us in mere seconds as he races to my side. "Are you all right?"

"Yeah, fine," I say with a grateful smile.

Despite everything, despite how serious this is and how quickly it could devolve, I'm grateful for him. For his concern. To be so fiercely adored by someone like Levi—that's a gift I cherish, former assassin or no.

Tucker exits the closet and throws me a long shirt. I grab it and tug it on, grateful for something to cover me even though I don't have any underwear to put on underneath it, thanks to Tucker's rough idea of foreplay. I briefly eye the ripped shards of my underwear laying against the wall and smirk at the memory as warmth pools down my legs.

"Rory," Irena chides, as if she can read my mind.

"Right." I clear my throat, trying to rid my mind of the raunchy thoughts and the memory of Tucker's ravenous tongue between my thighs. "Give it here."

Irena frowns, watching me briefly before handing it to me. As the phone hits my palm, Jace and Drew charge into the room. Both men instantly look at me, and I can see the relief run across their faces as our gazes meet. In unison, their shoulders seem to relax, like they had both expected to find me bleeding out on the floor.

Once their shared moment of relief passes, Jace

glares jealously at Tucker. His jaw tenses, and his hand subtly balls into a fist, but he doesn't say anything.

With Zurie on the line, I don't have time for this.

I unmute the phone. "What's the plan, Zurie?" I ask, letting my voice drop a little in octave to meet hers.

Relaxed. Calm. Collected.

A little bored.

I try to enjoy every word, to speak slowly and clearly. The goal is to seem as though she doesn't faze me or bother me in the least, as if she's nothing more than a toy I'm quickly growing bored of.

I try to remember how Ian spoke—whenever he called to taunt me, he had a way of speaking that made it sound like he was playing with his food. It was like everything was beneath him and life was nothing but a dull game he had already mastered.

It was irritating as *fuck.*

And I can totally mimic it. Zurie's going to *hate* this.

With a cocky smile I use the memory of Ian's inflection as inspiration and quickly shift gears. "You really think a little goading is enough to lure Irena out of here? You think you're going to use her as bait against me? That's just lazy, woman. Don't get *sloppy.*"

The phone is silent—and, if I'm not mistaken, I

hear the subtlest intake of breath as Zurie betrays her surprise.

In all likelihood, she wasn't expecting Irena to share this information. In the past, even in cases like this, Irena and I did things solo. We would share and debate after the fact, but rarely in the moment. In the middle of the night when there was a risk, we simply dealt with it by ourselves and handled the fallout as needed.

But that was the old way. Before we knew better.

In the silence that follows, I know I'm right. I wish I could see Zurie's face. It would let me better gauge the situation and who currently holds the upper hand. Her expressions always betray so much more than her voice.

I'm just going to have to make do.

This conversation needs to go somewhere. I can't let Zurie off the phone, not yet—I need to manipulate Zurie into giving me something. She needs to betray a clue, anything at all. Even the smallest hint might mean the difference between life and death for us.

I have to trip her up.

"Silence, huh?" I yawn, making sure the sound is exaggerated enough for her to hear through the phone. "Figures. You're so predictable. Besides, I already know your plan," I add, lying through my teeth. "I just thought I'd give you the chance to do something *interesting* for a change."

"Enlighten me then," Zurie quips. "What's my plan, little Lorelei?"

I grit my teeth in anger at hearing my real name.

At the memory it always stirs within me.

My only memory of Mother is her leaning over my bed when I was little. A foggy gray room. A blurry face I can't recall. Brown hair and a broad smile, but that's it.

"Little Lorelei, my baby," she'd said, her voice echoing.

That's it—the whole memory, over in a flash—but it's something I've always cherished.

Low blow, Zurie. Low blow.

At least she didn't hang up.

I brace myself, trying to force a smarmy tone even though all I want to do is crush the phone in my hand. "You're going to try to lure one of us away from here and use her as bait against the other." It's my best guess, and I toss her snippets of the plan in an attempt to drag this conversation out. "You want to divide us and then dangle us in front of each other to get us out in the open." I pause, letting my theory settle in the air as if it's truth. "You were always terrified of how strong we are together, Zurie, and we can see right through you."

And that, right there, is the key to my plan.

Gods, I hope this works.

If I can jab at Zurie's few insecurities, I stand a real chance of getting her to spill something she didn't intend to share. I don't have many choices, but she does have a few wounds for me to rub salt against. Her fear of failure. Her fear that perhaps she isn't the one in control of the situation.

It doesn't have to be true for her to slip up and make a mistake.

"You're *afraid*," I say, goading her and stoking the fires.

I'm close.

"A Spectre has no fear," Zurie practically growls.

"Hmm," I say lazily, eying my fingernails to help sell the boredom I'm trying to weave into my tone. "What does that make you, then?"

Around me, everyone can barely contain their gasps of surprise. Even Irena's eyes widen, her lips parting slightly in shock that I would dare say such a thing to the Ghost.

But I'm not the scared little girl I was when I lived under Zurie's thumb. I'm not the obedient servant, controlled by my mentor and killing on demand.

My insult was a wicked blow, one I very much intended to give. One that's going to cripple the last of Zurie's resolve.

The woman's sole identity is wrapped up in leading the Spectres. Take that away, and I disrupt everything she stands for. Everything she is.

Take that away, and I can make her *weak*.

"How dare you," Zurie snaps. Her voice rumbles like thunder, and I can practically feel the hatred rolling off of every word.

My little plan is working.

My jaw tenses in anticipation as I barely hold back a retort. I need to wait, to let her sit in the silence, but it's excruciating. Almost breathless, I wait for her to make a rare but long overdue error.

"Every breath you take is numbered," Zurie barks. "I'm coming for you. For your men. For everything you've sacrificed so much to protect."

"And I'm waiting," I say calmly, firmly in control of the conversation. "Make your move, Zurie. I can wait as long as it takes for you to show your cards."

It's another lie, but it'll make Zurie impatient.

That's all I need to do right now.

With this simple phone call, we're two masters playing chess, and the question is simply which of us will make the first mistake.

"You could've had everything, Rory," Zurie says, her tone genuinely baffled. "Absolutely *anything*. I was going to give you the Spectres. I was going to make you the Ghost."

"And then what?" I counter, not bothering to mask my contempt. "Then what else would you have made me do? Who would you have forced me to become? You just want to control me, Zurie. And the moment I refused, you tried to *kill* me." I grit my teeth with loathing for this vile woman—this person I once thought of as a mother, in her own fractured way. "I'm not yours to own and control anymore."

"No, I guess you're not," Zurie says. Her tone shifts, and it's almost impossible to even recognize her anymore. She sounds almost—well, I would say sad, but this is Zurie. She doesn't feel grief or loss.

She just feels rage.

"My legacy is gone," she continues. "There's nothing left. No one to rule when I leave. No one I trained, anyway," she adds, and I can almost imagine her shrugging. "Diesel will take over when I die, and whoever he trains will take over after him. My only legacy depended on the two of you, and you both failed me. The least I can do is end what I started before my time is up."

I pause, thinking through the words I want to say

next and making sure they're perfect before I so much as open my mouth.

"If you come for me," I say with a deadly chill in my voice, "if you come for Irena or for my men, your time will be up much faster than you think."

I let the silence settle between us, more certain than ever that Zurie has to die.

She won't take this threat seriously because she's vain and blind to the truth—at least when it comes to me. I was the youngest. The screw-up. The one who didn't always blindly obey—the one who listened to intuition, rather than orders.

And that's what brought me here—to this new life. What she always saw as my weakness was in fact my greatest strength.

She just didn't realize it, and she's still oblivious. It's the one chink in her armor.

Any moment now, she will dismiss my threat like it's nothing. But that's because she has underestimated me for far too long.

"I gave you the chance for a truce, Zurie," I add. "You were a fool not to take it."

"You always did overestimate your ability," my former mentor says. "And now you're just cocky."

I chuckle. "Quite the contrary. I know *exactly* what

my limits are." I pause for effect, knowing my next words will *really* piss her off. "Do you?"

There's a moment of silence that follows, and in it is the quietest, most impatient sigh I've ever heard. I almost miss it, but it's there.

Zurie hangs up, and I win this round.

I watch the phone, imagining what she must be doing right now—the things she must be throwing across the room. The destruction that's going to come from her anger.

All because she thinks I'm still the obstinate little assassin I was under her care. All because she doesn't realize who I've become and what I can do.

I know my skills. I know my limits, and Zurie has absolutely no clue what she's up against. She's used to facing dragons—Bosses even—but I'm something else. Something different.

Something *more*.

I have allies, ones I know are here for me no matter what or when I need them. For the first time in my life, I know exactly what I'm doing—and, more importantly, why I'm doing it.

Zurie's greatest weakness is that she doesn't see the change in me.

Tucker grins broadly. "So your real name is Lore—"

"Don't," I interrupt, my voice dripping with warning.

Only Mother gets to call me that. Zurie using my real name was a cruel blow.

"Sorry," he says genuinely, kissing me on the side of my head.

"It's fine," I lie, trying to shove away the deep sense of loss that's trying to bubble to the surface.

With a deep and steadying breath, I fight the impulse to crush the phone in my hand. It's not mine to destroy, after all. I offer it to my sister, but she just looks at it and shakes her head. "No thanks."

I shrug, crushing it in my palm after all and tossing it in the trash bin by the door. As I throw it aside, I feel so much lighter, like I just cut the final ribbon that connected me to my former mentor—that small part of me that still cared about the woman who raised me.

"Zurie's plan is bigger than we thought," Irena says, biting her lip as she leans back against the wall with her hands in her pant pockets. She stares at the floor, lost in her buzzing mind.

I nod, crossing my arms. I have the same intuitive hit, the same idea that whatever Zurie's really up to, it's so much bigger than we can even conceive of at the moment. "She probably has a contingency plan," I add. "Something to make life hell for us if she's killed."

"Like what?" Drew asks, leaning against the doorframe.

I shake my head, as I honestly don't know. "Past Ghosts have done this, and every plan is different. It ranges from a full-scale terrorist attack to biological warfare."

"Oh, fun," Tucker says derisively, laying back in bed. "I love enemies that keep coming after me, even after they're dead."

"It's always a doomsday option," I continue, ignoring his sarcasm. "A total self-destruct that cashes in all favors, resources, and connections they have."

"Then we stop it," Jace says simply, his hands on his hips as he looks at me. "We figure it out, and we stop her."

"You make it sound so easy," I say with a little shrug.

"I have the best surveillance team and equipment in the world," Jace replies with a cocky smirk. "Easy might be an oversimplification, but we can do it."

I nod. "Find out what you can."

He grins. "Oh, you're giving me orders now?"

I roll my eyes, but I can't suppress a chuckle. "Jace, not now."

"What tech do you have left?" Irena asks, interrupting our banter.

I shrug. "A few voids, some override devices. Most of it's broken or gone. Drew?"

He shakes his head. "I used it all."

I hesitate, studying his face for signs of a lie, but there isn't one. He just has the one spent void—useless to us and impossible to reverse engineer.

I figure he will find that out the hard way, but he could've just asked.

Irena grimaces, setting her head back against the wall as a determined expression crosses her face. Her brows pinch together, and she stares at the ceiling with her lips in a taut, grim line. Her bright green eyes narrow, brimming with grit and resolve, and my heart twinges with dread.

Oh, *shit.*

I know that look.

She just made a decision—the kind I can't undo. The sort of choice that can never be undone. One she will see through to the bitter end, even if it kills her.

I've seen it on her face only three times in my life, and the months afterward were awful. Filled with bullets. Blood. Broken bones. A *lot* of cursing and gritted teeth as we tended each other's wounds—but in the end, she always got her way.

Every time she makes one of those choices, she succeeds.

So far, anyway.

In the past, she's always launched into her plan after she dons that expression. And this time, to my disappointment, she's eerily silent.

I wait, watching her as the silence stretches on, and it's clear she has no intention of telling me anything.

That means whatever choice she just made doesn't involve me.

It means she's going to go do something foolhardy.

"Irena," I say with a lethal warning in my voice, one that *dares* her to lie to me. "What are you planning?"

"Nothing," she says, glancing quickly away.

A tell.

She lied.

"Irena—"

"Nothing," she interrupts, her tone icy and curt. She glares at me, daring me to press this.

Oh, she's definitely up to something.

Something big.

Something I'm going to have to stop her from doing.

"Do you think Zurie is staying at a nearby safe-house?" Irena asks, clearly changing the subject.

I tilt my head and groan in annoyance, barely able to mask my irritation at the transparent sleight of hand. I'm tempted to dig in and argue with her until she gives away whatever she was planning, but I decide to just catch her in the act later.

It's the only way I'm going to snap her out of whatever suicidal bullshit she's trying to get herself into.

"No," I begrudgingly admit. "A nearby safehouse is too easy. Zurie will be in a new location and expect us to check all the safehouses we know of."

"Or expect us *not* to," Irena says, her gaze shifting toward me.

I frown as I consider the idea, but I just don't think it's even remotely plausible. Zurie never stays in the same safehouse twice. It was one of the first things she taught us—to keep moving. To be unpredictable. To never let anyone guess what you're about to do.

It keeps our enemies guessing—which works in our favor.

"We can check," I say with a halfhearted shrug. "I just don't want us to waste our manpower or resources on a goose chase."

"What about the Omega-3?" Irena asks.

It's the bunker in the hills of Montana. I shake my head. "That was destroyed on a mission shortly before, well, this," I say with a gesture to the embassy around us. "Some Palarne dragons found it."

"Huh." Irena rubs her jaw, thinking. "Beta-7?"

"Maybe," I admit. "I guess it's worth checking. Alpha-10?"

She nods. "Could be. What about Omega-4?"

I shake my head. "Zurie always hated that one. It's nothing but a swamp."

"She might go there just to throw us off," Irena points out.

I groan, and it takes everything in me not to shake her. She's just trying to make me forget about whatever she's planning, and it won't work.

This is all a waste of time.

I briefly scan the room, only to find my four men watching me with various versions of the same astounded expression. I figure they're probably surprised at the sheer volume of data Irena and I are sifting through, but this is our normal.

Although she's being a bit of an ass, I have to admit it's nice to have my sister back.

"Give me those locations," Jace says, looking at me with a barely veiled hint of awe. "All of them. Anything you have. We'll run simultaneous scans and send squads to sweep them. At a minimum, we can bug them. Best case, we find a Spectre and have a little talk," he adds with a grin, and I figure I know the kind of talk he wants to have.

It probably involves bloody knuckles and a lot of pain—for them.

"Just keep in mind they're probably vacant," I remind him. "But yeah, I suppose it can't hurt to check. Still, Zurie never stayed in the same place twice so I'm pretty sure this is all a waste of time, Jace. You won't get anything from it."

"We may as well try," the dojo master says with a shrug.

"Fair enough," I admit.

"If we're done, I have something to share," Drew interjects impatiently, lifting his phone. "This little nugget just came through my network." He taps the screen, and a recording pipes through the speaker.

"I didn't ask for excuses," a familiar man's voice barks.

The General.

Impulsively, I look at Tucker. The weapons expert freezes in place at the harsh grate of his father's voice, his features twisted and tortured as he stares at the floor. His ear twitches slightly as he strains to listen.

After Zurie and the General tried to kill us all, and after Zurie destroyed the Knights' base and blamed it on me, a small part of me had hoped he was dead. A small part of me had hoped the General was simply buried in the rubble somewhere, broken and no longer breathing, out of our hair.

But the man's a survivor, much to my disappointment.

"They can't keep me out of commission for much longer," the General barks again. There's a soft beeping in the background, something that sounds vaguely like a heart rate monitor, and I figure he's probably confined to a hospital bed somewhere.

"Sorry, sir, but you have three months left," a man says, his tone exasperated and pleading. "Please just stay in the bed. You've—"

"You've got *one* month," the General interjects. "Get me walking again, damn it. I don't care if I limp. Just get me on my feet!"

The doctor groans, exasperated. "Sir, you need to heal."

"No, I need to kill that bitch who brainwashed my son!" the General shouts.

"Classy," I mutter dryly.

The asshole can try to kill me—it would be nice to punch the man in the face. Besides, I would hardly call giving Tucker a way out of that hellhole an act of brainwashing.

"Is Brett in position yet? Get—" The General coughs furiously, the sound raspy and jarring. "Get him on the phone, damn it. I need to plan the joint-force assault. There's—"

"Sir, this isn't a secured line—"

"Shut *up*, damn you," the General interjects, coughing again. "Get... get... what did you..."

There's a moment of silence before the soft sound of snoring filters through the phone. A nurse breathes a sigh of relief as someone jostles the phone.

"He keeps fighting his meds, Doctor," she says, her voice getting louder as she speaks, as if she picked it up.

"Keep him unconscious as often as possible," the doctor orders. "If he keeps working himself up, he will never get better."

"Yes, Doctor," the nurse says, sighing. Seconds later, the connection cuts out.

I rub my eyes, frustrated and disappointed that we have to deal with this on top of Zurie. On top of everything else.

"I really hoped he was dead," Jace admits. He pauses for a second, glancing at Tucker as he realizes the reality of what he just said. "No offense."

Tucker shakes his head. "The feeling's mutual."

"Who's Brett?" I ask, watching Tucker's face as the grief slowly takes him.

Tucker sighs, rubbing his jaw as he tries to find the

words. "Brett Clarke is one of my father's favorites. He's been slowly climbing up the ranks, and when Carter was..." Tucker trails off, glancing at me. "Promoted," he continues, referring to Zurie recruiting the man from the Knights' ranks, "I heard that Brett took his place. As far as I'm aware, he's the General's Second-in-Command now. It's what Father was priming me for, but he never felt I was ready—because I wasn't. Because I didn't want the job at all. Now, I guess he's giving Brett the chance to prove himself, even though he's young."

"How old?" I press.

Tucker shrugs. "About my age. Sometimes I wondered if my dad thought of Brett and Carter as the sons he never really had." Tucker's jaw tenses, and he glares out the window, lost in thought once again.

"What else?" Drew presses.

I glare at the Darrington dragon, annoyed at his lack of compassion given everything that's happening right now.

Drew tilts his head in exasperation, frowning as I silently chide him.

I have to admit, he's probably right. We need to know who we're up against, and we need to know everything we can get our hands on. If these people are coming after us, we need all the information we can get.

"He's a sniper," Tucker says, staring at his hands. "Master of hand-to-hand combat and wickedly clever with war strategy, but he could never handle weapons the way I did. He was never as good with a pistol or rifle—all he could handle were the sniper missions. That's why he didn't progress as fast as me or Carter." Tucker pauses, his eyes glazed over as he sifts through his memories. "But what he lacked in skill, he made up for in sheer fire and grit. He's hated dragons his whole life, guys. He even killed one in front of a human, his old girlfriend. She was horrified, but he found purpose. He said God spoke to him in that moment." Tucker rolls his eyes—*hard*—and shakes his head in disgust. "A few days later, he shows up at the nearest Knights compound. He's been kissing my father's ass ever since."

"So, he wasn't raised in the Knights," I say, starting to piece it together. "He came to you guys later."

Tucker nods. "Unlike me and Carter, yeah. He was sixteen when he joined."

I pace quietly back and forth, briefly looking at Levi as he quietly leans against the wall, watching and listening to all of us. His clear, sharp eyes narrow slightly as he takes in all this information.

Our gazes meet, and I wonder what he's thinking. What concerns him most—and what he thinks is coming for us. But Levi only speaks when he wants to, and I learned a while ago that I can't press him to share until he's ready.

Jace absently rubs the stubble on his jaw. "So, they're sending Brett on an assault. Where? Toward what? It's clearly joint force, so it probably includes the Spectres."

"Zurie's call was probably a diversion," I say, starting to piece it all together. "Maybe to throw us off."

"Or maybe to keep us in place," Levi says, his voice dark and deep.

We all pause to stare blankly at him, baffled by the mere suggestion of an onslaught against the dojo. For a moment, I can't quite process what he said.

"She wouldn't attack here," Jace says, almost laughing at the idea. "It's suicide, even with two forces."

Levi shrugs, not fazed in the least. "Zurie's desperate. Rory said so herself. A desperate Spectre with nothing to lose? Jace, don't be blind."

I pause, debating the option even though I'm not quite willing to believe it.

Zurie's running out of choices, but she's not stupid.

There's no way humans could attack a dragon embassy and survive, much less win.

"Unless..." My voice is almost inaudible as I trail off. My ear begins to ring as I lose myself in my thoughts. A painful realization dawns on me, too big and too terrible to fully imagine.

Unless there were more than two forces.

Unless they found allies—dangerous ones with massive weapons and a big budget.

We have to face the facts. The General is alive, though badly injured. He has someone taking over for him in the meantime, someone green but anxious to prove himself. The Knights aren't losing any ground, even with the General out of commission.

More important than the General, however, is Zurie. Arguably the world's greatest assassin, but one has nothing to live for.

Whatever she does next, it'll be an all-or-nothing, last-ditch effort to destroy everything I love. So, yes, between the two of them, there's a chance they found more allies.

After all, a lot of powerful people want me dead.

Zurie is dedicated. Focused. Clear and utterly undeterrable. That's bad news for her enemies.

That's bad news for *us*.

CHAPTER ELEVEN

I lean against the wall in the stairwell leading down from the suites where Levi, Tucker, Irena, and I are staying.

With my leg propped against the wall, I simply wait.

I'm about to catch Irena doing something she's not supposed to do. As annoyed as I am, I have to confess that I'm actually kind of looking forward to the look on her face when she realizes she won't get away with whatever she's concocting.

My big sister isn't used to getting caught.

Whatever decision Irena made up there in Tucker's room, it's not good. I may have changed since coming here, but Irena hasn't.

Irena is still very much the same person she was

before she went into the coma. The heir to the Spectre throne. A woman who's used to doing things on her own—and getting her way.

What doesn't make sense to me is that Irena knows Zurie is trying to goad her into leaving. It'll weaken us if she goes before she has better control over her new abilities, but I know in my heart that her decision was to leave.

My question is *why*.

What choice could she have made that she didn't want to share in the room?

With *me*?

As the night wears on, I don't move. I'm alone in the stairwell, and that's the way I want it right now.

Tucker needed to be by himself, and no matter what I tried, nothing could make him smile. It's strange to see him so somber. So quiet. But I know what it is.

His father's alive, and I think a part of him had hoped the man would have just died in the rubble. A part of Tucker wished that he would never have to face his father again because then he could simply let the man fade away. If they never had to face each other, his only enemy would be the things that were left unsaid between them.

Since his father is alive, however, it means they will

meet again. And when that day comes, Tucker may have to kill the man himself.

I know firsthand what Tucker's going through right now. Up until Zurie tried to kill my men and the dragon within me, I wasn't even sure I wanted her to die. I was trying to save her. Trying to make her see reason.

In the end, I failed. Not because I could have done more for her, but because I saw the woman I *wanted* her to be, rather than the woman she *was*. The woman I was trying to save never even existed in the first place.

As difficult as it will be to kill the woman who raised me, I know in my heart it's the right thing to do.

Tucker's going through the same thing, and all I can do for him is give him space and compassion.

The General is awful, but he's still Tucker's father. I suspect there's still a sense of obligation and duty buried deep within Tucker, same as I felt for Zurie. However awful the man might be, they're still blood.

All Tucker can do, for now, is to grieve—he has to relinquish any hope of the man redeeming himself.

Because he never, *ever* will.

The General and Zurie are too much alike for redemption.

With Tucker needing space to himself, everyone

else quickly left. Jace is briefing his surveillance team as I stand here in the stariwell, while Drew is contacting his spy network to wring more information out of them.

Levi needed to go burn off some steam, so I suspect he's destroying a tree somewhere with a sword. I really wanted to go with him, but I knew I needed to be here.

To stop Irena.

The soft patter of footsteps—almost as silent as breath and just as easily overlooked by anyone else— slink toward me from the top of the stairwell.

Finally.

I relax my shoulders and lean my head against the wall, looking for all the world as if I'm comfortable even though I'm absolutely, positively *not*.

Irena rounds the bend, and the moment her gaze lands on me, she tenses. There's a brief and subtle widening to her eyes, like she can't believe I could have figured this out. Like it's impossible that I'm here.

But a moment later, she simply groans in exasperation.

I've been toying with what I wanted to say when I caught her. It was a tough battle, deciding how to start this conversation, and I couldn't settle on anything that really felt right.

So, I wing it.

"What are you afraid of?" I ask, narrowing my eyes as I study her face for signs of a lie. "Why wouldn't you tell me what your plan is? Why you're going to leave?"

Irena frowns, leaning against the opposite wall as she gives me a once-over. "A Spectre's never afraid, remember?"

"You're not a Spectre," I remind her. "Not anymore."

Irena's eye twitches slightly, and she simply looks away, down into the shadows of the stairwell below us.

I let out a small sigh. "You don't have to tell me, Irena, but I'm going with you unless you do."

My big sister rolls her eyes. "You really would, wouldn't you?"

I grin. She knows me.

Irena runs an impatient hand through her hair, shaking her head slightly, and it's clear she's given in.

Good. Maybe I'll finally get some answers.

"My only mission in life was to carry on Zurie's legacy," Irena says quietly, not looking at me as she confesses. "To make the Spectres even better than they were. Wealthier. More powerful. To spread our influence and network. To recruit. To do everything I could to ensure we lived forever. That we *survived* in a world that was actively trying to kill us all."

She leans her head back against the wall, pinching her eyes closed in frustration. "When Zurie was convinced of my loyalty, she gave me access to the secure files. She had to, after all—since one day, I would lead in her stead. I had to know everything. Everyone. Every lead. Every safehouse. Every weak link in the organization."

Irena gently massages her temples as she falls silent, and I wonder what she's remembering. What horrible things she read in those files—and the terrible confessions buried within Zurie's archives.

"I saw everything Zurie had," Irena continues, crossing her arms as she leans back once again. "Honestly, I read some files I don't think she realized she had. I connected dots she never even saw. I had everything at my fingertips, everything I would ever need to make the Spectres a permanent force in the world— and maybe more." She gently sets a hand on the gun at her waist, one Tucker provided her not too long ago just so she wouldn't feel naked in a dragon's den. "I had purpose, Rory. I had something to drive me. Something to do. People like you and me—we need that."

"I know," I say quietly.

And I do. I absolutely understand. Mine is to protect my men.

"When I discovered Zurie's plans for you, all of my purpose dissolved instantly," Irena continues. "I had nothing left but hate. Nothing to do but destroy the organization I had been raised to protect. But I didn't really care," she confessed. "As long as you and I got away, I didn't care what happened to the Spectres. As I was giving Mason everything he needed to take them down, I realized I was completely content with simply walking away. As long as you and I escaped, I'd be happy."

"No, you wouldn't have," I say, calling her out on the lie she was telling herself.

Her eyes dart to me, intense and a bit surprised that I would dare say such a thing. "What?"

"People like us..." I trail off, not quite sure how to phrase this. "We need something to drive us forward. We need direction. We need something to do, something to sink our teeth into. What were you and I going to do? Ride off into the sunset and live in a cabin?"

She frowns. "I had a couple safehouses lined up."

"That's not what I meant," I say, a bit impatient as the night wears on.

"I know," she begrudgingly answers.

I hesitate, something finally clicking for me, and my lips slowly part in disbelief as I study her face, wondering if it's true. I finally think I might know where this is going, but I almost can't believe it.

It's too big. Too dangerous. Too ambitious, even for her.

"Irena, you're not—"

"I am," she interrupts, her eyes closed as she waits for me to lose my mind. To yell at her and tell her to stop, even though I know she won't.

I don't even know where to begin. Maybe I'll chain her to a bed somewhere, or just throw caution to the wind and lock her in a tower.

"You can't be serious," I snap. "It's one thing to kill Zurie, but—Irena, you want to dismantle the Spectres *entirely?*"

At first, she doesn't move. She doesn't so much as breathe. But after a few moments, she slowly begins to nod her head. "I've been thinking about it for a while now, and up there, it just became so clear. There's no question in my mind. My purpose, my mission, the only thing left for me to do is shatter them from within. I'm the only one who can do it, Rory. I'm the only one with the knowledge and insight of their inner workings."

She pauses and watches me, those intense green

eyes studying my face, clearly wondering what I'm going to do.

If I'm going to try to stop her.

The sister in me wants to. The person who loves her and wants her to live a long life wants to beg for her to do anything else, to find a hobby or a boyfriend or anything at all that can occupy her time in a less self-destructive way.

But the fighter in me knows better.

"What's your plan?" I ask, tense and ready to discuss the little things, the details, anything at all that will help her stay alive a bit longer.

"I'll use their tech against them," she answers instantly, and it's clear this isn't some half-baked guess.

She knows what she's doing, and I have to admit that she is, in fact, the best person for this job.

I just wish it didn't have to be *her*.

"It's the best choice," she continues. "Besides pure skill, the one thing that makes the Spectres so dangerous is our advanced weaponry. Technologically speaking, we're the most advanced organization in the world, and I know everything about that tech. I know how it's made. I know where the resources are procured. I know it all."

I frown, furrowing my brow. "How—"

"Before I reached out to the Vaer," Irena interrupts, "I put aside a hoard of data and samples. I smuggled out everything. Prototypes, plans, resource lists, all of it. It was my backup plan in case things went south." She hesitates, her eyes glossing over briefly as she loses herself in thought. "They sure as hell did, huh?"

"That's an understatement," I agree with a small nod. "Why didn't you tell me about this? Why make me drag it out of you? You have all of the Spectre tech, all of their resources, but—"

"I know." She lifts her hand to silence me as she interrupts me yet again. "I didn't tell you because I knew you'd want to be involved. To help. Rory, can't you see that everything I've done—everything I've sacrificed—has been to keep you safe? It was just better if you didn't know."

My, doesn't *that* sound familiar.

She and Jace both think in obnoxiously similar ways.

I shake my head, biting my lip to keep myself from saying something I'll regret. As the anger bubbles within me, I try to suppress the resentment of being kept in the dark yet again by someone I love.

"That's not how we do things anymore," I say tensely. "Come with me." I start down the stairs, expecting her to follow.

"Where are you going?" she asks dryly.

"To talk to the guys," I say, pausing to look over my shoulder. "We're going to do this as a team, Irena. And that is *not* up for negotiation."

The six of us sit in Jace's war room, everyone gathered around the table as Irena finishes her admittedly terse and impatient briefing on everything she and I discussed in the stairwell.

Whenever she left out a detail, I would fill it in, and she would shoot me an annoyed glare.

Tough shit.

She's got to learn one way or another that this is how we do it now, and she's too damn stubborn for me to give her any space on this.

In the silence that follows, Irena leans against the wall and glares slightly at me for making her share any of this at all.

I don't react.

"This is incredible," Jace says as he takes it all in. "Absolutely incredible, Irena. The Fairfax dragons will, of course, manufacture anything you desire, and—"

"Hell no, you won't," Drew says, interrupting. "I'll do it. I have a faster network, and I'm not confined to just the Fairfax loyalists. I work with everyone. Humans, dragons—the best of the best. I'll get it done faster and more efficiently."

Jace impatiently snorts, glaring at Drew as he furrows his brow in contempt. "I'm not about to trust an unknown network that only you control to produce some of the most important technology on the planet."

Drew laughs derisively. "Oh, but it's better if we give everything to the Fairfax dragons? Let you all control everything. Right."

"Stop it," I demand, glaring at the two of them. "Focus."

Both men look at me briefly, each of them bristling with anger for the other, and I briefly wonder if a fist-fight is going to break out in this room at any moment.

Deep down, I know it's not about the tech. They both want it, sure, but they're more eager to have something to fight over.

For whatever reason, their feud is getting worse and worse with every passing day. Any chance they have to argue, they take it. Any chance they have to jump at each other's throats, they do.

I need them to cut it the hell out. We don't have time for this.

"If you guys don't get it together and compromise, Levi's going to get the manufacturing deal," I say with a nod toward my ice dragon.

The former Vaer tracker laughs, leaning back in his chair. "Don't drag me into this, dear."

I can't hide the small smirk that plays at the corner of my mouth at him calling my bluff. I look at him over my shoulder. "You were *supposed* to back me up on that."

He laughs.

Out of the corner of my eye, I see Tucker sitting at the far edge of the table, somber and quiet as he stares at the grains of wood in the surface. My smile falls, and my heart twists for him. He's grieving more than he did when he thought his father might have died, and this kind of pain is almost worse. To have family live, but to be forced to disown them. To know they're bad for you and everything you love, like toxic waste that will poison the world if you let it stay around too long—and yet, to still fight that little, loyal piece of you that wants them to be worthy of redemption.

"While you two figure that out," Irena says, jarring me from my thoughts, "I still have to reactivate some of my old contacts to see if the backups have been compromised or not. I need to ensure that no one betrayed me, and that everything I stored away is still there before we go get it. We'll be exposed when we go to retrieve everything, so we can't go in blind."

"Why did you make it so difficult to recover?" Levi asks, tilting his head slightly in curiosity.

"Accessing the backups was never my primary plan," Irena confesses. "Ideally, I would never have to retrieve it—and, just in case I left it, I wanted to make sure that nobody would accidentally stumble upon what I'd stowed away. I found an old storage facility in Oklahoma that has lifetime policies on their units and a security system with a broad overview of the entire facility, something that can let me assess risk before I go in. The location I picked was strategic and meant to ensure no one could ferry it away without me knowing—but, unfortunately, that also means I'll be exposed and visible when I go for it."

I frown, crossing my arms as I glare at her.

She knows exactly what was wrong with that statement.

"Ugh," she mutters. "Fine, when *we* go to get it."

"Whatever you need, we'll make sure you have it," Jace says, tapping his finger on the table for emphasis. "This is crucial tech, and we absolutely must ensure it's extracted safely. I'll make sure you have backup and air support, as well as whatever tactical support you may require. Just name it."

Irena tilts her head in subtle surprise, silent as she watches him and waits for the catch. When he doesn't say anything, she frowns. "And what's the cost? What are you trying to strong-arm me into doing? Because I don't give out favors to *dragons*," she says with a slight wrinkle to her nose.

I groan, rubbing my temples in aggravation.

Jace hesitates briefly, glancing between Irena and me as he tries to figure out what my sister is really asking.

"There's no catch, Irena," the dojo master finally says. "You're on our side. I'm going to support you and give you what you need because it helps all of us." He gestures around the room, though I notice that he doesn't motion toward Drew.

Irena leans her knuckles against the table, watching the dojo master with an incredulous expression.

And that's how you baffle a Spectre—show them loyalty.

Dumbfounded and shocked into silence, Irena seems utterly lost for words. She's not used to dependable people. Hopefully with time, she will realize there are good people in the world she can trust.

"Thank you," she eventually says.

And for the first time since she got here, it sounds genuine.

"Of course," Jace says casually, missing the magnitude of the moment. "This is solid, and we'll be ready to leave within twenty four hours. Irena, you check for leaks and compromised assets. Once you're sure it's safe to go in, we'll go with an army. In, out, and over. Our command center will survey the area with full tech and surveillance support to make sure that we can get in and out safely." He rubs his hands together, like he can't wait to get started. "Give me the address so that I can scope it too. I want to make sure my team's safe when we go in."

A small smile plays at Irena's lips, and it almost seems like something clicked for her. "All right," she says softly, clearly impressed.

"We have a lot to do, guys. Let's get going." Jace raps his knuckle against the table as he stands, heading for the door. As he passes behind me, he pauses and gently kisses me on the back of my head. My traitorous body leans toward him on its own, begging for more as the kiss leaves a lingering tingle of joy across my scalp. Before I can so much as say a word, however, Jace is gone—into the hallway and off to arrange a full-on military raid.

Drew grumbles under his breath as he stands. He

casually walks toward me, and I glance up toward him as he nears.

My lips part as I begin to ask him what he's up to, but before I can speak even one syllable, he grabs my jaw and presses his mouth roughly against mine.

It's dominating and deep, radiating with tension and anger from his ongoing spat with Jace. The sensation of his strong fingers pressed against my jaw ignites a flurry of desire within me, and I lean in to him despite myself.

As much as I hate their feud, Drew is hot as hell when he's angry.

"Are you going to come and keep me company soon?" he asks under his breath, his intense eyes locked on me.

"You act like I never go," I chide him gently.

He smirks. "I'm selfish."

I chuckle. "Well, maybe if you asked nicely, I'd come more often."

"I never ask nicely," he answers. "That's what you love about me."

He grins and walks off without another word, not giving me a chance to even reply before he's out the door.

If I'm being honest, there's a lot I love about Drew. But I figure it would inflate his ego if I told him.

Before I can so much as blink, Levi's beside me, silent as ever. It's still astonishing how he can sneak up on me, and I keep expecting to eventually learn how to pick up on his movements—but I just don't.

He's too good.

Levi tenderly brushes my arm, the skin of his knuckles grazing against my bicep as he smiles tenderly. Our connection opens, and a flood of devotion comes through, more enchanting and endearing than any kiss. The sensation swirls within me, filling me like sunlight, and I can't hide the smile that breaks across my face.

We'll talk later, he says through our connection.

With that, he walks out the door as well, leaving me and Tucker still sitting at the table. Irena, meanwhile, still leans against the nearby wall.

Tucker stands, lost as ever in his thoughts.

Quickly getting to my feet, I set my hand on his arm. "Are you okay?"

The soft question breaks through his brooding, and he tilts his head toward me. There's a moment or two of hesitation, but he eventually nods.

"I'll leave you two alone," Irena says, kicking off the wall and walking out the door, closing it behind her.

Tucker sighs. "Sorry if I seem distracted."

I shrug. "I understand."

"I know," he says, watching me. "Look, Rory. I meant what I said. The Knights are killers, and you're my family. These guys are my family." He nods toward the door, in the general direction of Levi, Drew, and Jace.

"I know, and it's okay to grieve. Grief is a funny thing," I say quietly, looking at the table as I sift through my thoughts, trying to piece together something that's been sitting in the back of my mind for a while. "It can come out of nowhere at any time, even when it seems like you should be completely happy." I pause, looking at Tucker. "Your father's an ass, but I understand why this is hard."

"My father might be alive, but he tried to kill you," Tucker says calmly. His voice is stronger now, more certain than before. "My father tried to kill them," he adds with another nod toward the door. "These men who I've come to see as brothers. So, as difficult as it may be, he's dead to me." Tucker frowns, his jaw tensing as he really sits with the thought. "I'm sure of it, Rory. My father is dead to me, and if I see him again, I will kill him. I just need some time to work through that."

"Take the time you need," I say gently, setting my hand on his arm again.

He gives me a small smile and leans in, gently

brushing his lips against mine as he kisses me lovingly. "You're the best, babe."

I wink at him. "Oh, I know."

He chuckles and gestures toward the hallway, letting me go in front of him. As we leave, I find Irena waiting nearby with her shoulder pressed against the wall, her arms crossed.

Huh. It would seem as though someone wants to have a little chat with me.

"I'll see you ladies later," Tucker says, nodding toward us as he takes the hint and walks off in the other direction.

As he leaves, I can't help but watch his gorgeous figure retreat down the hallway. My eyes linger a little too long on his ass, and I lose myself briefly in the memory of his naked body getting out of bed earlier tonight.

Irena chuckles. "It's a treat to see how you and your men interact."

I look over my shoulder at my sister. "Thanks. I appreciate you trusting them."

"I don't," she admits. "Not yet. But I think I can get there."

I shrug. "That's really all I can ask."

She nods, looking off briefly after Tucker. "It's good to know you'll be cared for when I'm gone."

I frown, a pang of alarm ringing through my chest at her choice of words. "And what exactly do you mean by that?"

Irena tilts her head impatiently. "I can't destroy the Spectres from here, Rory. I'll eventually need to leave. No amount of stairwell stalking is going to stop me."

I set my hands on my hips, ready to dig into her, ready to knock some sense into her and at least make her wait a little while.

But Irena kills my argument before I can even start by flashing me a brilliant smile.

She looks, well, *happy*.

"I'm proud of you, little sister," she says quietly. "You have your purpose. Let me have mine."

Ugh.

Unfair.

I pinch my eyes closed, and damn it all, that completely disarms me. My shoulders relax, and I just nod. As much as I want to fight it, to convince Irena to stay, she's right.

My sister is smart. Brilliant, actually, though I would probably never tell her that.

This purpose of hers, it's perfect. It works, and it makes sense.

I just hope it doesn't cost her life.

CHAPTER TWELVE

As I wrap myself in my blankets, my head against the soft pillow, I smile and savor the silky sensation of the cool sheets. Even as dawn slowly breaks across the horizon and creeps through the gap in the curtains beside my bed, it's nice to get some shut-eye.

Relaxing in the silence of my bedroom, finally alone and with a moment to myself, I hear the thundering clomp of heavy footsteps bolting up the stairwell and into the hallway.

Toward my room.

So much for getting a bit of much-needed sleep.

I groan and sit up, rubbing my eyes as the door to my suite opens, the hinges creaking slightly as whoever this is enters. I listen to the footsteps as they near, recognizing the gait instantly.

Tucker.

As my bedroom door creaks open, I chuckle. "Did you even *try* to be stealthy?"

He leans into the room, eyes wide with concern and his chest heaving as he struggles to catch his breath. One hand holds onto the doorknob and his other rests on the doorframe, like he can't quite keep his balance.

"What's wrong?" I ask, frowning.

"Jace and Drew are going at it," he says, his tone tense and urgent. "Drawing blood. Levi and I have already tried to stop them, but Drew nearly took my head off. We think only you can get them to back down. It's a full-on brawl, Rory."

I curse under my breath and throw on some clothes, running after him down the stairwells and through the hallways as we make our way to the center courtyard.

As we race toward the open front doors, the roars and snarls of what sounds like an epic battle filter through from outside. One of them screeches in agony, and the heart-wrenching tear of claws across skin shakes me to the core.

Oh, *great.*

As I race onto the front steps, I find two dragons locked in a duel in the center of the black stone.

Soldiers in their human forms fill the edges of the square, while dragons perch along the walls. Everyone leans forward. Those in their human forms grip swords and guns tightly, while the dragons among us dig their claws into the black stone. Teeth bared, growls rumbling in the backs of their throats, it's clear everyone wishes they could dive in and stop this.

And yet, no one is willing to try.

Faced with a bloody war zone, my training kicks in. I impulsively scan the crowd for any familiar faces, and while I recognize a few of them, Irena's not down here. Levi stands at the front of the crowd in a wide stance with his arms crossed, his back to me as he watches the fire dragon and the thunderbird duel in the center courtyard.

As I jog down the steps toward him, Russell makes his way through the crowd toward me and hops onto the bottom steps, blocking my way.

I don't care if he's Harper's favorite. I don't care if he's a contender for second in command of this dojo. I swear to the gods—if this man tries to stop me from intervening because of some stupid rule about honor, I will punch him in the *face*.

He leans in, his hand lifted between us to get me to

stop. I frown, eyebrows pinched as I wait for the inevitable request that I stand down.

"Please stop them," he says under his breath, his gaze shifting toward the two dragons locked in battle. "None of us can defy our master, and no one has any authority over Drew."

Oh.

What a nice surprise.

I nod. "That's what I'm here to do."

Russell steps aside to let me pass, and I jog toward Levi with Tucker hot on my heels. The ice dragon's arms are crossed, and even as I approach him, his gaze is locked on the dragons before us. It's almost as if he's not just studying them, but trying to anticipate what they're going to do next. Who they might hurt. Where they might go. What they might do that they'll regret later.

"No formal duel was declared," Levi says the moment I'm next to him, without so much as a glance toward me.

He can't afford to look away—at any moment, this could all get even worse. He—and all of us, for that matter—has to stay alert.

Only then do I notice a deep scrape across his cheek. It goes from his nose down to his jaw, and even though it's not bleeding anymore, the deep gouge looks remarkably painful.

I grit my teeth in an effort to choke back my fury. "Which of them did that to you?"

He shakes his head. "I honestly don't know. Stepping in to stop them didn't go very well for me."

I'm fuming.

It's almost impossible to describe the depth of my rage at this moment, to really feel it, to fully understand how deep and hot the anger goes.

I want to rip something apart, to shatter things, to break the world until these two idiots can finally drop this feud of theirs. I want to make them see and think clearly again. To be the men I remember and not the assholes they've become.

"Rory, relax," Levi says calmly beside me. "I'm fine."

My attention shifts to him, and I'm sure I look as livid as I feel. I know full well I'm glaring even though I'm not angry with him. He, for the most part, appears unfazed, and watches me as if he doesn't have a deep gouge on his face.

"How can I *not* be angry with this nonsense?" I ask.

"This will heal," he says, pointing to the wound on his face. "You won't even see it by tomorrow."

"They should never have hurt you in the first place," I point out as Jace and Drew wrestle. They dig their claws into each other, biting at each other's faces and necks, each of them trying to get the upper hand on the other as they quickly decimate the courtyard.

"We're dragons, Rory," Levi says calmly. "This comes with the territory. We're hot-blooded and angry, and sometimes a fight can break out just to settle little grudges." He shrugs. "It's our way."

"It's barbaric."

"You're one of us now, Rory," he reminds me with an endearing chuckle. "I can see how this is brutal to the human in you, but there's still a lot for you to learn about being a dragon."

"What started this?" I ask, not wanting a lecture right now.

"I don't think anyone heard the initial argument." Levi hesitates, absently scratching at the back of his head as he watches the fight. "They were angry and shifted. They just started going at it."

I narrow my eyes in suspicion, knowing full well he's hiding something from me.

He knows damn well what they were arguing about.

Levi frowns, studying my face as he seems to internally debate whether or not to tell me the truth.

"Levi..." I say quietly, a hint of warning in my tone.

He sighs deeply, the sound heavy with resignation

and a hint of regret. "You. They were fighting over who had *claim* to you."

Oh, *hell* no.

That's *it*.

I take a step toward the dragons as they writhe and wrestle in the center courtyard. Before I can go any further, Tucker grabs my arm and turns me toward him. He holds my shoulders, leaning toward me, his eyes scanning me intently. "Be careful, Rory. They're not themselves right now."

I nod and set my hand on his to reassure him, but I'm not about to let this go.

Jace and Drew have officially taken this too far.

I step into the fray as the two dragons duel. They snarl at each other, the black thunderbird pausing as he digs his sharp claws into the ground, cracking the black rock beneath him with effortless grace. His body hums with blue light and magic as he aims a blast toward Drew.

Apparently, claws and battle aren't enough for them anymore. Now, they're going to try to burn and dissolve each other into ash.

In that split second, everything gets so much *worse*.

Drew snarls, his growl rumbling in his chest like thunder, daring Jace to fire.

Jace is happy to oblige.

The sizzling beam of energy tears from his mouth, crackling through the air, but Drew doesn't flinch. He stands on his back legs, the mighty fire dragon spreading his broad wings as he leans into the beam. The magic breaks across Drew's skin, driving him backward and digging a path through the stone that cracks and crumbles around him.

Drew roars into the sky, unleashing a barrel of fire into the air—unfazed by a blast that would have killed most, if not *all*, other dragons.

Even as their anger rages, I find mine slowly morphing into something else—something strange. The anger simmers and stews, blurring and blending into an odd sense of calm. It's not peace, of course, just —*knowing.*

Knowing that I'm going to stop them.

Knowing that this is too far.

Knowing that this behavior is absolutely unacceptable.

Deep within me, my dragon is *just* as furious as I am.

As I walk toward them, a blast of fire shoots overhead, the billowing heat from the flames brushing against my skin and warming my face.

But I don't flinch.

These are my men, and I won't fear them. Not now. Not ever.

As far as I can tell, neither dragon sees me. They don't see anything but each other, but the hot fury of bloodlust and the desire to see the other fall before him.

I summon my magic, the white light flitting across my skin, crackling with power and life as I reach the center of the courtyard.

Both dragons step back, circling each other, their gaze is fixed on the dragon in front of them, completely overlooking me. They circle, waiting for an opportunity to attack.

With me in the middle of their duel, the two of them oblivious to my presence, they charge.

But I'm faster.

I summon my magic into my hands and aim it at the ground, shooting a furious blast of white light into the rock beneath me as I scream into the air.

"STOP!" I demand.

And the world around me trembles with the command.

The fury burning through my body makes my voice boom. I can hear it echo across the mountains. It comes from so deep within me that it feels ethereal. It feels *other*.

It feels powerful.

A burst of white light shoots from my hands, cracking the ground beneath us and drowning everything with its sheer, blinding brilliance. Even I have to shut my eyes to block out the light as a blast of air shoots in all directions from me. I hear the crumble of rock, the kick of dust and pebbles tumbling across the ground.

As the light recedes, I open my eyes to find the two dragons staring at me. Their heads hover near mine, barely a few feet away on either side of me. Their hot breath rolls over my face with every furious exhale as they softly growl.

Sparks burn along the black thunderbird as if he's desperate to unleash another blast. Black smoke rolls from Drew's nose as if he is anxious to let loose another torrent of fire at his enemy.

But both dragons wait, glaring at me. As furious with me that I would intervene as I am with them for starting this to begin with.

And yet, they listened. To me.

They stopped.

I want to dig into them, to find out what the hell is wrong with the two of them and what's really going on. This hatred they have for each other is getting out of control, and it has officially spiraled into something bigger, something even more deadly and dangerous than it was before.

I have to stop that, too. I just don't know how.

As much as I want to scream at them both, I have to save face for the dojo master in front of his soldiers. Jace rules here—not me—and I can't formally demand anything of him in front of all these witnesses. If I try, it'll just make everything worse.

"I would like to speak to you both privately," I say through gritted teeth, white sparks darting up my arm as I glare at them. "Now."

In Jace's war room, I pace across the floor as the two men sit at the heads of the table. The furious silence is tense and heavy as both men glare daggers at each other.

On the way up here, they manage to find pants, for which I'm admittedly grateful. Even as angry as I am, their gorgeous, naked bodies would be far too distracting for me to really focus.

"Figure this out," I demand, turning on my heel as I pace the length of the room once again, refusing to look at either of them. "I don't care how you do it.

Therapy, yelling match, it doesn't matter. But this has to stop!"

"It's simple enough," Drew says, leaning back in his chair as his biceps flex, his gaze fixed on Jace. "This asshole just needs to break the mate-bond with you and leave you to men who will actually *protect* you instead of trying to *own* you."

"Drew," I snap. "That's not helping."

"How *dare* you," Jace growls, his voice low and deadly as he stands and rests his fists against the table. "How dare you even *suggest* such a thing?"

"Do you want the dojo or a mate?" Drew snaps back, not missing a beat. "She's a partner, not your property. How hard is it to tell her she has fourteen death-bounties on her head? You're not training her, you're keeping her busy so she doesn't ask questions!"

I ball my hand into a fist, fed up and furious with them both. My magic burns in my blood, aching to break free.

"She's *my* mate and *mine* to protect as *I* see fit," Jace says, his jaw tensing as he squares his shoulders, daring Drew to disagree.

"She's not," Drew slams his fist against the table, cracking it. "She's mine as much as yours, and I won't let you steal her from me!"

"Enough!" I shout, bristling again, white light

racing across my arms as it pushes against me. I'm so angry that I can barely keep my magic at bay. Any second, it will force its way out of me.

They don't stop.

Drew leans forward, resting his knuckles on the table as he points at Jace. "He wants to take you to the capital, to store you away with the rest of the mates. He's actually making arrangements, Rory!"

I scowl, looking at Jace, wondering if it's true.

I can believe it.

"He's keeping secrets," Drew continues, not missing a beat. "Secrets left and right. He won't treat you as an equal. Is that what you want? Someone who will steal you away from the others? Not just from me, Rory. From Levi. From Tucker. From Irena. He will hide you away forever."

"No," Jace interjects, standing. "Just you."

My magic burns in my palms, and before I know it, I'm setting my hands on the table.

"Shut *up!*" I shout.

And with a surge in my anger, I unleash a torrent of white light that shatters the table to splinters. A thin cloud of dust lingers in the air where the table once stood, but most of the remnants lie in shattered heaps of dagger-sharp wood on the floor.

Both men impulsively step back from the remnants

of what was once Jace's table, and I can't find it within me to feel an ounce of sympathy for what I destroyed.

I'm too angry, too furious, too frustrated with *both* of them.

"Figure this out," I repeat, trying to deal with one thing at a time. "If not for each other, then do it for me." I pause, my chin lifting in irritated defiance as I give Jace a once-over. "And, in case you were curious, I won't go to the capital. If you try to send me off to live in hiding, it had better be in chains because there's no other way you'll get me to leave anyone here behind."

"Rory, I wasn't going to send you off," Jace snaps, offended. "We would talk about it, and—"

"Fucking *liar*," Drew snaps.

With the table no longer between them, both men bristle, clenching their hands into fists and glaring at each other as if they're about to fight again.

Drew even takes a step forward, slipping into a fighting stance before he hesitates and looks at me. I gently shake my head, practically begging him not to do it, to not start this.

Not again.

He groans in frustration and without a word, charges out into the hallway and slams the door behind him.

Jace is breathing heavily, still primed for a fight.

With Drew no longer there, that unfortunately means he turns his full fury toward me. "Why did you have to want us *both*?"

I glare at him in answer, not about to explain myself after everything he's done.

He seems to get the hint, and his shoulders relax ever so slightly. He begins to pace the far side of the room, shaking his head and looking anywhere but at me. "Rory, this is more than just a feud. It's hatred, and it's going to end in blood."

"It doesn't have to," I point out, setting my hands on my hips and wishing these two could just see sense. "You're both good men. You're aggressive, dominating assholes sometimes, but you're good at heart or I wouldn't waste my time with you. I wouldn't want you in my life otherwise. This grudge that divides you, it's there, yes, but you can heal it."

Jace turns toward me, his nose wrinkled in disgust as he points toward the door. "He killed my brother, Rory. I can never forgive that!"

But he *didn't*.

In that split-second of weakness, of just wanting to stop their hatred for each other, I almost tell Jace the truth.

Drew didn't kill Jace's brother, but he's saving face for the man who did. He's taking the blame because he knows the person who actually killed Jace's brother wouldn't survive if the world knew.

I grit my teeth and turn my back on him, wishing I could just tell Jace the truth. But if I did, it would destroy Drew's trust in me.

I need him to come clean, but I can't be the one to force him to do it.

"There's more to this than meets the eye, Jace," I say instead. "And I believe in you. I believe in you both." I turn toward him, scanning his handsome face as I try to make him see the truth in all this. "I need you to believe in yourselves, too. I need you to want to heal this."

Jace shakes his head, turning his back on me as if he can't even find the words to respond.

I look at the shattered table on the floor, the remnants of what was once a beautiful surface, and my mind wanders over the rest of the conversation.

"Which way are you leaning?" I ask, not wanting to look at him, not daring to hope too hard. "On the mate-bond, I mean."

With his back still toward me, he stops, freezing in place and groaning as he sets his hands on his head. "I hate Drew for telling you about that."

"I was in the tunnels," I confess. "I heard everything."

Jace groans furiously, his shoulders tensing as he loops his thumbs over the edge of his pants. His hard back tenses, the muscles flexing as his anger burns within him, and I figure he's wondering if giving me access to the tunnels was a mistake.

"I want a partner," I remind him. "Not just a protector. Not a warden. Do you think you can be that for me? Because if not—Jace, just choose the dojo."

My heart wrenches at the words. I hate them. I hate that they came out of my mouth, but Harper's right—this is as much my decision as his.

If I can't be his equal, then he can't have me.

He doesn't move. For several moments, he doesn't even answer and barely breathes. "Rory, I'm too angry to talk about this right now."

In the silence that follows, it seems like there's something else he wants to say, like he was working through something he can't quite form into words yet. But after a few tense moments, he just walks out the door, his bare feet unfazed by the splinters strewn across the ground.

When he leaves, I roll my fingers into a fist. I'm practically shaking with frustration, and I can't hold it back anymore. It takes over me, and I have to burn it off.

I have to do something.

I yell, angry and heartbroken, and punch my fist into the wall. I've only done this a few times in my life, and never when anyone could see—always alone, always when I can really let my anger free.

In the past, I've broken my knuckles.

This time, my fist goes clear through the wall. It shatters the black rock beyond the wallpaper, crumbling it into a fine gray dust.

I set my palms against the wall, head hanging as I try to catch my breath. As my heart settles, I have to admit that felt pretty damn good.

With everything that's going on, I need the men I'm growing to love to work together. It's like Tucker said —for this to work, they need to see each other as brothers.

But this—their hatred—it could destroy us all.

CHAPTER THIRTEEN

Around midday, I arch my back and stretch my arms wide, drinking in the warm sun. After the fallout from the battle between Jace and Drew this morning, everyone is avoiding both of them.

Including me.

I recline across a section of roof I'm unfamiliar with, somewhere above the dozens of balconies that lead down to the ground below. If I went to my old spot, I figured one of them would look for me there—and I need some space from them both.

As I stare at the clouds above me, my eyes glaze over. I'm trying to figure out what Zurie's plan is. For the last two hours, I sat up here and sketched out loose concepts on the pad of paper currently resting beside me.

This is something we used to do back when I was a Spectre, something Zurie taught me—a means of figuring out the plan of attack from every angle.

I'm trying to get in her head, and it's really, *really* not working.

I grumble in frustration, rubbing my eyes as I reach over and cross out yet another idea. This is like trying to predict lottery numbers. Everything Zurie does is just so random, and while there's always a thread of strategy running beneath it, it's usually not something you see until it's too late to change anything.

I furiously scribble out one of the sketches—a ludicrous idea involving hot-air balloons—and throw my pen off the roof in anger. It's one of those things that I instantly regret doing, but it's too late to go back on it now. I'll just have to find it later.

Deep within me, a strange flurry of desire swells and swirls from nowhere.

Oh, great. My dragon senses Jace.

The tug on my navel aches to lead me toward him. He's somewhere on the other side of the building, somewhere close, and I figure spying on him might be a little bit of fun since sketches aren't getting me anywhere. I climb the slope of the roof and peek over the edge, my ears straining to hear him if he's close enough.

He's not.

I ease my way down the other side of the roof, the slope on this side a bit steeper than I'm used to. I climb down a few sections of the roof, hopping onto stretches of flat area as I follow the tug on my navel until, finally, I hear his voice filter over the wind.

Keeping low, I inch toward a section of the roof that covers a balcony only to find Levi and Jace leaning over the railing next to each other, both looking out on the mountains and the mists.

I frown, not quite sure what to make of this. My impulse is to defend Levi, as some shifters may still see him as a feral dragon. To see the two of them so casually standing next to each other strikes me as odd.

"What if I can't figure it out, Jace?" Levi asks, a twinge of distress in his voice.

"You will," Jace says calmly, resting his elbows against the railing as he looks out across the embassy grounds.

Levi shakes his head, looking at his hands as if they have the answers he's looking for, if he could only decipher the lines in his palms. "Every time I try to shift, I just..." he trails off, groaning in frustration, unable to find the words.

"I know," Jace says, his tone gentle and understanding. "But that's what you do, Levi. The impossible. I know you're capable of figuring this out, too. You just need time. You need to trust your dragon, and only then can you heal this."

Levi sighs like he isn't quite sure he believes what Jace is saying.

Keeping close to the roof, I smile as a flurry of gratitude bubbles through me. Even though Jace is a jealous creature, he's talking to Levi with compassion and kindness. With *respect*, even though Levi adores me.

I never expected Jace to be this open, this compassionate. It's a deeper, warmer side of him that I wasn't sure was there. Truth be told, I'm grateful to see it.

Jace adjusts, trying to get comfortable, and I notice a long scar running from his ear down the back of his neck and into his shirt. It's fresh, red and raw, and I figure that's from the fight with Drew. I frown. Even though it seems that Jace is making progress with Levi and Tucker, it's clear that he and Drew are still very much at each other's throats. Those two are at risk for doing something unforgivable to each other.

"It's not just about trusting him," Levi says. "He wants to take over again. I can feel it. He's afraid I'll fail Rory like I failed…" His throat tightens, and he looks away, his voice catching.

My hands grip the edge of the roof as I remember

what Levi's commander did to his sister. The brutal murder right in front of him. The one that broke him. The moment that made him feral. I can barely contain the surge of hatred for such a vile man—and my sorrow for Levi for having to put up with him his whole life.

Jace slowly shakes his head. "Levi, you came back from the brink. You came back from a point everyone assumes no shifter can never come back from. You are one of the most capable dragons I know, and I have to admit I'm glad Rory begged me not to kill you." Jace grins, winking at Levi.

Levi laughs. "She never told me that. I mean, I figured my days were numbered the moment she brought me here, but I didn't realize how hard she was fighting for me."

I roll my eyes. I didn't *beg*. I gave him an order. At *best*, I asked him nicely.

"So, how do I do it?" Levi asks, his smile falling. "How do I reconnect with my dragon?"

Jace shrugs. "Remember what connected you in the first place."

"Fear," Levi answers. "The need to survive."

And just like that, I remember the story of Levi's first shift, the near-death experience when he was just a boy. I grit my teeth in anger, glad the man who did that to Levi is already dead because if he wasn't, I'd be out for blood.

No one hurts my Levi.

"No, man," Jace says, shaking his head. "It was love that connected you two in the first place. You knew your dragon would take care of you and vice versa." He lightly jabs his finger into Levi's chest, emphasizing his point. "You were both a team once, you two against the world. You need to find that place again."

Levi rubs the back of his neck. "But what if he blocks me? What if I give in, and he never gives me back the reins?"

Jace hesitates, studying Levi's face with a somber expression. "If you have a reason to come back, he won't."

Both men go quiet, and I have to wonder if they're referring to me. If this is Jace's subtle way of giving in, of learning how to share.

I try not to hope too hard.

"Thanks, Jace," Levi says quietly, patting the dojo master on the back.

Jace nods and leans once more against the balcony, looking out over the mists and the forest below.

With that, their conversation is apparently over. I don't always recognize the unspoken rules of guy-communication, but Levi just leaves without another word.

With Jace's back to me, I wonder if I should simply disappear. Maybe sneak back over the roof and go back to my sketching.

If I'm being honest, I want to savor this moment of compassion. I don't see Jace do this often, and I want to remember it. Appreciate it, even if he didn't know I witnessed the whole thing.

Plus, it's not often that Jace exposes his back to me, so I kind of want to mess with him, too.

Quietly, I sit on a crook in the roof where Jace will notice me when he does finally turn around. As he watches the mountains, he sets his hand against his chest like his own dragon is swirling and tugging him toward me.

Without a word, he looks over his shoulder— directly at me, like he knew where I would be.

And he grins.

"I always feel you, but I'm never sure where you are," he confesses.

I chuckle. "It's all part of my devious plan to keep you on your toes. I'm quite the evil mastermind."

He laughs as I slide off the roof and onto the balcony, landing lightly against the tile floor.

I nod back into the castle after Levi. "I didn't know you were such a softie, Jace."

"Yeah, well, don't get used to it," he says, returning his attention to the mountains beyond.

"Thank you for helping him," I say, leaning against the railing beside the dojo master, taking the place where Levi stood just moments before. "Even though, you know…"

Jace frowns and looks away. "I respect those who master their immense power and who can hone impressive abilities. Levi did the impossible and that means he earned my respect."

I can't help but think of all the power burning within me. Of my dragon, given to me by the gods themselves to carry because I'm worthy. I wonder why that's not enough for him, but if it's one thing I've learned with Jace, it's when to pick a fight and when to save something for later.

We stand there for a while, enjoying the crisp air and the warm sun without saying a thing. We don't need to.

"You're not going to pick just one of us, are you?" Jace eventually asks, breaking the silence.

No.

I won't.

I hesitate, not entirely sure how to answer. "I

would always feel like I was trying to be something I'm not," I confess. "It's not the world I know, Jace. Besides, you all have a piece of me—a piece I can never get back."

As gooey and uncomfortable as I feel for admitting it, that's the truth. They do.

He sighs, and even though I wait for him to be angry, he doesn't even look disappointed. Just... clear, like it's the answer he was expecting.

I tilt my head in curiosity. "You don't look as furious as I thought you would."

He chuckles. "I'm actually warming up to the idea. My dragon still gets possessive any time I see you with Tucker or Levi or..." He grimaces, his nose wrinkling in disgust. "*Drew*. And that will never go away, but if I had you as my mate, that's a life bond. That's forever. I would know no one could ever take you from me, and maybe then I could share."

I laugh, not quite believing what I just heard. "Did hell just freeze over?"

Jace grins, his face lighting up with humor and happiness as I poke fun at him. It steals my breath away, seeing him smile.

I wish he would do it more often.

"It's not fair to you." My heart twists as I bring up the impossible choice he has to make.

Jace shrugs. "Sometimes life isn't fair."

"Which way are you leaning?"

He shakes his head. "I can't even begin to decide, Rory. If I chose the dojo, I would always love you no matter what they did to break our bond. I would always think of you and wonder if I'd done the right thing."

My heart skips a few hopeful beats at his confession, but I can't bring myself to look at him. "And if you choose me?"

"I'm pretty sure I would drive you crazy protecting you," he admits with a smirk. "With no dojo to distract me, my full attention would be on you."

I laugh. "Oh, gods help me."

He grins and grabs me, pulling me close as his electric touch simmers across my skin. My body leans into him impulsively, aching for him, wanting nothing but him in this moment. I expect him to tease me, to dangle his lips near mine and watch me squirm, but he simply holds me close.

I try not to indulge myself or hope too hard, but I can't help my hands as they weave around his waist, holding him tightly. "You put female soldiers in the field all the time, Jace. You clearly don't mind putting women in the line of fire. So why am I different?"

"I don't mind if they've earned it," he says with a

shrug. "It's the same for all my soldiers, man or woman. They have to earn their place in the ranks."

"Considering my upbringing and all I've done so far, I'd say I've earned that much," I say, craning my neck to look up at him. "So, what's this overbearing protectiveness?"

He doesn't meet my eye. Instead, he looks off into the mists. "It's a mate thing, Rory, and it's self-protection. You control my dragon. He and I would sacrifice anything for our mate. You virtually control us."

"But I don't understand," I press. "You see those soldiers as capable. What would it take to see me in the same light?"

"No, it's different," he insists, taking a step back so that he can see me. "They take on the risk themselves when they go into battle. They choose to fight, and the only life at stake is their own. With you, you have the world after you, trying to kill you, and all my enemies are after you, too. Between us, we will never have peace. We will always be hunted. It's not enough to be able to hold your own in a battle. You need to be able to hold your own every moment of every *day*. You need to see the things even I miss."

I groan. He has eyes and ears everywhere, so I'm not even sure that's possible

Jace lets out a soft breath and holds me tight again,

toying with the ends of my hair as he leans his chin against the top of my head. "Mated life never interested me," he confesses, confirming my initial theory. "It was never what I wanted until I saw you. I never thought I could love a person as much as I love the dojo."

Yet again, there's a hopeful pang in my chest, and I indulge a small smile. "Which side of you is winning? The duty or the bond?"

For several minutes, he doesn't answer, and I'm surprised to find myself nervous. I give him the silence he needs, and I don't press it.

"You make me *feel*, Rory," he admits. "I feel more deeply for you than even a mate-bond should make me feel. It's insanely deep. If anything happened to you, I would instantly and irreparably snap. There would be no coming back from the brink. If, for whatever reason, you reject this bond and say it's not what you want, my dragon would pursue you to the ends of the Earth."

His dragon is pushy, so I'll give him that. "What would *you* do?"

"Try my best to honor your wishes," he admits, gently kissing the top of my head. "And fail miserably at it."

CHAPTER FOURTEEN

As the moon shines overhead in the jet-black sky, suspended between the thousands of stars shining in the darkness, I sit on my tower roof and enjoy the soft hum of wind through the silence.

My peace lasts all of five minutes, which is honestly a record in this place.

The rustle of somebody climbing up onto the roof catches my attention, but I recognize the sound. I don't look over my shoulder, since I already know who it is.

Irena pulls herself onto the roof and joins me, sitting beside me as she reclines and stretches her legs. We sit together in the stillness for a few moments, not needing to say anything to enjoy each other's company.

"You're glowing," she eventually says.

I look down in my arms, at the sleeves that I've pulled up to my elbow. True to her word, my skin glows faintly gold, as do the glimmering two-dimensional chains along my forearms. I lift my hands to study the magical tattoos as they glitter and glisten even in the darkness.

"Yeah, I guess I am." I shrug, as if they don't bother me even though they do. "You know, it's funny. Over time, you just kind of tune them out. Every now and then, I'll look down and suddenly remember they're there."

"What are they?"

"I don't know." I tuck my legs under me and look out over the dark forest once again. "They appeared when I got my magic. I'm not sure what they mean, and I just kind of assume I'll have them forever."

There's a lot I expect Irena to say in response to that. I know she has opinions, especially on this whole me *being the dragon vessel* thing.

Thankfully, she doesn't press it. She's quiet, keeping her thoughts to herself, and I have to admit I'm grateful for that. At least for the moment.

"I've reactivated most of my contacts," Irena says instead, changing the subject. "The good ones, anyway."

"Think we'll leave soon, then?"

For the Spectre tech. For the remote storage warehouse that unknowingly hides the specs on some of the most advanced technology in the world.

"Soon," she promises. "After talking with them, something's becoming clear to me, though."

"Oh?"

"You and I aren't the only ones who wanted out," she says with a knowing glance toward me. "There were others forced into the life just like we were. There's a growing resentment, something I can turn into a rebellion. Something that can destroy the Spectres from within."

Irena pauses, her green eyes darting toward me as I process everything she just said.

My sister wants to trust people. She wants to build a team, just like me.

I truly never thought I would see the day.

"I've never taken many lovers," she says, looking at her fingernails. "But the few I have are in the Spectres. Others like us who understood the life, the limitations, the risks. They want to help."

"And you trust them?"

For a moment, Irena doesn't move or speak. Her jaw tenses like she doesn't quite know what to say or if she should speak at all. "I don't know, Rory. You never know who might be a double agent. Who's ultimately in Zurie's pocket, or who she placed in my life just to watch me."

"That's true," I admit with a nod. "Do you have any guesses who might be on Zurie's side?"

She hesitates. "Everyone?"

I chuckle. "Deep down, you already know who's honorable and who's not. Trust your gut."

"But what if—"

Irena is interrupted by the chime on her phone, nothing more than a simple ding that catches our attention and is gone just as quickly. She tugs it out of her pocket, her thumb sliding across the screen as she pulls up an alert.

"There's chatter on the closed Fairfax network," she says, tapping her thumbs furiously across the phone screen.

I roll my eyes. "Do I need to hit you with a rolled-up newspaper or something? Bad assassin. *Bad*," I add, waggling my finger at her.

She flashes an irritated glare at me, but she can't suppress the small grin that falls at the edge of her mouth. "Let me have my fun."

Seconds later, a ripple of static cuts through the speaker on the phone, followed by the soft chatter of men talking over each other.

"Shut up, all of you," Russell snaps.

I lean subtly forward, surprised to hear his voice. Jace doesn't tell me much about the embassy or its inner workings, and I haven't yet been able to really figure out who does what around here.

It would seem as though Russell has his hand in every pot, a fact that becomes all the more interesting now that I know he's currently the front-runner for Jace's second in command. He's clearly capable, and I'm curious to see how he handles being in charge.

Pretty much anyone would be better than Guy Durand though.

"Anderson, report," Russell orders.

"We've spotted a Knights onslaught in the East Forest," a man answers. "Thirty soldiers. Possible reinforcements on the way. Anti-dragon tanks stationed along the perimeter, but we've had those in our sights for a while."

"Progress?" Russell asks.

"Making headway through the forests along one of the clearer paths. Team Bravo strategically downed trees around the tanks yesterday, which will funnel through a clearing in about five minutes so we can intercept."

"Good. Send Squad One."

"Yes, sir," the man answers.

Seconds later, a tightly knit formation of twenty dragons soars overhead from the far end of the embassy, stealing through the air as they bank eastward. They maneuver like planes in tight configuration, silent and stealthy. If I hadn't been up here on the roof to see them, to know where to look, I may not have even known where they were.

It makes me wonder how much I've missed in those moments where I'm sleeping or not constantly watching over the embassy grounds.

It makes me wonder what else Jace is hiding from me.

"Give me details," Jace orders, his voice cutting through the connection.

My heart impulsively skips a beat at the sound of his voice, at hearing the authoritative growl in his command. My dragon stirs and shivers, aching for him as he takes control of this military operation.

"Surveillance shows Brett Clark leading the assault," Russell answers through the connection. "It seems as though the Knights are trying to infiltrate, and chatter suggests they're coming for Rory."

Jace doesn't answer. Instead, a low and rumbling growl floats through the line, and his connection goes dead. Seconds later, a black thunderbird tears through the sky after Squad One, nothing but a shadowy blur of dark scales and blue magic through the night.

Irena briefly looks at me, her eyebrows raised in skeptical curiosity. I shake my head to stop her from asking any questions or saying anything annoying.

"Those poor bastards don't realize what they just got themselves into," a woman says, her voice cutting through the phone's speaker.

"They most certainly do *not*," Russell agrees, and I can practically hear the smile on his face.

"Squad One approaching," Anderson says. "Switching to live footage from the forest cams."

Through the speaker, the cold bite of wind blows across a microphone. It's quiet, almost to an eerie degree, without a hint of the creatures living in the forest to occupy the silence. I wait for the sound of the growl, for the leathery beat of wings hitting air.

But there's nothing.

Just the quiet.

I wait with bated breath in the silence, itching for something to happen.

There—the distant, stifled scream of a man caught off guard. Seconds later, more screams cut through the line, each of them cutting off before they can finish.

In the distance, a few trees shake, but it's so subtle that I almost miss it.

I don't, however, miss the gunfire.

It's far enough away that to me, the gunfire sounds like nothing more than distant, muted pops. Through the connection on the phone, however, it's blaring and thunderous. Irena flinches from the sudden noise, leaning away from the speaker as she turns down the volume.

"Damn it, they're escaping," a woman says. "Sir, what are your orders?"

"Send Squad Two," Russell demands, his tone both urgent and calmly in control. "Have them secure the Eastern Perimeter."

Moments later, a second squad of twenty dragons rushes off from the northern forests toward the east, heading in the same direction as the first. They fly low across the forest, each of them in tight formation as they follow one dragon that leads the way through the night.

"I want to help," I say quietly under my breath.

I ache to be out there, to do *something*. Anything at all, as long as it means not just sitting and waiting to hear what will happen next.

"They'll be done before we even get there," Irena points out, her shoulders tight and tense.

It looks like she wants to help, too—or, at least, she wants to get in a bit of trouble.

"I know," I admit, frustrated and restless as ever. A bright blast of blue magic tears through the air, scattering leaves into the wind. I stand impulsively, knowing full well who that is.

Jace.

"Goodwin found Brett Clark," one of the soldiers says through the connection.

"Send support," Russell demands.

"You know he won't accept it," a woman counters.

"I don't give a damn," Russell snaps. "Send it anyway."

"Yes, sir," she answers.

An explosion rocks the distant forest, and a plume of smoke rises through the trees. My heart pangs with worry, and I wonder if this time maybe Jace bit off more than he could chew.

All because he didn't want to accept my help. All because he thinks he can handle this better than me.

All because he doesn't realize we can be a *team* and do the impossible—together.

"Gods, he's a beast," Anderson says through the line.

"Focus," Russell chides.

"Yes, sir. It's just..." The man trails off as if he's debating whether or not he wants to finish a sentence.

Russell groans impatiently. "Fine. What is it?"

"I wouldn't want to be on the receiving end of a fight with Goodwin," the soldier admits. "He's brutal."

"That's why he's the master of the dojo," Russell says simply, as if Jace's brutal skill is basic, common knowledge. "Now focus."

"Yes, sir."

My shoulders relax somewhat, and even though I can't see the fight and judge it for myself, it's comforting to know Jace seems to be holding his own. If Brett really is as good as Tucker says, he won't be easy to take down.

In the silence that follows, I pace along the roof, my eyes locked on the eastern forest as I wait for an update.

"Brett's squad is escaping, sir," one of the soldiers pipes through the connection. "Well, what's left of them, anyway."

"How many remain?" Russell asks.

"Seven."

"Get Squad Three out there to drop that number down to *zero*," Russell orders. "Do a full sweep of the forest to make sure no one is playing dead."

"Yes, sir. Deploying Squad Three."

Almost instantly, a third group of dragons emerges from the mist that hangs in the ravine behind the embassy. They angle as they pass us, and I notice a familiar green dragon among them.

Eric.

The one who's been toying non-stop with Irena.

He briefly looks at us, his eyes lingering on my sister. But he doesn't stop, and he doesn't flirt.

He's on a mission.

Squad Three fans out across the forests, the dragons flying low over the canopy in a single line over the trees. Before I even have a moment to guess their plan, they dive into the leaves.

I have to admit, I'm deeply impressed. These dragons are good.

"Dunn found one, sir," one of the soldiers says through the connection.

"That's Eric," Irena says with a proud little smirk—one I think she believes I can't see in this darkness.

"Bring him in," Russell demands.

Irena's green dragon soars into the air with a man in his claws. Fast as lightning, the dragon tears through the sky as the man wriggles in his grip.

As Eric flies closer, the strange man's eyes land on me, and he freezes. He simply watches me even as the dragon dives back into the mists, and a cold shiver of dread snakes up my spine.

"Damn it, Clarke got away," Jace says into the line, seething.

"We saw his route, sir," Russell replies. "We can send—"

"We can't leave the embassy grounds," Jace interrupts, clearly irritated. "You know the law, Russell."

"Not even if they invade our lands?" Russell replies, barely biting back his fury. "There are loopholes in the law, sir! If we chase them now, when they're—"

"Those loopholes aren't strong enough to save us from public opinion," Jace says more calmly this time, a hint of disappointment in his voice. "We have to be the bigger men and let them go."

There's a tense moment of silence before Russell clears his throat. "Very well, sir. We did capture one of his troops. It would seem there's a lone wolf that was headed toward the castle on his own."

"Good. And the others?"

"Only Clarke escaped," Russell confirms.

"I can live with that," Jace says tensely. "Take the captive to Interrogation Room 3. I'm going to have a little chat with him."

There's an icy hatred in Jace's tone, something dark and dangerous. It reminds me of the kind of growl you hear before a wolf attacks, the frantic rage-filled anger that can drive a man to murder.

He's livid. Whatever happened out there in the forest *really* pissed him off.

"Come on," Irena says, switching off the phone and standing. "We need to find out what happens in that interrogation room."

"I know where to go," I admit, standing and taking the lead.

Irena hesitates, glancing me over briefly. "You've been in the interrogation rooms?"

"Once or twice," I admit with a wry smirk, intentionally leaving out the details just to mess with her. "Now, let's *go*."

I n the tunnels beneath the embassy, with our backs pressed against the wall, Irena and I pause in the darkness to listen.

We wait in the corridor beyond the primary door —the one Drew and I used to spy on Harper's ultimatum to Jace. This stretch of hallway holds most of the interrogation rooms, and while it's not a surefire bet, I'm fairly certain Interrogation Room 3 is somewhere nearby.

The meaty thud of knuckles hitting a face filters through one of the vents, along with a groan of pain.

Irena looks at me, her green eyes bright in the darkness, and points to the vent she heard it come from.

I nod. The subtle pull at my navel is also yanking me in that direction. Even though my connection to Jace is fuzzy at the moment, I know he's close.

I kneel, peeking through the slots in the vent near the floor, but there's no visibility even as another punch lands. I can see shadows dance across the ground, but nothing more.

My ear straining, I listen intently.

Footsteps pace across the ground as the captive groans in pain once again. "You're not the first, you know," a man says, his voice growly and deep.

Jace.

"I've intercepted twelve of these failed missions since the dragon vessel arrived," Jace says, surprisingly formal despite the cutting grate in his tone. He must not want them to realize the depth of his connection to me, in case this one is released. "Every time you try to take her, you fail. Every time you come here, more of your people die. When will you Knights learn to give up?"

"When the girl's dead," the captive says, gurgling slightly through what I figure must be blood in his mouth.

There's a pause, and I can only imagine the look on

Jace's face. Seconds later, another punch lands, this time harder and heavier than before. The chair creaks, and the guy hits the ground. He lands on the floor in front of the vent, the back of his head covered in sweat and dirt. A small puddle of blood forms beneath him.

He, however, laughs.

I grimace, briefly sharing a brief glance with Irena as I listen to the Knight laughing through his own blood.

He sounds insane.

"It's just a matter of time before we have her," the captive says, still laughing. "The General is going to break her when he gets her. He will bleed her dry, refill her and bleed her again. Over and over. He will have his way with her, and then let the rest of us do the same. Anyone who wants a ride."

I grit my teeth in disgust at the vile thought, wishing I could be in there, wishing I could beat some sense into this man myself.

Lucky for me, Jace has no qualms about doing it, too.

He grabs the man's collar with one hand and brings his fist down on the man's nose with the other. Over and over again, Jace beats the man with a raging fury I haven't seen in him before. It's unfiltered and uncontrolled, fueled by wrath and loathing.

When he finally pauses, the man is wheezing. It's like he can barely breathe through the blood in his broken nose, but it's hard to care.

This is a man who came to kill me, who wants to not just kill me but break my spirit first.

I don't have a lot of sympathy for people like that.

"I'm going to give you a chance to be useful," Jace says, his voice low and deadly. "And if you're useful, you might not die. Where's Brett Clarke?"

"You played into my hands, you know," the captive says, ignoring the question. He wheezes, the soft whistle of air through his broken nose a bit distracting each time he tries to talk. "Bringing me in here was exactly what I wanted you to do. I'm where I want to be. How long do you think you can hold me in this cell, Goodwin?" He laughs, the sound sputtering out into a coughing fit as he chokes on his blood. "I'll find her, drag her back to the General, and kill the traitor while I'm at it."

He snickers, and I figure the "traitor" he's referring to is Tucker. If that's the case, that means the General has officially written off his son.

It's hard to tell which of us the General hates more —me or Tucker.

Probably me.

"I'll bring back his head," the soldier continues.

"Bring back the girl. I'll be a legend, Goodwin. A hero. So, go on, beat me senseless—you'll only make the story I share when I get back all the more impressive."

I grimace in utter revulsion. What a *freak*.

I expect to hear more punches. Instead, Jace kneels.

Through the slits in the vent, I can see the stubble on his jaw as he gets close to the man's face, his voice a deadly growl. "I've stopped four dozen attempts to kill her, *Knight*. Four *dozen*. You're no hero. You're just another one of the masses, a pawn the General will discard and forget. You see, you just made this so much easier for me."

"How so?" the soldier asks, the arrogance in his tone daring Jace to continue.

"You're threatening my mate," Jace replies, his nose wrinkling in disgust as he inches toward the man's face. "And that's a death sentence. I don't have to keep you alive anymore—I can just kill you."

"You wouldn't dare." The man laughs again, wheezing. "You need me. You need my intel. You need my knowledge. You won't kill me until you learn it all."

"You haven't been especially useful," Jace says, his tone sharp and warning. "So, right now, it doesn't seem like I need you at all."

"Of course, you do. I have everything—movements, locations, names. Besides, don't you dragons have ethics?" The captive wheezes again and spits blood across the floor. "I heard you don't kill prisoners. Or have I always been right about you lot—you're just monsters, thirsty for blood any chance you get?"

"Oh, I kill prisoners," Jace says calmly. "I kill them when they threaten my woman."

He grabs the guy's throat with one hand and hoists him into the air with his enhanced dragon strength, effortlessly lifting both the Knight and the chair he's tied to.

From my angle near the floor, I can't see anything but shadows along the concrete ground. I lean forward, trying to get more information, but all I hear is wheezing laughter.

With a snap of bones, the laughter stops. A second later, his body thuds against the floor, the chair shattering to splinters from the force. He doesn't move, and the wheezing whistle of his breath finally stops.

Heavy footsteps hit the ground, and I see Jace's bare feet pass by. Seconds later, the door slams, and there's silence once again in the room.

I stare at the body on the ground, not quite sure what to say or what to think. I do, however, know exactly how I feel.

Astonished.

Jace stopped four dozen attacks on my life without telling me about any of them.

"I never thought I would say this," Irena admits quietly, squeezing her eyes shut as if she's about to say something that pains her to admit. "You're lucky to have someone like that looking out for you. To have someone protect you like that." She hesitates, her bright green eyes watching me. "To love you that fiercely."

Still dazed, I stare at the corpse on the floor and simply nod.

Jace is strong and sexy as hell, and he will do anything to keep the people and things he loves safe. I just wish he could trust me enough to tell me these things.

There's still so much he hides from me—and so much I don't know about Jace Goodwin.

CHAPTER FIFTEEN

J ace won't tell me the truth—but there's one
dragon in this embassy who knows *exactly*
what's going on.

It all clicked for me, downstairs in the tunnels.

The truth.

Drew has been keeping things from me, just like
Jace.

After everything he's said about me being his equal,
this feels like the ultimate betrayal.

There's no way he missed this chatter on all of the
different bounties on my head. He can't possibly have
overlooked the sheer volume of hit squads that have
come after me. There's no way he didn't see Jace
deploy the troops.

My question is why he never told me.

I kneel at the door to Drew's bedroom, picking the lock. I seamlessly juggle the tools, holding the ones I'm not using between my clenched teeth as I fight with the keyhole.

For some reason, his doorknob is a difficult one. I figure he gave himself a nice little upgrade when he got here, but it's not sophisticated enough to keep me out.

The mechanism clicks, the door finally unlocked, and I strain my ear in the lingering silence as I tuck my tools away. The hiss of running water filters faintly beneath the door, and I figure he's probably in the shower—that is, until I hear the subtle footsteps across the carpet in the hall. There's the creak of skin on a gun handle, and the footsteps stop.

He's probably at the tail end of the hallway, facing the door, armed and ready to fire on whoever would dare enter his room.

I smirk. This will be fun.

I kick open the door to find Drew just where I figured he would be, at the far end of the hallway with a handgun aimed at my face. Water drips along his gorgeous and *very* naked body, and his left hand holds the ends of a white towel strung loosely around his waist. His eyes are narrowed, ready to fire at a moment's notice, and it's not until our gazes lock that he relaxes his shoulders.

"Come in," he says sarcastically as he lowers his gun.

I slam the door behind me, trying to ignore his bare chest and the defined muscle in his abdomen. Drops of water slide along his biceps as he watches me.

"Tell me the truth about the bounties," I demand. "Everything you've picked up that Jace won't tell me. Everything *you've* been hiding from me."

He groans, tilting his head backward slightly as he realizes what this is going to be about. "You found out."

I nod, taking a few steps toward him even though it's next to impossible to keep my gaze trained on his face. I keep wanting to examine his hard abs or admire the way his tight grip on the towel is the only thing keeping it around his waist.

"How'd you do it?" he asks, lifting one eyebrow in curiosity.

"You don't get to change the subject," I snap, admittedly sounding far more irritated than I really am.

It's difficult to maintain composure around a naked Drew. He's just so damn distracting.

He grins, clearly caught in the act. "What do you want to know?"

"Everything," I repeat.

"You're going to have to be a little more specific," he says, turning on the safety on his handgun before he tosses it onto the bed.

"How long have you known?"

"A while," Drew admits.

"That's not what I—"

"This is what Jace and I've been fighting over," he interrupts, his dark eyes locking on me and snaring me in his intense gaze. "We agreed at the beginning that you needed to focus, that we shouldn't tell you because you needed to train. You needed to get clear on your powers, your limits, and your abilities."

I grit my teeth in anger, furious and annoyed that Drew's in on this, too. I open my mouth to speak, but he cuts me off yet again.

"The tide, however, is changing," he says, standing a little taller and rolling his shoulders back. "People are being more brazen. There's more competition, and the longer we wait, the more people come after you. The less you know, the more enemies you make." He lets out an exasperated groan and runs a strong hand through his gorgeous hair. "Rory, half of these people —you don't even know their names. You wouldn't recognize them in the street or know the organization they work for. But they know you. They know far too much about you."

I shake my head in irritation, furious that it's gotten this bad. I've been so disconnected from the world out there that I've lost touch with the people who are after me. In his effort to protect me, Jace just took away one of my most important weapons —information.

"You're my equal," Drew says, his tone hard and serious. "I told you that before when you and I made this pact of ours, and it's been true ever since. Even now. I might not tell you things I deem irrelevant, but if it impacts you, if it threatens you, you need to know about it."

I study his face briefly. "Then why didn't you tell me this?"

He scoffs, his nose wrinkling briefly in disdain. "Because Jace swore that if you so much as hinted at knowing, he would throw me in a cell in the capital. He would forbid me from ever seeing you."

"That's not even possible," I counter, hardly believing it. "That isn't how the embassies work. There are laws—"

"There's a loophole in the law," Drew interjects. "If I give him reason to kick me out, and if there just *happens* to be soldiers waiting at the edge of the embassy to carry me off, there's nothing against him giving me a ground escort right to them." Drew cracks his neck, his jaw tense. "Or, as he put it, knocking me the hell out and letting me wake up in a cage. It was a very real threat, Rory."

I bristle at the idea of Jace using me as leverage against Drew. I don't even quite know what to say, but I do know that there's a certain neck I want a wring right now.

Drew watches me, and it's almost like he can read my thoughts. He debates something for a moment, frowning slightly. But in the end, he sighs. "Rory, the mate-bond makes thunderbirds do incredibly stupid things. Don't be too hard on him."

"Has hell been freezing over a lot lately?" I scoff. "You told me yourself how much you hate him. Why are you defending him now?"

"I thought this over very thoroughly," Drew admits. "Jace is still an invaluable asset, even if he *is* a royal asshole."

I set one hand on my hip, shaking my head as I think through this again. "I don't think he would have done it, Drew. That's just too far, even for him."

Drew shrugs. "You forget how much the Fairfax

dragons hate me, Rory. Jace's brother was a legend, and they all think I killed him."

"And yet you won't tell them the truth," I counter, narrowing my eyes at him in disappointment. "That would solve all of this, Drew. Tell him the truth. Tell him what really happened."

"I thought about it," Drew admits, taking a few steps toward me. "I've kept it a secret to keep Milo alive. He travels a lot, and you never know when even a Darrington might go missing. My brother relies too much on his security detail," Drew says with a huff of disdain. "Until I met you, my priorities were always to honor my family—and have a bit of fun," he adds with a wry grin. "But my priorities are changing. You're more important than Jett or Milo, Rory. You're in my world, now. And if Jace is going to be in your world, too—if you really believe he's good for you, for *us*, then…" He groans, rubbing his eyes in frustration. "Then I don't know. I'm not sure what the best move is, yet, and I'm not used to not knowing. One thing is for sure, though," he says, looking me dead in the eye. "I take care of my own."

His intimate tone disarms me, and for a moment, all I can do is study his face. The intensity of his gaze. The way his eyes gently soften as he drinks me in, like I'm a priceless portrait he loves to look at.

Before I can say anything, he drops the towel at his waist and reveals that he is, in fact, delightfully and deliciously naked underneath. My eyes impulsively flit downward, taking in his thick cock as it begins to harden. Droplets of water trail down his toned body, and I bite my lip to keep the rising tide of desire at bay.

We're not done talking, damn it, and it isn't fair for him to use his gorgeous body against me.

Then again, it's not like Drew *ever* plays fair.

He grins mischievously, knowing full well what he does to me, and closes the final few steps between us. His strong fingers weave through my hair, his hands engulfing me as he tenderly holds my head.

"I can tell you, however, that you're safe here at the dojo," he says quietly, gently pulling me closer. He presses his lips against my forehead, and I can't help but drink in his delightful scent—like smoke and sweat. He radiates power and strength.

"Maybe," I concede, trying to regain at least some of my composure even as heat snakes between my thighs. "For now, at least. It won't be long before the other Bosses use political and trade pressure to try to force the Fairfax dragons to hand me over."

Drew reflexively tenses, and though he relaxes almost as quickly, I still caught the subtle movement.

"Gods, they already are, aren't they?" I press.

"Uh…"

He clears his throat, his gaze darting off to the side like he's debating whether or not to lie.

"Yeah, they are," he ultimately admits.

"We should leave," I say quietly, not wanting to really consider the option even though I know I have to. "It isn't fair to put so much pressure on Harper and Jace. They—"

"We need to wait," Drew interrupts. "As much as I hate having little to no control over my environment, and despite how little I enjoy giving the others so much access to my *woman*"—his grip on me tightens as he says the word—"Zurie is a real threat. At least here, we have the resources to truly handle her."

"We don't know how much longer that could take," I point out. "It could be years."

"Do you really think she will wait that long?" he asks, leaning back until he can see my face.

I hesitate, and though my impulse is to say yes, I know better. She's desperate—and desperate people don't dally.

Tenderly, Drew trails a hand down my neck and along my spine. His strong fingertips press against my skin, marking their path with a ribbon of warmth that kicks up the deepest, most primal flurries of lust deep within my core.

He leans against me yet again, and this time his hard cock presses against my leg. Warmth pools at my entrance, and my treasonous body aches for him. My legs want to spread apart. My hips want to tilt toward him, to let him inside of me.

This man knows *exactly* what he's doing—and what he wants.

My dragon stirs within me, curling with glee and mischief as my fire dragon toys with me.

She *loves* it. And *him.*

A burst of energy blazes through me, and white light shimmers along my arms along with the surge of power. The wisps of magic blur across my skin as my dragon aches for us to get on with it already.

"Beautiful," Drew says gently, his eyes on my arms as the white light begins to fade. "Shift, Rory."

"What, here?" I laugh, gesturing to his suite. "Just... right now?"

He nods, smirking as he watches my face.

"I don't even know *how.*"

"Listen to her," he commands, gently pushing me until my back presses against the wall behind me. "Trust her. Touch her."

Briefly, I debate shutting him up with a kiss and

just wrapping my legs around his waist to get things started, but I decide to indulge him.

I close my eyes as his warm hands slip to my waist, holding me in place as he peppers kisses along my neck.

I can barely focus on my dragon—all I can feel is the fiery delight of his touch.

"You're distracting me," I say with a grin.

"Oh, am I?" he asks mischievously as he nibbles my jaw. "How rude."

Without warning, he lifts me into his arms and carries me into his bedroom. I laugh, caught off guard with the sudden movement, but he doesn't lay me on the bed like I expected.

Instead, he carries me into the bathroom where the hot water is still running in the shower. Steam billows around us as he nudges open the door with his foot. He carries me into the sauna, despite the fact that I'm still fully clothed.

"Drew, what—" I laugh, trying to squirm out of his grip, but it's too late.

The water blasts me, drenching me instantly from above as it seeps into my shirt and clear through to the bra and underwear beneath it all. I close my eyes, laughing as I try to shake the water off, but he's on me instantly.

My fire dragon presses my hips against the wall as the water slides over us. Wordlessly, he grabs my thighs and spreads my legs apart, and the only thing keeping me upright is his chest pressed hard against mine, pinning me to the tiles.

His thick cock hits my entrance, the fabric of my loose dojo pants the only thing between us. I can feel myself getting wetter the longer he holds me there, suspended in anticipation and desire—and it's not from the shower.

He leans toward me until his mouth is by my ear. "Is this better?"

"You're such an ass," I say, laughing.

"You love it."

Drew grabs the back of my head, snaring a fistful of my hair as he roughly kisses me. His fiery kisses are full of hunger and need, like he can't possibly wait another second. Like he has to have me—right *now* —and will never have enough.

Yes, I love it. I truly do.

As my clothes get heavier from the water they're absorbing, Drew reaches for my shirt and rips it clean off. I can't suppress the gasp as he tears into my clothes, leaving nothing but rags behind, and I love it.

The force. The strength. The power.

No one dominates me like Drew.

In seconds, the ribbons of what were once my clothes are tossed aside, nothing but heaps of fabric in the corner of the shower. Drew presses his naked body against mine. His hard muscle pins me to the wall as the full length of his cock glides across my entrance, teasing me with his length even though he won't let me ride it yet.

He weaves his hands down my waist and to my ass, gripping me tightly as he effortlessly lifts me into the air. I'm spread eagle and at his mercy, pinned against the shower tile as the water drips over me.

At this moment, I can't think of anywhere else I would rather be.

The tip of his cock presses against the sensitive folds between my thighs, inching inward as if he can hardly hold himself back. Somehow, he manages to restrain himself.

It's torture.

He kisses my neck as he pins me there, his dick slowly forcing its way into me. He's barely giving me a taste, and I arch my back to invite him in. Anything at all to make the torment stop.

"When you do shift," he says, gently nibbling my ear. "Your IUD won't work anymore."

"What—"

With that, he thrusts himself into me.

I gasp as our hips meet, the full length of him stretching me in delightfully sinful ways. He waits for a moment, gently pumping his cock into me as he rocks his hips against mine. His hands grip my ass and hold me in place as we become one.

Slowly, tantalizingly, he pulls out of me, and I can't help but moan in pleasure as his cock slides through me, raw and unprotected. The thought of my IUD failing is both terrifying and exhilaratingly *wrong*.

Drew sure knows how to talk dirty.

I freaking *love* it.

When his dick finally slides out of me, it bounces slightly before he presses it once more against my entrance. And just like that, he's ready to go again, to continue this delightful torment.

"You'll have to brew a special tea," Drew continues calmly, like he didn't just rock my world with a single thrust.

I look at him, my brain foggy with lust and the unyielding need for him to be in me once again.

He's really milking this.

I smile, too horny to fight him on this. "Tea? That's—"

He rams into me, and my back arches against the warm tile wall as he once again fills me to the brim. I moan, wrapping my legs around him as my clit slides along his body, buzzing with delight and desire.

Gods, he's so damn good at this.

This time, he doesn't stop. He thrusts into me again and again, somehow picking up speed and power every time he bucks into me.

"You have to stay regular with it," he says through heavy breaths as he fucks me hard in the shower.

The hot water rolls over us, filling my lungs with steam as he drives his cock into me again and again.

I moan, barely able to *think*, much less listen.

"If you don't take it daily," he continues, gently biting my neck between words. "You might get a little surprise nine months out."

I can barely handle this.

Lost in him, in his cock, in the way he thrusts again and again into me, I moan in pleasure. My hips rock against his, milking every motion and movement for every ounce of ecstasy his body can give me.

He's never ridden me this hard before—and with Drew, that's saying something. He rides me like he *wants* my IUD to fail.

With his hands on my ass, his powerful grip keeping me rooted against his body, I spread my legs as wide as they can go. Anything at all to get closer, to feel *more*, to be even more filled by him.

The ribbon of delight and pleasure builds slowly, deep within me, blooming more every time his cock slides deep inside of me. I gasp, enchanted and ensnared, feeling my orgasm build long before it hits.

I love every second of this rapture.

It's heaven.

When I come, it's unrelenting. I moan and tighten my legs around him, riding the orgasm as his cock continues to dive into me again and again and *again.*

I hold him tightly, my arms around his neck as I kiss him fiercely between delightful moans.

I lose all track of time. For all I know, I came for several minutes straight—it's so intense, so all-encompassing, that I don't care about anything but the moment.

The sensation.

Him.

When the orgasm slowly begins to fade, he picks up speed. He almost sends me spiraling into another orgasm as he rails into me, his grip on my ass so tight my skin begins to tingle.

But I don't care. This feels too amazing to ask him to stop.

With one final thrust, he forces his cock as deep into me as he can go, and I feel the hot surge of him releasing deep within me. It's rough and raw, and he sighs with contented delight as he reaches his own orgasm.

Drew holds me pinned against the wall, my feet off the ground and my legs wrapped around his waist. With his mouth near my ear, he breathes heavily, apparently unable to move.

I smile and kiss the side of his head, releasing my legs as I try to slowly slide off of him.

He doesn't allow me to move.

Instead, he tenses and thrusts his hips forward, his cock still semi-hard and buried deep within me. The motion keeps me frozen in place, lifted off the ground as the water continues to roll off us both.

"I didn't say you could leave," he growls into my ear.

Playfully, he bites my jaw and trails a string of kisses down my neck. His chest presses hard against my breasts. Inside me, his cock fully hardens once again.

Apparently, he's ready for round two.

"Let's see how many orgasms I can give you in a row," he growls into my ear, his voice thick with lust. "And see if I can beat Tucker's record."

I grin. Gods above, I love my life.

CHAPTER SIXTEEN

The next morning, brilliant sunlight shines through the windows along the hallway as I walk back to my room. I can't help the contented smile on my face, and I know my hair is still a bit messed up from the adventures I had with Drew.

I just can't bring myself to care.

"I know that smile," a woman says from behind me.

I pivot the moment I hear the voice, lifting my fists and settling into a fighting stance as I prepare to take down whoever managed to catch me off-guard. I hadn't even heard footsteps or a whisper of breath, and I don't appreciate being snuck up on.

It's...

Irena.

I relax the moment I recognize her. She smirks, her

bright green eyes locked on me, and I let out a relieved breath as I shake my head in surprise.

"You're getting better," I confess.

She nods and begins to walk down the hallway in the same direction I was headed. "I'm getting my mojo back, yeah. It's nice." She looks at me as I catch up to her, matching her gait. "Which of your men gave you that grin?"

I smirk but don't say anything.

She chuckles. "Fine. Keep your secrets. We have work to do anyway."

"Oh?"

"It's time," she says with a nod. "The tech is clear. Chatter about us at the moment is minimal, so now is the time to strike. Are you ready?"

"Oh, I've been ready," I say, rolling out my shoulders and loosening my neck.

I've been itching for a mission—for a hit of that addictive adrenaline—and I'm more than ready for battle.

"What are we waiting for?" I ask. "Let's go steal Zurie's precious tech, big sister."

I t doesn't take long to get everyone together, and before I know it, we're all circled around the table in Jace's war room.

Well, the new table anyway. I'm not entirely sure when it happened, but he's already managed to find a replacement.

Part of me wonders if he keeps heaps of tables in a storage room somewhere, just in case one of the heated conversations he always seems to have in this room gets out of hand.

I have to admit, the speed with which he replaced it makes me feel a little less guilty about breaking it.

Irena leans against the table, her eyes scanning the various maps she laid out across the wood. The collection of drawings and sketches gives us a bird's eye view of not just the storage facility, but also the surrounding area.

In addition to a little green dot representing her storage unit, every possible Spectre safehouse has been marked in yellow. I have to admit I'm not altogether pleased with the amount of yellow highlighter covering the maps.

But that's what makes it fun.

The risk.

"This is the route we need to take," Irena says, dragging her finger along the map. "Security in this place is minimal, and we can tap the camera feed rather easily to get a clear picture of what it'll be like before we go in."

"But they have voids," Jace points out. "Can't they just loop every camera and make the entire system moot?"

"It's possible," Irena admits with a nod. "However, I doubt it. The chances that they know we're coming are incredibly low. To be safe, I've planted a few cameras throughout the facility as well, set to record on a motion sensor basis to preserve battery and prolong life. Those cameras will tell me the moment anyone goes in, and they're hidden to the point where no one can see them. I didn't tell my contacts about them, and no one knows they're there."

I grin. "Clever."

Irena feigns a little bow. "I try."

"Have you seen anything yet?" Drew asks, leaning his elbows on the table.

"Nothing interesting," Irena says. "People going in, people coming out—standard patrons. No Spectres, and no known Spectre allies."

Levi leans forward. "How do you know if—"

"I know," Irena says darkly, rolling her shoulders as she tilts her head. "I know them *all*."

"She does," I confirm.

Levi chuckles and leans back in his chair. "Continue."

Irena taps her finger on the little green dot. "If they know we're going to recover this, they're being careful and not going anywhere near it. My guess is, if there is somebody waiting for us, they're waiting outside." She drags her finger around the edge of the compound to drive her point home.

"Comforting," Tucker says sarcastically.

Briefly, I steal a glance at him, only to find him studying the maps. His eyes are focused and clear, and it's nice to see him alert.

I'm sure there's still grief stewing in that gorgeous head of his, but he's not letting it show.

"I managed to secure the tech in four cases that are locked with a special code," Irena continues. "I tried to compact it into fewer trunks, but with everything I needed to cover my ass, that's what it had to be. It has everything in it. Everything we could ever need."

A soft laugh escapes Drew, and he watches Irena with an amazed expression. "Even the voids? The override devices?"

"All of it," Irena says with a small nod. "Absolutely everything."

I impulsively lean forward, my shoulders tensing as I zero in on the little green square that represents the storage unit full of information on Spectres. Every-thing we could ever need to destroy them is in there.

That's my ticket to killing Zurie. To dismantling the Spectres from within and keeping Irena alive through it all.

"What's our way out?" I ask, nodding to the center of the storage facility. "If this all goes south, what's the backup plan?"

"Hopefully, we just walk out," Irena says with a shrug. "If we're attacked while inside, we have a few options. Our best bet, and I can't believe I'm saying this," she adds, squeezing her eyes shut as if this pains her to say. "But our best bet is to simply shift and fly off. It's fast, and it's the safest way to escape with the goods intact."

"Out of the question," Jace says with a stiff shake of his head.

"Think about it," Irena demands, never one to give up. "If we're under heavy fire against humans without the ability to fly, why on Earth *wouldn't* you use that advantage?"

"Oh, I don't know," Jace says, his voice dripping with sarcasm. "Maybe because there are dozens of peace accords that keep this world from devolving into war? Us shifting in human territory would violate all of them."

"So?" Drew and Irena say in unison.

I chuckle.

"It's not an option." Jace's voice is firmer, now. Angrier.

"Guys, look," I say calmly, my gaze drifting from Irena to Drew. "These are his troops, and he faces the greatest risk if we're in any way caught. If so much as a camera feed shows any of the dojo soldiers, the world will come after him and Harper. They'll become the poster children for dragons behaving badly, and no one will care why we were there. They'll get all the blame, lose lucrative business deals they need to keep their family functioning, and possibly start an all-out war. Human-dragon tensions are bad enough as it is. Let's not make this worse, okay?"

"Fine," Irena says, her shoulders drooping as she pouts.

"Thank you," Jace says quietly, leaning toward me with a small smile on his face.

I nod. "Don't make me regret sticking up for you, now."

He grins. "I wouldn't dream of it."

"Option two is the roofs," Irena says with a heavy —and rather dramatic—sigh. "The facility is comprised of two dozen single-story buildings, each with roads between them. These two on the end funnel into a forest," she says, pointing to the buildings at the edge of the facility. "That's our best bet. We get on the roofs, fire down at anyone coming our way, and bolt."

"Going in, what are the risks?" Jace weaves his fingers together as he leans his elbows on the table.

"I'd like to say the risks are minimal," Irena confesses. "But that would be a lie. If one of my contacts betrayed me, the Spectres will not only know what is here but where it is. That was part of the danger I had to assume in getting this information in the first place. Getting it out meant trusting people."

"I thought that's not something Spectres did," Drew says with a wry smirk.

"I'm not fond of it, no, but I had to," Irena admits.

"If that's the case," Jace interjects, "what's stopping them from taking it back right now? Are we sure it's even there?"

Irena nods. "There's no doubt. I rigged it to explode if the wrong code is entered, and only I know it. Plus, if it's moved for more than five minutes, it also explodes unless a code is entered."

"Oh, great," Tucker says wryly. "There's a very literal chance that this could blow up in our faces."

"Only if I don't enter the code," Irena says again.

"The rest of us should know it, too." Jace crosses

his arms as he leans back in his chair. Irena watches him, her green eyes narrowing slightly as she frowns.

"Take baby steps, Jace," I say quietly.

He shakes his head in irritation, turning his attention on me. "We need to know—"

"Rory and I will know it," Irena interrupts. "If anything happens to me, she will be able to disarm the explosives."

I glare at her, hating that she would even consider the possibility of something happening to her.

"Ah." Jace rubs his jaw. "That brings me to my next concern, actually," he confesses.

Despite the entire room quiet and waiting for him to speak, he hesitates. His gaze shifts toward me, like there's something he wants to say, but he knows I'm not going to like it.

"Spit it out," I say dryly.

"I don't suppose you'll stay behind?" he asks.

"No," everyone else in the room says, all of us in unison. More than a few eyes roll.

He groans in annoyance. "Fine. Forgive me for trying to protect my woman."

"You mean *our* woman," Drew interjects, glaring at the dojo master.

For a moment, the two men simply glare at each other, and I can feel the tension crackling through the air. I need to stop this before it devolves. More importantly, however, I need to make sure this doesn't get in the way of a very important mission that could change everything for us.

"I need you two to work together," I interject, snapping them both out of it. "There's no room for grudges here. Not on this mission. Can you two do that?"

"I'm a professional," Jace says as he stands, the legs of his chair grating along the floor as he pushes it backward. "I can't speak for the caveman, though."

Drew grimaces in disgust as he glares at the dojo master, and a ribbon of thin black smoke shoots out of the fire dragon's nose even in his human form.

I rub my eyes in frustration.

This should be fun.

I lift a rifle from the armory wall and rack it, lifting the barrel toward one of the lockers as I get a feel for the weapon in my hands.

Heavy. Effective.

I like it.

With a few adjustments to the scope and grip, I flip on the safety and swing the heavy gun over my shoulder.

"You're so damn hot," Tucker says.

I chuckle and glance over my shoulder at him as he hides the fourteenth handgun on his body, this time down by his ankle. He covers the holster with his pant leg and adjusts the bulletproof vest strapped to his ripped torso.

"The feeling's mutual," I admit with a flirty wink.

He grins and slides four knives into the various pockets on his cargo pants before sliding a fifth into his boot, for good measure. Apparently satisfied with the various deadly weapons already strewn across his body, the former Knight grabs a standard rifle off the wall and adjusts the scope, frowning slightly as if it's not good enough for him.

"What's the matter?" I ask playfully. "Not big enough?"

"Not really," he confesses with a sheepish grin. "I like the dragon killers, personally. More heft."

My smile falls.

His gaze shifts back to me, and he frowns instantly as he realizes what he said. "No, not—not *killing* dragons, babe. Just, the guns are called dragon killers, so—"

"You're fine." I chuckle.

He's so damn adorable.

Tucker returns to his rifle, and as I watch him

adjust the grip and check for ammo, I lean against the lockers with my arms crossed.

"You got something on your mind, babe?" he asks, lifting his brows inquisitively.

Instead of answering, I watch him all the more intently.

Studying him. His face. His features. His square jaw. His broad shoulders, covered with weapons and Kevlar.

His eyes.

There's still a hint of sadness in them. It's mostly gone, but I know him.

I can still see it.

"Are you good?" I ask. "For this mission, I mean. Are you clearheaded enough to be out there? Because I can't..." I clear my throat, not even able to say the words.

Because I can't lose you.

I can't let him out there if he's distracted in any way. He will be in the line of fire, and I'll never forgive myself if he doesn't come back from this.

He sighs, jaw tensing a little as he swings the massive rifle over his shoulder and gently lifts my chin. "Babe, listen. If there's one thing I will *always* do, no matter what, it's show up for you. Nothing in this world will stop me from protecting you in any way I can. You hear me?"

"You can stay—"

"I swear to the gods—or whatever it is you dragons say, I don't know—that if you tell me I can stay behind, I'll pull a Jace and lock you in a tower just to see how you like *staying behind*, woman," he says with a firm shake of his head.

I bite my lip and slowly grin.

"That was pretty hot," I admit.

He chuckles and kisses me, his lips hot and fierce against mine. "You just like getting me fired up, don't you?"

"A little," I admit.

"Well, you get your way, then," he says, grinning as he racks his rifle. "Let's go steal from Spectres, babe."

"Oh, Tucker," I say, fanning my face with an exaggerated little flourish. "You say the most romantic things."

CHAPTER SEVENTEEN

In the woods outside a storage facility in the middle of Nowhere, Oklahoma, I lay on the ground with Jace at my side, swallowed by the shadows of the forest.

The moment we arrived, we scanned the barbed-wire fence along the outskirts of the facility but found no infiltration points or overt risks. Just the owner, locking up on his way out the door.

The people who regularly walk through this facility have no idea what it really holds—and the money they could get for what's inside.

If they don't die trying to steal it, of course.

A team of Jace's soldiers fan out behind us, everyone keeping close to the ground as we wait for the signal to move.

Squad One. Jace's best fighters, all of them ready to spring at a moment's notice.

As he's prone to do, Levi appears suddenly at my side. He nods once to me, and though his focus is primarily on the facility in front of us, it's comforting to know he's here. He simply refuses to be on any other team but mine, and I have to admit I kind of love it.

Drew and Tucker are leading Squad Two, which is approaching from the north while we approach from the south, and Russell is on a nearby hill waiting for the signal with Squad Three in case they're needed.

This facility isn't large enough for the sixty-seven of us to swarm in at once. It would create bottlenecks that would put us all at risk, so we need him to be backup.

Hopefully, he never has to move a muscle.

The whisper of footsteps along the dirt catches my ear. Levi and I both turn to look as Irena joins us. A few of the soldiers nearby flinch as she appears suddenly next to them, seemingly from thin air.

It's nice to see her getting her mojo back.

"The security system is uncompromised," she says quietly, her bright green eyes scanning the facility as she speaks. "The guard is taken care of as well."

I frown, not quite enjoying her choice of words

when it comes to an innocent security guard whose only job is to keep an eye on the facility.

Irena seems to catch my irritation and rolls her eyes. "He's tied up and unconscious, Rory. I didn't kill him. I even put him a little off property in case things get... *fiery*."

"Good," I say, returning my attention to the storage area.

"It seems like no one's here," Irena adds.

"Or they're lying in wait," I reply.

Something feels off about this. Deep within me, my dragon wriggles, clearly uncomfortable by something I can't fully understand or put into words just yet.

It's just an inherent *knowing*.

She can tell that something isn't right. In the past, I would have ignored this hit of intuition and simply pushed through, per Zurie's orders. But now that I have the magic of dragons, I can't simply ignore it anymore.

It's too damn loud.

"Something's not right," Irena admits quietly, apparently sensing it, too.

"Do we abort?" Levi asks simply.

"We can't," Irena says with a shake of her head. "We'll probably never get another opportunity. If this *is* a trap and we don't walk in, Zurie might blow this place to hell just to keep us from getting it."

"There's no point going in if we can't get out," Jace says tensely.

"We'll never take down the Spectres unless we get that information," Irena counters.

"Rory, what does your dragon say?" Jace asks.

I sit with the question for a moment. I want to make sure I give an honest answer. So, for a little while, I simply watch the storage facility and think.

After a moment, I realize everyone is watching me and waiting for an answer.

I frown, not entirely enjoying being the final say on this, but I close my eyes and listen intently to the dragon deep within me.

She's wary, yes, but she's also primed and ready for a fight. There's the pump of adrenaline, the eagerness to dive into the fray.

It's dangerous, but I know in my bones there's going to be a way out once we go in.

"We go," I say quietly. "But everyone has to be ready. I get the feeling we're going to walk into a fire-fight. Jace, that means we shift if we have no other way out. Are we all clear on that?"

He frowns, his eyes narrowing as he clearly

disagrees, and I have to confess he knows more about politics and treaties than I do.

In terms of this mission, however—in terms of what's going to save the most lives and ensure that we're successful—we have to know there's a Plan B.

"Let's hope it doesn't come to that," Jace says simply. "The soldiers here are the best of the best. If there's a way out that doesn't involve shifting, we'll find it."

"Zurie's bringing the best of the best, too," I point out.

Jace's eyes start briefly toward me, and his frown deepens before he returns his attention to the storage facility. "Tech team, do we have anything?"

"The signal's jammed, sir," somebody pipes through the comm in my ear. "We can't get a good signal or a good read."

"Damn it," I mutter. "She's here."

"They're *definitely* here," Irena says with a small nod.

I scan the unassuming storage facility, wondering where they're hiding, what they've set up for us, and if this is really worth going.

It is, but I kind of wish it wasn't.

The Spectres have survived thus far because they have advanced technology and stealth training, as well as information and secrets that set them ahead of the pack. If we can take away their core advantage, we can destroy them once and for all.

This is dangerous, but we absolutely have to do it.

"Keep to the shadows," I order raising my gun as I get to my feet. "Stay low."

"Move out," Jacc orders, and his soldiers jump to obey.

We slink through the shadows toward the hole Irena cut in the fence not long ago. Before long, we've moved from the darkness of the forest into the shadow-ridden gloom of the facility.

With almost no moon, there's very little to give us away. These soldiers move with stealth and perfection, barely giving away so much as a footstep as they cut through the night, and I'm grateful to be working with some of the best soldiers in the world.

It's a treat, honestly. Under any other circumstances, I would be practically giddy.

With Irena leading the way, we charge through the corridors of the open facility, darting past identical rows of buildings riddled with padlocked doors. She takes us through the labyrinth, leading us into the middle—toward the most exposed section of the facility.

I know she did this intentionally. She wanted to

make sure the cases were protected and that if anyone but her got to them, she would know right away. But, damn it, this location just makes them harder to retrieve.

"Squad Two moving in," Drew says through the comm in my ear.

My heart flutters a little bit with gratitude and relief that they're coming because the longer they're out of my sight, the more at risk they are of being hurt.

They probably think the same about me.

When we finally reach Irena's locker, the soldiers fan out around us with their backs to the door, guns raised to give us cover.

Irena enters a code on the padlock and tosses it aside when it opens. For a moment, she hesitates with her hand on the door handle, briefly waiting as the padlock thuds on the asphalt road that runs between the storage buildings.

With a steadying breath, she opens the door.

Inside the twenty-by-twenty storage room are four cases, each about five feet long. They're bulky, and they won't be easy to carry.

"That's a lot of stuff, Irena," I confess, scanning the cases.

"It is," she says with a nod. "And we need all of it."

"All right then," I mutter, not loving this.

She types in the code on a small pad at the top of the nearest case, and I do the same on the others. In moments, the cases are disabled—and now, we're prime targets.

This is the hairy bit—with the bombs deactivated, there's more incentive for the Spectres to attack.

We know they're here. We know they're waiting. And I suspect they were waiting for us to do *this*.

With the motion bombs disabled, we'll actually be able to carry these out of here. This is the most vulnerable time, and at this point, anything could go wrong.

Irena whistles softly, alerting the eight soldiers who are going to carry these cases out. They dart in, each of them holding a gun with one hand and grabbing a handle with the other. One by one, they funnel out until the storage facility is finally empty.

Now the hard part. Getting these back to the dojo.

"We're not picking up any chatter about you guys," a soldier says to the comm in my ear. "As far as we can tell, it's all clear."

But I know better.

It's not.

We sweep through the facility again with the goal to leave the way we came in. With the butt of my rifle planted firmly against my shoulder, I take the lead once more, scoping all the space ahead of me with my gun raised.

A fight is coming for us, and I'm ready.

Somehow, I feel worse than before. I feel like we opened up Pandora's Box, and all of hell is about to fly out at us.

We pause at the next corner, taking it slowly and making sure it's clear before we move. The fence is getting nearer, and a small part of me flickers with the hope that maybe we can actually leave without anything happening.

But that's the hopeful part of us that can get us killed. I'm not about to let my guard down.

In my periphery, I catch the barest hint of movement ahead. I tense, my finger hovering over the trigger, itching for a chance to blow someone to hell, if only to release some of this pent-up tension.

As I scan the area where I saw the movement, nothing happens. No one else seemed to notice—not even Irena, who stalks beside me and effortlessly scans the world around us.

We continue to walk toward it, taking every step slowly, alert as ever. But I focus on this area.

Something about it is off. Even though it's just a shadowy dip in the wall, I don't like it. With the way the light plays around us, it looks like an impossible trick of the eye for it to be so dark.

All of my Spectre training screams that it's the perfect hiding spot—just a little gap between two buildings, barely wide enough for a person.

Hmm.

It would be wide enough for *me*.

If I were here, that's where I'd hide.

That's where I'd wait for my prey to come to me.

Jace walks beside me, his shoulders tensed and rifle at the ready. His eyes narrow as he scans the road ahead, his gaze darting occasionally to the roof. He's never still, his focus constantly shifting and totally aware of his environment.

Except that he doesn't see this shadowy void, either.

Just me.

As we near, most people don't even look at it. No one else seems to notice or care about it at all, but I watch it just to be careful.

Just to be safe.

As we pass the small gap, a shadow springs at us. No one else even seems to see it, but I see the glint of light across metal as whoever this is swings at Jace.

Running on pure instinct, I drop my rifle and block the shadow's arm. In that moment, the shadow becomes a man, and his bone shatters beneath my hands. He groans in agony, and the metal in his hand falls to the ground.

Glass shatters as whatever he was holding breaks across the asphalt, and the sizzling crackle of burning acid fills the air.

I briefly look at the ground to find a shattered syringe with green liquid pouring over the road. White smoke fizzles upward as it begins to eat away the ground.

And this asshole was about to inject that into Jace.

I punch the man in the throat. With a black scarf covering his mouth, I can't recognize him—I've worn that same scarf before on many a mission.

It's standard Spectre attire.

I don't care who this jackass is.

He tried to kill Jace, so he's going to die.

The stranger swings at me, a lightning-fast jab aimed for my neck. A second syringe glistens in the low-light, and this one apparently has my name on it.

Nope. Not today.

I duck his blow. Still choking and disoriented from my original attack, he swings again at me. This time, I grab his wrist and snap his hand backward. His wrist cracks, and he lets out a muffled scream.

In a fluid, seamless movement, I grab the syringe as

it falls from his hand. I sweep out his leg, and as he falls forward, I jab the needle into his throat before he even has a chance to move.

With my thumb against the end of the syringe, I inject the whole thing into his body in the blink of an eye as he falls to the ground.

The moment he hits the asphalt, he spasms. His face twitches as his skin slowly turns green. White froth foams at his mouth, and the choking gets worse. He looks up at me, but as he does, his eyes roll back into his head, and I see nothing but white. Moments later, he goes still, and the white foam slowly drips from his mouth onto the ground.

I pick up my rifle, ready for another attack should the need arise, and turn to find Jace watching me with wide eyes.

He looks briefly at the man before returning his attention toward me. "Are you okay?"

"Yeah, of course," I say calmly. "Let's go."

But we don't get the chance to even move.

One second, the path is clear and quiet—the next, we're swarmed.

Hooded figures cloaked in black come from everywhere. From every shadow.

The pop of gunfire fills the air.

Our response is reactive, and I shoot at everything

the moves. The recoil from my rifle jolts my shoulder again and again as I fire. I wish to the gods that I had cover. Right now, the only thing keeping me alive is the fact that I can fire faster than my opponents.

We're in the middle of a firefight with four bombs at the center of our party.

This could not be worse.

"Russell, get in here," Jace orders into the comm. "We need backup. Now!"

"Already on our way, sir," Russell responds, and I can hear the rustle of clothing and leaves as he races to join us.

Movement in my periphery catches my attention, and I look up to find a Spectre on the roof. With one shot, I take him out, and his body thuds against the ground beside us.

"Retreat!" Jace shouts, ushering us into one of the only pathways that isn't currently being swarmed by figures dressed in all black.

The attack is fierce and furious, and we barely take cover behind one of the buildings before a hail of gunfire explodes across it. Sparks light the night, and I curse under my breath.

This could *not* be *worse*.

A louder thunder of gunfire catches my attention from another direction, and I peek around the corner to find Drew and Tucker leading the charge of Squad Two as they join us. The Spectres begin to fall back, taking cover and jumping onto the roofs to get out of the line of fire, and I let out a slow breath of relief.

"You trying to have fun without us?" Drew asks as he joins me, kneeling at my side.

Levi chuckles. "Wouldn't dream of it," he says as he lifts his gun and fires off a few rounds into the shadows.

"They're going to swarm us soon," I warn as I reload my rifle. "We can't let them separate us. Everybody stick close."

"We have to get out of here," Irena barks as a hail of gunfire rains across the nearby wall. "These buildings aren't going to last much longer, and it won't be long before the sirens come. The clock is ticking because Zurie would rather blow up everything here than let us escape."

"Fair point," I admit.

The patter of footsteps across the roof catches my attention, and I raise my rifle as four Spectres dive at me. One hits me in the chest, knocking my gun away as I fall to the ground. The Spectre lifts a knife, and the dark sultry eyes of a woman with a scarf across her nose and mouth glare at me as light glints off the metal.

Without missing a beat, I punch her in the throat. She chokes, but the pain isn't enough to stop her. She brings the knife down at my face, but I don't give her the chance to stab me. I lift my head out of the way, and the metal hits the cement hard, casting a few sparks into the night before I grab her wrist and twist it.

The snap of cracking bones bursts through the gunfire around us, and she winces. I lift my knee and kick her hard in the gut, knocking her backward before she can so much as stand.

With her distracted, I grab her knife off the ground and hurl it at her. It lands solidly in her chest, and her eyes go wide as she takes a few steps backward. She falls, crumbling to the ground, and I pick up my rifle as another Spectre aims a handgun at the back of Irena's head.

Irena seems to sense him, and she twists around.

She's not fast enough.

I fire off a bullet before he can do anything, and he collapses to the ground. Irena's gaze quickly darts between me and the corpse before she nods to me in thanks and steals his handgun.

She and I press our backs together, guns raised as we systematically take out anything that moves that's not one of my men or one of Jace's soldiers.

As I scan the area around me, I find Tucker and Levi doing the same, both men bantering and grinning as they fire into the night. I can't hear what they're saying over the rattle of gunfire, but it doesn't matter.

As long as they're alive.

Not far off, Drew and Jace fight fluidly next to each other, each man watching the other's back as the battle wears on. As my eyes briefly roam across them, Jace fires a head shot at a Spectre who has his gun aimed toward Drew's chest. Drew nods briefly in thanks before returning the favor, taking out a soldier on the roof who was coiled and ready to spring at the dojo master.

I wish those two could get over their hatred for each other and see what a brilliant team they are.

"Jace, we need you all to shift!" I shout.

"It could start a war, Rory," he snaps back. "There's a way out of this. I know it."

"Yeah, shifting!" I shout back as I fire off around at a Spectre who's climbing over the roof.

I grimace in annoyance and look upward. I need to get a clear view of everything that's going on. If we're going to get out of here, we need to do it soon.

"Irena, cover me," I order as I jump toward the roof, grabbing the edge and lifting myself onto it.

Jace loudly curses, but I don't care. I'm not about to

get myself shot. That's really not the goal of this. I just need a better view.

I keep low, scanning the paths around us, only to discover that all of them are covered with various Spectres at every strategic point. There must be dozens, and I wonder how it's even possible Zurie was able to coordinate all of them.

Come to think of it, I can't figure out why I haven't run into her, yet.

It makes me wonder if, perhaps, she isn't even here. I can't tell if that's a good sign—or a truly horrible one.

To my disappointment, I notice three open lockers across the facility. Several Spectres are wheeling something out of each of them, and for a moment, I can't tell what kind of weapon or machinery they've brought with them.

Seconds later, however, they roll an anti-dragon artillery gun out of the nearest locker, and I shake my head in frustration.

This just keeps getting better.

Someone spots me, and they fire off a few rounds in my direction. I drop to the roof and slide off, landing on my feet in the middle of my team.

"There are anti-dragon guns being wheeled out. Three total," I say. "They're trying to keep us grounded, and we only have a few seconds before they get these things op—"

An explosion rocks the ground, throwing us all off-balance. A large chunk of the far end of the building goes up in flames.

"I think they're operational," Tucker says dryly.

I grimace. "We destroy them, and then—Jace, we've *got* to shift. Zurie's counting on us not to!"

"Fine," Jace admits through gritted teeth as he shoots the last of the Spectres in our stretch of the facility. "I'll give the order."

"Good. Thank you," I say. "Irena, which—"

Irena peeks around the edge of a building, her gun raised, and a gunshot echoes through the air. Though I initially figure it's from her gun, she grimaces and holds her side. She drops her weapon on the ground, doubling over with her hand at her waist.

She's been hit, and if she dropped her weapon, it's *bad*.

I run to her, holding her in my arms as I check the wound. I lift her hand to find a pool of blood staining her fingers, and a dark red liquid rhythmically pulses from the hole in her side.

"We need to get out here," Drew says as he kneels beside me, ripping off a makeshift bandage from the bottom of his shirt. He wraps the fabric around Irena's waist, keeping pressure on the wound itself as he looks at me. "We need to get out of here. Now."

I nod. "Will you carry her?"

Irena grimaces, her jaw tense. "I will *not* be carried out of—"

"Shut up, Irena, and let him help you," I demand, standing. "We're moving. Go, team! Go!"

Squad One slips into a tight formation, every gun raised while the eight men at the center once again carry the cases through the now-cleared asphalt road toward the anti-dragon guns.

It's not usually smart to go *toward* the thing that's trying to kill you, but in this case, we have very few other options.

I pause at the corner that will lead us to the nearest artillery gun. As I carefully peek around the edge, I find a familiar man standing in the center with his gun already raised toward me.

Diesel.

He fires off several rounds into the corner of the building, no doubt hoping it'll go through the siding and clear into me. The facility has been shot to shit so far, and it's probably not going to hold up much longer.

I dart backward out of the line of fire, cursing

under my breath. If he's here, that means Zurie's not far behind.

"We have to get out of here!" I say tensely as I glare at Jace.

"Yeah," he says with a short nod. "There's no other option."

"Russell, where are you?" I ask into the comm line.

"Nearly there," he answers with the grunt of effort. "We encountered some difficulties along the way, but we're handling it."

"Get ready to fly," Jace orders through the comm. "The moment those anti-dragon guns are destroyed, we're out of here. Is that clear?"

"Yes, sir," dozens of voices say through the line.

"Rory," Diesel shouts in a singsong voice. "Did you ever think this would be how you die?"

I reload my rifle and rack it. "I could ask you the same thing, Diesel."

"I never would have guessed it," he admits. "I always figured you'd die by drowning, to be honest."

That's... remarkably specific.

If I had to guess, I would say he was probably the one drowning me in those messed up daydreams of his.

What a charmer.

With my rifle in my right hand, I summon my

magic into my left. White light flutters across my skin, glimmering like the Northern Lights as I prepare to give Diesel a fight he will never forget.

Before anyone can stop me, I summon a massive blast of magic into my hand and round the corner. The plan is to use myself as bait, and sure, that's risky —but I only do it because I'm faster than him. I want him to stay in place so that I can use my magic to blast him to hell.

Diesel's finger hovers over the trigger, about to fire at me yet again, but I don't give him the chance.

My magic burst and crackles in the air above my skin, and I let it free. The beam soars through the storage facility—not at him, but at the anti-dragon gun sitting in the storage locker behind him.

It explodes.

A cascade of fire shoots into the air, billowing and smoking into the sky. The blast knocks the nearby Spectres off their feet, and even Diesel falls to his knees, rolling across the asphalt from the force of the explosion.

With him dazed, I aim my rifle at his head and fire. Since he's a moving target and I'm doing this one-handed, my aim is a little off—I only catch him in the bicep.

He grimaces and darts for cover, taking refuge behind a nearby building as I race toward him.

Soldiers flood out behind me, a swarm of fury and bullets that takes out every Spectre they see.

I, however, am focused on Diesel.

This is my chance to end him, and I won't miss it. If he gets out of here alive, that's bad news for me. That's bad news for everyone I love.

My gun runs out of ammo, and I curse under my breath. I duck for cover, hiding behind a building seconds before Diesel emerges and shoots. His bullets ricochet off the walls as he stalks toward me.

His footsteps thunder across the ground amidst the patter of gunfire in the war zone around us, ever closer.

Tucker, Levi, and Jace fight nearby, while Drew guards Irena. My sister grimaces in agony, holding her side and trying to keep from bleeding out.

To my horror, Tucker goes down. He groans in pain, grimacing as he holds his shoulder. Jace covers them while Levi pauses to check on the former Knight. My ice dragon pauses to fire off a few rounds as he kneels beside his friend, checking the wound.

My team is losing.

The people I love are getting shot, and with every

passing second, there's a greater chance one of them is going to die.

I can't allow this.

I want to kill Diesel, but it's more important that we get out of here. Diesel's gunfire stops, but I can hear his footsteps getting ever closer. He's probably just reloading. If I can blast him with my magic and then head toward the guns—

Before I can even finish the thought, a massive explosion rocks the building across from me.

The force blows me backward, and I roll across the ground, sliding to a stop as Diesel rounds the corner with a rocket launcher on his shoulder.

"Bye, Rory," he says, grinning.

I summon my magic and fire at him, but he manages to duck out of the way with seconds to spare. My blast hits the roof of the storage facility across from us instead, lighting it ablaze.

Fine. I meant to kill him, but I can use it as a distraction instead.

I grab the edge of the roof and hoist myself on top of the building, knowing full well it could put me in greater danger depending on who else might be up here. However, for the moment, I just need to get out of his line of fire. I need him to not know where I am, even if only for a second.

From this vantage point, I can spot the other two anti-dragon weapons and the additional Spectres beginning to file into the storage facility. If there's backup, that means Zurie could come at any moment, and I need to get us out of here.

The other two anti-dragon guns are aimed in the general direction of the rest of my team. I still don't have eyes on Russell, and I hope he and his team aren't dead. He's probably stopping additional Spectres from filing in, and right now, that's the best we can hope for.

Any longer in this mess, and we're all going to die.

I scan my team, trying to think of a plan, and I catch sight of the four bomb-laden crates we came here to get. They're lined up beside Irena and closely guarded by soldiers.

After all, that's why we're here.

We can't exactly let *those* get blown up.

I have an awful idea, but at this point, we're desperate.

I run across the roof toward my team and dive, rolling as I hit the ground and join them. I would have loved to break Diesel's arm or shatter a leg or just outright kill him, but I don't have the time to indulge such a thing right now.

Besides, he's never going to let me get close enough for a fistfight, not with a rocket launcher.

I kneel beside Irena as she grimaces in pain.

"Which crate is the least important?" I ask.

"They're all important," she says through her gritted teeth.

"Pick one. If you had to sacrifice one of them, which one?"

"Rory, no," she says, narrowing her eyes at me as she arches her back in pain. "We came all this way!"

"And we're about to die because of it, so pick a damn crate!"

She groans in frustration and even a hint of grief. Given everything she must have gone through to get those crates together, I understand why she doesn't want to sacrifice even one of them. I can only imagine what she had to do, who she had to kill, and what she had to sacrifice to make it happen.

And I'm about to blow one of them up.

"That one," she says, pointing to the second crate.

I tap Drew and Jace on the shoulder. "Guys, I need you to throw this between the two anti-dragon guns."

"What?" Jace asks, his brow furrowing.

Drew laughs. "You've got to be kidding."

"Do it," I shout, summoning my magic. White light races across my arms and burns in my hands like fire.

Jace fires off a few rounds into the fray, pausing only when his gun runs out of ammo. "Rory, what—"

"Do it!" I roar.

"Fine," Drew snaps, though it's clear he's not convinced this is a great idea.

The two men grab the crate, and I hover near the corner, peeking into the firefight as I wait for a good shot.

"Jace, the moment we throw it, I need everyone to shift and get out of here. We can't leave anything behind. No bodies, no weapons, no tech. That clear?"

"Clear," he nods. "Did everyone hear that?"

"Yes, sir," dozens of voices say through the comm.

"Get ready," I say, scanning the open path between buildings as several Spectres reload the dragon guns. "Aim right in the middle."

"We got it," Drew says.

"Now!" I shout.

The men hurl the massive crate into the center of the two guns, and I watch with bated breath as the massive bomb flies through the air. With the enemy distracted, I take the moment to step into the open path, aiming at the crate, tracking where it's going to go.

Just as I step into the path, Diesel does the same, lifting his rocket launcher and aiming it toward me.

Now or never.

I fire off my magic. It seeps from me as I let the full brunt of my power free. I barely try to control it, and the blinding white light that streams from me is possibly the most massive blast I've shot thus far. It tears through the air toward the crate and, in seconds, hits.

A massive explosion rocks the facility, shaking the very ground and making the buildings themselves tremble. Fire and smoke billows into the air, swallowing everything around it—including the anti-dragon guns and the Spectres who were managing them.

The blast throws Diesel to the ground as the missile launches from his rocket launcher, throwing off his aim. It explodes above us like a firework, and the rocket launcher slides across the asphalt.

I'm tempted to grab it. I'm tempted to run over there and shoot him. To destroy him. To make sure he's dead.

I don't get the chance.

A black thunderbird wraps his claws around my waist and lifts me into the air. I look up as Jace carries me through the sky, the blue light glowing in his wings and along his chest, and I know he didn't want this. He didn't want it to come to a shift because, if any of this can be traced back to him, the Fairfax family will face the full brunt of a world desperate to go to war with them.

By leaving behind no trace, we mitigate that risk. If all goes well, the Spectres will be blamed for this. Not dragons.

As sirens near the chaos, all of Jace's dragons are already in the sky. The blue and red lights flash across the road, but we're too high to even see.

And if all went right, we left no trace we were even there.

CHAPTER EIGHTEEN

I pace the living room in Jace's suite, slowly circling the sofa as I bite my nails.

Everyone is injured in some fashion, and it's chaos down in the medic ward. The nurses ordered me up here, and I can't sit still.

All I can do is think about everything happening just a few floors below me—and all the ways I can't help.

I hate waiting.

Irena and Tucker were immediately wheeled into the emergency operating room. As the chaos devolved, Levi was helping a soldier who had nearly lost his foot and somehow also ended up in a surgery room, though he was thankfully assisting instead of being operated on.

I caught glimpses of a furious Drew trying to bat away his doctors, insisting he was fine despite the deep gash in his chest. Jace, of course, was directing everyone through the ocean of heads and shouting, coordinating the chaos and keeping it from devolving into something worse.

And yet, I'm stuck up here.

Even though I tried to help, there simply wasn't enough space. It wasn't long before I was shooed away.

With everything going on, I could have probably put up a fight and stayed to help, but I would rather the nurse's attention be focused on making the people I love healthy again, rather than trying to deal with me.

The door to the hallway opens, and an exhausted Jace enters. He rubs his eyes as he closes the door, and for a moment, it seems as though he doesn't even know I'm here.

Deep within my chest, my dragon curls with long-ing, aching to be closer to him. Though I'm still pacing and restless, I stop mid-stride. I tense, watching his face and waiting for an update.

Given everything he's endured tonight, I don't want to push him, and I certainly don't want to hound him for answers.

Without a word, he walks toward me. Only in the

final few steps do his eyes land on me, but just as my dragon sensed him, his probably senses me.

He pulls me into his powerful arms and hugs me tightly, cradling the back of my head with his massive hand. He kisses the side of my face and breathes me in, drinking in my scent like he wasn't sure he was going to see me again.

My traitorous body impulsively relaxes into him, and I wrap my arms around his waist.

We simply stand there for a while like this, just him and me. Enjoying the silence and the fact that we're all still alive.

"Everyone's fine," he says quietly, without moving a muscle. "Irena and Tucker will both have full recoveries. They're sleeping off the anesthesia right now, as their surgeries were pretty intense. I'm fairly certain Levi has stolen the heart of everyone in the ward with his willingness to do anything and help anyone who's hurting," Jace adds with a small chuckle.

"That sounds about right," I admit, grinning with pride.

"Drew's being an asshole, of course," Jace says, the humor dropping from his voice. "He's trying to tell the nurses to leave him alone so that he can figure out what happened and what went wrong."

"I already know what went wrong," I admit, my

grip impulsively tightening on his shirt. "Someone betrayed us. Specifically, someone betrayed Irena."

"I think you're right," he admits.

"I'm grateful everyone else is fine," I say, leaning backward until I can see his face. "But how are you?"

He hesitates, his eyes darting between mine as his mouth opens. It's clear he wants to say something but hasn't found the words yet, and for a moment, he just struggles to think of how he wants to phrase this.

It's strange to see Jace speechless, and I'm not sure what's about to happen. My fingers tighten around his arms, both out of comfort and curiosity as I study his face.

"I'm impressed," he admits after a moment, his hands falling to my waist. "And confused."

"What?" I ask, admittedly baffled.

He doesn't answer right away. Instead, he gently brushes his knuckle along my jaw as he studies every inch of me, like he's seeing me for the first time. Every curve. Every freckle. He drinks it in as if he's amazed by every detail. It's like he's building a map of my face in his mind, and I'm not really sure what to make of this.

"You saw something I missed back there," he finally says, breaking the silence. "You saved my life when that Spectre attacked. I didn't see him coming." Jace pauses, his jaw clenching, and I figure admitting that is a bit of a wounding blow to his pride. But he's man enough to learn from his own mistakes, and I respect that.

"Oh," I say, shrugging. "Sure, Jace. I mean, I'm not going to let you get hurt. I know Spectres, and I knew we weren't alone. I was ready."

"So was I," he points out, a somber look crossing his face.

I pause to really look at him, to really study the subtle changes in his expression.

There's something... *different*.

There's been a clear shift, though I'm not yet sure what it was and what it means. There's something in the way he looks at me that's changed.

He's looking at me like he looks at Harper. Tucker. Levi.

He's looking at me like I'm his equal.

"I won't lie to you," Jace says quietly, briefly looking at the floor. "I have always thought of you as a treasure to hoard, as something to stow away and protect. And as often as you made fun of me for it and as often as I denied it, that's the truth," he confesses. "I thought I knew this world better than you, that I knew the *risks* better than you. But Rory..." he hesitates, his gaze serious and focused as he watches me. "Rory, I was wrong."

"Be still my heart," I say, fanning my face as I make fun of him. "I didn't know you could even say those words."

Jace laughs, his eyes crinkling a little with the joy of the moment. Gods, I love it when he smiles.

"So, what does this mean?" I ask, not entirely sure where he's going with this. "What does it mean for us? For the dojo? For this choice you have to make?"

He takes a step, closing the already small gap between us as he towers over me. For a moment, I think he's actually going to answer me, even as his mischievous gaze rakes over my body.

Without a word, his lips brush mine. It's tender, at first, more so than I expected from a man as dominating and authoritative as him. Ribbons of delight weave through me with every breath of his that rolls across my face. He holds my arms tightly, pulling me close as the kiss deepens.

"Use your words, Jace," I chide between kisses, grinning as I poke fun at him.

"This is more enjoyable," he answers.

With that, he lifts me into the air. My stomach churns as I lose my balance, and I arch my head back with laughter and delightful surprise. He sets me gently on the couch, laying over me as he kisses me yet again. His fingers weave through my hair, caressing me with fierce passion.

I open my mouth to speak, to crack a joke or make him laugh again, but he presses his lips against mine to silence me. I have no choice but to give in to him, and I love it—his possessive grip on the back of my neck, the way he presses his hips against mine, the way the bulge in his pants grows as I wrap my legs around him.

I very much like this new and improved Jace Goodwin.

He abruptly stops, his hot breath rolling over me as his grip on my neck tightens. It's soothing, his strong fingertips against my skin a reminder of his power. His strength. His devotion.

His lips hover an inch above mine, taunting me at how tantalizingly close they are.

"I want you," he says simply.

"You still haven't answered—"

"Forever," he interrupts. He gently bites my neck to drive the point home, and the almost primal sensation pushes me over the edge.

My dragon practically roars within me, begging me to give in, to go all the way, to give him any and everything he wants so that she and I can finally have him.

Our mate.

"In my world," he continues, his lips hovering just above mine once again, "that means you're mine—and I'm yours. Just the two of us against the world, forever."

My heart skips with simultaneous joy and dread. I'm gutted to be so close to something I've wanted since I came here—him, as my equal, my partner—and the other three men I've grown to love.

And I wonder.

I wonder if he would *dare*.

I wonder if an ultimatum is coming—and worse, what I'll do. I need him, pure and simple. He does things to me no one else can, and he has a powerful influence over my dragon no one else can match.

He may be the key to me shifting. He, and he alone, might very well be the key to mastering my magic.

To give him up is unthinkable. I can admit that, now.

But Tucker has been at my side from the start. He taught me to trust. To love. To laugh.

Drew has pushed me to be better. To grow. He made me realize what it means to give in. To not need to control the world around me, but to use what's happening to my advantage.

And Levi—my darling Levi. In a world that's so harsh and unforgiving, he gives me hope. He makes me *feel.*

I can never let go of any of them.

They're my team. My family.

My men.

And I want Jace in that world, too.

The dojo master sighs, his stormy eyes snaring me as they rake over my face. Tenderly, he brushes his nose against mine, and I feel something within him shift. It's a soft change, just a subtle one, but it's there.

"We're not in my world, anymore," he says. "If you and I do this, if we give in to what we both want, I can't just live in my world, by my laws. I have to honor your past, too. We come from different cultures, and we came into this—whatever it is you and I have— with different expectations of each other. So what are we going to do, Rory Quinn?"

"Compromise?" I ask softly, knowing my eyes betray every sensation rippling through my body. I try to hide the breathless shutters in my chest, but I don't do a very convincing job of it.

He leans toward me, pressing his hard chest against mine as he breathes me in once again. It's like smelling a bouquet, and he smiles as if it's the most delicious scent in the world. "I suppose we can try."

I grin, almost unable to believe what's happening. "What do you need to be happy, Jace?"

"You," he says simply. "To know you're mine. That you're in this life with me, for eternity. That we're partners in crime and have each other's back, no matter the cost. To know that when we go into battle, you'll be there at my side. To have you, now and forever. And," he adds with a soft sigh, grinning a little as he looks down at me. "To know that when I'm with you, I have you fully to myself—that you're not thinking of anyone else. That when I'm with you, I'm enough."

He pauses, and his hand trails to my face. He gently holds my jaw, his possessive grip beautifully dominating as he smiles down at me. "Can you give me that?"

I smile, beyond blissfully happy that I can finally give in to the fluttering and overwhelming *need* I've felt for this man from the start. "Forever."

He kisses me, wild and fierce. I weave my fingers through his hair, hoping this isn't just a beautiful dream. It's almost surreal, like it can't possibly be happening.

But it is.

Jace Goodwin is *mine.*

He pauses, setting his hand gently on my neck as his thumb gently strokes my cheek. "I can't believe I'm doing this," he admits, laughing. "Tucker, Levi, and I will have to figure out some boundaries, but we'll make it work."

"Thank you," I say, grinning. "Does that also mean you and Drew are..."

I trail off as I notice something change in his gaze. His expression hardens, those stormy eyes narrowing with hatred at the mere mention of Drew's name, and it's clear there's another element of this agreement that needs to be ironed out.

The blood feud.

"I don't understand it, Rory," Jace says, practically growling in his rage. His grip on my neck tightens, and the possessive fury returns. "I can't share you with a *monster.* He's bad for you. Bad for the *world.* I can't forgive him for what he did."

"But he didn't—" I grimace and snap my stupid mouth shut before I break my vow.

I swore I wouldn't betray Drew's trust, and even now, I won't do it—even with so much at stake, I can't shatter his faith in me.

"Didn't what?" Jace presses, lowering his head until his stormy glare is inches from my face. He narrows his eyes with suspicion, and an eerie darkness crosses his face.

I don't fear Jace Goodwin. He's my mate and my man. But that withering look would make grown men tremble—and I doubt he even knows he's capable of such an expression.

Somehow, his hatred has only gotten worse since Drew came here.

"I can't," I say quietly, setting my hands on either side of his head as I try to drive my next point home. "But he can tell you everything. You two need to work this out. We'll sit down, and—"

"No, Rory," Jace interrupts. Even though his face brims with rage, he pauses and kisses the inside of my wrist as my hands hover by his face. "Our grudge can only be settled one way."

He can't mean...

I gasp.

"Jace, don't," I plead.

"I think it's time he and I finally settle this," Jace says, ignoring me. "Once and for all."

"Now, you wait just a damn minute—"

"Rory," Jace interrupts.

Hearing him say my name sends both chills of dread and shivers of delight through me. Just that—

just my name—it's enough to silence me, and I find myself watching him with breathless anticipation.

I was so close.

So close.

But this feud—this hatred they have of each other —it could cost me everything.

"This ends tonight," Jace says, standing.

I feel suddenly cold as he leaves me, my body missing the warmth of his chest pressed against mine, but I try to ignore my dragon's traitorous aches for this man and focus on the dire circumstance I've found myself in yet again.

The dojo master heads for the door without another word, and I can't quite process that this is really happening. That he's actually going to go through with this.

Carefully, I sit upright and try to make him see reason. "Jace—"

"Do you want us to hate each other forever?" he asks, turning on his heel. "Because if you're mine, Rory, I won't allow him to *touch* you. Not until this is settled."

"Jace, damn it—" I stand, entirely done with this entire conversation, when he reaches the door.

"I'm sorry," he says simply.

"What are you—"

Sparks dance across his skin, the electric current of his magic sizzling across the metal knob as he opens the door. He looks at me once more, a serious and somber expression on his face that leaves me unsettled.

It's the kind of face you make when you say goodbye—when you have to go do something you may never come back from.

"Jace!" I shout, bolting toward him.

He storms into the hall and slams the door behind him, leaving me alone in his room as sparks burn along the handle from the other side. The metal begins to fuse, and I realize too late what he's done.

He's stowed me away in his room the only way he knows how—by giving me a lock I can't pick.

I bang my fist against the door, and it trembles under my enhanced strength. I can hear his footsteps retreat down the hall, calm and controlled on this death march he's taking, and I practically growl with rage.

I can feel my dragon burning deep within, simmering in her own fury, and the two of us are shattered.

The grudge Drew and Jace have with each other will end in fire and lightning. Bones and blood. These two men I've grown to adore—to *love*—they're two of the most powerful dragons in the world.

They're going to fight each other, and this time, no one alive or dead will be able to stop them until one concedes—or one of them *dies.*

CHAPTER NINETEEN

When I finally break down the door, it splinters across the hallway. Nothing remains but the fiery fury burning within me. The melted doorknob, nothing but a molten chunk of metal now, slides across the ground.

It takes everything in me not to blast my magic throughout this entire embassy. I just want to destroy something, and one door is not enough right now.

Jace knew it would only delay me, not stop me, and I'm pretty sure that was his point. His goal. He wasn't trying to protect me from this—from what he's about to do to Drew.

He's trying to keep me from stopping it.

Despite the adrenaline surging through my body, I force myself to pause and close my eyes. I want nothing more than to punch someone in the face, but instead, I force myself to listen.

To my dragon.

She knows where Jace is.

His presence flickers to light within me like a candle's flame suddenly lit in the darkness, and I can feel him somewhere nearby. His energy is different right now, more powerful and utterly ablaze. He's burning with magic.

He's burning with *hate*.

As I feel for him, I try to get a more specific idea of where he is. After a few moments of searching, I'm pretty sure I can narrow it down to the front courtyard.

It's a start.

I race to the nearest window facing the front of the embassy, and sure enough, I see two figures circling each other on the black stone below. Even though it's too far away to clearly see their features, I recognize their gait as they circle each other. I recognize their builds and the muscle along both men's bare chests.

It's already started.

By now, I've memorized most of the embassy, and I race downstairs toward the main door. With most of the dojo still tending the wounded, not many soldiers fill the hallways, and for that I'm grateful.

I don't want very many witnesses to what's about to happen, especially if I have to whip Jace's ass in front of his soldiers.

As I reach the front doors, I kick them open. I half expect them to shatter like his bedroom door did, but these are sturdier. They simply slam against the black stone walls as I storm down the stairway toward the courtyard.

Both men turn briefly to look at me as I walk toward them. I know they can see my fury. They can see my anger sizzling across my skin. Ribbons of white light run up and down my arms as I desperately try to hold my magic at bay.

But they're hardly worried.

Despite the magic crackling across my skin and through my core, both men return their attention to each other almost immediately. They're focused, their eyes sharp and clear.

All they want in this moment is to *begin*.

And that's when it hits home for me.

They want this.

For them, whatever is about to happen means finally getting closure.

That slows my raging pace, and before I know what I'm doing, I stop walking altogether. I'm close enough to see them, to hear the steady breaths and the rustle of fabric as they slowly circle each other, waiting to see who will take the first blow.

My intention when I came here was to charge in and stop this even if it meant a flurry of magic and the threat of facing down a dragon or two. But the chilling realization of what they need to do makes my blood run cold.

They *need* to draw blood.

It's taken me until now to see it, but they've both been subtly warning me that this was coming. Even if they didn't do it consciously, both men knew this fight of theirs was inevitable.

I just didn't want to listen.

Soldiers begin to gather, keeping mostly to the edge of the massive courtyard walls. There seems to be an unspoken understanding that this battle is somehow different—because no one gets too close.

I'm the only one standing in the courtyard, and I am definitely in the line of fire.

Levi appears suddenly beside me, and I flinch slightly as he steps abruptly into my periphery. My heart skips a beat in surprise, but it really shouldn't at this point.

He glares at the circling men, his hands balled into fists. "Rory, what's happening?"

I shake my head and open my mouth to answer, but I don't even know how to put this into words.

"I should shift," Levi says when I don't answer. "I can stop this. I can—"

"No," I say softly, setting my hand on his chest to make sure he doesn't try. "They need this, Levi."

He looks at me with a baffled expression, but all I can do is watch my two men as they circle each other, ready for blood and battle.

If I keep stopping them, it will only get worse. If I keep getting in the way of their closure, then maybe it *will* get to the point where neither man can forgive the other. At that point, I would have to choose.

Deep within me, I can feel my dragon itching for war. She's angry and furious, her very soul buzzing with energy I've never felt before. She's so close to a shift that I can taste it.

It gives me an idea.

It's desperate, of course. Maybe a bit foolhardy, but I don't exactly have a ton of options.

Even though I keep most of my attention on the fight about to break out in the center courtyard, I reach toward her. Inwardly, I try to connect.

Just in case.

Just in case they take this too far.

Jace thinks Drew killed his brother Garrett, and Drew is just trying to protect his brother Milo. But dragons believe in an eye for an eye, and this won't end pretty.

Jace pauses, his eyes scanning the courtyard as more of his soldiers watch from the walls and windows.

"Leave!" the dojo master shouts. "This doesn't involve any of you. If you have nothing to do, I'm sure there are doctors in the medic ward who can fix that."

It's astonishing how quickly the crowd disperses. But their master has spoken, and none of these soldiers want to face his ire, especially given the fury that radiates from him right now.

In moments, the courtyard is empty except for Levi and myself—but I'm pretty sure they'll still be watching.

When the last soldier leaves, Jace lifts his fists. Drew does the same, and it's clear.

It has begun.

Jace throws the first punch, and Drew takes it. Jace's fist connects with Drew's side, and though I suspect Drew figured he could take the blow easily, he lets out a groan of pain and doubles over.

In a vicious double-whammy, Jace lifts his knee, aiming for Drew's nose. This time, Drew ducks and rolls out of the way. He lands with one leg extended, his palm on the ground as he regains his balance. Seconds later, he launches, tackling Jace to the ground. Jace hits the black stone hard, his head raised to protect his skull.

And he takes the blow like a beast.

The two men duck and swing at each other, their brutal dance almost hypnotizing, and I find myself leaning forward with breathless anticipation as I wait for it to end. It's a daydream, of course, to think it would end so quickly or so neatly, but a girl can dream.

Jace's fist hits Drew's temple, and the crack of bone hitting bone thuds through the courtyard. I wince, sucking in a sharp breath through my teeth.

But I can't look away.

Drew takes a step back, shaking out his head to clear the fog as a trickle of blood races down his face and along his jaw. He narrows his eyes, glaring at Jace, ready for the next blow—and more than ready to give one.

"I can't let you stay," Jace says through clenched teeth as he lands a kick in Drew's stomach.

Drew grabs Jace's leg and twists. Jace flips in the air and falls to the ground.

"*Let* me?" Drew asks, smirking.

With his back on the ground and his foot still

pinned under Drew's arm, Jace nails a brutal kick on Drew's knee. Drew falls, grimacing, and releases Jace's other foot.

"I refuse," Jace says, rolling away and jumping back to his feet. "I won't be reminded of my loss forever. You can't have her."

"This is not up for discussion," Drew says, wiping away a trail of blood from his face. "You can't steal her from me."

The two men launch at each other, their hands on each other's shoulders as they grapple, each trying to get a slight advantage on the other despite being so evenly matched.

As they fight for dominance, Drew slowly begins to win. He pushes against Jace, trying to take him down. In a move so fast I almost miss it, Jace twists, throwing Drew to the ground and rolling with him. His opponent on his back, Jace cocks his arm to land a blow.

In that moment, Drew is faster. With one arm lifted to protect his face, he lands a deadly accurate blow in Jace's throat.

Jace coughs, backing up as he tries to catch his breath, and this is a moment where the whole fight could turn. If Drew cut off Jace's windpipe, then…

I pinch my eyes shut, and I almost wish I wasn't watching this. I almost wish this was just a bad dream.

Thankfully, Jace recovers, lifting his fists once more. He's ready for battle even as a red trickle escapes the corner of his mouth.

These two men are bloody and brutal. With every blow they land on each other, I wince. I feel for both of them, and I can't imagine how much longer this will go on.

In most battles, there would be a winner by now, someone clearly better, clearly more capable.

But these two are the best, and they knew going in that this fight would be vicious.

Beside me, Levi is as still as a statue, stoic and silent as he focuses on the fight. He doesn't want to see this any more than I do, but I think deep down, he also realizes there's more at stake than just pride.

"Why would you kill Garrett over a business deal?" Jace sneers as he throws Drew onto the ground. "Tell me why. Does life mean so little to you?"

"No," Drew says, rolling out of the way as Jace's fist hits hard against the black stone, cracking it. "I did what I had to do to protect my family," Drew snaps.

With my heart practically in my throat, I lean forward, on edge.

Just tell him, I think to myself.

"That wasn't protection," Jace sneers as he throws another punch. "That was murder, and you know it."

His blows are crippling and lightning-fast, but Drew manages to duck out of the way each time, just seconds before getting nailed in the face.

"You just didn't like the fact that you might not get your way," Jace continues, seething. "Darringtons are vile, selfish bastards. All of you."

"I never wanted that damn business deal at all," Drew says, parrying another one of Jace's blows. "Milo's pride drove us out there. Jett's approval means so much to that idiot that I had no choice."

Say it, I think. *Tell him the truth.*

Fast as lightning, Jace kicks out Drew's knee. Drew falls to the ground, grimacing even as he tries to roll out of the way, but Jace is just a hair faster. The dojo master wraps his arm around Drew's throat, grabbing him in a headlock and pinning him in place.

"You won't just leave," the dojo master seethes. "No, you won't just go away. You insist on being a daily reminder of everything I lost even as I try to start over and move on. I've had to battle my hatred for you every day since I lost Garrett. Every damn *day,*" Jace says, lost in his anger. "All I wanted was justice and revenge, and I never got it all because a Darrington royal killed my brother. You got away with murder." Jace pauses, letting the words sink in. "Again."

"All I want is to move on, Jace," Drew says, choking slightly as Jace's arm tightens against his windpipe.

I want to dive between them. I want to stop this. It takes everything in my power not to, but I don't know how much longer I can hold out.

Drew looks at me, struggling to breathe, and I can tell he's debating. He's trying to figure out what he wants to do, what matters to him most.

I swallow hard and force myself to keep my mouth shut.

Drew, please! I think, wishing he could hear me.

Jace summons magic into his free hand and lifts it above Drew. The dojo master's gaze never leaves the back of Drew's head as he tightens his grip with each passing second, cutting off more and more of Drew's air.

It looks like this might be the end. The final blow of the battle.

Just as Jace summons his magic, I summon mine.

No matter the outcome, no matter what I lose, I cannot let either of these men die.

Jace is so lost in his anger that he doesn't notice me. Sparks burn along his arm as the last bit of his magic floats into his hand.

"At least I'll finally get a bit of justice," he says, gritting his teeth.

He looks resolved and absolutely certain of what he's about to do.

As am I.

Before either Jace or I can do anything, however, Drew stands with an earth-shattering groan of effort and pain. As he forces himself to his feet, he twists his body, giving everything he has into the maneuver and throws Jace off of him.

Jace staggers, hands lifted, still burning with magic, but Drew kicks him hard in the chest. Jace falls backward, rolling away—and just like that, the tide has turned again in the fight.

"I didn't kill him!" Drew shouts into the mostly empty courtyard.

I stiffen, and beside me, so does Levi.

Yes, I think to myself. *Fucking finally.*

"What?" Jace asks in disbelief. He stands, his hands balled into fists as he glares at Drew. "I *saw* you do it, you lying sack of—"

"No, you saw Milo and Garrett attack each other!" Drew snaps, pacing back and forth and utterly lost in his anger and adrenaline. "You saw Milo losing. You saw me rush to my idiot brother's rescue. And I assume you saw flames after that."

"Yes," Jace says, his voice breaking as he watches Drew with a combination of hatred and earth-shattering grief. "You burned him to ash. There was nothing left to even bury!"

"It wasn't me," Drew admits, pausing with his hands on his hips. He hangs his head and pinches the bridge of his nose. "It was Milo. My fire was aimed at my stupid brother, to stop him. It would have knocked him out, and you and I could have retreated. You and I could have made a truce. But no, I wasn't fast enough." Drew sighs, the sound laden with frustration and regret as he runs his hands through his hair. "I wanted to end the fight that had already cost a dozen lives. I wasn't trying to make it worse."

Jace is still as a stone, his full and furious gaze focused on Drew. It's like he's fighting something internally, like he can't quite believe what he's hearing even as it starts to make sense.

"I couldn't comprehend what he'd done," Drew admits, rubbing his jaw. "Garrett was a hero, a man even I respected. We'd met on the field half a dozen times, back in the days before Jett made Milo the general." Drew's shoulders relax, and I can all but see him surrendering to the truth.

Finally.

"But you admitted to it!" Jace snaps.

"I didn't *deny* it," Drew corrects, glaring at Jace. "You wanted so badly to hate someone that you heard what you wanted to hear. The Darringtons get away with murder, yet again. That's what you said. Those big bad brutal bastards, right? The world believed it. You just needed somebody to blame. You just like hating us. You want to. It makes the grief easier to bear."

"You make it easy to hate you," Jace says, wrinkling his nose in loathing.

Drew shakes his head, like Jace just hasn't figured it out yet. "Your hate gives us power, damn it!" The Darrington dragon takes a few furious steps closer to Jace. "How have none of you figured this out, yet? The more you all hate us, the more we *get away with*. The more injustice there is, the more people *fear* us. That's what Jett has always wanted, and everyone has always played right into his hands."

"If that's true, why lie?" Jace's back arches as he gestures toward the clouds above us. "There's no reason to lie at that point. Milo is still a royal. He still would have gotten away with it. Nothing would have changed."

Drew scoffs. "Everything would be entirely differ-ent, and you know it. Milo's a politician, not a fighter. The Fairfax dragons respect warriors, not statesmen. You don't fear him. You fear war with Jett." Drew pauses. "You fear war with *me*."

Jace lifts his chin in defiance, but he doesn't deny it.

Drew slowly nods. "It's why Jett wants me to go back. He's seen his mistake with Milo. It took longer than I expected, which makes me wonder if this was all a bluff on his part, some failed manipulation tactic to get me to act the way he wanted me to act. He knows Milo will never be a true Darrington Boss and never show up in a way that honors Jett's legacy. He made a prideful mistake trying to pit me and Milo against each other, all because he assumed I gave a shit." Drew laughs humorlessly. "But I couldn't care less. I don't want to sit in a capital building, making decrees all day long."

Drew's gaze drifts toward me, and he pauses. I can practically hear all the things he wants to say, all the things he wants out of life. Instead, he simply closes his mouth and sucks in a deep breath, watching me all the while.

Jace rubs the back of his head, pacing a little as he tries to calm down. "So, Milo killed Garrett?"

Drew nods.

"And you let us believe it was you?" Jace continued, his gaze focused on the Darrington heir in front of us. "You faced the wrath of every living Fairfax dragon, including the Boss herself," Jace pauses, almost in disbelief. "All to protect your brother's life?"

Drew hesitates, like he's trying to decide if this is a trick question. After a moment, with his hands on his hips, he nods again.

Jace shakes his head in disbelief. "That's—"

"Stupid?" Drew glares at Jace, daring the dojo master to insult him. "Foolish? Moronic?"

"Noble," Jace says, his tone genuinely baffled that a Darrington could act in such a way.

Drew takes a step back in surprise, his frown dissolving as his brows lift in mild shock.

"You sacrificed everything to protect family," Jace says, briefly glancing at me. "I didn't think you were capable of that, Drew."

Drew frowns, tilting his head slightly as he watches the dojo master. "That almost sounded like a compliment."

"Almost," Jace admits quietly. He sets his hands on his head and turns his back to us, his shoulders heaving as he finally starts to catch his breath.

He's processing.

Drew looks at me like he's asking me to step in, to maybe back him up.

Instead, I tilt my head gently toward Jace, urging Drew to finish this. He hates feelings, sure, but he's just going to have to suck it up and get to it.

Quickly.

Drew frowns in irritation that I'm making him do this, but he lets out a resigned groan and rubs his jaw as he dives in. "Jace, look, I'm not one for words or apologies, but I can only imagine what you dealt with. The hate that brewed for so long with no way to burn it off. I'm..." Drew trails off, pinching his eyes shut as he braces himself for what he's about to say. "I'm sorry."

Jace turns around abruptly, eyes narrowing in disbelief as he stares at the fire dragon. "Say that again."

Drew scowls, and I know that expression. He's telling Jace not to be such an asshole. The Darrington dragon looks at me again for support, but I just shake my head and gesture again toward Jace, urging Drew to finish what he started.

Drew rolls his eyes. "I'm sorry. For all you endured so that I could keep my idiot brother alive."

Jace's entire body relaxes, and it looks for all the world like a heavy weight just lifted off his shoulders. He stares off at the forest beyond the walls through the main gate. After a moment or two of silence, he returns his attention toward us.

Toward *Drew*. And he looks at the man without even a hint of irritation.

"I see why you did it," Jace admits. "You were

keeping your brother safe. You were doing something I couldn't do. Something I failed at, a failure I've regretted every day since." He sighs. "I don't think we're that different after all, Darrington."

Drew playfully grins and mockingly sets a hand on his heart. "How dare you insult me, sir."

Jace laughs, and I almost can't believe what I'm watching.

For a moment, nothing happens. The two men stand on opposite sides of the courtyard, not quite sure what to do next. But then, as Levi and I wait in the silence, they walk toward each other and shake hands.

I let out a slow breath of relief.

"You're still an asshole though," Jace says, raising one eyebrow as if daring Drew to deny it.

Drew laughs and wipes a bit of blood from his jaw. "That's fair."

"Truce?" Jace asks.

Drew nods. "Truce."

I smile, admiring them for how far they've come, and my body finally relaxes. What a relief.

They walk toward me and Levi, and all I can do is look happily between the two of them. I'm not sure what to say or, for that matter, what comes next after a fight like that.

I don't get the chance to ask.

As they reach us, Jace pulls me toward him and kisses me fiercely. As his lips press against mine, I hear Levi chuckle. I can imagine him rolling his eyes and grinning, and as I take a peek out of the corner of my eye, I see him doing exactly that.

Drew laughs. "Get a room."

"That's doable," Jace says, and before I can do a thing, throws me over his shoulder, carrying me back up the steps and into the embassy. I shake my head, laughing as I blow a goodbye kiss at Levi and Drew before they disappear from view.

It's a little disorienting to go through the embassy backward, and for a moment, I'm not sure where we are as Jace takes us down a side hallway. Seconds later, however, he puts me on my feet.

Without a word of warning, Jace presses my hips against the wall and kisses me fiercely, his warm lips buzzing with need. My body burns for him, aching to complete the bond we've refused to indulge.

Well, I'd say it's time to indulge.

He pauses and holds the side of my head, his stormy eyes watching me as he smiles softly. "Do you want this? Me? I'm an imperfect jackass, but I'll love you and be by your side until the bitter end."

"Maybe," I say with a playful grin. "If you truly see

me as your equal. None of that stow-me-away bullshit."

"I'll never so much as think about it again," he promises.

"Then yes." I grab his shoulders, the muscle hard beneath my palms, and pull him into a rough kiss. He gives in, igniting the deepest fires of lust and love burning at my core.

My thunderbird.

He's finally *mine.*

Jace growls possessively, his grip on my waist sliding up toward my breasts. "As much as I want to rip off your clothes and take you right now, we have to wait." He gently bites my neck, barely able to contain his primal need. "The dojo master cannot have a mate, and the moment I enter you, the mate-bond is complete. I have to find my replacement first before we can take this all the way."

My hips tilt toward him as I ache to have him inside of me, and I bite my lip to stem the rising tide of desire that swirls through my chest. "You tease."

"I can, however, help you blow off a little steam." He says, grinning mischievously.

With that, he grabs my jaw and kisses me deeply. The powerful, possessive movement stokes the craving deep within my soul for him, and the warm between my thighs only builds.

I *need* him.

Now.

Deep within my body, at the source of my power and magic, I can feel my dragon stir at his touch. At the shift in him. In *us.* She's louder this time, and I can practically feel her pressing against me like a bird trying to break out of an egg.

It freaking *hurts.*

I gasp, holding my hand to my chest as a second ripple of pain shoots through me. My heart stutters, and just like that, all is calm once again.

"What's wrong?" he asks, brows furrowed with concern. His fingertips brush aside a lock of my hair so that he can see my face, and as his skin brushes mine, my dragon pushes against my very *soul.*

As another blast of pain shoots through me, I realize what this is.

It's—it's *Jace.*

She's reacting to *him.*

His touch alone nearly helped her break free.

I knew he had power over my dragon and my magic, but this is something else entirely. Something new. Letting down my guard, giving in to him—it gave me access to her in new ways, and deep in my bones, I can tell he somehow makes me even more powerful.

"I think I nearly shifted, just then," I say breathlessly, my hand still on my chest. "It—damn it, that *hurt*, Jace."

"The first time is incredibly painful," he admits, brushing his lips against my forehead tenderly. "I can tell you're close. Even I could feel that one. We'll have to practice more," he adds with a dashing smile as his eyes wander over my breasts. "It seems like the more intimate we get, the closer you are to a shift, so I'm more than happy to do my part."

"Oh *gods.*" I grin. "You're going to be insufferable without the dojo as a distraction, aren't you?"

"Oh, you have no idea," he replies, smirking as he loops a strand of my hair around his finger. "You're going to need all the luck you've got to deal with *me*."

CHAPTER TWENTY

It's not until the next morning that the nurses finally let me see Irena and Tucker.

As I walk through the hallway of the medic ward, nurses and doctors buzz around the corridors, ducking in and out of rooms as they flip through papers on their clipboards and scribble notes across the pages. Barely anyone recognizes or addresses me, and the general hum in the air is one of overpowering urgency.

Every room is full. Some of them have two or three beds despite the small space, and most have the curtains drawn across the windows on the far wall. Heart rate monitors beep, getting louder and softer as I pass each door.

A nurse charges out of the nearest door I'm about

to pass, and I barely duck out of her way before the two of us collide. If she notices me at all, she doesn't say a thing or look my way.

I don't take it personally. These brave shifters have been up all night, tending to the wounded, and all I have for them is gratitude. These people saved my sister and one of the men I love most in the world. I owe them, pure and simple.

I scan the room numbers beside each door, looking for either 17 or 20. Surprisingly, I come across Room 20 first and duck my head in to find Irena lying flat on a gurney with her head on a pillow. Her eyes are shut, her chest falling and raising in a soothing rhythm as light streams in through the open window beside her.

My heart pangs impulsively at the calm expression on her face because it reminds me far too much of how she looked when she was in a coma. I have to force myself to notice the warm tone to her skin, the calm and steady pattern of her breath.

She's not in a coma. She's just asleep. She's just healing.

As I hover by the door, one of the nurses darts inside, flipping through the pages on her clipboard. Her red hair is pulled back in a ponytail, and she doesn't so much as look my way as she gets to work checking the various machines and IV drips around Irena's bed.

"Will she wake up soon?" I ask the nurse.

The nurse flinches like she genuinely hadn't realized I was there and holds her hand to her chest as she tries to catch her breath. "I'm sorry, Miss Quinn. I didn't see you."

"It's fine," I say with a small smile, pointing again to my sister. "Is she going to be okay?"

"Yeah, she's a fighter," the nurse says with a nod.

I chuckle. Talk about an understatement.

"If you give her another fifteen minutes, she should be awake," the nurse continues, adjusting the IV bag as it hangs beside the bed.

"Thanks." I pat the doorframe absently as I force myself to walk away.

I want to make sure Tucker's all right, and it won't do any good to sit at Irena's bedside and twiddle my thumbs. I figure when Irena does wake up, she will want some time to herself.

I meander through the corridor until I get to Room 17, and when I peek in, I find Tucker laying in a bed almost identical to Irena's. His curtains are drawn, the sun streaming in through the windowpanes and filling the room with a warm light. A few chairs line the wall opposite him, and I grab one, carefully setting it beside him.

I sit in the chair and lean my chin against the railing of his hospital bed, watching him as his heart rate monitor beeps steadily in the background. His bare chest rises and falls, half covered by a sheet, and I find myself simply watching him, hypnotized by every breath and grateful he's okay.

For once, I have nothing immediate and urgent I need to do. Jace told me to take the day off from training, and since we won't mate until he's found his replacement, he's focusing his full attention on securing a new chain of command for the dojo with Drew and Levi's help.

And that leaves me with surprisingly little to do.

It's nice to just sit here, to be with a man who has risked his life for me time and time again and be grateful that he's going to be all right.

As I rest beside Tucker's bed, listening to the steady beep of the machines around him, I find myself surprisingly tired. My eyes get heavy, and even though the cold metal of the railing isn't exactly comfortable, I find myself beginning to doze off.

The rustle of sheets captures my attention, and I jolt awake, not even realizing I had actually fallen asleep and with no idea of how long I was out.

"Hey, babe," Tucker slurs.

I rub my eyes to clear my vision, and I find him watching me with his eyelids only half open. He grins as I wake up and reaches for me, his palm facing the ceiling as his fingers twitch slightly. I set my hand in his, holding him tightly as his grip tightens around my palm.

And with that one little touch—just our hands grazing—I hum with gratitude and love.

Real, true love.

Tucker put his life on the line, as he has so often, for me. Love is a loaded word, but I think for him, it's the right one.

I clear my throat, still not entirely comfortable with all this emotion and feeling.

"So, you're hurting yourself for attention now?" I ask with a playful grin.

He laughs. "That's a good one."

Seconds later, he cringes in pain and holds his free hand against the shoulder where he took the bullet. His face scrunches in agony, and I figure he probably needs another dose of morphine to help with the pain.

"Nurse!" I shout into the hallway, hoping someone can hear me.

"I'm fine. I'm fine," he says, shaking his head and

dismissing my concern with a wave of his hand. "Really, Rory."

I frown, not completely believing him, but I leave it alone for now. I'll tell one of the nurses on the way out that he should probably get a few more pain meds.

My grip on his wrists tightens possessively. "Tucker, look. I'm sorry," I say quietly, not quite able to look at him. "I blame myself for letting you get hurt. You should never have to take a bullet for me, and—"

"Rory, stop," he chides me softly.

I look up to find him already studying my face, wearing a drugged grin as he admires me. It's charming and endearing, and I find my mind slowly going blank as that charming expression dissolves everything I wanted to say.

"This is the life we chose," he says calmly. "Bullets and facing down death every day, that's what we do. And Rory, I'll give anything to live that life with you."

I smile, utterly and completely enchanted by this foolhardy and adorable man. I stand, leaning toward him, and kiss him gently—even though I want to straddle him and hold his face. I need to be tender with him for now since humans don't heal quite as quickly as dragons, and he might be a little fragile for a day or two.

"I'm so damn lucky," I say, brushing my nose against his.

"You really are," he says, grinning. "I'm quite a catch."

I chuckle. "And modest too. Don't forget that."

"Oh, the most modest," he says, smirking as he brilliantly plays along.

The clack of heels against the floor catches my attention, and I look up as a nurse walks in. She rifles through the pages on her clipboard, frowning slightly as she studies Tucker's monitors.

"Miss Quinn, you needed to tell me when he woke up," she chides. "Mr. Chase here needs lots of rest and a lot more meds. Out, out," she says in a slightly sing-song voice as she gestures toward the door.

I chuckle. In this domain, I have no control. What the nurses ask for, they get, and I'm not about to argue with them. Not when my man's life is at stake.

"I'll see you later," I say, kissing him gently.

"Don't worry, babe," he says with a lighthearted shrug. "We'll get plenty of exercise later when you help rehabilitate me. I think I'll need lots of physical therapy."

He winks.

I laugh on my way out the door, shaking my head at my adorable idiot.

"Oh, Miss Quinn," the redheaded nurse says as she passes me in the hallway.

I pause, turning around as she stops mid-stride and points at Irena's room.

"Your sister's awake," she says with a smile. "She's asking for you."

"Thank you," I say, eager to see how Irena's doing.

I peek into Irena's room to find my sister sitting upright in bed, stretching her fingers. She studies her hands, flipping them over again and again as she examines every inch of them. It's almost like she can't quite believe they're there, but I'm not entirely sure what she's doing.

"Hey," I say quietly, knocking gently against the doorframe so as not to startle her.

Irena slowly lifts her head and winces, tenderly touching her temples as she fights a headache.

"You doing okay?" I ask as I shut the door behind me.

I have a feeling that whatever Irena and I are going to discuss won't be lighthearted or playful. She's going to want to get down to business, and it's better if nurses don't overhear it.

"I don't hurt as much as I normally would after an ass-kicking like that," she admits with a small sigh.

"That's the dragon healing," I say, pulling a chair

from the far wall up to the foot of her bed. I spin it around so that it's facing away from her and sit on it backward, with my elbows leaning against the back-rest of the chair.

Irena scoffs. "Well, at least the dragon blood is good for something, then."

I'm tempted to lecture her. The more she rejects her dragon, the greater her chances of killing it. But what she said was vaguely positive, and I'm going to take it as a win, however small of a win it might be.

"The doctor says I'll be back on my feet by tonight," Irena says, lifting her eyebrows in disbelief. "It's crazy to think about. Before the coma, I'd be out for two weeks easily after something like this."

"Yeah, that's dragon healing," I say again. "You have a lot of gifts now that you didn't have before."

She quirks one eyebrow, daring me to scold her or ask about training with Harper, and I take the not-so-subtle hint to shut the hell up.

"Do you want to talk about what happened back there?" I ask instead. "What went wrong at the storage facility?"

Her shoulders droop slightly, and she bites her lip as she stares out the window. Her jaw tenses, and I can see the muscles in her neck tighten. "A lot went wrong."

That's an understatement, but I don't say anything. I sit with the silence, letting her speak when she's ready.

"We were betrayed, Rory."

"Yeah," I say bitterly, looking at the floor as I absently brush my thumb against my jaw.

"I've been trying to figure out who did it," Irena admits, her voice deadly serious. "As I fell in and out of consciousness and the pain was too much to bear, the only thing that kept me going was figuring out who would do this to me. Who I shouldn't have trusted. There were a few vulnerabilities in my network, some people I wasn't quite sure of, but one stands out as the obvious weak link."

"Who?" I press.

Irena shakes her head, looking at her palms as if she can't bring herself to say the name. She pinches her eyes shut, her lips finally parting, but even still she hesitates.

I've never seen her like this. She looks—well, vulnerable. Exposed, and a little raw. Whoever this person is, they meant a lot to her.

"Benjamin," she says quietly after a while.

I frown because I have no idea who the hell that is.

"You never met him," Irena continues, still not

looking at me. "I kept my lovers secret as much for your sake as mine."

Oh.

Oh, *shit*.

"Irena," I say softly, leaning toward her. "You're not saying this is someone you love?"

"Yeah," she admits, her voice breaking as she looks out the window yet again. "I guess his loyalties lay elsewhere."

I shatter for her because the thought of being betrayed by the men I love—even just the thought—breaks me. I stare at the floor, trying to get my bearings and figure out what to even say. "What makes you think it's him?"

"There's no one else it could be," she says simply, squaring her shoulders. "I gave every contact a different location for the cases. It was a test, Rory. To see who I could trust and who I couldn't. But Benjamin, I had to give him the real location. He was the one who helped me get it there in the first place," she says, catching my eye. "I figured if I could trust anyone, I could trust him, and—" Her jaw tenses painfully as she squeezes her eyes shut. "I guess I couldn't," she finishes, swallowing hard.

I sigh, rubbing my eyes, not sure how to handle this. I don't care about Benjamin. I care about Irena. I care about what this is going to do to her, how it's going to break her to be betrayed by someone she trusted so intrinsically.

"That's why Zurie wasn't there last night," Irena says, breaking my train of thought. "I had four contacts, and based on the chatter, it looks like two of them betrayed me. Zurie went to one location and Diesel went to the other, both with massive forces and both with one goal." She pauses, looking me dead in the eye. "To kill us."

I let out a slow and heavy sigh as I process what she's telling me. "What are you going to do?"

"I have two men to kill," Irena says, her eyes narrowing as she glares outside.

We sit in the lingering silence for a while, mostly because I have no idea what to say. I don't know how to make this better because that's not something that's even in my power to do. This is Irena's battle, her wound, and all I can do is be here for her.

"Rory, I can't believe I'm about to ask this," Irena says, pinching her eyes shut as if she's bracing herself to ask the impossible of me.

"Yeah?" I ask warily, preparing myself for the worst.

"Can you call a meeting with your men?" Irena asks, wincing as if the words literally hurt her. "This is something we need to discuss before any action is taken."

For a moment, I just watch her with a small smile on my face, not bothering to mask how impressed I am with her growth.

"Yeah," I say with a small nod. "I think we can do that."

"Good," she says, shaking out her shoulders uncomfortably. "If you don't mind though, I could use some time alone beforehand."

"Of course," I say, standing and returning the chair to where it was originally. I head for the door, pausing only briefly as I leave to check on her over my shoulder. She's still staring out the window, stiff and uncomfortable, battling her demons alone.

I don't blame her, of course. I was the same way before Tucker. Before Levi. Before Drew. Before Jace.

Love changes you, but only if you let it.

I sigh and walk into the hallway, closing the door behind me as I leave. I duck my head in Tucker's room one more time to find him out cold, snoring slightly as he no doubt rides another wave of pain medication.

As I leave the medical ward, the double doors slowly closing behind me, I notice a familiar soldier lounging with his back against the wall. When he lifts his gaze from the floor and sees me, he abruptly stands upright, smoothing out his shirt as if he's been waiting here for me.

Eric.

"Is Irena okay?" he asks, briefly glancing at the doors.

I nod, grateful that there's at least one man around here that Irena can trust. "She's fine. You can go see her."

He shakes his head. "She won't let me in."

His shoulders droop slightly as he speaks, and in that moment, everything clicks for me.

I sigh deeply, rubbing my temples as I realize just how badly this Benjamin person messed Irena up. Two of her lovers just betrayed her to our former mentor, to the woman who wants us both dead in the most painful way possible.

Of *course* Irena is closing herself off. It's all she knows how to do.

I set my hand on his shoulder. "It's not you, Eric. She doesn't trust easily, and she's shutting down right now because—well, because…" I trail off, not even sure where to start with this. It's not my story to tell.

"Thanks," he says, clearing his throat as he looks again toward the medic bay doors.

He seems to get it, and I'm thankful I don't have to explain anything more than that.

"Tell her I'm here," he says, looking at me. "When she's ready."

I offer him a half-hearted smile and a small nod. At that, he walks away, disappearing around the corner.

I need to have a talk with her. She can't shut out all love just because her old life betrayed her. She's a new woman now, with a new future. She just hasn't accepted it yet.

She will in time.

...I *hope*.

CHAPTER TWENTY-ONE

A s the moon rises over the mountains surrounding the dojo, I once again walk into Jace's war room. It's just me, the dojo master, and the Darrington heir—and this time, those two aren't at each other's throats.

It's surreal, I won't lie. Welcome, but strange.

They sit at the far end of the table as I enter, already laughing at some joke Drew's finishing up. Both men smile at me as I get comfortable in my chair.

I figure they're probably swapping playful insults, and I'm just grateful to see the two of them getting along for once.

It's a nice change of pace.

I went to check on Tucker again an hour ago, and he's out of commission. The nurses said he needs more rest, so, unfortunately, he won't join us tonight. I figure Irena will be on her way soon, though, as I assume she's been ignoring the doctor's orders to sleep and heal.

We Quinn girls don't usually do what we're told, anyway.

The door opens, and Levi enters. He smiles warmly as our eyes meet and sits beside me, gently brushing his knuckle along the exposed skin on my arm. As we touch, our connection opens, and a flurry of affection swarms through from him. It fills me with sunshine and joy, and I allow myself to simply sit with it, to enjoy it.

Hi, I say through our connection, smiling as we speak without saying a thing.

He grins, a flirty glint to his eye. *Hey.*

The door swings open, and Irena enters. Despite the bandage still wrapped around her wrist, she seems completely normal. There's no limp, no blood stains, and not even a hint that she was ever seriously wounded in the first place.

Across the table from me, she leans her palms against the wooden surface, not bothering with a chair. Her bright green eyes seem sharper than usual.

Clearer.

Focused.

Angry.

It's surreal to think my sister has Kinsley's magic in her. That, in some small way, Kinsley is somehow in there.

It's a sudden thought, the kind that comes out of nowhere but won't leave. I never really thought about it that way before, but something in the way her bright green eyes rove over the table makes me realize how quickly she's adopting the little traits of a dragon. It's subtle, but I can see it in the way she moves, in her posture.

The way she walks.

The way she thinks.

Even if she hasn't accepted what she is, her body is changing.

There's nothing she can do to stop that.

"How far along are you in producing the Spectre tech we acquired?" she asks, her eyes darting between Jace and Drew.

I chuckle. It's just like her to get right down to business, to assume control of the room and immediately start making demands of people.

Jace seems to get as much of a kick out of it as I do, given that this is not only his dojo, but his *room*. A small grin plays at the corner of his mouth as he briefly looks at me, surprised Irena has the guts to take control.

Everyone here is used to handling stressful military matters, and we're fine with just getting right down to business. Only Tucker would have said something, maybe—*Hey, Irena. We're great, thanks. How are you?*

But since he's asleep, I bite my tongue, resisting the impulse to make a sarcastic crack.

"I found the materials," Drew says, reclining in his chair as he taps his finger on the table. "However, it's difficult to get a steady supply without raising all sorts of eyebrows. I need a bit more time and a few shell companies to make it all happen with any kind of consistency. Otherwise, we risk all sorts of investigations across dozens of countries, and we don't want any of this tied back to us."

"Exactly," Jace says, leaning his elbows on the table. "The Fairfax production facilities are nearly ready. We're clearing out a few of our military weapons compounds to prepare and produce this tech you've given us, Irena. Once Drew procures the resources in a steady fashion, our factories will be able to manufacture most of what you gave us. Not all of it though, so we're still figuring out how to get some of it working."

"Like what?" she asks, her eyes narrowing.

"The override devices primarily," Jace says with a

small shrug. "They're the most intricate, complex machines we've ever seen. Even with the detailed specs you gave us, we're not entirely sure how they work. It'll take reverse engineering several of the components before we can get those up and running."

"I can give you a few of my guys," Drew says, looking at Jace. "I have a few human tech experts who might be useful."

Irena frowns, her bright green eyes darting between the two of them with a hint of confusion on her face. "You two are working together now? Did I miss something?"

The four of us laugh.

Yeah, I would say she missed a *lot*.

"I'll tell you later, Irena," I say, grinning.

I half expect her to laugh along with us, but her frown only deepens. Her gaze settles on Levi's knuckle as he gently strokes my arm, and there's a sense of loss in her expression as she quickly looks away.

She wants that.

Irena wants what I have. My men. This connection we share. She aches for it even though she tells herself otherwise. She aches to trust, to let her guard down, and I figure she still hasn't come to terms with Benjamin's betrayal.

Seeing how well we get along, how strong our

bond is—it must be like salt in a wound for her right now.

It'll take time for her to heal from this, and my heart hurts for her.

Never one to sit too long with a feeling—especially an unpleasant one—Irena cracks her knuckles. "I spent today reaching out to my network and confirmed the names of the two people who betrayed us on the storage raid."

The last of the laughter dies, and the room becomes quickly somber. There's an eerie silence as we wait for names like bloodthirsty hounds, thirsting for the scent so we can hunt.

"Who are they?" I ask, breaking the tense silence.

"You don't know them," Irena says, shaking her head.

Hmm.

Interesting, since I know at least one of them.

I get the distinct impression she just lied to me, but her tells weren't there. If she lied, she hid it expertly well.

"So, what are you going to do?" I ask, baiting her, daring her to say what I think she's going to say.

Irena squares her shoulders. "I'm going to see what else they know, and then I'm going to kill them."

Around me, Jace, Drew, and Levi all nod. Their

mouths are grim lines on their handsome faces, and their eyes are all focused on her.

But the unspoken agreement that these men must die, well, it's just a given.

It's a bleak reality of our world that we can discuss death and murder in such a blasé fashion. It's just the reality of our lives as warriors. As dragons. As former assassins.

If we let traitors live, there will never be a truce. Down the line, it will always become a choice: us or them.

Even though we're all looking at her, it seems like only I'm able to see the deep hurt in the way Irena can't hold my gaze—in the way she keeps tensing her jaw and shifting her weight. They're subtle movements that most people would miss entirely, but to me, they betray her deep discomfort.

Apparently, she really liked this Benjamin guy.

It makes me want to kill him all the more for breaking her heart so completely.

At this point, it's obvious she wants to go alone, but I'm not even going to consider it.

"When are we leaving?" I ask casually as if it's a given that I'm going. "I figure it should be just me and Irena though, since these traitors will probably be spooked if we bring any more company than that. We still want to get intel from them, after all, and we can dangle my presence there as a bit of bait."

"Good idea, Rory," Jace says, relaxing into his chair. "What sort of weapons will you guys need?"

The room goes silent, and everyone instantly looks at Jace with various dumbfounded expressions.

He quickly scans the room. "What?" he asks, genuinely baffled.

Drew laughs, shaking his head as he rubs his eyes. "You've spent the last how many months trying to lock her away, and now suddenly you're throwing her into the line of fire?"

Jace rolls his eyes. "Well, I'm not *throwing* her—"

"Is there any middle ground with you?" Drew interrupts, still chuckling.

"Rory, you're not coming," Irena interjects, crossing her arms as she looks at me intently.

I scoff. "The hell I'm not. I won't let you go out there alone."

"It's non-negotiable," she says slowly, shaking her head. "I need to go underground to get to him, to get to them both. I need to..." She trails off, her eyes quickly darting around the room. "Begin," she finishes vaguely.

Around me, my men narrow their eyes with

skeptic concern, but I know exactly what she's talking about.

I impulsively stiffen, leaning forward as I try to think of how I can convince her not to do this. Not yet anyway.

The beginning—of her destroying the Spectres from within.

The beginning of her death march.

She's going to work her contacts and get things started. In her mind, it's time to unravel the Spectres from within. But in my mind, she's not ready. Until she accepts what she is—a *dragon,* not just a former Spectre—she won't be.

"You can't stop me," Irena says before I can get a word in edgewise.

"Irena, you're not ready," I snap.

"I'm fine," she says, her tone even and steady.

"You were just shot." I gesture toward her abdomen, toward the bandage I know is still there. Toward the wound I *know* still hurts her.

"Yeah," she says, a hint of boredom in her tone. "And I'm better. Dragon blood or whatever. Right?"

I roll my eyes and rub my face, not entirely sure how I can make her see reason. "Jace, order her to stay."

The dojo master laughs. "I'm not getting in the

middle of this, Rory. You Quinn girls need to work this out."

"Rory, stop this!" Irena barks.

The harsh demand cuts through the room, and tension builds in the lingering silence.

No one talks to me that way.

Especially not since I became the dragon vessel.

I bristle at the very idea that she could give me such a dismissive demand—and even more so that she thinks I would listen. I slowly stand from my chair, the wooden legs scraping over the floor as I lean my palms on the table.

Our gazes lock in silent challenge.

"You're running away from your problems," I say, my voice dark and deadly.

A warning.

To sit the hell *down.*

"I'm facing them," she corrects, her eyes narrowing.

I scoff. "No. You're facing your problems like a *Spectre.*"

By snuffing them out as brutally as she can—when, in reality, facing her problems would mean staying here. *Facing her problems* would mean healing things with Eric.

So, no. She's absolutely running away.

And—as much as it pains me to admit this to

myself—I know in my heart that I can't actually stop her.

With a long, slow breath, I relax my shoulders and hang my head. I know this woman better than anyone else on the planet, and I know when my efforts will be wasted.

No matter what I say, no matter what I try to do, nothing at all could possibly keep her here a moment longer.

I'm disappointed, heartbroken even, that she's already trying to leave. I really thought I had more time with my sister, but I know her too well to live in that fantasy anymore.

"Try not to be an idiot," I say through the knot forming in my throat.

"I can handle this, Rory," she says calmly. "I won't give Zurie the chance to capture me, and if anything is compromised, I'll come back immediately."

I lift my head, studying her face in surprise. "Really?"

Usually, she would find a safehouse and retreat for a little while to let the trouble die down or move on.

For her to come back shows growth—however small.

It's progress.

"I promise," she says with a nod. "I won't let Zurie

use me against you, even if that means coming back here." She hesitates briefly, looking at Jace. "No offense."

He shrugs. "None taken."

"Okay," I say, nodding as I cross my arms. "Good luck, Irena."

She smirks. "Won't need it."

I sit on the carpet in the living room of my suite, my back against the door. My head rests against the wood as I listen to the silence.

And I wait.

I'm waiting for the inevitable patter of Irena's footsteps as she leaves.

It's the middle of the night, and as the evening wears on, a beam of moonlight slices through the shadows of the dark living room. I rest my arm on one knee, my other leg stretched in front of me.

It's difficult—forcing myself not to intervene—but it's already been decided, and there's nothing I can do.

Around two in the morning, a door creaks open down the corridor, and I hear the soft thud of footsteps through the hall, heading toward the stairs.

I expect them to just keep going, but they don't.

They pause at my door.

I close my eyes and hold my breath. Silently, I wish for her footsteps to recede back to her bedroom, but I know my sister better than that.

She's debating saying goodbye. Out there, right now, she's deliberating as to whether or not she should ask for one last hug before she leaves.

But *she* knows *me* too well.

She knows I'll try to make her stay.

Her footsteps steal down the stairwell, and after a few moments, they fade into the silence once again.

I let out the breath I was holding, and my shoulders fall as I relax against the door. A ball forms in my throat, and I swallow hard to clear it.

It doesn't work.

Irena and I have always stayed one step ahead of Zurie, and if Irena does this, she might come back with intel that can turn the tides in our favor. It's ironic to think that intel from the very traitors that tried to kill us may, in fact, betray our mentor's next move.

I shut my eyes, exhausted from the day—but mostly, I fight grief. I finally got my sister back, only to have to sit and listen as she leaves again.

But that's our way. It was always us against the world, back when we were Spectres. Our missions, our purposes, were always the same. Now, however, we lead different lives—lives that often don't intersect at all.

I have my life, my men, and my reason for living. Now, she's driven to fulfill hers.

I can't stop her from doing that.

CHAPTER TWENTY-TWO

The midday sun shines across the center courtyard, filtering in through the windows of the room Jace tried to lock me in when Mason Greene came to threaten me all those months ago.

He and I have sure come a long way since then.

I straighten his collar, mostly just fiddling with his shirt just because I like the way being near him ignites the deepest parts of me. He allows me to do it, grinning slightly and watching my every movement like this is somehow entertaining.

"Are you sure you want to do this?" I ask, looking up at him.

He grins and kisses me in answer, the brush of his lips on mine igniting fire and magic deep within me.

"Stop asking that," he demands, his voice playful and light.

"Once you announce that you're stepping down from the dojo, there's no going back," I point out even as he holds me tightly to his chest.

He studies my face for a moment as he holds me, his grip firm and strong on my back. "I know."

I smirk, lost in his stormy gray eyes and drunk from his touch.

Gods, he's so damn hot.

Movement outside catches my attention, and I peek over his shoulder as the crowd forms beneath the balcony. The double doors onto the terrace sit open, letting in a cool breeze on the otherwise warm day, and the courtyard is practically full. Dragons line the walls, but most of the soldiers huddle in their human forms, standing below on the black tile as they wait.

Only Harper, my men, and I know what the announcement is about. I almost can't believe this is happening—that Jace and I really got to this point.

There's no turning back after he steps out there.

With one arm still around my shoulders, he lifts my chin with his other hand until our eyes meet. The air between us crackles with energy and desire as our unfulfilled mate-bond drives us ever closer. Our dragons are aching for us to do this already, to finish what we've resisted for so long, and there's not a doubt in my mind that this is the right thing to do.

After all, this is the choice he made. I'm not forcing him to do anything.

The door to the hallway opens, and Harper walks in as we hold each other.

"Ew, stop making out," she says, grinning.

"Is it time?" Jace asks, ignoring her jibe.

The Fairfax Boss nods. "Go get 'em, tiger."

Jace squares his shoulders and winks at me. He kisses me once more tenderly on the forehead and smacks my ass hard before heading out onto the balcony.

There's a slight tingle in my rear from his touch as the skin goes briefly numb, but I laugh. Jace Goodwin plays rough, and I have to admit I *really* like it.

Harper stands next to me, watching as he exits onto the balcony. "I've never seen him this happy," Harper admits, leaning toward me. "I'm proud of you both."

"Thanks," I say with a small smile.

Outside, the soldiers cheer as Jace walks onto the balcony. The dragons along the wall roar in welcome as their general and master takes center stage. He lifts his hand, and that simple gesture instantly settles them into silence.

"As many of you know," he begins, his eyes scanning the crowd below him, "I've trained at this dojo since I was a boy. For as long as I can remember, I fought within these halls and wandered the tunnels below the embassy. I learned everything I know from the masters who have taught here before me. So, when I say serving in this dojo is all I ever wanted, know that this has been a lifelong dream come true."

He pauses, puffing out his chest ever so slightly with pride. "Serving as your master and as the Fairfax General has been the honor of a lifetime, and one I do not take lightly. However, my dragon has made a choice for me. One I cannot refuse."

Jace pauses, and I suspect this is carefully orchestrated silence. The only sound is the wind whistling by, and I imagine that everyone below is starting to figure out what this announcement is really about.

"As of today, I will be stepping down as the dojo master," he says, arching his shoulders. "And I'll be taking my mate."

I expect disappointed murmurs, or maybe even some heckling. Instead, the crowd cheers.

I lift my eyebrows in surprise, and I'm not entirely sure how to take this. After all, they deeply respect him. These are people who would die for him, and they're cheering that he's stepping down.

"Is that a good thing?" I ask, pointing outside. "Shouldn't they be, I don't know, upset?"

Harper laughs. "They're happy for him, same as me. For a thunderbird, finding your mate is one of the highest honors. It doesn't happen to everyone, and when it *does*, it's to be celebrated. Most of them out there want mates, Rory. They're as proud of him as I am."

Jace laughs while the soldiers cheer for him, beaming as he steals a look at me over his shoulder. I smile back at the goofball and gesture for him to finish his speech.

He returns his gaze toward the crowd, and as he speaks, the rising tide of their cheering drowns him out. He continues talking over them, but I only catch every few words.

"He's explaining what's going to happen next," Harper says, probably reading the confusion on my face. "He's telling them that he's choosing a replacement, one that'll do his legacy proud. We've already chosen our candidate."

"Russell?" I ask.

Harper nods. "He's accepted the trials, and we begin tonight."

I frown in confusion. "What trials?"

"It's our selection process. The trials are intense,"

Harper says as she cracks her knuckles, shaking out her hand to loosen the tension. "But that's the point. If he passes, the next time he walks among the other soldiers, it will be as their master. He will have to prove himself before he can be deemed their leader, though. It's going to be a difficult few days for him."

"And if he doesn't pass?" I ask.

Harper lets out of frustrated sigh. "Then we'll have to do it all again. It happens more often than you think. I almost didn't pass mine."

I lean slightly away from her, scanning her face skeptically. "There was a trial for you to become the Boss?"

"Oh, *hell* yeah," she says casually, shrugging. "Why wouldn't there be?"

"I don't know," I admitted. "I figured that it just sort of… *happened*. You know, like an ascension to power."

Harper scoffs. "Not for Fairfax dragons. We're all about adrenaline and honor. We have to earn our place and continue to do so to maintain the respect of the people. There are no handouts with us."

"What were your trials like?"

"Brutal," she admits quietly. "When my father died, I only had two weeks to grieve and then prepare for the Great Trial. The ultimate one, so to speak—gruesome, difficult, and painful. That's how the Boss is selected. I had about forty competitors, and even Jace competed just to mess with me."

I laugh. It's something Jace would do.

"It lasted for three weeks," Harper continues, her gaze briefly slipping out of focus as she remembers. "The final battle of the Great Trial is a fight to the death amongst the two most competent challengers. It's the final proof of strength and pretty much a given in any Fairfax trial. I was up against my younger brother."

My heart pangs, and I look at her in horror. "You had to kill your younger brother?"

"No, no," she says, gently shaking her head. "Sorry, I always forget how brutal that sounds to outsiders. A 'fight to the death' for the Fairfax dragons can also be a fight to surrender, since in many ways it's the death of others' respect for you."

Gods above.

The Fairfax dragons are so much more brutal than I ever realized.

Harper crosses her arms, smiling as she reminisces. "In my case, I'm grateful I fought him. He knew I was fit to rule. Knew I would win. He just wanted to make sure no one ever doubted my authority. It's not common for female dragons to be Bosses, Rory. And anything less than a full and total battle wouldn't have convinced the world I deserved my place." She hesitates, squaring her shoulders and standing a little taller. "I needed to make sure no one ever challenged me, and in that final battle, I proved my worth."

I don't really know what to say to that, so I let the silence between us be filled by the occasional roar of the crowd outside.

"Do you remember the tattoo on my forehead when I was in my dragon form?" Harper asks, leaning toward me. "When we sparred?"

"I do. It was beautiful," I admit, and it was—a gorgeous, glowing symbol in the middle of her forehead. "I didn't recognize it."

"They call that the Anointing," she says, tapping her own forehead. "It's the tattoo of the Boss, and I wear it until I die. It's carved by magic, and it's forever. If someone wants to take the crown from me, they have to literally take off my head to get it."

"That's dark as hell," I admit.

"Yeah," she says, laughing. "It really is. But that's the Fairfax way. Hardcore to the end."

"Can't deny that," I say absently, returning my attention to Jace.

As Jace wraps up his speech, I steal another look at Harper. With her arms crossed, she simply watches her cousin with a small smile on her face. It's a combination of gratitude and pride, and I can tell she's wanted this for him for a long time.

But the longer I'm here, the more Fairfax dragons I put at risk.

"I figure the other Bosses aren't too happy that I'm still here," I casually say, watching Jace even as I lean toward Harper to speak in low tones.

"It's fine," Harper says dismissively, not even looking at me. As I study her face, I notice her eye twitch slightly. The corner of her mouth briefly pulls upward, and it's clear she just lied.

"You know you can't lie to a Spectre, right?" I ask, grinning slightly.

At that, she finally looks at me, raising one eyebrow skeptically as she dares me to challenge her.

"I could always find out for myself, of course," I admit, shrugging lazily. "Rifle through a few top-secret computers, scope out some confidential information. Shouldn't be too hard."

Harper laughs, shaking her head in defeat. "You're insufferable. You know that?"

"Yeah," I admit, grinning.

"It's becoming difficult," Harper confesses. "The other families are starting to pull out of trade deals, claiming that they'll continue to boycott us until you're in neutral territory. They say it's to make sure you're not favoring one family over the other or being controlled by anyone. But come on," she shrugs, looking briefly at me. "We both know they just all want a chance to steal you away. I'm not going to let them hurt you, Rory. I'm not going to let them come for you."

"I pity whatever idiot tries to come after me, but I appreciate the sentiment all the same. Thanks, Harper."

She nods. "You're always welcome here, Rory," she says, looking at me with a serious expression. "Remember that. If anyone ever tries to come for you, they'll have to go through me first."

As the crowd cheers outside, I study the Fairfax Boss's face, wondering how this is my life. Wondering how any of this is real.

But somehow, by some beautiful miracle, it *is*.

"Thank you, Harper," I say genuinely. "And the same is true for you. If you ever need me, you know I'll be there for you."

It's the truth.

I will be.

I don't have many friends in this world, and I can't trust very many people. But those I do love—I will protect them with my *life*.

CHAPTER TWENTY-THREE

The moon climbs into the sky on a warm night as I wander the empty halls of the embassy.

It's been two days since Jace's announcement, and there's an excited buzz running through the castle—mostly from the hushed conversations about who the candidate could be. Russell can't say anything until he's officially named, so to everyone else, it's a mystery.

I smirk as I pass a group of soldiers huddled together in the hallway, all pausing as I walk by. They know that I know, but I suspect they don't realize I can tell they're not-so-subtly watching me as I go by.

It's kind of fun knowing the secrets of a dragon embassy for a change. Thus far, they've usually been *about* me, and kept *from* me.

Tucker has one week left in the medic ward, and then he can finally get back on his feet. He's antsy as hell as he keeps trying to get up despite the gaping wounds in his side and shoulder. I've been visiting him several times a day, and they're beginning to threaten sedation if he doesn't just sleep and heal.

Even though I know exactly where Tucker is, I have no idea where to find Levi, Drew, or Jace tonight. They've been missing for the last few hours, and I figure if they're *all* missing, they're up to something.

I can't for the life of me figure out what though— and more importantly, why I didn't get invited.

I *love* getting into trouble, and those men *know* that.

As I wander into another corridor, trying to figure out where they could be, I pause and listen for Jace. Turning inward, I touch the dragon deep within me, asking her for help.

She's happy to oblige.

The vague sensation of Jace's presence flickers to life, and even though the connection is a little fuzzy, there are blips and surges of energy that indicate he's below me, somewhere in the tunnels.

Hmm.

I wonder what he could be up to.

Maybe I can find Levi and spar with him. It's not often that my ice dragon gets into mischief with Jace and Drew, so I figure I'll check the back courtyard to see if he's there.

As I make my way toward the stairs that will lead me outside, I unconsciously watch my periphery for movement. It's an old habit from my Spectre days, one that has kept me alive in more situations than I can count, and I'm not about to give it up.

Even if I'm *not* a Spectre anymore.

A familiar blonde steps into the hallway from a side corridor, and I pause, turning on my heel as she walks toward me.

Harper.

"There you are," she says, smiling warmly. "I've been looking for you."

"Well, I hope you want to make some trouble because I'm itching for something to do."

The gorgeous shifter laughs. "Yeah, actually. Do you want to get into some mischief?"

"Yeah," I say. "Duh."

She giggles and gestures for me to follow her, and the two of us slip silently through the hallways of the embassy. After a short stairwell and a few minutes of ducking through various hallways, she pauses at a long stretch of wall with a few portraits of past Fairfax dragons hung along the elaborate wallpaper.

With a few quick glances on either side of us, she

lifts a portrait of a woman in an elegant purple gown to reveal a keypad hidden beneath the frame. Harper taps in a code, activating a secret panel in the wall that leads to yet another secret tunnel—and, I suspect, connects with the others that weave through this place.

Score.

I grin mischievously. "I can already tell this is going to be fun."

We duck into the dark tunnel, and seconds later, the panel closes automatically behind us. To anyone who might have noticed us walk into that corridor, it will seem as though we disappeared into thin air.

That's the way I like it.

Harper leads me down the corridor, taking us deeper into the mountain and the tunnels that carve through it. She walks with the confidence of someone who was taken this route a hundred times before.

It's clear to me, then—Harper must have grown up here, same as Jace. This place must hold special meaning for their family.

And Jace gave it up. For me.

I can't help but walk a little taller with pride.

As the corridor weaves and bobs through the castle, we take several flights of stairs that connect to other secret hallways. For the most part, we walk in silence, with Harper's focus entirely on the hallways.

Before long, I find myself in a familiar stretch of the tunnels. I stretch out my fingers in anticipation as I began to recognize the shape of the vents along the floor, and adrenaline buzzes through me as I eagerly debate what we're going to see.

I've been here before. Long ago, when Drew brought me to secretly watch one of Jace's training sessions with his soldiers.

Harper pauses at a tall grate that runs from floor to ceiling. A variety of levers and switches are set against it, and she flips one of them. Thin slits in the grate open at eye level, revealing a wide view of the room inside—a much better view than I would get peeking through one of the grates.

I lean toward it, peering into the room to find a familiar training area. Yep, this is exactly where I thought we were. I've not only spied on training sessions in this room before, but Drew and I sparred in here. This is where he told me the truth about his feud with Jace—and what really happened between their brothers.

Only four men stand in the room, however—Russell, Jace, Drew, and Levi.

So, this is where they went off to.

Russell stands in an empty stretch of the massive training hall, and from this angle, I can see the massive doors that lead into the corridors and tunnels below the castle. I can't see the wall of weapons from where I'm standing, so I figure they're somewhere along this stretch of the tunnel.

Jace and Drew circle Russell, the three men wielding staffs as they watch each other intently. Russell stands at the ready, his weight shifted slightly forward onto the balls of his feet. His shoulders relax, and his eyes sweep the floor as he blatantly watches them both from the corner of his eye.

With two opponents on opposite sides of him, he has no choice. He can't look at either of them directly, or the other will attack.

Levi stands on the platform in the center of the room, his arms crossed as he watches the three men intently. A pile of weapons covers the platform around him—from swords to throwing stars and everything in between. He has his own little arsenal at his feet, and I can tell he wants to join in the fun.

My question is, why hasn't he?

"Can they see us?" I ask quietly.

Harper shakes her head. "This is a secret viewing panel. From their perspective, we're just grout and mortar between the stones."

"Fascinating," I mutter, leaning in to get a better look.

Jace attacks first. Russell parries, the two staffs connecting with a thundering crack. Before Russell can recover, Drew swings his weapon at Russell's face. Russell is barely able to lift his staff in time, but he manages, and another resounding snap thunders through the room.

The three men dodge and parry, Russell darting between the two warriors with impossible speed. The cracks of the staffs hitting sound a bit like fireworks, one after the other, again and again.

I can only imagine the pain shooting up Russell's forearms with every blow.

Jace and Drew are two masters. For Russell to hold out even this long is impressive.

Even though I'm curious about Russell's fighting habits and methods, I'm continuously drawn to Drew and Jace. It's surreal to see them working together, and they move in a seamless formation. It's like they were born to fight side by side, every now and then landing a blow on Russell's shoulder or back despite his clear skill.

For the most part, Russell defends brilliantly, always rolling away to give himself space or blocking another blow in the nick of time.

I never realized the depth of Russell's talent until now, as I had never really gotten the chance to see him fight. I heard him coordinate troops and lead, sure, but in terms of actually getting to see his ability—this is the first time I've had the honor.

And he's impressive.

Drew swirls the staff around his head and comes down hard on Russell's shoulder. Russell grimaces as the staff hits his skin, and I'm not quite sure if the crack I hear is the staff or Russell's bones.

Russell goes down, hitting the floor hard, and Jace doesn't give the man a moment to breathe. He lifts his staff, about to bring it down on Russell's head when the man rolls out of the way. The staff hits the ground, shattering as the resilient wood meets its match with Jace's strength.

"Jace, here," Levi says from the center ring, grabbing a staff from the many weapons at his feet and tossing it to the dojo master.

Jace snatches it out of the air, swinging it expertly as he returns instantly to the fray. The masterful movement was so seamless, so elegant, that he didn't miss a beat. He returns to the fight as if he never left, despite his destroyed weapon now laying in splinters on the floor.

Levi resumes his wide stance, arms crossed as he intently watches the fight.

Oh.

I see what he's doing, and why he's here.

I've seen that expression on his face before—he's looking for weaknesses, calculating the odds of survival for each person involved, and looking for any way to break their opponent.

It's a chilling expression. He's so focused, so ready to kill that it takes me a moment to remember he's on our side.

As the men spar, landing blow after blow against each other, I look at Harper with a playful pout. "This looks like fun. Why wasn't I invited?"

Harper laughs, her smile lighting up her face as she watches through the slits. "The trials aren't to be taken lightly, Rory. And they're never to be spoken of unless you're directly involved. Usually, we whisk someone off to aid in the trial without telling them until we even get there. That way, they can't accidentally let slip that they're involved." She shrugs. "It's nothing personal. Those three will probably tell you about it the next time you see them."

The dragon Boss rolls her eyes, and it's clear they're not supposed to. It would seem she has accepted the inevitable, however, and chosen not to fight it.

Without warning, Levi grabs a sword from the many weapons at his feet and hurls it into the fray. Drew catches it easily, tossing aside his staff in one fluid motion as he now swings the blade at Russell.

In a fluid movement that's probably mostly instinct, Russell blocks the blade with his staff. The sword slices his weapon in half, and he stands there in a momentary beat of shock.

"You cheater," he says, looking at Drew with a wry grin on his face.

"He's a Darrington," Jace says, twirling his staff around his head as he prepares to go again. "They always cheat."

Drew laughs and flips Jace the bird.

The three men chuckle as the fight continues, mostly with Russell dodging the sword blade as Jace continues to attack with a staff from the other side. Russell fights with the two broken halves of his staff, and I wonder why he hasn't asked for a replacement.

Huh. Odd.

With a hefty swing, Drew slices at Russell's stomach with enough force to gut him.

Damn. They really aren't pulling any punches—not in *this* fight.

There's too much at stake.

Russell, to his credit, doesn't need anyone to go easy on him. The man ducks Drew's attack and slides across the floor, putting space between him and his opponents so that he can finally have a few seconds of respite.

"Care to join us, Levi?" Jace asks, chest heaving as he momentarily pauses to grab his breath.

"Happy to oblige," Levi says, his voice dark and deep as he grabs a bo staff of his own off the ground. He leaps off the platform, grinning as he joins in the fun.

The three of them attack Russell in quick bursts, one after the other. It's vicious, fast, and merciless. Even though Russell takes a few blows to his shoulders and side from the staffs, he never stays down long.

"Brutal," I mutter, admittedly impressed.

"It is," Harper admits a little wistfully as she watches the fight. "There's only one rule in this trial. He can take no weapon but the one he was given, and he must go until all three of them stop."

"So, he could shift?" I point out.

"Yeah, but it's considered bad form," Harper says with a shrug. "Especially indoors. He's trying to impress Jace—and me, since the trials have secret judges the contender can't see. He knows he's being watched right now. He just doesn't know by whom."

"Who are the judges?" I ask, scanning the walls to see if I can find anyone else peeking through any other secret grates.

I can't, of course. But I can't fight the impulse to try.

"Me, Jace, Drew, Levi, and you," she says with a nod toward me. "A few others you haven't met yet."

"When were you going to tell me I'm a judge?" I ask, lifting one skeptical eyebrow.

Harper chuckles. "What do you think we're doing now?"

Fair point.

"What other trials are there?" I ask.

"I can't tell you," Harper says. "We just went over this, Rory."

"Fine. You're no fun."

"I'm a *little* fun," she says, smirking as she returns her gaze to the fight. "I can tell you this, I guess—we test him by pushing him to his absolute limits for a week straight. It's grueling. Honor, ability, intelligence, resourcefulness. The man will barely sleep over the next seven days, and that's the point. We'll push him to the limit, and it all culminates in a final exam of sorts. Something that will test his moral fiber." Harper pauses, her eyes darting toward me. "You want to help?"

"Of course. What do I need to do?"

"Just trust me," she says with a smile.

"I don't know," I say, playfully shaking my head as I set my hands on my hips. "You're a dragon Boss. I've heard they're very dangerous."

Harper laughs, returning her attention to the fight as another thundering crack echoes through the hall.

In my pocket, my phone vibrates. I pull it out to find the screen lit with Irena's name.

As a former Spectre, it's surreal and uncomfortably strange to actually have someone in my contacts, much less listed under their real name. We used burner phones and never had any contact saved. Every number had to be memorized.

Yet again, I have to remind myself that this is a different world.

"I need to take this," I say.

Harper nods, still watching the fight as I walk away from the grate, just in case they can hear me.

I hold the phone to my ear, lips parted to speak when Irena interrupts me.

"The traitors have been dealt with," she says simply, her voice grim and dark.

I pause. "Are you okay?"

"Fine," she says quickly.

Too quickly.

"Irena," I chide softly.

"I sustained a few injuries," she says, and I can practically imagine her shrugging. "Nothing major. Nothing worth telling you about."

"You know that's not what I mean."

She hesitates and a small sigh filters through the phone. "I've been better, Rory."

"Was it hard?" I ask, hoping she knows what I mean.

Was it hard to kill someone you loved?

Was it hard to look at someone who used to share her bed, and kill him? Who made her happy at a time when there was very little to be joyful about?

"Of course, it was hard," she says quietly. "Especially Benjamin." She sighs, and I hear the rustle of fabric as she leans against a wall. "But this is the kind of lover I'm used to, Rory. I never know if I can trust him or not."

"It doesn't have to be that way anymore," I point out.

"Yeah. You've definitely figured it out," she says, and I can hear the smile in her voice. "You learned how to trust. Maybe someday I can too," she says, pausing briefly.

"Eric's a good man," I point out. "He can help you with that."

"Not now, Rory," Irena says, her voice getting a little distant as her mouth moves away from the phone. "Now, listen. Zurie has some secured lines she's been using to discuss this attack the General is planning. It's pretty clear she's involved. I just need to figure out how."

My throat tightens with concern. My sister is playing with fire. "Has she spotted you?"

"She knows I'm a threat," Irena says, not really answering my question. "I'm staying ahead of her."

"I know I don't have to tell you to be careful," I say, squeezing my eyes shut with dread. "But—"

"I know. Be careful," Irena says, laughing. "I am, and I'll come back the moment things get hairy. Promise."

"Thanks." I sigh and rub my eyes. "Were any of your contacts viable and trustworthy?"

"That's a stretch, but I can at least say they're useful." She hesitates. "I won't give anyone the level of access Benjamin had. I've learned *that* lesson."

"Well, no, that's not what I meant." Out of habit, I lift my hand to stop her before this goes any further, even though she's not here to see it. "This is a new life for us both, and it's going to take a little bit of opening up and trying something new for us to really figure this out. Live a little. See how Eric makes you feel." I pause, wondering if my next suggestion is taking it too far, but I say it anyway. "Train with Harper."

"Let me handle one thing at a time," Irena says, chuckling.

"I just don't want you to run from this forever," I admit as I absently play with the ends of my hair. "Don't let this Benjamin guy keep you from being happy. Don't let Zurie's brainwashing from when we were kids keep you from accepting who you are now." I pause. "*What* you are now," I add.

Irena groans playfully. "Yes, Sensei Rory."

I roll my eyes. "Just come back to me in one piece."

"I'll try," she says, and the line goes dead.

CHAPTER TWENTY-FOUR

I n the week since Jace's announcement, it's been tough to keep myself busy. The men disappear regularly, only to come back with stories of how they've tested Russell in new and fascinating ways.

Battle strategies played out on a large scale, like a life-size game of chest.

Sparring in the mists, on the mountains, in deadly regions.

Mind games that test his resolve and his limits.

Basically, *fun,* and I'm not allowed to be a part of *any* of it.

I've been able to watch a few of the trials, giving Harper my notes and thoughts on Russell—his weaknesses and his strengths, mainly. For the most part, I simply train by myself.

The time away from the chaos is kind of nice, and I often enjoy the solitude of the late nights I spend on the back courtyard running through forms.

I keep thinking about Zurie. About Irena.

About what's coming for us all.

Irena has called me twice this week—which is a lot, given how deep she had to go into our old network of Spectre associates. Always keeping one step ahead of Zurie has been a daunting task, but Irena's capable.

She always ends every call the same way.

"Don't worry, baby sister. I'm not going to let myself get caught."

Irena's close to figuring out Zurie's plan.

I can feel it.

I just hate how close to the Ghost she's getting as she figures it out.

As the midnight moon wears on, I spin a blade over my head in the back courtyard, exhaling as I run through another familiar form. One Zurie taught me.

With my eyes peeled, I scan my periphery while I decapitate imaginary enemies, moonlight glinting off the cold steel of my sword as I spin it around me.

Tucker will be released from the medic ward tomorrow. I've been checking on him several times a day, and the poor man is bouncing off the walls, eager to get back into the fray.

I can't blame him, and I'm grateful for the dragon magic that helps me heal more quickly than I did as a human.

But that's one of the many things I love about Tucker. He reminds me of where I came from. He keeps me grounded. No matter how much dragon magic I possess, he helps me retain my humanity and keep a connection to the past, even if it's only to teach me something about the future.

There's a rustle at the top step overlooking the small courtyard I'm currently training in. I lift my blade on impulse, glaring at whoever made the sound, only to find Harper leaning against the railing above me. She watches with a small smile on her face.

"That's a kickass form," she says, nodding to the sword. "Will you teach me?"

"Maybe another time," I say, relaxing my shoulders as I look up at her. "What's going on? You're not usually up this late."

"Remember how I said I would need your help with the candidate's final exam?" she asks, casually glancing off at the mountains.

A hit of adrenaline buzzes through me and my breath quickens with anticipation. "It's time?"

Harper nods.

I grin, shaking out my shoulders. "Finally! I get to *do* something."

I jog up the stairs, bringing my sword with me. Together, we walk into the embassy and through the halls, Harper leading all the while. I casually carry the sword in my hand, the blade occasionally reflecting light against the wall as we walk through the darker hallways.

It's a little surreal to me that a Fairfax royal can be so relaxed at my side, especially when I'm armed. It's a strange feeling—a dragon Boss and a dragon assassin, walking shoulder-to-shoulder through a dragon den. Sometimes I forget she leads one of the most powerful dragon families in the world.

To me, she's not a Boss. She's just my friend.

Harper pauses at a door deep in the heart of the castle. With her hand on the knob, she hesitates, looking back at me with a strange expression on her face. One I don't entirely recognize.

"You trust me, right?" Harper asks. "You know I'll never let any harm come to you? No matter what the situation may seem like?"

I hesitate, my intuition flaring slightly at the odd phrasing. There's something off in the question, something leading, and I wonder what exactly this test is going to be.

But this is *Harper*. Time and time again, she's looked out for me. For Jace. Even for Irena.

"Yeah," I say with a small nod. "I think by now you've earned that."

Harper smiles, genuine gratitude on her face as her eyes wrinkle slightly with appreciation. The door swings open, and she leads me into the room.

There's a chair against the far wall with latches and iron embedded in the wood. It reminds me a little bit of an electric chair with its Spartan appearance. Iron orbs sit on the armrests, and it takes me a moment to recognize the same cuffs that Ian put on me are bolted to the chair.

The cuffs that dampened my and Jace's magic until I shattered them both.

I hesitate by the exit as Harper shuts the door behind us.

"That had better be for Russell," I say, nodding toward it. "Not me."

"I'm sorry, Rory," Harper says, her brows twisting slightly upward as she pats the backrest. "This is part of his exam."

"What's the plan, Harper?" I ask, my eyes narrowing in suspicion, not liking this at all.

I expect her to instantly answer. To dismiss my concerns with a wave of her hand.

Instead, she looks at me with a strange sort of disappointment on her face, like I failed *her* test of *me*.

Even if I did, I don't care.

I set my hands on my hips and roll my shoulders back, chin lifted slightly in defiance. This is the sort of situation that could go downhill fast, and it is *not* too much for me to expect her to explain what she plans to do before I go sitting in a chair that could dampen my magic and keep me contained.

"I'm not supposed to tell you," she says, tapping her foot a little bit as she bites her lip. "I can't tell you what the test is or he might be able to pick up on the reality of what's going on, Rory. I—ugh." She hesitates, her jaw tensing as she massages her temples and struggles to figure out what she wants to say. "Look, Rory. I need to test Russell's greed. I'm sorry, but that's all I can tell you. Please. I *need* you to trust me."

I frown, studying her big green eyes as they slowly dart between mine.

Eventually, I just sigh in frustration.

"Fine," I concede. "But I swear to the gods themselves that if this gets weird, I'm going to beat your *ass*. You hear me?"

A soft laugh escapes her as she taps the backrest of the chair again. "Fair enough."

I sit in the chair, hating every moment of this. My dragon curls in discomfort, though it's thankfully not in warning. My dragon's not scared, but she *really* hates this.

Me, too, babe, I think. *Me, too.*

I tense slightly as Harper slides my hands into the cuffs bolted to the chair.

With a sweet and comforting smile over her shoulder, Harper leaves. For several minutes, I'm alone in the room. I keep fidgeting, unable to sit still in the uncomfortable wooden chair, and sweat pools across my palms as my fingers graze the inside of the iron cuffs. My nails drag along the metal, and I grit my teeth in irritation and discomfort.

I don't like this at all.

Just to test the cuffs, I summon my magic. White light pools across my skin, but it's harder to reach than usual. It's like I'm drunk and can't quite touch the ribbons of light within me, the ones that are the source of all my power.

This is—well, different than the cuffs Ian put on me. My magic's there, it's just distant. Like the cuffs aren't quite working right.

I grit my teeth through the strange sensations, forcing the magic to come to me, asking it to obey. After a while, it does. The cuffs vibrate as I pull my magic in my palms, shuddering like they might break at any moment.

But they hold.

I let out a slow breath, releasing the magic, and the vibration slowly stops. I shattered one pair, and if I have to, it's comforting to know I can shatter another.

I close my eyes, bracing myself, trying to remind myself that this is just a test. A test for someone *else*, for that matter. Not me.

After what feels like an eternity, Harper finally opens the door again, and this time she leads Russell inside. There's no smiling. No light in her eyes. She frowns slightly, a forceful intensity in her gaze as she looks at me and slams the door behind them.

She's in Boss Mode.

The test is on. She's serious. No laughter. No light-hearted banter.

Even though I hate this chair with a passion, I put my game face on, too. It's the focused glare I don anytime I'm on a mission and prepared to kill.

And I give Russell the brunt of it.

My jaw tenses slightly as I glare at them both, my eyes darting from one to the other as the silence wears on.

Russell tenses as his gaze washes over me, and he takes an unconscious step toward the door. I can tell he doesn't like this, either. He isn't sure what's happening, but to him, this doesn't look good.

"What is this, Miss Fairfax?" he asks, narrowing his eyes slightly as he looks at the Boss.

Despite the situation, it's so strange to hear him call her that. The rules and laws of the embassy are that he can't use her title—in the dojo, everyone is *Miss* or *Mister*. Formality reins, and everyone's equal.

Even down here, with no one else watching but the two of us, he's an incredibly respectful and formal man.

Harper crosses her arms, leans against the wall, and nods lazily toward me. "Kill her."

"What?!" Russell and I shout in unison.

I pull against the bindings holding me to the chair, my hands curling into fists within the iron cuffs that keep my magic at bay. The heavy, icy sensation of dread sinks clear to my toes, weighing me down as a surge of adrenaline darts through me.

What the hell kind of test is this?

I summon my magic again, and even though the iron cuffs tremble beneath my power, the chair manages to keep it at bay. The magic burns in my veins, pushing the limits of the chair.

I know this is supposed to be a test, but it feels remarkably real.

There's no way this is how I die.

Russell squares his shoulders, his mouth set in a grim line as he looks at his Boss—at the woman who runs the family he's belonged to all his life. "That would make Jace go feral," he says, his brows furrowing as he glares at her. "There's so much wrong with that order."

"Jace had his chance," Harper says flatly, looking at her fingernails. "He betrayed us, Russell. A Fairfax general serves for life, with no greater love than the family. That's the law, and he broke it." Her gaze shifts toward Russell, her glare heavy and intense. "He's a criminal, Russell, and a selfish one at that. He betrayed *you*. He betrayed *all* of you. Now, I can't kill him outright, but if he goes feral…" She trails off, nodding subtly toward me once again to hint at what she's trying to do.

I pull on the straps keeping me in place, the leather and metal straining to keep me at bay.

"You can't be serious," I say practically snarling.

"She's your friend," Russell says, his brow twisting upward as he looks between me and Harper.

"Friends are for children," Harper says flatly. "I got what I wanted. Now it's time to cash it in." She studies Russell's face, calm and composed despite the horrible things she's saying. "Now, *kill* her."

"This isn't what we stand for," Russell says, pointing at the ground to emphasize what he's saying. "This embassy is built on the idea of protecting those who need it. Of being a refuge and a force for good."

"And I'm giving you a chance to control it," Harper says, lifting her chin defiantly. "I'm giving you power. Authority. Running this dojo is your lifelong dream, isn't it?" She takes a few steps toward him, her hips swaying in a sultry and seductive manner as she looks him dead in the eye. "If you do this—if you kill her—I will give you everything your heart desires. Fame. Honor. Infamy. Only you and I will ever know about this little... *mess* down here."

She hesitates, and from this angle, I can't see her expression anymore.

But I *can* see Russell's.

His square jaw tenses as he looks at her with a strange expression I've never seen on his face before.

Desire.

For her.

Oh, *shit*.

I don't know how I missed it before—how I missed the subtle twinge of need in his gaze when he looks at her. Maybe he's learned to expertly hide it over the years. Perhaps he only betrays it on his face when he's pushed to his limits.

The fact is, Russell wants her. Despite his ability to mask his desires, it's suddenly very clear to me that he wants her *badly*.

That he might even do anything for her.

Like kill me.

"No human should have that much magic," Harper whispers, and I can barely hear her as she leans toward Russell. "The dragon vessel has brought us nothing but pain and misery and the threat of war." She circles him, letting the silence settle between them as his gaze shifts toward me.

Gods above, he's actually considering it.

She pauses beside him, the two Fairfax dragons watching me as tension crackles through the room.

And there, the bait is set.

Now, all we have left to do is wait to see what will happen next.

"Kill her," Harper says for the last time. "I need to watch her die."

I study Harper's face warily, looking for the tells of a lie. Practically *begging* to find one.

And—there, at the corner of her mouth, I finally see it. The lie. Her lips twitch slightly, almost imperceptibly, and that's all I needed.

Oh, thank the gods.

This really is just a test.

She's lying. This whole Boss Mode experience, the order to kill me—it's all a show. A farce. She doesn't really want me dead, but damn—she's one hell of an actress.

Russell squares his shoulders, and it's clear he bought the play she's putting on. I caught the lie on her face, but he didn't.

He thinks this is real.

The candidate for dojo master studies me, his eyes narrowing as he barely breathes. He's clearly going through a horrible internal ordeal, battling the commands of his Boss—the woman he adores—with his own honor and values.

"No," he says quietly, still looking at me.

Harper wrinkles her nose in disgust, really selling this. "What did you say to me?"

"I said *no!*" he barks, his voice tense and commanding as he glares at her. "No honorable man or leader would ever do that, and if that's what it takes to be the general of this place—if that's what Jace had to do to get to where he is now—I want nothing to do with it."

Harper squares her shoulders, glaring at him as they stare each other down. Her eyes drift lightly over him as she lets the silence stretch on, daring him to change his mind.

"Then I guess we're done," she says darkly. "You've spent the week pushing your limits, torturing yourself, nearly killing yourself twice. Just to turn this down."

"That's right," he says quietly, his fingers curling into fists at his side.

He radiates regret.

Disgust.

Disappointment.

But this is his boundary. His line. The one thing he won't compromise for anyone.

Not even her.

The tense silence carries for another moment or two until Harper lets out a slow breath and smiles broadly. "Thank the gods because I did not want to go through all that again with someone else!"

Russell, to his credit, leans slightly backward, his brows furrowing in confusion as he studies the Boss's face.

Harper looks at me, beaming. But her smile falls as our eyes meet.

"Why are you mad, girl?" she asks, genuinely baffled. "I told you it was a test. Look, the cuffs aren't even really working." She pulls a small remote out of her pocket and taps a button on it. The cuffs and handles around my wrists and arms loosen, letting me free.

That was too similar to my encounter with Ian. It was too wounding—to have a friend even feign betraying my trust like that.

I wriggle out of the restraints, rubbing my wrists as I stare her down. I take a few menacing steps toward her, still fuming from the grueling experience she just put me through, all with barely any warning.

Russell steps protectively in front of her, but Harper sets a hand on his arm and gently moves him aside so that she and I can face each other.

I narrow my eyes at her, still rubbing my wrists from where the iron had dug into my skin. "You're such an asshole," I bark at her. "And if you ever do something like this to me again, I will hit you. Hard."

Harper lifts an eyebrow skeptically, a wry smile on her face as she watches me. "Oh, come on. That was fun."

I shake my head, my lips parting slightly as the adrenaline begins to fade now that the threat is gone. I can't deny how much of a rush that really was.

Despite myself, I chuckle, and she laughs along with me.

The two of us—we must be crazy.

But, yeah, I have to admit—that was a little fun.

Russell lets out a slow breath, finally relaxing.

"Russell," Harper says, looking up at the man beside

us. "You are an incredible candidate. Honorable, noble, skilled, patient, and above all, you're a good and right-eous person." She shakes Russell's hand, her fingers tiny compared to his. "I nominate you as my general."

He grins, clearly baffled, like he can't quite believe what she said. "I passed?"

"With flying colors," Harper admits, setting a hand on his shoulder. "There's just one thing left to do."

He nods, rolling out his shoulders with excitement. "I'm ready."

I watch the two of them, grateful this whole ordeal is over. I'm ready for the announcement, too, because the moment it comes, Jace will be free.

He will be mine.

CHAPTER TWENTY-FIVE

I sit on the roof of my tower, my arms around my knees as I suck in a deep breath and enjoy the sky. This is as close as I can get to flying until I finally shift.

Someday.

Someday, I'll fly.

Dragons swirl overhead, trailing and snapping at each other as they soar through the clouds. There's a celebratory buzz in the air, full of adrenaline and energy, and it reminds me of the festivals I used to sometimes slink through when on a mission.

Sometimes, Zurie would send me to tail someone through a carnival or even an occasional wedding. I never got to enjoy the party itself—never got to be a part of the reverie—but it was at least fun to watch other people be happy.

This time, however much I want to let my guard down and celebrate with the rest of them, all I can think about is my former mentor. She's been silent for too long, and that never bodes well for me.

Until she's dead, I can't bring myself to truly relax. Until she and I face off for the last time, there really is nothing to celebrate. To relax right now would be to let my guard down.

I can't afford to do that, not with Zurie out for blood.

I can, however, enjoy watching the Fairfax Dragons have fun.

A dragon above me lets out a mighty barrel of flame into the sky, and heat rolls over me from the flame even though it's a hundred feet or so above me. The dragons around him roar, cheering for the fire as he spins through the air, showing off.

Everyone can't wait to find out who the candidate is. Today is his final test, and if he passes, he will be their general.

Naturally, I've been kept entirely in the dark as to what the last test could be. The Fairfax family sure love their secret traditions and clandestine rituals, but I guess that's part of the fun.

I lean back on the roof with my palms against the tiles as I stretch out my neck. It's bizarre how much I like this dojo, how much I consider the embassy to be my home. I spent my entire life moving around from place to place, from safehouse to safehouse, and I thought that's how it would always be.

Just me, my sister, and our mentor, darting from place to place with whatever we can carry or steal.

Despite myself, I try not to think of the embassy as home. I can't, not really. With the mounting political pressure, it's just not fair to the Fairfax family for me to stay much longer.

Drew said he was finding information on Ashgrave —figuring out if the ancient home of the dragon gods is even real. If it *is* real, we also need to know if it's safe. If it's functional.

We've had so much on our minds that the hunt for Ashgrave has taken a backseat to the chaos. However, I think it's time we dig a little deeper.

After all, Jace won't be the dojo master anymore after today. There's no reason for us to remain here.

I frown, fighting a surge of both excitement and sadness.

What a strange thought.

The rustle of fabric against skin catches my attention, and I tilt my head as two strong hands grip the edge of the roof. Drew pulls himself onto the shingles, flashing me that devilish grin of his as our eyes meet. "I figured you were up here brooding."

Gods, not this again.

I laugh. "Ass."

He chuckles and sits down next to me, planting a rough kiss on the side of my head. "Are you ready for today?"

"As I'll ever be," I admit, closing my eyes to drink in the warm sun.

"It's starting soon. Harper had chairs brought out to the balcony, so I guess we get the VIP seating," Drew says, and I hear him stretch out on the tiles. "We'll have a better view of the fight."

"Oh, so the final test is a fight?" I ask. "Harper mentioned that her final test to become the Boss was a duel, but I wasn't sure if it would be different for Russell. No one's really told me anything."

"You and me both," he says with a scoff. "I did manage to find out a little bit about it though."

"Of course you did," I say, grinning.

He laughs. "Our contender will have to face off with someone the soldiers respect. He's already passed the formal trials, but this is more for them than him. It's a final proof of fortitude, to defeat someone they admire and prove that he deserves the title of their general."

"I think the Fairfax dragons just like competing," I admit.

"That too," Drew says, chuckling.

He sets his strong hand on my lower back, slipping his fingers beneath my shirt. The warm touch of his fingertips against my skin shoots tendrils of desire through me, distracting me from the beautiful day around us. A surge of lust warms the space between my thighs, and I impulsively stiffen as his touch trails up my spine, tender and teasing.

It's not fair how easily he can push my buttons. How easily he turns me on.

I peek out the corner of my eye to jokingly glare at him, only to find him smirking with his eyes shut as he pretends not to notice how my body's reacting to him.

This man knows exactly what he does to me, and he enjoys every minute of it.

He grips my waist possessively, his strong fingers pressing against my skin in a dominating way that suggests he has a few ideas of how we can pass the time before the fight begins.

I almost laugh in disbelief. We have maybe fifteen, twenty minutes tops before this begins, and that's not nearly enough time for him to have his way with me.

I'm tempted to straddle him, and it's hard to

refrain. Denying him what he wants is the best way to tease him, and it's high time I get him back.

As his fingertips possessively rove over my spine, he takes a deep breath. "Brett's on the move," he says, trying to turn me on while simultaneously distracting me.

Gods, this man is such a tease.

"It seems like he's rallying troops," Drew continues. "And the more I look into it, the more certain I am he and Zurie are somehow working together."

"Irena confirmed that," I admit.

He gasps, exaggerating the sound as he watches me with wide eyes. "Are you keeping *secrets* from me, woman?"

I laugh and push him playfully. "I wouldn't if I'd *seen* you at all this past week. You were always off having too much fun."

"Fair point," he says, shrugging. "What else did she say?"

"Not much," I confess. "We've been chatting when she can call me, but Zurie hasn't given a lot away." It's difficult to ignore the way his fingertips tease the edge of my underwear, but I manage to give a convincing show of absently looking off into the clouds. "It just seems doubtful. Last time they worked together, everything went south. We nearly killed them all."

"The General really hates you, Rory," Drew points out, his tone shifting.

He presses his palm flat against my back in a way that's more comforting than possessive, and I hear the twinge of warning in his tone. I look over my shoulder to find him already studying my face, his mouth a grim line as he watches me with concern.

I want to tell him that I'll be careful. That I'm safe. That there's no way I'll let the General or Zurie touch me or the men I love.

For some reason, however, the words die in my throat as I drink in his intense and doting expression.

After all we've been through, I take the moment to simply watch him. To enjoy him. To love that he's here with me and on my side. To know that no matter what comes our way, he will be there fighting beside me.

I open my mouth to finally say something, but as I do, his gaze darts behind me. I look over my shoulder to find the dragons beginning to land along the wall surrounding the center courtyard, while soldiers still in their human forms fill much of the space below. The bodies along the black stone leave a large circle that I suspect will act as our arena for the day.

"It's starting," Drew says, lifting his hand off my back. A cold chill washes over the space he was touching, and I'm a little sad to see his hand leave my skin.

But we have a fight to watch.

He and I slip through the window and jog downstairs toward the balcony. Before long, we walk into the parlor to find Levi and Tucker already sitting in two of the five chairs set out on the terrace.

Bandages stick out from the sleeve of Tucker's shirt as he looks over his shoulder at me and grins widely. His eyes are clearer than they have been all week, and it would seem he's finally off the heavy pain meds.

"Glad you two finally decided to join us," he quips. "We saved you a seat, Rory," he adds, patting the empty chair between him and Levi.

I shoot Drew a playful look as I take the seat.

The fire dragon sets a hand over his heart, letting out a mocking gasp as he pretends to be offended. "After all I've done for you, woman, this is how you betray me?"

I laugh and nod to the seat next to Tucker. "Quit being a baby."

"Yeah, Drew," Tucker says, patting the seat. "I have love enough for two!"

Drew chuckles and shakes his head, sitting in the chair as he shoots one last mischievous glance at me.

My eyes rove the seats on the terrace, and I confess I'm surprised to find only five chairs instead of six. I figured Harper and Jace would be up here already, but neither are around.

That would suggest they're going to be in the arena, but even that doesn't quite make sense. I thought only *one* person was to fight Russell.

"Where's Harper and Jace?" I ask.

"I'm not sure," Drew admits, looking around. "Harper was up here when I last spoke with her."

"Think they'll be fighting?" Levi asks with a nod to the arena.

"Nah," Drew says, shaking his head. "They've already sparred R—" He stops abruptly from saying Russell's name, briefly glancing around to see if anyone overheard. "Our *contender* dozens of times this week."

"But never as dragons," Levi points out.

Drew tilts his head as if he hadn't considered that yet. "That's true."

"It sounds like I missed a ton of fun," Tucker says, pouting.

"You and me both," I mumble, crossing my arms. "These guys got all the fun."

"Says the *judge*," Levi adds with a grin, calling me out.

"I gave Harper a few pointers and comments," I say, shrugging. "Nothing major."

Drew snorts derisively. "Harper created three tests purely based on your feedback from the first *day*," Drew says, lifting his eyebrows. "You know that, right?"

Huh.

I didn't, actually. That's kind of flattering.

Below us, the thud of wooden doors slamming against stone cuts through the courtyard. Footsteps echo off the stairs, and moments later, Harper appears below us, walking through the crowd as they part for her.

The Fairfax Boss steps into the open circle at the middle of the soldiers and lifts her hands in welcome. "Our contender has passed with flying colors," she says, her voice echoing off the stone. "I am pleased to give you all your candidate for master of the dojo—Russell Kane!"

Below us, the thundering cheer of soldiers shakes the very stone beneath us. The dragons along the wall roar in welcome as Russell appears on the stairs below us, the crowd parting for him as he walks toward Harper in the center of the ring.

Footsteps behind us catch my attention, and I look over my shoulder to find Jace entering the room.

"Are you all ready for this?" he asks with a nod outside.

"We thought you were going to be in the ring," Drew says, ignoring Jace's question. "Is it going to be Harper, then?"

"Nope," Jace says playfully with a quick glance at me.

I narrow my eyes skeptically, wondering what he's playing at.

Because this is *Jace.*

He's up to *something.* It's just a given.

Jace leans against the balcony railing, ignoring the chair that's been set out for him as the crowd cheers around us. "Russell's been a favorite captain of pretty much everyone here for as long as he's had the role," Jace says crossing his arms. "Steady promotions, beloved by all. We even went through the Academy together. Same year."

"The Academy?" I ask.

"The capital's military school," Jace explains. "Every winter we would train here in the snow to stretch our abilities and skills. He and I practically grew up here," Jace says with a nod to Russell as he enters the center of the ring. "He will make a great leader."

Even so, the soldiers need to see him as an equal to Jace or else they might not remain, and they might not follow him. Russell's undergone intense trials this week, but I figure this last one is the most important of all—not because of the people in the ring, but because of the people in the audience.

"Now for the final test!" Harper's voice booms over the din. "To face and win against a master of the art. The final fight!" she adds, lifting her fist in the air.

Applause and roars thunder through the courtyard, booming and almost impossibly loud as Russell rolls out his shoulders, ready for his opponent.

But he's nervous—that much is obvious. To me, anyway. Even from here, I can see the subtle fidgeting. Even with his considerable skill, he knows this will be savage.

And considering that Jace is most certainly up to some sort of mischief, Russell absolutely *should* be apprehensive about the final test headed his way.

"It's strange to think I won't be the dojo master after today," Jace says a little wistfully, looking at me. "That this is it."

"It's fine," I say, grinning playfully. "I'll find ways to keep you busy."

Jace laughs, as do Tucker, Levi and Drew. Jace leans forward and plants a kiss on my cheek before standing on the railing.

Below, heads turn toward him as he spreads his arms wide. It takes a minute for everyone to realize what's about to happen, but the moment they do, the crowd roars even louder.

"You're so dramatic," I chide Jace.

He did this on purpose—letting us wonder who would go into the ring, even though we suspected all along it would be him.

My thunderbird looks over his shoulder at me and winks. "Let me have my fun."

He jumps off the railing, and I lean over, fully expecting to see him land gracefully on the stairs below.

By the time I peek over the railing, however, he has already shifted. His claws dig into the stone stairs, his wings stretching over the crowd. He roars into the sky and lets loose a fierce blast of crackling blue magic that cuts through the clouds above.

In the arena, Russell stiffens. His face goes a little pale, and I wonder if he truly didn't see this coming. As Drew said, Russell had been sparring pretty much all week with Jace, but it would seem they don't fight in their dragon form very often.

It's clear he fiercely respects Jace, and the current dojo master isn't really one to tap out.

If I didn't know better, it would seem like this was a fight to the death. A victory against Jace Goodwin has to be hard won.

Whatever happens next, I know in my heart it's going to be merciless.

Harper shifts into her beautiful lilac dragon, the violet scales glistening in the bright sun as she paces the edge of the arena. Jace soars into the open circle in the middle of the courtyard and slowly paces the edge, his eyes on Russell in the center.

Harper gently brushes her wing against the edge of Jace's, and I figure she just told him something through the subtle and silent connection dragons share in their primal forms. He nods even as he watches Russell, and she takes that as her answer.

Apparently satisfied, she leaps onto the stretch of wall that towers over the front gate and sits there with her wings spread, watching the two men in the center.

It would seem she's going to be referee.

She shoots a blast of magic into the air, and it explodes above us like a firework.

The start of the fight.

Russell's form shimmers and twists in the center ring as he shifts as well. His body morphs as he allows his jet-black dragon to take over, his scales dark as night. His broad, angled wings glow with a subtle, golden magic—as do the vibrant golden stripes along his legs and face.

As he takes his first steps in the arena in his dragon

form, his body glows with warm light. His chest and wings shimmer with magic as bright and brilliant as the sun.

He's—he's a *thunderbird.*

I had no idea.

I lean forward. This is going to be *good.*

The two warriors circle each other, their chests rumbling with fury and fire as they prepare for their duel.

Russell attacks first.

He snaps, teeth sharp as daggers, barely missing Jace's head as Jace dodges out of the way. My thunderbird slides across the ground, his claws digging up the black tile as he avoids a second attack from the razor-sharp teeth and powerful claws of Russell's dragon. Sparks dance along Russell's skin as he coils, ready to spring again, and it's clear that magic is fair game in this fight.

Russell shoots a blast of crackling light at Jace, but yet again, Jace is faster. The magic shatters the wall behind him as he ducks out of the way. Black rock spews into the air, shattering to dust from the fury of Russell's attack.

Jace snarls, blue light burning in the back of his throat as he prepares an attack of his own. It simmers and surges, barely contained as he waits for the right moment to spring.

Russell snarls, diving toward the dojo master, and Jace lets his magic free. Russell dodges it, and the magic flies into the air.

Holy shit.

Jace *missed*.

Russell is even better than I realized.

They dig into each other, firing blasts of magic at each other's chests as their claws draw blood. Their tails and wings cut through the air, powerful and fierce.

Never stopping.

Never slowing.

Barely pausing for even a breath.

Every now and then they pull away, pacing in a slow circle as they wait for another chance to strike.

This is the deadly dance of two masters, and neither appears willing to give in. For Russell, everything is on the line—everything he's worked for, everything he's ever wanted.

Jace, on the other hand, fights for his legacy. This is how he will be remembered. More importantly than even that, though, is what this battle means for Russell —Jace can't be merciful here. He fights for Russell, to make sure that those in the dojo honor the man's word as law.

For him to be the dojo master, it must be fully and completely earned.

I lose track of time as they dig into each other again and again. Puddles of blood stain the cracked black stone across the courtyard, gleaming each time the sun glints off the surface of the blood freely spilled in this match.

The two dragons' chests begin to heave as they start to tire, but neither backs down. The crowd watches breathlessly, tensing with every blow that lands, with every attack that draws blood, with every blast of magic.

It's a ruthless final battle.

Something shifts in Jace. I can see it in the way his eyes dilate and the way his nose wrinkles as he snarls with every breath. He charges at Russell, who meets him head-on.

They dig their claws into each other's shoulders. The claws rip apart their thick scales, drawing even more blood as they growl and snap at each other.

Russell digs his teeth into the base of Jace's neck and launches into the air, carrying Jace into the sky as Jace digs his claws into Russell's hide. Both men spread their wings, magic brewing in their throats.

Yellow and blue—sunshine and night—the magic of the most fearsome warriors on the planet.

A crackling blast of blue magic soars from Jace's throat, hitting Russell on his back. Russell roars in pain, releasing Jace impulsively as he tries to recover from the surge of agony. They both soar away from each other, blood dripping from their claws and teeth to the ground below.

A slow roar begins to build in the crowd, and I feel it too.

The final blow.

The deciding moment.

Jace's body hums with light and power. His veins glow, and I can see a massive blast of magic brewing in his chest.

Not to be outdone, Russell summons his own magic. Yellow sparks fizz across his skin as his body hums and glows.

They hover in the air, evenly matched, aiming their deadly magic at each other.

Jace fires first, but Russell isn't far behind. The rays of light crackle and sizzle through the air, aimed at each other.

The two beams collide.

An explosion rocks the courtyard, shooting heat and air past all of us. I squeeze my eyes shut hastily as the force of the blow kicks dust across the crowd and cuts through my hair.

A brilliant white light engulfs the world, and for a moment, I can't see. My ears ring in the sudden silence.

When the blinding light clears, both dragons are on the ground in the center of the arena, panting heavily. Their skin smokes and smolders as their chests heave. They're spent from the fight, each of them having pushed themselves to the absolute limit.

The silence that follows is deafening.

No one moves. No one breathes. No one speaks.

We simply wait.

As the two dragons stand in the arena, exhausted but ready to go again, their wings curling slightly with every heavy breath, Jace lifts his head. His intense gaze —all of his focus—is trained entirely on Russell.

The blue glow recedes from Jace's throat as he calls his magic back.

Russell hesitates, the yellow glow of his own magic still burning bright in his throat as he waits to see what will happen next. I suspect he wonders if this is perhaps a trick, or merely some technique he's unfamiliar with.

Good. A dojo master should always be ready to fight, even if he suspects his adversary is done.

Because I know the truth.

Jace relaxes his shoulders, and after a moment longer of pausing and watching his opponent, gently bows his head in surrender.

Russell relaxes, his dragon letting out a hearty sigh of relief.

Russell won.

Harper roars into the sky, declaring Russell the new general of the dragon dojo as the crowd erupts with cheers.

Jace stands, watching Russell proudly as the new master of the dojo bows his head in thanks to the man who mentored and taught him all these years.

My thunderbird tucks his wings at his side, and his head tilts toward me. I lean toward him in disbelief and joy, and I can practically see him smiling.

Just like that, he's free—and *mine*.

CHAPTER TWENTY-SIX

As evening falls, the celebration of Russell's promotion echoes through the hallways. Drinking songs float through every corridor, and I'm honestly a bit surprised at the sheer number of soldiers that stumble up and down stairways without falling to their deaths.

But these are dragons, and if anyone can handle a bit of heavy drinking, it's them.

I lean against the railing of the balcony adjacent to Jace's suite, and it's strange to think this is the last time we'll be in here. It is reserved for the dojo master after all, and Jace is starting a new life with me.

He leans against the balcony beside me, listening to the celebration as it filters through every window and clamors across every path below. One of the trails below us curves toward the dining area, and three men stumble across it, unable to walk in a straight line as they try to maneuver their way back to the kitchens for more beer. With their arms around each other, they manage to vaguely move in the right direction, and I figure they should probably be cut off.

That said, no one seems interested in stopping the party tonight.

I laugh as one of the men hiccups and falls backward, landing in the grass beside the trail as he stares up at the sky. His eyelids are half closed, and there's a drunken smirk on his face as he hiccups again.

I chuckle at their shenanigans, and at his two friends as they try and fail to get him back on his feet. They tug on his hands, but the man won't move.

Jace laughs, looking over the railing at the three of them. "From that, you'd never realize those are three of the most capable fighters on the planet," he says, shaking his head as he rests his forearms against the railing. "All of them are on Squad Two."

I snort. "No way, really?"

He nods. "They went into the storage facility with us and Rodgers down there saved my ass when you were off fighting Diesel."

Jace flashes an annoyed glare at me, but his proud little smirk gives him away.

He loved it—watching me fight.

"That's a Fairfax dragon for you," he continues with a shrug as he nods toward the three of them. "They can take on ten fighters at once and then drink anyone under the table right after. Just don't ask them to get up the next morning."

I grin as they finally get their friend up on his feet and slowly maneuver in the vague direction of the kitchens once again.

"They deserve this," Jace says with a broad smile. "This party. This time off. They've earned it."

I scan the horizon as the drinking songs start up again, echoing through the corridors below. "This would be the perfect night for an ambush," I point out. "Distracted soldiers. Guards are down. It would make sense for Zurie to attack, if she's paying attention— and she's *always* paying attention."

Jace grins, his gaze sweeping over me briefly. "You're so depressing."

"Oh, you've thought of it too," I say, casting a playful sidelong glare at him.

"Of course, I have," he admits with a shrug. "This celebration is my parting gift to Russell. One last night where he doesn't have anything to worry about, before he takes on the full responsibility of an army and the safety of a nation. I have my best soldiers along the perimeter, keeping watch the whole night."

"Is that where Tucker, Levi, and Drew are?" I ask.

Jace nods. "We didn't tell you because we figured you would want to go."

"You're right," I say, chiding him as I quirk an eyebrow,

He grins. "I know. But I wanted you to have this too. A night off."

I try and fail to hide the small smile playing at the edge of my lips, but I have to admit I'm kind of grateful. It's a sweet gesture, something I'm grateful the four of them decided on together, even if I didn't get any say in that.

They made a choice for me, but they had good intentions.

I'll allow it—this time.

"So, Tucker, Levi, and Drew are among your best soldiers, huh?" I nudge him playfully, trying to get him to admit it.

Jace laughs. "Don't you dare tell them I said that. I'll deny it if you do. I can't have their egos getting any bigger."

"Not Drew's anyway," I admit with a grin.

"With them watching the perimeter, I can sleep soundly and know nothing will get in or out. So, the dojo can relax—if only for this evening," He hesitates. "So, *you* can relax."

I smile. "I don't know if I can relax, Jace, but that was a kind gift to give Russell." I pause, intentionally brushing my arm against his as I look up at him. "I kind of expected you to be out there too, though."

With an exaggerated sigh, he stands and wraps his arms around me, pinning me to the railing. It's a swift and sudden movement, and before I know it, I'm engulfed. My back hits his hard chest as he holds the railings, enveloping me with his body. He brings his mouth to my ear and gently nips at my jaw, sending an electric current of desire clear down my neck and into my core.

"I was tempted," he says, "but I had a previous engagement planned for this evening."

I grin, letting my eyes flutter closed as I just enjoy the sensation of his touch. My body crackles with lust and energy, and I unconsciously lean into him, my dragon shivering with glee at how close he is.

Familiar laughter carries through the air, carefree and relaxed. I impulsively turn toward it, surprised to hear Harper so close by.

She and Russell share a balcony below us and off to the side, their view overlooking the misty ravine as they talk in hushed tones. Russell gestures wildly as he tells whatever story he's telling, and with each gesture, Harper laughs a little harder. Both of them hold glasses, occasionally sipping the brown liquid inside.

That girl sure likes her whiskey.

As Russell finishes his story, he looks out at the ravine, and in that moment, Harper watches him with deep affection. It's playful and light-hearted, but all the more meaningful because she thinks he isn't watching her face. I manage to catch the moment where she lets her guard down—the sort of moment where the truth is undeniable and obvious.

I've seen that look before, and I recognize it instantly.

It's the way my men look at me.

The way I look at them.

And just like that, what I saw in Russell's face when I was strapped to that wooden and iron chair—it's confirmed.

These two want each other. Badly.

"I hope they get a happy ending," I admit, watching the two of them as they stand in a moment of silence, looking out at the ravine.

Jace snorts. "What? Them? No, they're just friends, Rory."

I twist around to look at him like he's blind because he has to be to miss those signals. He frowns at the expression on my face and looks again, studying Harper's features as if he's somehow going to be able to prove his point.

"No, they're... It's just..." He trails off as he stares at them, really studying them this time, his eyes narrowing in disbelief the longer he watches.

"Gods above—they're absolutely into each other," he mutters. "When the hell did that happen?"

"See?" I say, gesturing toward them, basking in how freaking *right* I am.

"That's just weird," Jace admits, holding me a little tighter as he watches them. "They grew up together. I always thought of them as—I don't know. Related, maybe. Not romantically interested in each other. When they were kids, they fought like siblings."

"They're not kids anymore," I say, smirking as Harper throws back the last of her bourbon.

Russell leads Harper inside, pausing at the door so she can enter first, and I wonder if my friend's going to get lucky tonight.

"They shouldn't really indulge their affection for each other," Jace says quietly, setting his hand on the railing again as he leans into me once more. He peppers a few kisses on the back of my neck.

"Why not?" I ask, my heart hurting a little as I think

about Harper denying herself of something she so obviously wants.

"As a general rule, the dojo master shouldn't indulge romance," Jace admits. "That's why I fought this for so long. Why I fought against you," he confesses with an apologetic kiss behind my ear. "That said, it's sometimes permitted On occasion, the dojo master can even keep his position and have a family. But for Russell to fall in love with Harper..." Jace trails off, pausing to take a deep breath as he holds me tighter. "That could pose problems down the line, but it's hard to know for sure. After all, it's his duty to protect the Fairfax family. To protect *her.*"

The conversation lulls as our minds wander, and another surge of drinking songs echo through the air. Someone probably brought out another round of beer.

"I don't like this, Jace," I admit as my mind wanders yet again to my former mentor. "You do realize that the longer we hear nothing from Zurie, the worse her attack is going to be? It means she's mobilizing. Planning. Preparing."

"Of course," he says calmly. "I have every available soldier working on it day and night, some even monitoring the chatter during this celebration, when they should be off drinking. They volunteered for it, Rory —they want her dead as much as you and I do. We're doing everything we can to find her. To figure out what her plans are."

I don't answer. I can't, not with the possibilities buzzing around in my brain.

All the ways she can kill us.

All the things she wants to do—to me. To Irena. To the men I love.

I won't let her.

"You need to relax," Jace says in my ear, his voice a sultry growl as his hands grip my shoulders. "I've handled everything. Taken *every* precaution. So, take just *one* night, Rory. One night away from the dread and brainstorming. One night away from the obsessive brooding—and you can obsess to your heart's content tomorrow morning."

I snort derisively. "I don't *brood* nearly as much as you and Drew try to make it seem like I do."

Jace chuckles, gently biting my neck as his hands wander down the sides of my body. Sparks of desire and need burst through me beneath his touch, aching for more.

His fingers reach the hem of my pants, and he inches his strong hands past the fabric, sliding along my bare skin as he takes what's his. His hands press against my thighs, his thumb brushing ruthlessly along my entrance, and I suck in a deep breath of surprise.

"Tease," I say breathlessly.

"It doesn't have to be a tease," he says into my ear, his voice low and deep. He kisses the crook of my neck, his warm mouth exploring my body as his fingers glide between my legs, tormenting me with the possibilities of what else they can do.

Of what he's capable of.

No—I *should* be focused on Zurie.

I *should* call Irena.

But the longer he touches me, the more my magic swirls and buzzes through my blood. The more my dragon rumbles. The more I lean into him, my mind going blank.

As my dragon gets her way, I find myself relaxing into him. I gently press my hips forward and arch my back to give him better access. His strong fingers tenderly part my sensitive folds, exploring parts of me I've been dying for him to visit.

"Not fair," I say, gasping as his thumb brushes against my clit. "You know what your touch does to me."

"Yeah," he says shamelessly. "But it's for a good cause."

"And what cause is that?"

"The *Rory-just-relax* campaign," he says with a growly chuckle. "Can I make a donation?"

He thrusts two of his fingers into me, stretching me slightly as his thumb rubs harder against my clit. I quietly moan with delight and surprise as he enters me, giving me just a taste of what's to come.

He and I don't have to fight this anymore. I can finally give in—and screw his brains out.

Jace slides his fingers out of me and lovingly grabs my chin with his other hand, turning me around to face him. He watches me with a doting expression, his stormy gray eyes drinking me in as he briefly pauses to study my face.

Before I can say a thing, he kisses me. The embrace is deep and affectionate—the kiss of someone who's going to be there forever, beside me through thick and thin, through blood and war.

Nothing will stop him.

Nothing will keep him away.

He holds the back of my head, like he can't get enough. Like nothing in the world can ever compare to this. To having me.

His other hand grabs my waist, pulling my hips toward his, and the bulge in his pants presses hard against my entrance. With only a few thin layers of fabric between us, warmth pools between my thighs, as hungry for him as he is for me.

Something clicks for me, in this moment.

I can trust this man.

With everything. With my life. He's my partner in crime in all things, to the end of my days and beyond.

For the first time since we met in that courtyard, I really let my guard down.

For the first time, I truly give *in*.

I lean into his touch. To his kiss. Our lips brush against each other, and a current of electric need bubbles through me. Instead of fighting it, I let my body ache for him. I let my body *crave* him. I give into the demands of my dragon and let him hold me, let him drink me in.

A flurry of devotion flutters through me as we hold each other, rooted in place. The intensely intimate moment deepens the longer we stand there. The kiss becomes so much more than just a kiss—I feel as though he's reaching into my soul, and I into his.

We connect, in this moment—almost merging, in a way. Connecting on a level I didn't know was even possible.

In the bliss of this moment, my dragon and I align. We want the same thing—Jace Goodwin—and I won't deny her that anymore.

As I lose myself in Jace's kiss, a pang hits my chest hard. I flinch, but the joyful feeling I have in this moment doesn't stop even as I pull away from him.

"What's wrong?" he asks, his brows twisting slightly in concern.

"I don't..." I pause, looking at my hands, trying to figure out what's happening. "I don't know."

A flood of energy bubbles through me, cascading like a tsunami, engulfing me completely. My skin glows brighter as the sensation hits harder. It's a flood. A stampede—of love, of light, of power.

Along my arms, the glowing tattoos of the chains that I've had since I first fell into the pits glow brighter than ever.

A surge of energy hits me, stealing away my breath. My muscles tense as the sensation takes over.

I have no control in this moment. No mobility. Nothing. I can't even speak, and it feels so similar to when the magic first hit me. I feel like something is fusing to my soul, merging with my very existence.

Something permanent. Something unchangeable.

Jace speaks, his tone urgent and tense, but I can't hear words. My brain hums, tuning the world out, and everything goes fuzzy.

The most powerful surge of magic I've ever felt in my life runs through me like a lightning bolt, grounding me to the floor of the balcony—paralyzing me as it still steals the air out of my very lungs.

And, as the energy hits me, the chains along my arms shatter.

The tattoos dissolve into the air like salt into water, and a small white cloud lifts from my skin. It's subtle, almost invisible.

But I saw it.

With that, my body screams. I can feel something within me—pushing, twitching, breaking. My skin tightens, and suddenly, I feel as if every bone is about to fracture. I feel the world around me surge and bubble, the ground unstable.

A flash of white blinds me, and my world tumbles. I feel myself sliding down something. I feel rock scraping my skin. It's like I fell.

Oh, crap. I *am* falling.

Disoriented and dizzy, I reach for anything near me to slow my descent. My claws dig into the side of the roof, to the shingles themselves, cutting through the stone like butter until I finally slide to a stop.

Wait.

Claws?

I open my eyes, and my arms are thicker than they were before. I'm covered in glimmering scales that glisten like diamonds in the setting sun. Iridescent claws protrude from what were once my nails, a sharp contrast to the black stone shingles along the roof.

With a baffled glance upward, I can clearly make out the line I've cut through the black rock. Above that is the balcony where Jace and I were standing moments before. The railing is shattered, bits of it missing, and it looks like I made quite a mess.

As the disbelief slowly shatters, I look once again at the claws. The truth hits me in a sudden, crashing wave of realization.

I shifted.

My heart thudding in my chest, the pulse loud in my ear, I study my body—as much of it as I can see anyway. A soft roar builds in my throat, as I try to speak, my words lost in the rumble. I lift my wings, stretching them for the first time, and it's like stretching a tired limb.

I feel relief.

Joy.

I almost can't believe I really did it.

I shifted.

And with my first breath as a dragon, I *roar.*

A familiar black thunderbird with glowing blue light running the length of his wings lands on the roof above me. He effortlessly slides down the roof, slowing his descent with his powerful wings as he watches me with concern and joy all at once. His head bobs excitedly as our eyes connect, and he growls softly as he nears.

I try to say his name, but a roar comes out instead. It rumbles like thunder and shakes the tiles beneath me. What a surreal sensation—to not even be able to speak.

Everything about this is so bizarre, so strange that I shake my body from head to tail just to shake out the strangeness. Every muscle, every claw—it all just feels right. Like *this* is my real body.

It's like stepping into the sun for the first time and experiencing what warmth and joy are really like.

It's beautiful.

Exhilarating.

And I want more.

I let out a happy little growl, the sound short and sweet as I cling to the side of the building, stretching and getting familiar with this new body.

My dragon.

Jace nips happily at the air, stretching his wings for balance as he slides the rest of the way toward me. He gently rubs his nose against mine, and the second our skin touches, the magical connection of the dragons opens.

You're beautiful, he says to me. *I can't stop looking at you. Are you okay?*

Amazing, I say, beaming.

Try to fly, he says, nodding toward the sky above us.

The motion breaks our connection, and I look down at the hundred-foot drop to the hard ground below.

My eyes narrow in annoyance as I glare at him, trying to silently make my point.

He doesn't get it—or, more likely, he just doesn't care. He nods to the sky again, nipping once more in the air before he takes off. His wings creating a small gust that drifts over me as he does what I've wanted to do for so long.

Fly.

With an annoyed huff, I get my bearings. It's a bit difficult to stand as I dig my claws into the side of the roof, and I can't help but look over the edge once again.

The ground seems to get farther away the longer I stare at it, and I frown in trepidation.

If I fall, this is *really* going to hurt.

Jace growls softly in encouragement as he flies just above me, teasing me once again with something he knows I want.

Only this time, it doesn't involve his devious fingers.

I flap my wings hard, hoping against all hope that

my dragon instinct kicks in and keeps me from tumbling to my death.

My body lifts almost effortlessly as my dragon instinct kicks in. At the last possible second, I release my grip on the black shingles and take to the air.

Even though I'm wobbling, I don't really care.

I'm flying.

It's like heaven.

I can feel my dragon guiding me. Instinct warns me to turn this way or that, to even out my wing on the downturn or tighten it as I coast. The instruction and correction on my form keep me from wobbling as much as I would have otherwise, but I'm still fairly unstable.

Jace soars through the air, making it look effortless and easy, and I snarl in playful annoyance.

Show off.

True, he's had a lot more time to practice this than I have, but what can I say? I'm a perfectionist.

My wings beat the air, lifting me further skyward as I roar with glee into the clouds. Jace lets loose a triumphant blast of blue magic, and it crackles into the sky above us like a firework.

As he dives over the forest, I try to follow. I'm not nearly as graceful as him, but I don't really mind. The momentum of my wings along the air casts me over the trees around the dojo as we circle the castle. It's not until he circles ahead of me, guiding me in a slow bend around the embassy, that I take my mind off my form long enough to realize what he's doing.

He's showing me off. Showing everyone what I've done.

How *embarrassing.*

I briefly close my eyes to tune out the world, simply enjoying the cool rush of air as it hits my face. The wind up here smells like honey, almost—crisp and clean, with a little sweetness.

An air current hits us, and I wobble again, my eyes snapping open as a brief wave of concern runs through me. I look down at the ground far below and flap my wings a little harder, eager to stay in the sky.

Jace chuckles, the small puffs of air blowing over his nose as he watches me struggle to stay airborne.

I chuckle as well, swishing my beautiful tail at him, smacking him in lighthearted annoyance.

He effortlessly dodges my blow, flipping as he soars over me and to my other side. Gods, he just can't contain himself—he has to show off any chance he gets.

On the ground below, several soldiers run underneath us, cheering as he and I fly over the grassy knolls surrounding the dojo.

With our victory lap apparently complete, Jace leads me toward the misty ravine. I bank, wobbling again as he angles us toward the second island that has always looked kind of like it was floating across the mists.

It would seem the devious Jace Goodwin has someplace he would like to take me—and it appears to be a surprise.

Wherever we go, I'm happy as long as I get to fly there.

I love this. I've dreamed of flying since I first came here. Since I first accepted that I was a dragon. Since I came to understand that the shift may eventually happen.

Even as I tremble, still figuring out how to listen to the dragon instinct burning within me, I let myself enjoy the sky.

Up here, with the air rushing across my face and the cool, sweet scent of the sky, I'm free.

CHAPTER TWENTY-SEVEN

As I soar through the air, one with the sky, I lose track of time.

The moon rises as the night wears on, slowly creeping across the sky while Jace and I enjoy ourselves. He spins around me, his wing catching tufts of cloud as he shows off. Trails of white mist spiral from the edges of his wings as he gently roves through the air. His black scales shimmer now and then in the moonlight as the glowing light overtakes us.

It's heaven.

After a while, my wobbly balance starts to settle. The peaceful rush of wind fills my ears, crisp and clear, and I often simply close my eyes to enjoy the sensation of air rushing across my face.

It's bliss.

Every now and then, the glimmer of moonlight against my scales catches my attention—the way the light glints off my claws like sun off a diamond. It's mesmerizing. I wish I could see my face, to find what I really look like, but that will have to wait.

For now, I'm too happy in the sky to come down.

Jace rolls above me once again, ever the hotshot as his broad black wings stretch into the night. At times, all I can see is the soft blue glow of the magic in his veins, stretching through his wings like a spider web of light.

As he sails through another cloud, the tip of his wing brushes against mine.

Let's land.

I let out a sad little rumble at the idea.

He chuckles, his wing brushing mine again. *You need to rest.*

Fine.

I growl softly in agreement and nod toward the forests below us, suggesting he take the lead.

He banks against the air, wings taut as he glides downward. I try to follow, trusting the little voice in my head that instinctively guides me through the movements.

Wings tight.

Stretch them wide, now.

Tilt.

My dragon, guiding the way.

We slowly circle the forest and come upon a river that cuts through the trees as Jace leads me toward the ground. It's a slow and gradual descent, one I'm sure he's carefully orchestrating judging by how often he looks back at me, checking my position.

We follow the river, our noses still angling slightly downward in a slow and steady descent, and I have to confess—I am *not* looking forward to this landing.

I'm all for pushing myself to the limit—hell, it's the only way I know how to do *anything*—but I think I need to set my expectations, here.

My goal is more along the lines of a well-orchestrated fall, rather than a genuine landing.

Mist rises up ahead, obscuring the river. The closer we get, the louder the thunder of water becomes, and I realize we must be approaching a waterfall.

Sure enough, Jace dives into the mist, the blue glow of his magic illuminating the fog with a soft, sapphire haze.

I follow. The mist hits my face, soft as silk, and I resist the impulse to close my eyes in gleeful delight at the sensation.

Every feeling is more vivid as a dragon. Brighter. Louder. Crisper.

Just… *more*.

I *love* it.

The mist quickly dissolves, and I very suddenly see the pool below. Instinct kicks in, and I beat my wings against the air to slow myself.

It doesn't work very well.

I tumble into the water, hitting the surface with a hefty splash. I dip below the waves into a deep channel, holding my breath as I squint up at the moonlit surface above me.

Desperate for air, I swim upward, using my claws as much as my wings. The closer I get to the surface, the harder it is to swim—and as I break through the water, I burn through the last of my air.

I suck in a deep breath as soon as I'm able, only to hear myself gasp as I tread water. I look at my hands in surprise.

Hands.

I shifted back.

I look up at the stars as the water thunders into the deep lake, my hair sticking to my face as I drink in the night. The milky way stretches above me, brilliant and eternal without any lights out here to pollute the sky.

As I tread water, I glance around, trying to get my bearings. I've never been here before, nor do I have any idea where we are in relation to the embassy. I

assume we're somewhere on the dojo grounds, though
—Jace wouldn't have taken me anywhere else, not
with everything at stake.

He told me to take one night off from worrying—I
guess I can indulge him on that.

A cluster of boulders line the shallows of the lake,
and a bank covered in soft white sand stretches along
the other side.

I don't, however, see Jace anywhere.

My heart stutters with concern. With nowhere else
for him to have gone, I peer into the pitch-black abyss
below me.

A current sweeps below my toes, and before I can
even react, two strong hands grab my naked waist.
They tug me briefly downward as Jace breaks the
surface, splashing water against my face.

"You scared me," I admit, grinning as I splash him
back.

He grins mischievously, his grip on my waist tightening as he tugs me closer to him. "Now, I believe we
were in the middle of something before you so *rudely*
shifted. Where were we?"

I laugh as he kisses me in the middle of the moonlit
lake, his hands roving across my skin while we float.
His grip slides up my thigh—which makes it hard for
me to tread water, I'll admit—and he takes control. I'm

depending on him, now—on his strong kicks through the water as he keeps us both afloat.

Jace wraps my legs around his waist, his hard abs flexing as he works every muscle. With his firm grip on my ass once more, he presses my hips against his.

His erection slides over my entrance, thick and hard. Impulsively, I bite my lip, a happy little smile spreading across my face.

We've both wanted this for *a while*.

Apparently satisfied with how much he has teased me, Jace breaks away. It leaves me a little breathless, and I impulsively reach toward him, aching for more.

"This way." He takes my hand and nods toward the rocks, droplets of water caught in the stubble along his jaw as he grins.

We swim toward the boulders, and as we near, I notice a shallow shelf of rock at the base of them. About waist deep, the shelf creates a small table for us to stand on. Jace and I step onto the flat boulder submerged in the water, feeling weightless as our bare feet brush against the smooth surface.

Gently, Jace presses me against the nearest boulder, pinning me to the warm rock as the crystal-clear water laps at our waists. He once more presses his hips to mine, his cock sliding between my legs. It brushes my entrance, teasing me with what's to come, and my eyes flutter closed with delight.

He brushes aside my hair, the electric buzz of his touch igniting me with desire as he lovingly tucks a lock behind my ear. He holds my face, and I open my eyes to find him watching me.

His thumb brushes my lips, leaving a sizzling sensation of joy and lust with every flick of his finger, and I'm lost.

Utterly and completely *lost*—in him.

His lips press against mine, and he inhales my scent like he can't live without it. Like he can't live without *me*. The embrace gets more intense as his hunger deepens, and his other hand grips my waist tightly to keep my hips in place.

It would seem he plans to make up for lost time.

He pulls his cock from between my thighs, the length of his shaft running along my clit as I lean into him. The tip of his dick presses against my entrance, parting my sensitive folds as it teases my channel.

Mercilessly, Jace tilts my hips, controlling my body as he torments me with his incredible cock, refusing to enter me just yet. Preferring to torture me, instead.

I moan as his grip lowers to my thighs. Effortlessly, he lifts my legs until they're wrapped around his waist once more. His thumbs press against my inner thigh as he adjusts me, spreading me to give himself better access. His hard chest pins me to the smooth rock, his muscles flexed as he controls every inch of me.

I'm lost in the sensations blurring through my body as he kisses me, my eyes closed as I surrender to him completely.

To us.

He's tormenting me, playing with me until I'm putty in his hands. Jace knows what he's doing to me by making me wait, and now he's just being mean.

"Take me, Jace Goodwin," I softly demand.

He smirks devilishly. "Thy will be done, woman."

His cock slides into me, slowly at first, stretching me inch by glorious inch as he forces himself inside. I gasp as he slowly takes me, savoring every second of it even as his thick cock stretches me to my limits. Just when I think he couldn't possibly go deeper, he does—time and time again.

His mouth explores mine, lips hungry and unyielding as he continues to stretch me, fill me, enter me.

Slowly.

When my clit finally brushes against his body, his cock fully immersed, I arch my back in utter ecstasy. He waits, burying his face in my neck, enjoying the sensation as much as I do.

As we stay there, my legs spread with his cock buried deep within me, he slowly tilts his hips forward and back, gently pumping his dick through my channel. It's a subtle sensation, but it sends shockwaves of delight and lust through me as he pushes me to the brink.

We press our foreheads together, losing ourselves in the moment. In each other.

I run my fingers through his hair, holding him to me, refusing to let go as he continues to slowly rock against me. I kiss him fiercely, and his hands slip to the small of my back as his lips move against mine.

In that moment, our dragons are finally happy.

There's a bubbling sensation of happiness in my chest, and I can feel the very second when our souls meld.

With him deep inside of me, we become one—fused now and forever. Always. The serene *knowing* that he will always be there is overpowering, unlike anything I've ever felt before.

It's calm.

Comforting.

Absolute and unchangeable.

With our bond complete, my dragon is happy and at peace.

"I'm yours for life, Rory," he growls into my ear as my grip tightens in his hair.

For life.

I sigh happily, leaning into him. I want to give him everything. I want to tell him how devoted I am.

But as I open my mouth to speak, he doesn't give me the chance to say a word.

His hands grab my waist and he pulls slightly out, only to thrust deep within me. I gasp, swallowing everything I wanted to say as he takes over.

His cock slides out of me once again, and he bucks into me with even more fervor. More fire. He rides me with smooth, powerful strokes.

A man like him, a love like ours—he doesn't need to rush.

After all, we have forever.

With every thrust, he tilts my pelvis downward. The motion sends tendrils of delight through me every time as my clit rubs against his skin, a sensation that spirals clear down to my fingertips. I moan as he rides me, the slow and sensual thrusts overwhelming and beautiful.

He possessively grabs the back of my neck as he forces his way into me, the water surging around us as he fills me to the brim. I moan, back arching, lost in the utter bliss of his rock-hard body against mine.

The sensation builds, steady and constant, as he gradually picks up speed. Every thrust is somehow stronger than the last. His grip on my waist tightens with every plunge as he pulls me against him, creating even more friction. Even more ecstasy.

My orgasm starts to build, a slow flicker of bliss deep in my core as he rides me to my climax. It's steady, like a flame that slowly flickers to life, growing brighter every time he thrusts his cock deep into me.

He never once stops. He never once pauses. He just bucks into me again and again, more powerfully every time, his gorgeous abs tensing against me as his cock dominates me.

As my climax tortures me, so close and yet refusing to hit, I lean into him. I try to say something, to crack a joke, but all I can do is moan louder.

I arch my back and press my palm against the smooth rock behind me, riding him as hard as he rides me. I spread my legs wider, taking him in, giving him control. Giving him whatever he desires, anything he asks.

And then it hits.

My orgasm rocks through me, and as it does, my brain shuts off. All I can do is ride the tide of utter bliss. Of joy. Devotion. Love. Ecstasy. I'm lost in the sensation, in the overwhelming delight that shoots through every toe, every fingertip. With my legs still spread wide against him, my hips arched against his, giving him all of me, I moan into the sky.

I lose track of time as he continues to ride me through my orgasm, driving it harder, higher, longer.

When the blissful sensation finally begins to fade, I collapse against the rock. I'm completely spent and utterly exhausted.

His cock pauses its ride, still buried deep within me as his grip on my waist keeps me upright.

My eyes flutter open, and I'm delighted to find him watching me. His expression mirrors how I feel—devoted, in love, lost in the moment.

"Your turn," I say softly, exhausted and exhilarated all at once.

"Yes *ma'am,*" he says with a wry smirk.

He thrusts into me, somehow even harder than before, and I gasp with pleasure as he rubs his hard body against my sensitive bud. Before I can help myself, I moan, leaning into him as my over-stimu-lated clit takes me almost instantly into a second climax.

I wrap my arms around him as I come a second time, grinding my hips against him as he holds my back. His grip on my waist tightens, and he shoves his cock into me one last time. I feel a hot rush as he releases himself inside, his cock stretching me as he gives in to his own orgasm. He sighs with relief and leans his head against my neck.

We stay there for quite a while, breathing heavily as we try to catch our breath.

His biceps flex as he wraps his arms around me, holding me tightly. The movement is possessive, almost primal.

As his arms weave around my back, holding me tighter, his cock still buried within me, it feels very much like I'm being *claimed*.

"You're mine for life," he says, gently brushing his nose against my jaw. He plants a few kisses along my neck. "That's the only reason I'm okay with sharing you, Rory—the men you brought here, they're worthy of you. I might still get jealous from time to time, but that's a dragon's right."

I laugh breathlessly, my shoulders still heaving from our fun.

Crickets begin to chirp nearby, the sound soft and soothing as it fills the night. Jace lets out a slow sigh, and as his hard chest presses against mine, I can feel his pulse returning to normal.

He affectionately runs his hand through my wet hair, watching me with a small smile as he studies my face.

"What?" I ask, smiling back at him.

"From the moment you arrived here, Harper has been bugging me to carry you off and mate with you. It's been utterly aggravating—but now I have to tell her she was right."

I laugh. She would.

"I'm glad I can tell her that finally happened," he admits. "But first, I have business to tend to."

I tilt my head, a little confused. "Oh? What's that?"

Instead of answering, he winks and runs his fingers down the length of my body. He slips two of them into me, his thumb teasing my entrance yet again as he helps himself to the space between my thighs.

My hips impulsively tilt toward him, giving him access to whatever he wants, and I gasp in delighted surprise as he gets me ready for round two.

Deep within, my dragon curls with delight—and I have to agree.

My life *rocks.*

CHAPTER TWENTY-EIGHT

The next morning, I wake to the soft buzz of insects fluttering through the bushes nearby. The thunder of the waterfall coaxes me awake, as does the gentle breathing of the man sleeping next to me in the soft white sand.

His strong hands weave around my waist, his fingertips brushing my navel, sending tendrils of joyful delight through me every time he twitches in his sleep.

I adjust my position on the bank of the water, rolling over until we're face-to-face. With his eyes closed, his brows scrunch in his sleep, as if he's about to lecture the people in his dream.

Still serious, even when he's sleeping.

After the shift, we have no clothes, so we're still

lying naked in the sand. I look up at the sky, gauging that the sun must have only just risen, so we haven't wasted too much of the morning.

In the serene atmosphere around me, I can't help but hum with delight as the world feels so beautiful. So right.

I lean toward Jace, our noses almost touching as I admire him. The stubble that runs along his square jaw. His handsome features.

And those stormy eyes. Even though I can't see them, I know they're there.

I run my fingertip along his cheek, just drinking him in as the silent morning stretches on.

My mate.

He stirs at my touch, blinking awake and instantly snaring me with his gaze. The corner of his mouth curls slightly, and he growls a little in pleasure. His hand tightens around my waist, and he drags me closer to him, kissing my jaw as I land against his bare chest.

With one fluid motion, he pulls my leg over him and rolls onto his back. Now straddling him, I feel him start to harden between my legs.

I laugh. "What? Six times last night wasn't enough for you?"

"It's never enough," he says, admiring me. "Not when I have you."

"So romantic," I say, grinning as I tilt my head slightly to admire this man.

Just to tease him, I stay exactly where he put me and stretch my arms into the sky. It feels good to let the muscles relax and loosen, especially given the workout we had last night.

As I stretch, my stomach rumbles, and I wonder what they have for breakfast this morning—or if anyone is sober enough to cook anything.

While I stretch my biceps and shoulders, a painful cramp shoots through my pelvis. I grimace, holding my hand to the area as I breathe through it, wondering what the hell that was.

As a second cramp hits me, a rush of dread sinks clear to my toes.

The warning.

The tea.

Crap.

Drew warned me that my IUD would fail after I shifted for the first time.

Cold dread flutters through me.

"My IUD must have come out," I say as a third cramp rocks through my body.

I'm not sure what I was expecting Jace to do or say,

but I definitely wasn't expecting him to smile as broadly as he is now.

He sits upright, looking delightfully excited as he keeps me rooted in his lap. "Did I get you pregnant?"

I smack his shoulder playfully, but I can't keep from laughing. "We are *not* ready for that. Are you kidding?"

He chuckles, still holding me in place and brushes his nose across mine. "I'm ready, but I'll wait until you are, too."

Jace kisses me deeply, briefly chasing away the dread even though I most certainly am not ready for a kid just yet.

"Don't worry," he adds. "You have about a twelve-hour delay with a tea. Sure, it's better to drink it every morning, just in case, but you should be fine this time. There's some back at the embassy, so let's get going."

I stand, on a mission to not get pregnant.

Not right now. Not with everyone coming after me.

I shake out my hands and shoulders, rolling my head as I reach deep inside, trying to connect once again with my dragon. She's there. I can feel her, but for some reason, she's not responding.

"How do I do this, Jace?" I ask. "On purpose, I mean. What do I do?"

Last night was impulsive. Instinctual. I had no control over the shift when it happened, and I would really like to learn how to summon my dragon on my own terms.

"Reach toward her," Jace instructs, effortlessly adopting the stern voice he always uses when we train. "Try to find that same alignment you felt with her last night."

I frown as I face a wall of resistance inside. Like I know where she is but can't reach her. My jaw tenses as I get more and more annoyed the longer nothing happens.

Behind me, Jace take a smooth and steadying breath, and I already know what he's going to tell me to do next.

Breathe.

In an effort to calm my raging annoyance, I take a deep breath and peek at him through a half-closed eyelid as he smirks.

"Exactly," he says, nodding.

This time, I manage to get through to my dragon. I can practically feel her curled up in a ball deep inside, groggy and very much wanting me to go away so she can sleep.

I chuckle. Nope.

"The first few times are really rough on her," Jace

says, his deep voice rolling over me and soothing me as I try to coax her awake. "She probably doesn't have much energy left after last night. It takes some getting used to, but you'll both get it."

He walks behind me and brushes his fingers along my shoulders, his fingertips just barely touching my skin. It shoots tendrils of desire and glee through me, the sensations curling through my body like rays of sunshine.

At his touch, my dragon stirs, ignited by him. I can feel her start to rise. Start to rumble.

"Try again," Jace says in my ear.

I let out a slow sigh, and with my eyes still closed, reach for her once again.

Let's do this, babe, I tell her.

The longer Jace holds me, running his fingertips along my arms, the more powerful her flurry of excitement becomes. I feel her shake deep within my core, finally waking.

Jace's touch disappears from my skin, leaving me cold where he was holding me, but my body begins to hum and vibrate. Flickers of pain shoot through me, both agonizing and invigorating, all at once.

My world tilts, and I get briefly dizzy as my head spins. I fall forward, but instead of landing on my hands, instead of feeling awkward and off-balance, the ground thunders slightly beneath my front claws.

Just like that, the painful hum is over. I stumble, feeling so much bigger and entirely off-balance. My wings stretch instinctively to help me stay on my feet.

"Yeah!" Jace shouts triumphantly, and as I open my eyes, I find him jumping in the air, pumping his fist into the sky.

I shake out my body, feeling the tension release as my muscles relax. I feel amazing, like all is right with the world once again, and I lean into the sensation.

Out of curiosity, I look at myself in the reflection on the lake, only to pause with stunned disbelief as my scales glisten brilliantly—like diamonds in the light. Four elegant white horns curve from my brow, framing my golden eyes that glow with fire and magic. As I spread my wings, they dazzle me. Every curve of my body— every detail—is beautiful, regal, and powerful. Refined talons curl from the tips of my wings, extra weapons that shine with just as much brilliance as my scales.

I lean toward the water, my nose hovering over the surface as I study my new face. I huff in awe of her—of my dragon—and a flurry of white sparks sizzle in the air on my breath.

A soft growl beside me catches my attention, and I

lift my head to find Jace standing in the water not far away in his dragon form. His stunning thunderbird watches me, the blue magic of his dragon glowing beneath his skin.

He brushes his head against mine, our necks arching as the connection opens at our touch.

Do you know what you are? he asks.

No idea, I confess.

You're a diamond dragon, something so rare they were thought to be a myth.

Whoa. I blink in surprise, not quite sure what to make of that. *What does that mean, though?*

That you are truly unique, he says, brushing his wing lovingly against mine. *And drop-dead gorgeous, inside and out.*

I laugh, huffs of air rolling through my nose in short bursts. *You charmer.*

He nudges me playfully and takes to the sky, the gust of air from his wings brushing across my face as he hovers over the water, waiting for me to join him.

Right.

I spread my wings, still awkward and new to this whole flying business. I focus intently on them, flapping as hard as I can, and I slowly lift into the air. My claws drop a little with every beat, grazing the water as I take off with wobbly imperfection.

It's not pretty, but I do it.

I'm starting to get the hang of this. But damn, it's hard.

With every wing beat taking me a foot or so more into the air, it takes me a little while to reach him. He effortlessly flies ahead, his powerful wings angling and banking through the air currents with practiced ease. After an awkward start, I manage to keep up with him, but it's obvious he's going slowly for my benefit.

I try to go easy on myself for not getting this instantly, but I'm not used to things taking very long to understand. Zurie never gave me the leisure of learning at my own pace.

As we soar across the sky, I often pause to close my eyes and drink in the warm sun as it beats across my skin. The cool, sweet air rolls over me, and once again, I feel at home flying through the clouds.

Before long, dragons begin to tail us, roaring in celebration. At first, it's just a couple, but before long, there are dozens on every side, above and below and behind. Their roars are like an ongoing rumble of thunder that never stops, filling my heart with pride and accomplishment as the embassy approaches.

I did it. I shifted.

And Zurie can suck it.

If my former mentor comes for me, she will *die*.

CHAPTER TWENTY-NINE

I slowly pace my bedroom as I sip a murky green tea from the massive teacup in my hands. It tastes like matcha and dirt, but I don't care as long as I don't get pregnant.

Yet.

I smirk a little, remembering the excitement in Jace's eyes at the prospect of a baby. It was adorable, and I can't help but wonder what kind of dad he will be. What kind of fathers all my men will make.

Something to consider, perhaps, when we're not actively being hunted.

With every sip, the cramps subside a little more, and the dread of a pregnancy scare starts to fade.

In the suite beyond my bedroom, the door to the hallway creaks open. I've started playing with the idea of leaving it unlocked as I get more and more comfortable here, but I still expect whoever wants in to at least knock first.

There isn't the whisper of footsteps along the ground, and as far as I can tell, the creak was the only indication that someone's even in there.

My training kicks in, and I chug the last of the tea before setting the cup gently on my bed. I rest my palm against the handgun at my side and stiffen, my eyes on the door to the living room.

Levi walks in—much to my delight—and I relax my shoulders.

Damn, he's stealthy.

I wonder if I'll ever be able to pick up on his movements, or if he will forever be able to duck and dodge me, somehow more silent and surefooted than anyone else I've ever met.

He smiles as our eyes meet, watching me with an odd expression somewhere between trepidation and desire, like he's afraid I won't recognize him. He hesitates by the door, awkwardly stretching his fingers as he waits for me to break the silence.

I tilt my head in confusion. "What are you up to?"

"Checking on you," he admits. "How are you feeling?"

"Great," I admit with a broad smile.

And it's true.

After all the chaos and stress, I'm glad Jace convinced me to take one night away from it all. I feel renewed, like the world is fresh and bright.

Part of that is probably the mate-bond magic giving me rose-colored glasses and a temporary high, but I figure most of it comes from the fact that I finally shifted.

That I truly am a dragon, in and out.

Levi walks slowly toward me, and flurries of excitement dance through my chest the closer he gets. He gently sets the back of his hand against my arm, and as our skin touches, our rare and beautiful connection opens.

As the mind link opens between us, a flood of devotion and affection bleeds through from him into me, blended with the occasional ribbon of concern.

Of dread.

I have a confession, he says through our link, and another flutter of dread bleeds through with the words.

What's wrong? I ask, setting my hand on his bicep to comfort him as I study his face.

I was worried I might lose you, he admits, his eyes roving over me as his brows tilt slightly upward. *Once you mated with Jace, we were all worried we might lose you forever.*

Oh, Levi. I let out a slow sigh of relief, grateful that's the only concern in this conversation. Tenderly, I hold his face in my hands. *Never,* I say through our connection. *That was the deal. No mating if Jace expected me to live life his way.*

The mate-bond does things to people, he says, apparently not convinced yet as he holds my wrists. *It changes you—*

Not me, I interrupt, grinning. *I'm too damn stubborn.*

With that, I open my heart to him.

I let my guard down, truly and completely.

Through our connection, I try to make him feel what I feel for him. The devotion. The respect. The admiration for all he's done, and all I know he will do in the future.

As my emotions filter through into him, he smiles, and his shoulders relax with relief. He kisses the heel of my palm, and it's clear that we're good.

Nothing can take him away from me.

My phone buzzes in my pocket, and I fish it out to see a text from Drew.

Did you get laid?

I laugh and type out my reply while Levi holds me tight. *Yes.*

A moment later, my phone buzzes again. *Good. I've got dibs on you tonight though.*

I shake my head, laughing at these ridiculous men.

Levi wraps his arm around my shoulders and reads the text, only to chuckle under his breath. "He wishes."

The phone buzzes again. *Irena just arrived. She's in the downstairs corridors and nearly snuck by me. Did I beat Jace to telling you that?*

My heart pangs with excitement at the idea that my sister's back, but at the same time, I know this can't be good. She told me if she returned, it would be because something big happened.

Something bad.

As excited as I am to have her here, I know how much resistance she has to coming back.

Something's definitely wrong.

I begin typing my reply to Drew, but a text from Jace pops up on the screen before I get the chance.

Irena. Downstairs corridors, it says simply.

I chuckle. "He's not much of a texter, is he?"

"Nope," Levi says with a smirk.

"I need to go," I say to Levi, kissing him on the cheek as I head out the door.

He stops me, his hand on my wrist as he pulls me back toward him and kisses my forehead. "Go see your sister, but I *definitely* get dibs on you tonight."

Even with the threat of something terrible hanging over my head, I can't help but grin as I kiss him playfully on the nose, in love with my life.

I jog down the stairs, heading for the corridors Jace and Drew mentioned in their texts. This stretch of hallways is almost never used, and I find it odd that she would come through here. She clearly didn't want to be seen, and I have to wonder why.

The murmur of voices whispers down the tunnel, and I steal through the shadows toward them. As I near, the voices get louder, and I start to recognize Irena's. She's talking to a man, and it takes me a moment longer to recognize who.

Eric.

"I'm just worried about you, Irena," he says.

"Don't be," she answers, her voice chilly.

"Why are you pushing me away?" he asks, his tone tense and angry. "Do you think I endured that little audition of yours because it was *fun?*"

She pauses, and I can imagine her scrunching her brows. "Well, it *was* fun."

He chuckles, and I peek around the corner to find him running a hand through his hair. "Yeah, I guess it was," he admits. "But still, woman, I care about you. What happened that's making you push me away?"

"I don't want to talk about it," Irena says, squaring her shoulders as she lifts her chin in defiance.

"I do," he says, pressing the matter. "You can't keep running away from me. If you don't want me, say so. Otherwise, tell me what the *hell* is wrong!"

Irena's bright green eyes narrow, her dark lashes a sharp contrast to the brilliant emerald. "I don't run away."

"You just did," he snaps, and it's clear he doesn't give a shit about her tone.

I smirk. Good. Irena needs a man who can keep her honest, if only with herself.

"We're done," Irena says coldly. She turns on her heel and storms off down the hallway.

"If you walk away now," he shouts after her, "you walk away from me forever."

Irena pauses mid-stride, her body stiff and still even though she still has her back turned to him.

I hesitate, watching the exchange. I should probably give them space, but I'm too morbidly curious about what will happen next to pull away.

"I'm not going to force you to talk to me," Eric continues. "But I will absolutely set my boundaries. You have a choice right now. Either you can be real with me or you can run away. So, what's it going to be, Irena?"

"You want real?" she says quietly, her voice low and deadly as she looks at him over her shoulder. "You want the truth?"

"That's all I've wanted this whole time," he says, lifting both his arms and spreading them in frustration. "How bad could this *possibly* be?"

She turns toward him, taking slow and steady steps as she glares. "The people I love betray me, Eric. Every time. Every *fucking* time." She pinches her eyes shut, grimacing with the words. "I'm done with being hurt. I'm done with lovers. I'm done with friends. I'm done with everyone who could betray me. Only my sister has my back."

Oh, gods.

My heart twists for her, and I feel palpable pain in my chest.

She's in agony. She's taking this so much worse than I realized, and in a small way, I'm glad I heard all of this. She would never have admitted any of this to me. She would have let me think she's okay, that she's healing in her own way.

But what she did was make stories about the world based on a small subset of people. She nearly fractured, and by the look of things, only Eric can save her now.

"Love isn't for me," Irena says, her voice shaking

slightly as she pauses a good six feet away from Eric. "It's just better this way."

For a moment, he simply watches her face. From this angle, I can't see much of his expression. Based on the way Irena's eyes dart across his features, I suspect he looks somewhat tortured. I'm guessing he looks wounded and raw, and Irena can't handle it.

She can't handle that kind of vulnerability, not in her or anyone else. Zurie tried to beat that out of us, and I suspect Irena took more of the beatings than I did.

"If love isn't for you," he says gently, *tenderly*. "Then why didn't you walk away? You could have just left and let that be that."

She stutters, apparently unprepared for that comeback. "I... well, it's obvious that..."

"Yeah?" he presses, clearly waiting.

Calling her on her bullshit.

He takes a few careful steps toward her, his palms lifted as he reaches for her shoulders. Irena, however, is apparently done. She turns on her heel and walks away, but Eric grabs her wrist. She twists her hand, escaping his grip only to have him grab her other wrist immediately after.

They spar and parry for a minute, equally matched and capable. He twists her arm, spinning her into his chest as he holds her face with his other hand.

Despite all of her resistance, Irena relaxes at his touch. Her eyebrows tilt upwards slightly in longing and agony. She stiffens in his grip, chest to chest, looking up at him even as she wriggles and tries to get away.

"The people in your old life aren't like the ones here," he says quietly.

She hesitates, still as a statue for a moment as she studies his face. "I don't know what you mean," she lies.

"You're what? CIA?" he asks, shrugging.

She frowns, wriggling in his grip. "Don't go there, Eric."

He doesn't allow her to get away, and even as she tries to slide beneath his arm, he twists her hand again and pulls her back.

Damn, he's even better than I thought he was.

"No, you can't be CIA," he says casually, as if they're simply sitting on a bench talking about life. "You're too knowledgeable about dragon culture." He pauses, looking off down the corridor as his eyes gloss over in thought. "Knights?"

He's certainly getting closer.

Irena grimaces, still wriggling, still fighting—but

admittedly not very hard. If she really wanted to, she could break his arm and disable him. That would stop him from pinning her in place.

But she doesn't.

Deep down, she still wants him.

"You should stop," she warns, her voice chilly and cold.

"No, not Knights," he says with a sigh, shaking his head, ignoring her completely. "You're too talented." He shifts his attention back to her, studying her face as she squirms in his grip. "Spectres."

She stiffens almost imperceptibly, and I know her well enough that I see the lie. I see the tell. I see the truth. Her jaw tenses, and she very convincingly shakes her head, her eyes narrowing as if he's getting closer but hasn't yet figured it out.

She's always been a brilliant liar. She just can't lie to me.

Eric, however, buys it. With a sigh, he once more shrugs. "Fine, Irena. Don't tell me. I don't care, anyway. I'm just trying to make a point. It doesn't matter to me who trained you or where you come from. I'm here for you *now*."

Irena scoffs. "Right," she says, her voice dripping with sarcasm. "Like you would actually love a Knight or Spectre or any of those monsters."

"I love *you*," he snaps, releasing his grip on her hands and shoulder as he instead reaches for her face. His fingertips are light across her cheeks as he holds her tenderly and stares into her eyes.

Irena watches him, her jaw and shoulders tense as she studies him with a guarded expression, like she's waiting for the axe to fall.

Instead, Eric kisses her. At first, she watches him with her eyes open, letting him embrace her without indulging anything in return. He holds her tightly, and she simply stands there, letting it happen.

After a few moments, however, her eyes slowly flutter closed. She leans in, running her fingers through his hair as she gives in.

I relax my shoulders, grateful that the deep wound in Irena's heart is starting to heal.

That's my cue to leave.

She obviously has big news if she's here, but whatever's happening between her and Eric is also important. I need to give her space to heal—and probably to get laid.

Careful and quiet, I take slow steps away, making sure that she won't hear me.

There's a sharp intake of breath and a subtle gasp as lips part.

Eric huffs in confusion. "What—"

"Hush," Irena says quietly.

I freeze, astonished she heard me. Her senses must be getting better if she could detect the whisper of a footstep.

Hell, maybe her senses are even better than mine.

"Rory," Irena snaps, her voice tight with warning.

Crap.

I got caught.

With a frustrated little sigh, I shake out my shoulders and peek my head through the corridor. I lean against the wall as I grin at them. "You two are adorable."

Irena briefly looks at Eric and pauses, clearly torn between desire and duty. But duty always wins out with her.

"I have news," she admits, looking at me.

"I figured."

She lifts her chin, watching me warily as if she isn't sure she should share this with me. "I wanted you to have this information last night, Rory. But I couldn't risk it being intercepted. Zurie can't know that we know."

I stiffen at the mention of our former mentor's name. "Know what?"

"Her plan," Irena admits, squaring her shoulders.

"She's on the move, Rory. She's coming for us both. Coming for every Fairfax dragon in the world."

"Where?"

Irena pauses as if she can't quite believe what she's about to say. "Here."

"That's suicide," I say, not quite believing it. "Maybe your intel was wrong. Maybe she was leading us on or—"

"It's not wrong," Irena says confidently, shaking her head.

And I've seen that look before. That resigned knowing. The way she frowns, like she wishes it weren't true.

Zurie has nothing to live for, so a suicide battle to end the war is all she has left.

I stand a little straighter, my fingers curling into fists as I slowly nod, accepting the truth of the situation.

"It looks like we have a lot to do to get ready then," I say.

CHAPTER THIRTY

I t's surreal to sit in the war room attached to Jace's suite—only to realize it's not his suite anymore.

This time, Russell leads the meeting, pacing along the far wall as he rubs his jaw and processes everything we've shared with him thus far.

In the last hour, he's gotten a full debriefing of the entire situation involving Zurie—except, of course, for how Irena and I know her. He eyes Irena suspiciously, and then his gaze slowly trails toward me.

It would appear he's piecing things together, and I'm not sure how I feel about that.

The dojo master needs to be smart, suspicious, and aware, and the fact that he's already picking up on the hints as to what Irena and I really are shows that he truly is the best choice for this position.

I just don't know how that's going to affect me and the people I love.

Irena sits to my left, with Jace on my other side. The three of us lean back in our seats, each in various positions as we slowly watch the new dojo master pace on the opposite side of the table. Harper sits across from me with her back to Russell and her eyes glazed over as she thinks through the situation. Levi, Tucker, and Drew sit nearby, spread across the length of the table.

The three of them sat close by—and as much as I'd like to think it's my magnetic personality, they all lean subtly toward me. They must feel the tension. With the news of Zurie's imminent attack and Russell's growing suspicions, they must be as concerned as I am. I suspect they're trying to be a little extra protective, whether it's conscious or not.

It's endearing, if misguided.

If Zurie comes for me, she will have hell to pay. She's put me through too much, threatened the people I love and the dragon within me to the point where she cannot be redeemed.

As the silence wears on, Russell groans and rubs his eyes. "So, the Ghost is coming for us."

"Yes," I confirm with a small nod.

"She will bring an army, probably a combination of

Spectres and Knights, on a suicide mission to destroy us."

"That's right," Jace adds.

"I doubt the others realize the depths of this danger," I admit, tapping my finger absently on the table's polished surface. "The Knights, anyway. The Spectres probably know, but it's death to defy the Ghost. If she asks something of them, they must obey regardless of the cost to themselves."

Russell's eyes narrow in suspicion, but I don't have time to care.

We need a plan.

"The Knights, however," I say continuing as if I don't notice Russell's growing distrust of me. "They probably don't realize what they're doing or what they're getting themselves into. Zurie has a way of making you think you'll have a way out, even if you don't."

"Maybe they do," Harper says ominously, leaning her elbows on the table as she looks intently at me.

"Not possible," Russell says, shaking his head as he pauses behind the Fairfax Boss. "The tunnels are being thoroughly searched as we speak. From the forest to the perimeter, we have the entire dojo on lockdown. We're combing every inch and leaving nothing unturned. There's no possible way anyone can enter without us at least seeing them coming." He squares his shoulders as he resumes pacing, his back arched and strong, and his voice confident.

Russell's firm and in command, and I have to admit, impressive. He will do well in Jace's stead.

As Russell once more walks the length of the table, he pauses again behind Harper's chair, looking down at her with a grim frown on his face. "You're leaving."

"What?" she asks, craning her neck to look at him.

"Please go pack," he says, his voice firm.

"I'm not missing out on this," she says matter-of-factly.

Russell sets his hands on the back of her chair, leaning down until their noses almost touch. "This battle will be intense, and I won't let the Boss be harmed—or worse, killed."

And there it is—the protective fire in his eyes. The smoldering desire he won't let himself feel.

This isn't just about protecting the Boss of the Fairfax family.

This is about protecting the woman he loves.

Harper's cheeks burn with fury, and she sits upright in her chair, returning her gaze to the table as if she won't even consider what he's saying. "Absolutely not. I won't let my people fight assassins by themselves, or—"

"That's an order," Russell snaps, his voice unyielding.

Despite the tension crackling between the two of them, Jace laughs.

Both of them glare at him.

Unfazed, Jace crosses his arms and nods at Russell. "You picked up on the perks of being the dojo master *very* quickly."

Harper grits her teeth in anger, glaring at Jace with all the fire of a star. "You're not helping."

"Harper," Russell says softly. "Go." There's a request in his voice, an almost pleading, but he doesn't actually *ask*.

It's still very much a command.

Outnumbered and at risk for defying an order from the dojo master in the one place where he ranks above her, Harper growls in anger and stands. She walks with the grace of a queen, her chin gently lifted as she leaves.

As she opens the door, however, she pauses ever so briefly to look back at me. Her gaze is full of mischief and fire, and the expression feels incredibly familiar. I'm sure I've given that look to Irena more times than she can count, and it strikes me how similar Harper and my sister are to each other.

Harper is silently asking for my help. She wants me

to keep her updated, despite the fact that she's being cut out of the entire plan.

I nod almost imperceptibly, but she catches it.

Apparently satisfied that I'm on board, she storms off into the hallway and slams the door behind her.

With the door closed and his woman safe, Russell lets out a slow breath, like he can finally think and relax now. He leans his fists against the table, shaking his head. "The chatter isn't good," he confesses. "And it has come to my attention that Harper is as much a target as Rory."

I frown, wondering if he's going to kick me out next.

"Harper is safer in the capital," Russell continues. "Not in the heart of a battle. And besides, if we hold the two women in different locations, there are two targets. They'll have to choose."

"And let me guess," I say, grinning, "I'm the better bait."

He shrugs, smirking a little. "Your words, not mine."

"You're not using her as bait," Jace says, his voice dripping with danger and warning.

Russell watches Jace for a moment, studying the former dojo master as he considers what he's about to say very carefully. "This is not your dojo anymore, Jace."

Beside me, Jace bristles with ire, and he conveys his threat without having to say a word.

If Russell tries to dangle me to lure in the assassins, he will have to go through Jace.

I set a hand on Jace's shoulder.

"Hear him out," I say quietly.

Gently.

His touch ignites a flurry of light and joy that chases through my fingers and up my arm, and I suspect he felt the same thing as I touched him. He instantly relaxes, leaning back against the chair as he looks at me, the anger slowly dissolving from his face the longer I hold his arm.

He returns his attention to Russell, his mouth set in a grim line as he waits for the rest of the plan.

"These are the facts," Russell says firmly, tapping his finger on the table for emphasis. "The Spectres are moving, but we don't know how many of them there are or where they're going. Their chatter is almost impossible to detect, and the only information we have about them comes from the elder Miss Quinn here," he says with a nod toward my sister.

From the way his voice tightens as he addresses Irena, I suspect he's highly wary of how exactly she gathered the data and whether or not it's true. The fact that we all rally behind her is the only reason he's even considering what she has to say.

"The Knights, however, are moving," he continues. "We know that for certain."

Out of the corner of my eye, I spot Tucker lean forward just a little, listening more intently at the mention of the organization that wants him dead.

Russell gestures out the window, clearly frustrated. "They're mobilizing, but it seems for all the world like they're moving away from us, which doesn't make any sense."

"It's a distraction," Irena says dryly.

"I thought so too," Russell admits.

"That's not all," Drew admits, leaning his elbows on the table as he joins the conversation. "My network is finding hints of a third party that's somehow involved in all of this. We have no idea yet who it is, but we're going to find them," he adds with a confident nod as he looks briefly toward me. "They're leasing or outright buying weapons—dragon killers, and a few rumors of long-range missiles."

"Missiles?" I ask dryly, my eyebrows shooting up my forehead. "Are you *kidding*?"

"Wish I was," Drew admits with a disappointed shrug.

"But who could the third party be?" Tucker asks, his brows knitting in confusion. "Not even the Knights have weapons that big, and no one in the *world* will work with them. Legally speaking, it's a war crime to side with the Knights in *any* matter. Whoever has these weapons, whoever's giving these to the Spectres and Knights, they either don't know these organizations are involved, or they don't care."

"That's a problem," Levi admits, frowning deeply as he rubs his jaw.

Russell, surprisingly, says nothing. He simply watches Tucker as if he's noticing something for the first time. There's a suspicious glint in his eye, and his knuckles crack slightly as he leans them against the edges of the table.

Damn, Russell is way too smart.

"This is turning into an all-out assault," I say, in part to distract Russell, but mostly because it's genuinely concerning me.

I don't like this at all. It's a full-on war.

I bite my lip, my mind buzzing with ideas until one becomes clearer than the rest. I look at Russell, my shoulders relaxing a little as I realize what we need to do. "We should lead them away."

"Absolutely not," Russell says quickly, shaking his

head as he crosses his arms. "I won't allow it. It makes us look weak to have you running off."

"No, it doesn't," I argue, gesturing vaguely toward the door. "It throws Zurie off her game at the last minute. It changes the plan, which means she's less prepared. It means we all have a better chance of survival."

"No, it means there are better chances she will ambush you," Russell snaps, glaring at me. "This is not negotiable, Miss Quinn. The dojo's duty is to guard Jace, our former master, and his mate, *you*. I will not allow you to leave. None of you," he adds, his gaze sweeping over us all.

For a moment, the tense silence settles on the room as everyone leans forward, stiffening in defiance at the thought of being trapped within these walls.

Jace, however, laughs.

"And *what* is so damn funny?" I ask, looking at him like he's gone crazy.

"I get it now," he says, still chuckling. "This is how you felt, Rory. Every time I threatened to lock you away."

Oh.

Well, yeah.

I can't help the smile that cracks across my face as I

roll my eyes. "Yeah, Jace, this is exactly what it feels like."

"If you try to leave, you will be found," Russell interrupts, his voice firm and tense. "We have troops everywhere in the tunnels, in the air, in the forests, on the walls. The entire perimeter is on absolute lockdown." He hesitates, rubbing his temples. "I'm not threatening you. I'm just letting you know that this is the safest place for you to be. No one will be able to sneak up on us, and if anyone is stupid enough to try to attack, we will obliterate them."

Around me, everyone begins to relax into their chairs. Not out of relief, however. Mostly out of resignation.

He's on our side, and he's doing what he thinks is best—not just for us, but for all of Fairfax.

But Irena and I, we share the same mission to kill Zurie. Wherever she goes, we'll be. It's time for us to end this. To end this threat against not only us, but everyone we're learning to care for and love.

Our former mentor raised us to be assassins. The best killers in the world.

Irena and I are going to make her regret that.

As my mind buzzes with ideas on how take her down once and for all, I consider something I hadn't before—a way the Spectres might try to screw us over. To destroy us from within.

I'm not sure how to word this, but I know I need to speak up—no matter the cost to me.

"What's the policy on prisoners of war?" I ask, rubbing my jaw as I intently watch Russell's face.

His jaw tenses, and he narrows his eyes in confusion for a moment. "We accept them if they surrender. They go into the cells, separated and isolated, but well-cared-for."

"And then what?" I ask, lifting my chin in defiance, urging him to tell me the truth.

"They're interrogated," he admits, setting his hand on his hips as he slowly realizes where I'm taking this.

"And if they comply?" I press.

"If they play along, they survive," Russell says simply. "And if they don't..." He trails off, his gaze darting toward Jace, and I know exactly what he's thinking of.

All of the Knights who've come for me over the last few months—all the ones who *haven't* complied, who threatened me and the dojo and everything Jace loves.

They found themselves in early graves.

Frankly, it takes a certain obstinate stupidity to threaten someone who has you locked up and tied to a chair.

I frown, crossing my arms as I lean back in my seat, knowing that no Spectre would ever make a threat in a situation like that. They would play along. They would lie, and they would be *especially* convincing. They would say whatever they needed to say to appear compliant. They might even slowly make friends with the guards, let the dragons think they're just an innocent person in a bad situation.

And then, when their enemy's guard was down, they would strike.

I bite my lip, not sure what to share with Russell at this point. Jace isn't the master of the dojo anymore. If Russell doesn't accept me as a Spectre, Jace may not be able to protect me here. Russell said it himself—this entire place is on lockdown, even more so than before. If they try to lock me away, if they consider my Spectre past as dangerous and worthy of imprisonment, there may not be any way out.

Doesn't mean I wouldn't try, but it does mean we have a lower chance of success.

And if there's one thing I learned from Zurie, it's to measure risk carefully before any action is taken.

However, I don't want these people hurt just because they don't understand the full fury of what's coming for them.

Out of the corner of my eye, I look at Irena. Her

bright green eyes dart toward me, and they narrow a bit as she realizes what I'm about to do. She frowns, subtly shaking her head, but I just nod.

We have to.

We have to warn them of what's coming.

"Promise me something," I say, studying Russell's face as I speak. "If Zurie surrenders—if *any* of the Spectres surrender—kill them immediately."

The room goes still as everyone holds their breath and looks at me in shock.

I know it sounds brutal.

I know it sounds cruel, even, but this is the way it has to be.

"That's against our code," Russell says, shaking his head in baffled disbelief.

I open my mouth to speak, but the words die in my throat as my training kicks in and warns me to shut the hell up. There are about forty Spectre rules warning me not to share what I'm about to share.

However, I want to protect the Fairfax dragons who have done so much for us. More importantly, I want to protect my men.

"Honor is a weapon Spectres use against their opponents," I say simply. "It's a weapon that Zurie trains her Spectres to look for and manipulate at any chance because honor allows you to pit someone's values against them if you're clever enough."

I hesitate, resisting the impulse to look at Irena as she stiffens beside me.

"Look, Russell," I say leaning forward. "If Zurie's attack fails, she *will* surrender to buy time. Once she's inside, she *will* escape, and once she escapes, she will try to implode the building from within even if it kills her. This is how the Spectres think. They're trained to do this, to use surrender as a form of delaying the inevitable. To them, it's just a way to manipulate their opponent into an early death."

In the silence that follows, Russell's eyes narrow. He slowly arches his back, standing taller and watching me as if he's seeing a side of me for the first time—and he doesn't like it.

"You know a remarkable amount about Spectres, Miss Quinn."

"I do, don't I?" I say evenly, unfazed and holding his gaze.

Russell is tense, and it would appear that something has clicked for him. In that moment, his suspicions have been confirmed. But as he looks around the room, his gaze sweeping across everyone else here, his expression slowly corrodes into one of calm understanding.

Everyone here already knows what he just pieced together.

He sighs, rubbing the back of his neck as he slowly shakes his head. "Being the dojo master is going to take some getting used to."

"There's no one more capable," Jace says confidently.

"Thank you," Russell says, his gaze darting toward his former mentor. "Sir."

"What are you going to do?" I ask, and he knows damn well what I mean.

He watches me again, studying me, but the dangerous intent from before is gone. "I protect those who seek haven in these walls," he says simply. "And that includes you."

I subtly let out a slow breath as I relax, grateful I don't have to fight the master of the dojo. Grateful we're still allies.

I just hope that doesn't change.

"And for the Spectres who surrender?" I ask, pressing the matter.

"I'll think about it, Rory," he says simply, shaking his head, and I know I've asked him to do the impossible. With that request, I've pitted two of his values against each other—his vow to protect those who come here seeking haven with his vow to protect those who are already here.

"We're done for now," Russell says simply, gesturing toward the door. "There's a long fight ahead of us, and we have no idea of how quickly or slowly it will come. All we can do is prepare."

The rest of us take the hint, standing, but he nods toward me and Jace. "You two wait."

Irena, Drew, Tucker, and Levi hesitate, not exactly eager to leave us alone with the man who just figured out what I am. I look at Jace with wary concern.

"It's fine, guys," Jace says, nodding to them. "Go."

Instead of listening to him, the others turn toward me, and I subtly nod in agreement.

If Jace trusts Russell, so do I.

We wait in silence as the others leave, and I know they won't be far. They'll probably linger in the hallway, finding excuses not to leave, all of them ready to dash in at a moment's notice should the need arise.

I desperately hope the need does not, in fact, arise.

When the door shuts behind Irena and only the three of us are left in the room, Russell looks at me with his arms crossed and his chin raised in astonishment. "You're a Spectre," he says calmly, a hint of accusation in his tone.

I don't answer. Except in rare occasions, that's

never a question I answer. I instead watch him with a grim expression, daring him to press the issue.

"She *was*," Jace corrects after a moment, standing behind me and holding my shoulders firmly.

His touch sends shivers of pleasure through me despite the severity of the moment, and it's comforting to know he has my back through all things. Regardless of who I was and where I came from, he loves me. All he cares about is who I am now and who I can be.

Russell sighs in disappointment, his shoulders drooping slightly as he leans back against the wall behind him. "Does Harper know?"

I hesitate, tempted to ignore the question again, but I eventually nod.

The next time he talks to her, he's going to find out anyway.

"And Irena?" he continues. "She's a Spectre, too?"

I narrow my eyes skeptically, wondering where he's going with this and if there's an end in sight.

He takes my silence as his answer and nods as if I confirmed it. "Look, I meant what I said, Rory. If you're here, you're safe. Besides, Jace wouldn't mate with a monster." He hesitates, rubbing the stubble on his jaw as he stares out the window. "But when the other Spectres come, I can't have you recognizing your friends on the battlefield. I can't have you allowing for—"

"When they come, they'll die," I assure him, not letting him finish the thought. "I have no affection for any of them, and I didn't have any friends in the Spectres. They're here to kill me and the people I love."

Russell pauses, not acknowledging that he heard or understood my answer, and I wonder if that's a tactic of some kind to throw me off my game.

It's effective. I think I'll try that next chance I get.

"And Tucker…" he says, trailing off, waiting for me to finish the sentence.

Yet again, I'm tempted to simply ignore it. To say nothing. But I remember the trouble Tucker faced when he first came here, when Jace knew there was something off about him but wasn't quite sure what it was. I need to nip this in the bud to make sure that Tucker's safe.

"Tucker is dead to them," I say vaguely, even though I'm positive Russell knows exactly what I mean. "And they're dead to him."

Russell lets out a slow breath, and when he looks up, his full and intense focus is on Jace. "Is this what being the dojo master is like?"

"Yeah," Jace says with a nod as he pats Russell on the shoulder. "You're doing great, Russell. Just don't let

Harper get her way. That's all you've got to worry about."

The three of us chuckle, a bit of tension lifting from our shoulders as Russell accepts the sordid pasts of Irena, Tucker, and me.

He was right about one thing—we don't know when the war is coming, and the wait is going to be agonizing. I can feel the battle on the horizon. I can taste the blood and smell it in the air.

I'll face off with Zurie again, and as I promised her the last time we met, one of us is going to die. There will be no escape for her, no way out, no chance to retreat and come after me again.

This is it. Come hell or high water, she's going to die—by my hand, or preferably, by my *claw*.

CHAPTER THIRTY-ONE

I sit on the roof of my tower with Levi beside me, and I'm fidgeting because I'm just so freaking *antsy*.

Four days have passed since our meeting with Russell, and it's always the same news—every morning and every night.

The troops are mobilizing.

An attack is imminent.

And then absolutely *nothing* happens.

Beside me, Levi stretches out on the roof with his eyes closed, his hands behind his head as he takes deep and serene breaths.

"Try to relax, Rory," he says with his eyes still closed.

"I can't, damn it," I say, pushing myself to my feet. "How are you so calm, Levi?"

A little smile plays at the corner of his mouth, but he doesn't answer, and he doesn't open his eyes.

I pace the stone shingles two hundred feet in the air, glaring at the horizon with deadly focus. Adrenaline buzzes through me like it has for the last few days as I wait for something to happen.

And wait.

And *wait.*

I just want to *do* something.

In the distance, a tight formation of twelve dragons bank in perfect synchronicity above the forest, scoping the perimeter. As I pace along the roof, I zero in on them, my ears ringing slightly as I focus and tune out the world.

Waiting for a sign. Waiting for them to act.

It looks like they might have found something as they circle the same area twice, and I wonder if they're going to dive.

If it's starting.

If Zurie is here.

There are troops deployed across the surrounding area, even more than were here a few days ago. As General of the Fairfax army, Russell summoned troops from the capital itself to ensure we had enough firepower.

We have so many soldiers crawling these woods and camping on the mountains around us that if someone so much as sneezes out there, a dragon will bite their head off within ten seconds.

These troops are armed and ready to defend their home.

The squad hovers, banking again around the patch of trees in question before they continue their patrol.

False alarm.

It took some convincing, but Russell allowed my men to go on patrol as long as they remained within the lands closest to the embassy itself—no perimeter patrols for them. Tucker, Drew, and Jace are currently leading a squad through the forests as they help where they can. Levi, however, said he wanted the night off.

Uh huh.

Sure.

It's almost like they think I haven't realized they always leave one man behind to stay with me.

To protect me.

It's sweet, but again, unnecessary. I would rather be along the walls, out in the forest, doing something useful, rather than just standing here pacing and brainstorming various ways Zurie can break in.

Every time I try to help, however, I get an earful from Russell and a call from Harper, asking me to go drown myself in chocolate ice cream and just relax already.

It's getting annoying.

Behind me, Levi groans and stands. I don't hear any other movement, and for a second or two, I figure he's just standing there looking out at the horizon like I am.

That is, until I feel his hands on my shoulders.

I flinch slightly in surprise, and I don't know if I'll ever get used to his stealthy silence. As his fingers run along my arms, his cool touch soothes the bubbling tension within me. My treasonous body impulsively leans backward into his chest, and I have to confess I'm happier simply with him nearby. I'm able to breathe a little easier, but I still don't rein in my intense glare across the horizon as another squad makes their rounds.

"Irena said they're coming," he says calmly. "So, they're coming. It won't do any good to obsess over it."

I shake my head. "Russell went overboard. He shouldn't have called in the other troops! He should have asked me first, and I could have told him that it would tip off Zurie. We lost the advantage, Levi," I say, looking over my shoulder at him as I once more start to pace. "She knows that we know."

I curse under my breath, furious at Russell, knowing full well what Zurie is doing out there now.

She's debating moving forward. If she does, she risks being outnumbered. If she can wait us out, she can hang around until we let down our guard.

Or, after assessing the danger, she might simply leave.

Zurie is desperate, but she also knows when to fight another day. Killing me and Irena is her only reason for living, and she will wait as long as it takes to ensure it happens.

Levi's hands once more brush along my shoulders, and this time he kisses me tenderly along my neck. His lips on my skin open our connection, and a swirling storm of calmness seeps into me.

The zen and peace he's feeding into me both settle my heart, even though I know they're not my emotions at all. Through our connection, and by using his own emotions against me, he soothes the dread in my gut and fogs my mind.

"That's not fair," I chide even as I relax into him. "We have to be poised and ready to go at a moment's notice. I can't *be* calm."

"Poised, yes," he says. "Obsessive, no."

I frown, not entirely agreeing as I continue to survey the forest around us.

As I scan the horizon, a handful of troops change shift. Dozens of exhausted soldiers filter over the bridge and into the barracks for a bit of sleep before they have to do it all again.

I stiffen as I watch them enter the embassy, one after another. I hate that so many people's lives are in danger because of me, and I'm still tempted to leave to draw Zurie away. I'm getting frustrated about all the risk Russell is taking on, all in the name of protecting their former dojo master.

All in the name of protecting me.

Levi abruptly spins me around, and for a moment, I'm dizzy—which is never a good thing when you're standing two-hundred feet in the air, on a roof. But he holds me tightly, his blue eyes watching me with an intensity that steals my breath away.

Shit. He must have heard all of those thoughts, since our connection is still open.

I'm so focused on Zurie that I simply forgot he could read my mind with the connection open.

"Zurie is coming with an army," Levi says seriously, his eyes narrowing as he dares me to debate him. "You need to have one, too."

"But it's not *my* army," I remind him, gesturing to

the soldiers funneling into the embassy behind me. "It's Russell's. It's Harper's. Who am I to ask them to put their lives on the line for me?"

"They're not doing it for you," he says gently, his gaze softening just a little as he runs his fingertips lightly along my cheek. "They're doing it out of love for their home. Harper is being threatened, same as you. They're protecting their Boss, the woman who runs their family, who makes them strong and wealthy. They're protecting *her*."

I frown, my gaze falling to the roof tiles as I think about what he's saying. "Maybe, but—"

"The dojo stands for peace in a world that tries to take it from them regularly," Levi continues, not letting me finish. "So, these soldiers are fighting for Harper, yes. But they're also fighting for that right to simply *live*. Besides, these people would die for Jace—which means yes, they would die for you, too. But you're one of just many reasons they're fighting, Rory. Keep that in mind and give yourself a bit of grace."

I don't want to.

Truth be told, I want to do everything in my power to convince Russell to let us leave—or, hell, maybe just go.

But as I think through everything Levi's saying, I can't deny that he has a point.

"The truth is…" Levi trails off, gently rubbing my arms as he stares off into the horizon, trying to form his words. "The truth is you're not just some dragon, Rory. You're not even the dragon vessel anymore."

"What do you mean?" I ask, genuinely confused.

Wherever he's going with this, I'm not following.

"Rory, diamond dragons were lore until yours came into being," he points out, studying my face as he speaks. "The only ones ever thought to exist were the gods themselves."

He pauses as that sinks in, and for a moment, I simply can't comprehend it.

"You don't mean…" I trail off, not even able to finish the thought.

"Yeah," he says, nodding.

I may not just have the gods' magic.

I might be a fucking god *myself*.

"That's a bit heavy, don't you think?" I ask, looking at him, wondering if that could possibly be true.

"Perhaps," he admits. "But one thing's for sure, Rory, you're meant for more than this dojo."

I run my hand through my hair, taking a few steps away from him to clear my head and settle my racing heart.

"You've been saying for a while now that you're not sure we should stay here," Levi continues, letting me walk away and collect my thoughts. "I think you're right, especially now that Jace can leave. After this mess with Zurie, we go."

Despite the heavy topic of conversation, I look at him over my shoulder and smirk. "So, now you're bossy, too?"

He grins. "I might be picking up a few things from Drew, yeah."

I chuckle, admiring him for a moment. The dark hair. The brilliant blue eyes. The way he leans ever so slightly forward, like he wants to pull me close and hold me tight, but is just barely holding himself back to give me the space I need right now.

"We should find Ashgrave," he continues. "Drew's been looking for it, but now I think Harper is looking, too. And Jace. And Russell. Everyone wants to help you find your new home."

I smile, watching him affectionately as he sets his hands on his hips, trying to make me see reason.

"Okay," I say with a small nod.

His brows lift in surprise, as if he expected me to fight this harder. "Really?"

"Really," I promise.

We're going to find Ashgrave come hell or high water, and I just hope it's more than ruins and legend.

"For now, though," I say, gesturing toward the

forest. "Let's just focus on stopping my former mentor, who keeps trying to kill me."

"Yeah," he says, laughing. "That's fair."

From the mists behind the dojo, a jet-black dragon soars into the dark sky. Golden magic glimmers along his body, glowing just beneath the thunderbird's scales.

Russell.

He flies directly toward us, and I square my shoulders as I prepare for bad news.

The new dojo master lands on the roof, cracking a few tiles beneath his talons as he lowers his head toward us, inviting us to speak with him.

I set my palm against his forehead, and Levi follows suit by setting his hand against the dragon's neck.

The connection opens, and a blur of Russell's thoughts tumble through. I catch snippets of him flying through a forest, branches snapping under the heavy force of his wings. The brown and green blurs of the woods around him whiz by, disappearing as quickly as they come into vision.

Are you staying out of trouble? he asks, his voice cutting through the fragmented memory.

I smirk. *Trying to.*

He chuckles, the hot breath snorting through his

nose as his dragon laughs. *Wanted to let you know since you probably already saw it, but movement has been detected in the southern woods. We've taken care of it already,* he adds with a stern look toward me. *Some bounty hunters. Nothing major.*

It might still be Zurie, I warn him. *It could be a distraction or a test of your forces and response time.*

I considered that, he admits. *I sent the response team in a little slower than they wanted to go, simply to give false intel.*

"Thank you," I say, grateful he's taking the threat seriously.

We also found traces of explosives along the base of the cliff beneath the dojo, he admits, stiffening slightly in his ire that someone could get so close. *Security has been doubled, and the bombs are being quickly dismantled as we—*

"Wait," I order.

He snorts impatiently *Wait? What on earth for?*

A wicked little grin creeps across my face. "Let them think they've won this round."

Levi and Russell both watch me, the two shifters confused as my plan slowly forms.

But this—this is perfect.

"That's Zurie's style," I confess. "She loves a good explosion, and I suspect that's one of her failsafes. She spent a lot of money and cashed in a lot of favors to get those explosives down there, and I assume she strategically planted them?"

Along structural lines, yes, Russell admits. *At first, we thought little of it—these explosives are so small, I couldn't see what good they would do. As our explosives team began to disconnect them, however, they realized these are highly advanced. If they all were to detonate at once, the entire island holding the dojo would crumble.*

"That's the plan," I promise him. "She wants to wait until as many people are there as possible and implode it."

Why hasn't she already? Levi asks.

"She wants to watch me die," I say, my eyes darting toward him. "She has to know for a fact that I'm dead."

She sounds charming, Russell says dryly.

"Oh, the best." I roll my eyes. "Russell, look for the GPS on each explosive. There will be one, I guarantee it. Leave those behind, and if possible, don't let them move."

Russell hesitates, but he slowly nods as he pieces together where I'm going with this. *We trick her. We let her think this worked.*

"Exactly," I say, smirking. "That gives us the upper hand, for now anyway."

His bright eyes shift toward me, electric and fierce,

and he nods, my hand moving slightly with the subtle movement of his head. *We're ready, Rory. And when the time comes, I want you to stay out of the fray.*

He hesitates, waiting for me to agree. Even Levi looks up at me, waiting to see what I'll say.

I choose to say nothing because I don't want to lie.

Not to them.

CHAPTER THIRTY-TWO

I stand on a balcony looking over the vast forest around the dojo as the moon climbs across the sky.

I couldn't sleep if I wanted to, and as I lean against the railing looking out into the night, all I can do is wonder where Zurie is. What she's thinking. What she must have planned. Why she's waiting, and how she's spending the time.

With Jace asleep in the suite through the open double doors behind me, part of me wishes I could join him. This is a new bedroom, close to the wing where the rest of us sleep—but this stretch of the embassy is reserved for war heroes.

An honor Jace has certainly earned.

As a gust of wind blows by me, ruffling my hair, I

stand upright with my arms crossed and my legs in a wide stance. I'm ready for a brutal war that just won't start, and anticipation for the battle buzzes through me, making me restless.

I might as well channel this energy into something productive.

With only the occasional blustery wind and chirping cricket to keep me company, I reach inward toward my dragon.

Come on, babe, I say to her. *Let's shift.*

I feel a surge of resistance, like she's actively building a brick wall between us so that she can get some sleep. Annoyed, I curse quietly under my breath.

She's so damn stubborn. I have *no* idea where she gets that from.

With a deep and centering breath, I try again, reaching for her, asking for her, opening up to her.

This time, I wait just out of reach, wondering what she will do. Wondering if she will close the gap between us.

This time, I feel her come to me. It's slow at first, like waiting for an animal who isn't sure of your intentions yet. But as I keep my breath calm and steady, I feel her sink into me, trusting me.

My shoulders relax as the two of us merge, and I once more ask for the shift.

She leans in, fully listening, actually wanting this. Together, we lean forward. My skin buzzes, and my body aches. I can feel the ripples of pain shooting through me, the tell-tale sign of the pending shift.

But nothing happens.

The shift doesn't come.

On impulse, I hold my breath, trying to force it. The harder I push, however, the more light-headed I feel. Before I know it, I fall forward—my hands outstretched, reaching for the railing so that I don't fall a hundred feet to the ground below.

Two strong hands grab my shoulders, and a familiar voice lets out a relieved sigh as his strong head leans against the back of mine.

"Please don't fall to your death, damn it," Jace says quietly.

I chuckle. "Sorry."

His strong fingers ignite my core as they press against my arms, rooting me in place. His touch is like silk, and it calms my soul. Inwardly, my dragon swirls with glee, wanting more.

"Are you trying to shift again?" he asks.

"Trying and failing," I mutter, not bothering to mask the small pout of my lips as I think over my failure. "I want to be able to shift for the battle."

He peeks around me until I can see his face, and he

lifts one eyebrow skeptically. "You mean the battle Russell ordered you not to join?"

I grin sheepishly. "Yeah, that one."

He laughs and kisses my cheek, wrapping his arms around me as he holds my back tightly to his chest, hugging me from behind. "I knew better than to think you'd obey that command."

"Are you going to try to keep me in a tower?" I joke.

"Hell, no," he says. "You and I are going onto that battlefield and sending those assassins to their maker."

I nod, grateful for my partner in crime. "Damn right, we are."

My dragon stirs again within me, louder this time, and I set a hand on my chest as my heart pangs.

"She really reacts to you," I say, taking a moment to study myself after her surge of power.

Even though I can't see his face, I hear the flattered chuckle as he holds me a little tighter.

"I want to try to shift again," I say.

"Or we could just enjoy the night," he counters.

"I kind of feel like we should get ready for the war that's coming our way," I say, not bothering to mask my sarcasm.

He laughs. "Must you be so damn *serious* all the time?"

I pause. "Yes."

He chuckles and sighs in defeat. "Fine. But Rory, I don't think you should be in your dragon form for the fight."

I frown, pivoting on my heel to stare him down. "Why not?"

"You won't have control over your magic yet," he points out, lifting his hands as he gestures vaguely toward the sky. "Your magic is your most powerful weapon, even over your diamond dragon. Even if you're able to access it in your dragon form, there's no guarantee you'll be able to control that power. You could hurt one of us," he adds, gesturing toward himself. "Besides, you're still learning to fly. To control your new body. It's just too soon."

My gaze drops briefly to the balcony floor as I think about what he's saying and really process the risk. When I fly, I feel so powerful, so strong. In my dragon form, life just feels right, even if my flying is wobbly and my access to my magic is inconsistent at best.

There's just something so right about it.

"Trust me, Rory," he says, setting his hands on my shoulders as he smiles gently. "You'll get the hang of it. But for now, trust your human body." He gently taps his finger against my chest. "Trust yourself."

"I should still know how to shift," I point out. "If I fall, I'll need to fly. If I need to save someone…"

"Fair points," he says, shrugging. "I trust you, Rory. Listen to yourself and listen to your dragon. That's all I'm saying."

"Okay. I concede."

"Now close your eyes," he orders. "It's easier to shift in the beginning if your eyes are shut."

Despite his playfully bossy tone, I play along and indulge him. I feel for my dragon as she swims and tumbles within me, eager and ready, just waiting for a chance to stretch her wings.

"How is she feeling?" Jace asks.

"Restless," I answer.

"Is that you or her?" he challenges.

I pause again, frowning slightly as I listen a little more intently, filtering past the impatience to the dull pulse of her energy deep within.

She's brimming with power and light. Ready for war. Ready for blood.

Ready to fly.

"Eager," I answer, more confident this time.

"Good," Jace says as I hear him slowly pace around me. "Feel how that's different from your own energy. Listen for that difference. Really get to know it."

I scrunch my features as I focus on trying to implement what he's suggesting, knowing he's watching me all the while.

I have to confess that, with my mate circling me, I want to show off a little.

Come on, girl, I ask her. *Come on.*

Once again, my dragon leans into me, opening her heart as we merge into one.

And this time, we shift.

My body buzzes and hums with power and magic. My ears pop as ripples of pain tear through me, followed by surges of relief and adrenaline. The balcony gives a little underneath me, and I instinctively beat my wings on the air to lift myself into the sky. I take off, the stars glimmering above me as the wind cuts against my face, crisp and sweet.

I briefly look down as my wings beat the air, watching the moonlight glimmer off my iridescent scales.

Victory.

I roar into the sky triumphantly, once more connected to my dragon. Seconds later, Jace joins me, his jet-black skin almost invisible against the night sky except for the soft blue glow of his magic cutting through his wings. He effortlessly soars past, flying in literal circles around me as he growls in encouragement.

I began to feel more in tune with my wings as I carry myself into the stars, ever higher.

Movement in my periphery catches my attention, and I look down to see Tucker waving from the roof. Levi stands beside him, arms crossed, but I can't quite see the details of their features. A red fire dragon dominates the roof beside them.

Drew.

My fire dragon takes to the air, soaring toward me and Jace, and the two of them spiral around me as I soar higher.

It's a magical moment, one I feel like I'm stealing from the night. I can let the obsessive worry of when Zurie will attack slide off of me and just enjoy the moment. I stretch my wings and bank, the three of us circling the embassy as the crisp, clean air soars past me.

I feel so free. It's like soaring through heaven, and I feel like I was meant for the sky.

Below us, Tucker cheers as Levi watches quietly. As we near, I catch a broad grin on Levi's face, and I feel a swell of pride.

Even though I know he wants to be up here with us —that he and his dragon are still learning to see eye to eye—I'm grateful he can be happy for me. For my flight. For my connection to my dragon. For my shift.

Jace and Drew slip into formation around me, letting me lead as they keep to my admittedly slow pace. It's a kindness, one I figure they won't extend to me for much longer, as I know they're both going to want to train me to fly properly.

That's something I can worry about later.

There's a subtle shift in the air, and my joy quickly dissolves.

Even though nothing has changed, I feel a flicker of warning as my intuition detects something in the night that I miss. I look at Jace, and he tenses as well, scanning the horizon warily.

Something's off.

I just don't know what.

Drew seems to catch the hint, and even though he briefly scans my face, he quickly turns his attention to the world around us.

Twelve dragons sail by in tight formation, a scout squad that flies by Jace as they check on us. The leader of the pack nods to Jace, and it strikes me as the sort of subtle motion that's supposed to mean everything is fine. As they trail by, a few of them steal looks over their shoulder at me.

An air current cuts past me, and I wobble, still not used to my wings yet. Drew impulsively flies beneath me, ready to catch me if I fall, and I flick my tail at him playfully. He returns to my side, black smoke trailing from his nose as he watches me through the corner of his eye.

An alarm cuts through the air.

The warning.

The attack has begun.

Jace roars at me, nodding toward the roof, and we angle toward it. I know what he's doing—he wants me to shift back. To be human for this battle.

I still don't know if I agree.

Not to sound cocky, but I'm a *diamond dragon*—a creature of lore and magic. That's got to count for *something.*

Around us, hundreds of dragons take instantly to the air, breaking through the forest canopy as they fill the sky. Drew nudges my side, angling me toward the roof.

Ugh.

Fine.

I angle downward, hoping I don't drive a hole through the roof as I land, but kind of expecting it to happen anyway.

As the other dragons soar through the air, one of them dives toward us. He's as dark as shadow, and the yellow light of his magic leaves streaks through the midnight sky as he darts toward us at a blinding pace.

Russell.

He roars in warning, the sound almost desperate and panicked. He knows something—something we missed.

Something we haven't yet seen.

He roars again, but I have no idea what he's trying to tell us.

Moments later, explosions light the sky. Whistles tear through the clouds, and it takes me a moment to realize what's happening.

Missiles.

I roar into the air, brimming with fury and frustration that they were able to attack us without us noticing—after everything we've done. After all the precautions we took.

But this is Zurie.

If anyone can undermine a fortress and destroy it from within, it's *her*.

The three of us bolt toward the roof as Russell races to meet us.

I need to go get Tucker and Levi, to make sure they're safe. They wave at us from the rooftop, shouting something we can't hear over the whistles and explosions in the sky.

Beside me, Jace rotates, flying backward as magic pools and burns in his throat. He fires off several blasts of blue light, destroying missiles before they can actually hit anything. Explosions thunder behind us, shooting hot waves of air over me.

And damn it all, I wish I could help.

On my other side, Drew does the same, a brilliant blaze of fire shooting from his mouth as he destroys three missiles in one blow.

Explosions burn through the sky like fireworks as the missiles detonate too early. The deafening blasts make my ears ring sharply, the high-pitched whine almost painful.

My dragon wants in.

Instinct pulls on my magic, drawing it from the depths of my soul. It smolders in my chest, hot and fierce. The warmth and energy climb up my throat, desperate to break free.

No, I warn her. *We could hurt people.*

If I summon the magic, there's no saying what my control will be like. I need to practice in a controlled environment, not in a war zone where I could hurt someone on our side.

The impulsive wave of magic simmers, fading slowly as she listens, and I let out a sigh of relief.

A dozen missiles clump together, soaring through the air. This—this was intentional. These missiles were definitely meant for the three of us.

Jace and Drew unleash their magic and fire on the missiles, and the thundering crack of explosions burst through the sky.

Four of them get through the brilliant yellow fire.

Three miss, sailing off into the forest. Yellow and orange flames burst into the night, flattening trees and igniting the canopy.

But one missile hits its target, and slams against Jace's chest. The explosion knocks him through the sky, away from me, and he goes limp.

My thunderbird falls.

I feel it—the bolt of pain ripping through me as he's hit. It's surreal to feel another's pain, but my world goes briefly white. I stumble through the air, hurt by the blow that hit him, and drop in altitude.

But I recover.

And I'm *pissed.*

A surge of adrenaline and dread pumps through me, as does the overwhelming need to protect him. Without even thinking it through, I instinctively bolt through the sky, flying impossibly fast as I try to catch him before he falls to his death.

Russell has the same idea, and the two of us race toward the former dojo master as Drew roars at us in warning.

I don't even register Drew at first. I just hear the

same roar, echoing again and again in my mind, cutting through the chaos.

Getting louder and louder.

Then, I hear a whistle.

It whizzes through the air, getting closer with every passing second.

As the more experienced flyer, Russell gets to Jace before I can. He dips below Jace's unconscious body and catches him, carrying the former dojo master on his back as they tumble harmlessly into the canopy.

But that whistling, it just gets louder.

I look behind me as a missile approaches, coming too fast for me to duck out of the way.

Shit.

It hits my chest, and the pain shatters me. I can't even breathe. Every muscle tenses, paralyzed and immobile.

My wings stop working.

My body goes limp.

I fall.

The roars of panic through the night begin to fade as the ringing in my ears gets worse.

My vision blurs, and the last thing I see is a familiar blue blur sailing through the flame-riddled sky before my world goes dark.

CHAPTER THIRTY-THREE

I wake to the hazy sound of someone calling my name.

My head aches.

Searing pain splinters through my brow with every breath, with every movement.

My head spins, and I can barely think straight as the world rolls around me. I sit upright, and a flush of nausea burns through my cheeks. I pause to keep it at bay as the memory of the assault flashes through my mind.

The explosions.

The missiles.

Drew roaring in warning.

Jace falling toward trees below.

Jace.

A surge of adrenaline shoots through me like fire as bloodlust and fury pump through my veins.

I open my eyes, but the world's still blurry. The hazy silhouette of a person hovers over me. In my confused daze, instinct takes over. I cock my fist back and punch them, expecting them to fall to the floor.

The blow is fast, but a strong hand catches my fist. Thin fingers wrap around my hand with surprising strength.

My vision slowly clears, the blurs sharpening into detail, and it takes me only a moment longer to recognize Harper's face.

She leans toward me, her brows knit in concern, surrounded by the shadows of a dark room.

"Oh, good. You're not dead," she says with a wry grin.

As another round of nausea floods me, I try to figure out where I am.

Indoors.

Darkness.

The room is mostly empty, the walls made of a familiar black stone. Thin slits line the circular room, windows to the outside that let in thin rays of moonlight. Other than the occasional beam of silvery light, shadows swallow most of the dark chamber.

I adjust, only to feel the subtle give of a spring

below me. My world shifts slightly as the rough cot gives with my movement. I toss the blanket off of me as I try to get my bearings.

Harper sets her hands on my shoulders, squinting slightly as she studies my face, looking for something I don't have the energy to figure out right now.

As I continue to survey the world around me, it takes me a minute to realize she's not wearing any clothes.

"Girl, you're naked," I say, slurring as my head continues to spin.

"Yeah, thanks," she says dryly. "I shifted and flew over to help you all, so I'm afraid the clothes didn't quite survive the flight."

"Russell said not to do that," I quip, smirking at her audacity even as I continue to slur.

I rub my temples, trying to clear my head.

That was a hell of a concussion.

"Well, if he survives, he can yell at me," Harper says, shrugging.

"Where are we?" I ask.

"A watchtower at the edge of the dojo lands, a relatively safe space—at least for now. They needed to make sure you were out of harm's way, as you took the brunt of one hell of a missile." Harper whistles, clearly impressed. "I really didn't think you were going to wake up for a while." She hesitates, her smile falling. "Or at all."

"I'm fine," I lie, trying to ignore the way the room tilts around me. "Jace got hit. Is he—did he—"

"He's fine," Harper says, her tone gentle and soothing. "Dazed, but not dead. And, of course, already back in the fray."

I sigh with relief.

Thank goodness.

"I've been listening in to see when the fight would happen, but I wasn't expecting it to be this bad," she admits.

My head snaps toward her as I narrow my eyes in surprise and suspicion. The sudden movement shakes my brain, making the room spin again. But I grit my teeth and force my way through it. "What's going on?"

"A simultaneous attack of the Spectres and the Knights," she says, hesitating as she watches me. She tenses as if she's about to deliver a heavy blow.

"Just say it," I demand.

"The Spectres, the Knights—and the Vaer," she finishes.

"What?" I stand, fighting the surge of disorienting vertigo as my voice drips with icy disgust.

Harper nods. "It looks like an orchestrated surprise attack, and only the Spectres seem to know what's going on. The Vaer and the Knights attacked at once from every direction. Definitely an orchestrated event, except that the Vaer and Knights are also attacking each other," she says, lifting a skeptical eyebrow.

"That's Zurie's doing," I say, stumbling a bit as I try to get my bearings. Harper grabs my shoulder, helping me stay upright, and I nod in thanks. "Zurie's pitting everyone against each other to create enough chaos so that she can swoop in, do what she needs to do, and swoop out."

"Yeah, that was my worry, too," Harper admits. "Come on. We're leaving."

She grabs my bicep, but I violently wrench my arm free. "I'm fighting," I say, daring her to tell me otherwise. "I won't let the men I love fight and die alone out there."

"Duh," she says, pinching her brows together as if it were obvious. "Where did you think we were going?"

"Oh," I say, surprised. "Well, I assumed since everyone's always trying to lead me *away* from the fights..." I trail off, but it's not important, so I shake my head and dismiss the thought. "Yeah, let's go."

"Good. I know Jace doesn't want you to use your magic or be in your dragon form for this. But, Rory..." Harper trails off, setting her hand on my shoulder as she looks me dead in the eye. "I need you in this battle as a diamond dragon, if you can handle it. Someone like you charging into the fray halfway through a fight?" She pauses, grinning roguishly. "That can turn the tides of this battle. Most of the world still doesn't know that your diamond dragon exists. They don't know what you can do, and we can use that to our advantage."

I grin mischievously as my head finally begins to clear. What she's asking for—this plan she has concocted—it's brilliant.

A well-orchestrated bluff.

"That's smart," I admit.

"Can you handle it?" Harper asks again. "Can you shift?"

"I'll try."

"That's all I can ask."

Apparently satisfied, Harper leads me into the hallway. We quickly weave through the darkened halls, and as we jog, I realize I'm not only barefoot—but also stark naked as well.

I guess I'm going to have to get used to that, now that I'm shifting.

As we charge through the corridors, a twinge of pain shoots through me, and I wince. The movement throws me off balance, and my shoulder hits the wall hard. Harper looks back at me, concerned, and I try my best to hide the pain.

"Keep going," I demand.

She frowns, hesitating, but ultimately indulges me.

Harper leads me outside and onto a broad cliff that overlooks the ocean. Waves crash below as the wind rips by us, carrying the salty scent of the water with it.

Above us, hundreds of dragons hover in the sky, the low rumble of their growls like a constant hum of energy. There are so many that they block out the stars.

It would seem that Harper brought an army of her own.

The dragons above us roar as their Boss steps into the night, and it would seem they're more than ready for this battle.

As Harper stalks onto the grassy knoll overlooking the ocean, another jolt of pain shoots through my neck and up into my head. I wince again, pausing as I hold my head. I have to lean against the wall for support.

This is *not* good.

A dark blue blur jumps down from the roof, landing silently on the ground beside me. I flinch as he suddenly appears, my instinct driving me to lift my fists and prepare for a fight.

But I know this dragon.

His royal blue scales practically glow as he steps out of the shadows, his soft growl a gentle rumble that shakes the earth beneath my feet.

Levi.

My heart pangs with dread.

He wasn't sure if he could shift again—he was afraid of going feral. Now, as my head clears, I realize that the blue blur I saw as I fell to the ground was him.

He saved me.

Maybe even at a dire cost to himself.

Carefully, I inch closer, lifting my hands as I reach for him, eager to establish the connection between us.

He gently sets his nose against my palm, and our mind link instantly opens. To my surprise, his mind is crisp, clear, and sharp—in fact, it feels the same as when he was human. I never quite realized the difference before between his feral and human minds, but now it's obvious.

His brilliant blue eyes focus on me, and it's obvious he's entirely present.

I'm glad you're okay, he says.

Are you feral? I ask in disbelief, just wanting to be sure.

No, he says. *Just keeping watch and staying ready in case I'm needed.*

I sigh with relief, and I know without a doubt that the surge of emotion flooded from me into him.

He growls softly, affectionately leaning into me.

What happened? I ask. *How did you shift? How did—*

Instead of answering, images flash through my mind, taking over the world around me and swallowing me in the experience.

Fragments of memory buzz through my brain, and I watch the missiles exploding through the air—only this time, it's from Levi's perspective on the roof.

I see myself flying in the sky with Jace and Drew on either side of me, the two of them blasting the missiles and trying to detonate them before they can hurt anyone.

The memory shifts, and I'm plummeting toward the ground, limp and lifeless.

The memory fragments again, and Levi is jumping off the roof without a care about himself. His only worry, his only thought, was about me. Tucker yells through the night, and the world around us blurs and vibrates. His wings cut through the air as he races toward me, and in that moment, he and his dragon align. They're united in their one mission, their one purpose.

To save me.

We snap out of the memory, and Levi closes his

eyes as he leans his forehead against mine. *I'm just glad you're safe.*

I smile and wrap my hands around his face. *I knew you could do it.*

He growls happily. *You make the impossible possible.*

"Hey, lovebirds!" Harper yells, snapping her fingers to move this along. "Let's go!"

I shoot her an annoyed glare, but I have to admit that she's right—even if she is being a bit of an asshole.

She's in Boss Mode, eager to save her people. I guess I can forgive it this time.

I let out a slow breath, knowing that I don't have time to indulge anything other than the shift itself. I reach into my core for my dragon, but it's hard to find her through all of the noise. Through all of the pain. Through the dazed way the world spins around me every now and then. My ears keep buzzing and ringing, and several times, I teeter off balance.

Levi sets his nose against my side, helping me stand upright as I reach inside one more time for her.

Just let me carry you, Levi says through our connection.

I shake my head. *Harper's right. A diamond dragon in the fray could rally any of our troops who are panicking and scare off our enemies. They don't know what my powers are, and they don't know how limited my magic is as a dragon.*

Gritting my teeth, I try to clear my mind. Every second I spend here is another second that Tucker, Drew, and Jace face an impossible army brought there to kill them.

But that missile nearly destroyed me.

I grimace, frustrated, reaching for my dragon even as my cheeks burn with nausea. I try to wade past my injuries to feel her, trying to remember what Jace taught me on the balcony. What he's been teaching me from the start.

Trust my dragon.

Soothe her.

Give in.

And there, deep within the murky agony of the lingering concussion, I feel her. There's a pulse of magic, soft and low at first, but it grows ever brighter the longer I listen.

She's hurt but furious—and ready to taste blood.

Let's go kick some ass, baby girl, I tell her.

She growls in agreement, the sound rumbling in my chest like thunder. My body hums and stretches as she takes over, my head spinning with the shift. But I grit my teeth and press through it, forcing myself to endure.

No amount of pain is going to keep me from doing what needs to be done.

A shattering burst of energy throws me off balance as the shift takes over, and I fall forward. Instead of falling on my face, however, I land on my front claws, my head spinning so hard I think I might pass out.

I snarl, refusing to let the pain win. Refusing to let Zurie win.

A low growl continues to rumble through my chest as I grit my teeth, my lips curling, and a flash of lightning cuts through the air.

I open my eyes, spreading my wings wide.

On the edge of the cliff, Harper looks back at me, smirking victoriously, her shoulders squared as she takes me in.

She's proud. I can see it in her face—in her stance and the way her eyes rove over my wings and my scales.

The soldiers above us puff up their chests as they watch me, snarling in welcome as we all prepare for the fight.

"Let's kick some Vaer ass!" Harper yells into the sky.

The hundreds of dragons above us roar in deafening agreement, and she leaps off the side of the cliff.

Her body blurs as she falls, letting the shift take her as she dives with perfect and controlled grace.

Her beautiful violet wings stretch wide as she sails across the rocks and thundering waves below. With a few powerful beats of her wings, she soars upward, a stunning lilac dragon amongst an ocean of color as her army follows her lead.

Levi nudges me, his forehead brushing against mine. *Ready?*

Ready, I say.

He and I leap into the air, joining the army, my wings still a little wobbly as my head continues to spin.

Something tells me that if I get hit again, I won't be able to shift without a few weeks in the hospital—if I'm able to wake up at all from another blow like that.

But with Zurie after everything and everyone I love, that's a risk I'm willing to take.

CHAPTER THIRTY-FOUR

Harper leads us over the ocean as its foamy spray mists across my face. The army keeps low, the dark sky masking our approach as we near the embassy.

I don't recognize this stretch of the coast, but that's not a surprise since I haven't often flown this way.

If I had to guess, I suspect Zurie wasn't expecting Harper to mobilize so quickly. If anything, the additional troops are very likely to push the tides of the battle into our advantage.

A thick mist rolls over us, and it's hard to see more than hazy silhouettes as we dart into the fog. Only the beat of leathery wings on the air and the crash of the ocean breaks the silence.

There's no breath. No growling. No indication at all that we're even here.

As we fly, we begin to hear the roar of battle. Snarls. Men yelling.

The occasional explosion.

With every beat of my wings, we get nearer to war.

Island rock appears through the mist as we funnel through a channel, and a tense surge of adrenaline warns me that we're almost there.

The battle rages on ever closer. Ever louder.

There's a shift in the air, just the silent and subtle indication that something is different.

I look above me as a familiar lilac dragon sinks through the mist toward me. She hovers overhead, perfectly matching my speed, and drops her tail until it touches my back.

Go in and make a scene, Harper says, briefly glancing down at me as she speaks through the open connection. *Make sure everyone knows you're here.*

I nod.

Now, that I can do.

She beats her wings harder, soaring ahead and disappearing into the mist once again. Moments later, the army around me banks suddenly upward, following a cue I didn't catch. Levi and I join them as we race away from the water.

The din of battle gets louder.

In a sudden rush, we break through the mist and into a war zone.

Flames rage from most of the embassy's windows. A few towers lay in ruin, nothing but rubble and dark rock. Fires rage in the forest, not yet uncontrolled but getting there. Black smoke curls into the sky from a dozen different places as the raging fires cast an orange hue across the fields and forests surrounding the embassy.

Anti-dragon tanks cover most of the open grass I can see, occasionally firing more missiles into the sky. Soldiers cover the ground, and dragons fill the air.

Explosions rock the sky from a thousand different battles, all happening at once.

It's chaos.

My favorite kind of crazy.

Harper leads the army into the fray, soaring high into the air as we break through the clouds—the reinforcements no one saw coming.

But she already gave me my mission.

I careen toward the roof and land, the black tile cracking beneath me as I don't even try to soften my fall.

Levi lands on the roof beside me as I prepare to make myself known.

And I *roar*.

I scream into the sky as firelight dances across my iridescent scales. I reach deep within, accessing every ounce of strength and fire I have within me to make sure the bellow is heard.

It screeches through the sky, echoing off every mountain, every tree, and I carry it to the end of my breath as my chest resonates with the mighty thunder of my voice.

Below me, silence settles across the battlefield as heads turn toward me in shock. I snarl, my lips curling, and I decide it's time for a little show.

My dragon burns with mischievous glee as magic builds in my throat. White light shimmers across my scales, ready and oh-so-willing to cause a little mayhem.

I'm ready to show these assholes what they're messing with.

I can feel the magic brimming, growing, stretching within me, becoming ever *more* and ever *stronger*.

I know this is going to be uncontrolled, so I'm careful to lift my head into the sky far above me, where no dragons are currently flying. I'm trying to show off here, not kill anyone, and I have no idea what my magic can even *do* in my dragon form.

Guess we're going to find out.

As my magic reaches a head and I can no longer hold it back, I release a blinding blast of light into the sky. It catches the low-hanging clouds and carries through them like a thousand bolts of lightning. The magic ripples through the stormy air, turning the clouds into an ocean of thunder and lightning.

Harper wanted a show—and I *gave* one.

A cheer rises from the troops below, and I see several tanks turn and flee. Ground troops begin to run away from the embassy—away from me—and I let them go.

I have more important things to tend to, and I did what needed to be done. With fewer troops, the Spectres, Knights, and Vaer have just lost a very crucial advantage.

Harper leads her troops into a sharp dive, her claws outstretched as she grabs the nearest Vaer dragon and digs her talons deep into its hide. The Vaer screams in pain, but Harper is beyond caring.

She's not even in Boss Mode anymore. She's in full-on war mode, and anything that's not a Fairfax dragon is at risk of dying tonight.

The panicked surge of battle rises again as the three armies of our enemies now have to contend with a second wave of troops from the Fairfax.

In the main courtyard down below, Russell takes

on five of the dark Vaer dragons at once, his claws and teeth a blur as he sinks them into his opponents. Dazzling yellow magic sparks across his skin as he aims a blast at one of the Vaer who tries to latch onto his back. The dragon is knocked backward, a hole in its chest as it takes out a section of the wall with its death throes.

Oh, good.

Russell's fine. I don't need to worry about him.

I scan the crowd looking for Kinsley, but as far as I can tell, she's not here.

Figures.

I scan the crowd next for Zurie, but in the chaos, I can't find a small human among dragons—and a stealthy one at that. I figure it'll be a little while before I can pinpoint where she is.

There's also no sign of Tucker or Irena, and I bristle with dread.

To my delight, however, a familiar fire dragon and a beautiful black thunderbird soar toward me. Jace and Drew land on the roof and nuzzle me briefly, flickers of gratitude slipping through their fragmented connections as they brush my skin.

It's enough to know I'm a welcome addition to the fight, and they're grateful I'm okay.

Solid entry, Drew says through the connection. *And*

I'm going to screw your brains out when this is over because that was hot as hell, woman. Good God.

I laugh, puffs of hot air rushing through my nose as he makes me chuckle. *Let's focus on not dying first.*

Are you okay? Jace says, his beautiful blue eyes locking on me.

I've been better, I admit. *I'm not at full power, but they don't have to know it. You?*

Never better, he lies, his eyes dancing with mischief.

With everything going on right now, I decide to pick my battles. *I'm just glad you're okay. Where's Tucker?*

Jace snorts. *Kicking ass in the south fields. That man is deadly with a rifle.*

Have you seen Zurie?

Not yet, Drew interjects. *Several Spectres, but no Ghost.*

And Irena?

Killing every Spectre she finds, Jace says. *She's all over. None of us can keep up with her.*

Yeah, that sounds about right, I admit. *Let's go give Tucker a hand.*

We leap off the roof and coast across the battle-ground to the south fields just beyond the embassy walls. Most of the grass is burning, and I don't even know how Tucker could have gotten out here.

But that's just how battles work. In the bloodlust,

you lose track of things—like where you are, and how you got there.

As we clear the tree canopy and come across the grassy expanse of the south fields, most of it's on fire. Ribbons of black smoke pollute the sky. At its center, two tanks lay overturned in a soot-covered patch of dirt. There, in the middle of it all and sporting a stockpile of rifles and ammunition, is Tucker.

He fires shot after shot at any dragon who goes near him. All around him, Spectres dressed in all black and Knights in silver Kevlar vests race toward him, unleashing a hailstorm of bullets on his position.

Never one to go down easy, Tucker ducks for cover and fires off seven shots through a gap in the tank. Instantly, six Knights go down—followed by a Spectre.

Somehow, Tucker's become an even better shot since we got to the dojo. Perhaps it's because he finally has access to the best weapons money can buy.

Even if he did technically *borrow* them from Jace.

We angle toward him, but as we careen toward the ground, an orange dragon falls from the sky.

I've seen him before. He's one of the dojo soldiers, and he hits the ground hard as a Vaer dives toward him. Stunned on the ground below, it looks like he either can't see or can't react to the sharp claws headed for his throat.

I veer away from my men, racing toward the soldier and snatching the Vaer out of the sky before he can get to the dojo soldier. We tumble toward the ground as I dig my teeth into the Vaer's neck. He screams in pain, scratching at me as he tries to get away.

Not going to happen.

I use our momentum to hurl him into the trees and catch myself by spreading my wings wide. I slow even as he careens into the woods, taking down tree after tree before he hits the dirt. A thick branch cuts through his chest, and he lets out a final scream before collapsing onto the ground.

I snarl in victory, white sparks dancing along the edge of my nose as I return my attention to the dojo soldier. He scrambles out of the small crater, his skin still smoking as he shakes his body to loosen up his muscles and get his bearings. He nods at me in thanks before taking off to rejoin the fight.

Levi and Drew land beside Tucker, roaring as Jace flies toward me.

But I don't need backup.

As I near them, Tucker lifts his gun.

At me.

But—but he would *never*.

The air around me shifts, a little warning bell going

off in the back of my mind as I look over my shoulder to find a Vaer almost on me.

Jace snarls, lightning building in his throat as he prepares to take the soldier out, but Tucker fires before Jace has the chance.

The dragon goes down.

I let out a slow breath. That was way too close.

Jace lands on the grass beside Drew while I land on one of the overturned tanks, my wings spread awkwardly to help me keep balance as I still figure out this whole flying thing.

When I'm sure I won't fall over, I stretch my long neck and nuzzle Tucker briefly in gratitude. *Thanks for the quick shot, babe.*

He winks at me, lifting his rifle as he returns his attention to the war around us. "I know how you can thank me later," he says, grinning as he fires off four more bullets.

Two Vaer dragons go down, their heads recoiling as they get hit.

A few bullets ricochet off my scales, but they feel more like bee stings. I snarl at the Knights nearby who dared to fire at me, and they hesitate, their eyes going wide with fear as I glare at them. They drop their rifles in panic, running away into the forest beyond, and I snort an annoyance.

Damn right. You *better* run.

I take the moment to survey the battlefield. Jace and Drew cover each other's backs, spinning effortlessly and blasting fire and magic into the air. It's a treat to watch them battle as a team. It's like they were built to fight together, two masters taking out anyone foolish enough to go near them.

Levi and Tucker fight as a seamless team as well, and I'm impressed. Levi freezes his opponents with icy blasts from his throat as he races through the battlefield like a ghost. Tucker covers him effortlessly, picking off anyone who goes near his friend.

I growl with pride.

The whistle of something cutting blindingly fast through the air catches my attention, and I lift my gaze as a Vaer barrels toward me and Tucker.

I snarl protectively and launch into the air toward the dragon. He fires a blast of ice at me, and I'm tempted to duck it. It would be fairly easy, after all, even with my awkward flying— but I can't risk it hitting Tucker.

So I decide to take the hit.

I grit my teeth, snarling as I let it break across my chest. Magic burns in my throat, my dragon doing its best to instinctively protect us both, and the blistering cold burns through me. I can feel my scales freezing, feel the muscles slowing as they tense, nearly paralyzed from the icy blast.

But my skin is thick, thicker even than most dragons. Though the icy blast burns furiously, eating away at my nerves and sending ripples of pain through my entire body, my magic builds brighter in my throat as the two of us barrel toward each other.

The ice starts to melt away, chipping and breaking off of my skin as I fly. As the two of us collide, the last of the ice breaks off.

Victory.

What would have utterly disabled others barely hurt me at all.

I dig my teeth and claws into the dragon, trying my best to keep my magic at bay and just kill this guy the old-fashioned way. His claws carve deep gouges into my skin—into my shoulder and back. He snaps at the air, trying to bite any part of me he can reach.

Not going to happen.

We tumble to the ground, both of us furiously flapping our wings as we try to recover, but I refuse to let go. My magic burns brighter within me, my dragon calling it forth even as I beg her not to.

There it is—the familiar lack of control I felt when I was first learning to rein in this incredible power.

Shit.

I can't hold it back. Not this time.

I pivot so that my back is facing the ground, my head to the sky as I grip the Vaer tighter. I dig my teeth into him, locking my jaw to ensure he can't wriggle free. I refuse to let go of him, even as my magic aches to escape.

If my magic is going to force its way out of me, it's all going to hit this guy.

He seems to realize something's wrong, and he begins to panic. He furiously beats at the air with his wings, clawing at everything he can reach. Even though he draws blood, breaking open my beautiful scales, I don't let go.

Not even a little.

My magic snakes out of me, hot and fierce. It burns through him as he takes the full brunt of my power.

He screeches into the air as the white light fills his every vein. It illuminates every inch of him from within, and as he arches his back to scream one last time, he dissolves into brilliant white dust.

With nothing to hold on to anymore, I tumble alone toward the ground.

Time to recover.

My wings snap open as I try to slow my descent. I beat the air hard, flapping furiously as I try to take once more to the air, but I can't make it happen in time. I hit the ground hard and tumble across the grass. My claws dig into the dirt, kicking up clumps of weeds and earth as I slide to a stop.

When my world is finally still, I pause and let myself catch my breath. My chest heaves, my wings lifting with each intake of air as I try to regain my balance. Above me, the wind carries off the ribbons of dust that were once a Vaer dragon, and he fades to nothing.

My magic—it's even more powerful as a dragon.

And, yet again, it's difficult to control.

This can destroy whole cities. This could probably kill thousands, all at once.

The thought shakes me. For a moment, I'm shaken by the very idea. The concussion still rocks through me, my head spinning, but I'm also dazed by the sheer power in my bones. In my blood. In every fiber of my being.

I take a deep breath to settle myself, puffing up my chest and spreading my wings with pride. I can handle this. No matter how tempting the magic might be to use, I won't risk the lives of the Fairfax dragons. Of my men.

I won't fail the people who count on me.

It's time for me to get back to my men in the south field—and before I can do that, I have to figure out where the hell I am. I stretch my wings, about to take off, when I see a familiar flash of dark hair in the firelight of a nearby blaze.

Next comes the glint of cold steel in the light.

Green eyes that practically glow in the darkness.

Irena.

My sister ducks a blow from a woman with dark hair who's facing away from me. As the two of them grapple for dominance, the woman throws Irena onto the ground and steps into the light.

Zurie.

Irena gets to her feet, but Zurie quickly kicks her onto her back again and lifts a long dagger. She's ready, then, to deal the final blow. My former mentor wrinkles her nose in disgust as she looks down at Irena.

No.

I won't let Zurie take my sister from me.

I *refuse.*

CHAPTER THIRTY-FIVE

D riven by instinct and a primal need to save my sister, I race toward Irena and Zurie.

I don't have much time, and I'm too far away.

But I try anyway, pushing myself to my absolute limit, stretching my wings and soaring harder, *faster* than I ever have before.

Zurie lifts the blade over her head and dives it into Irena. Even from here, I can hear the scream of utter, earth-shattering agony.

Zurie lifts her dagger again, and this time the blade is covered in blood. Red drops slink along the blade and trickle from the tip of the dagger. My former mentor braces herself in the dark night, lit only by the fires around and prepares herself to strike the final blow.

I'm so close.

I can almost taste Zurie's blood.

I push myself harder.

Faster.

Before I can make it to her, a green dragon barrels into Zurie, snarling as he tackles her to the ground. His claws dig deep into her side, leaving dozens of gouges across her body.

Eric.

A surge of relief shoots through me, but we're not out of the woods yet.

Irena groans in misery, stirring from her place on the ground, and I'm grateful she isn't dead.

Yet.

The fact that she's not getting up means she's hurt *bad*, possibly worse than I imagined.

I'm facing a choice, one with no easy answer.

Eric snarls as he recovers, his claws digging into the ground to slow his momentum as he faces off with the Ghost of the Spectres. He's good, that much is sure, but I truly wonder *how* good.

Irena might be dying, however, and my loyalty is to her above all else.

I bolt toward her, sliding across the ground as my face hovers close to hers. Her brows are scrunched in pain, her eyes closed. As I near, she peeks through her lids and flinches in surprise.

It takes a moment for her to recognize me, and I figure she must be in even more pain than I thought if she doesn't know who I am.

I mean, sure, I'm a dragon—but there aren't too many diamond dragons hanging around here.

She winces. "I'm fine," she says through gritted teeth. "Go help Eric."

I growl in annoyance at the blatant lie, watching as blood spews and bubbles across her fingers from the wound in her abdomen.

"Go!" she snaps.

I snarl, making my opinion of the matter very clear. She needs a medic.

I lower my head, nudging her slightly to help her sit up. As much as this hurts her, she needs to get on my back so I can carry her to safety.

"Fine then. Help me up," she says with her hands still firmly planted on her side. Her fingers press against the injury as she tries and fails to keep pressure on the gaping wound. It continues to drain across her hand with no sign of slowing.

Gritting her teeth, Irena sets her other arm across my nose and awkwardly gets to her feet. She limps, unable to walk in a straight line, and I press my stomach and neck to the ground so that she can climb onto my back. She limps along, moving as quickly as she can and staggering with every step. I use my wing to steady her as she slowly climbs onto my back.

I just hope I can find a nurse in time.

With Irena's arm holding tightly to the base of my neck, I take off, trying to fly as smoothly as I can despite my lack of experience. Otherwise, she might go careening off into the trees below.

As we approach the dark towers of the embassy, I scan the ground, looking for anyone who even closely resembles a medic.

To my relief, I spot one of the nurses who helped Irena and Tucker recover. She tends to a dojo soldier who's laying on the ground in his human form, still but breathing as she finishes tying a bloodstained bandage around his leg.

Thank the gods—they've created a field hospital in an alcove along the side of the embassy, one that forty dojo dragons are viciously defending.

This will work.

I dive. The dojo soldiers watch me as I fly toward them, flanking me to give me added protection as I head toward the makeshift facility.

Without much in the way of grace or elegance, I

land in the center of the small field. The ground rumbles under my feet, and the nurse's eyes go wide as she spots me.

Now that I have the woman's attention, I lower my head and tilt my back slightly so that she can see Irena. The movement says everything I need to say, all without speaking a word. As I lower my wing, trying to help Irena off, she doesn't move.

Bad sign.

I try to build a connection with her through her limp hand against my neck, but nothing happens.

She's out cold.

I growl with concern, nodding toward my sister on my back and looking at the nurse to get her moving.

The nurse races toward me and grabs Irena, gently lifting her off of my back and laying her on the ground.

"I need help!" she shouts over her shoulder at two other nurses I hadn't noticed before, who tend to other patients in the shadows beneath one of the many walls in this alcove. The two women look up, nodding as they briefly finish what they're working on before running toward us.

I hesitate, wondering how I can help. What I can do to make this better.

The nurse can tell.

She gently sets her hand on my nose. I pause, wondering what the hell she's doing. I allow it, though, and watch her with a blended flurry of concern and confusion buzzing through my brain.

If you want to help us, she says through our connection, *if you want to help your sister, then you need to end this battle. Now.*

I stiffen, wondering how the hell I'm supposed to do that. But with one look at Irena, I know that's exactly what I have to do.

She needs a hospital, not a field medic, and I growl with rage as her face slowly goes white.

I take off into the sky, my wings beating at the air as I race back towards Zurie and Eric. I reach them in moments, and I figure the one way I can end this is to kill Zurie. If she's dead, the rest will slowly filter out. She's driving everyone forward, all for her own selfish means.

The woman will *die.*

She and Eric are still dueling. Zurie rolls across the charred grass, and as she slides across the slick ground, she pulls a high-caliber handgun from a hidden holster. With deadly precision, she fires several shots from the weapon.

Right into Eric's chest.

No.

That's point-blank range.

Even with a handgun, that's a death sentence.

He roars in pain and fury, spewing blood as he snaps at her. She ducks out of the way, rolling to the side as she lifts the gun to fire again.

My wings carving through the air at breakneck speed, I race toward them, desperate to save this man. Irena is finally opening up to someone, finally learning how to love and trust.

I can't let the man who loves her die.

The cold air streams across my face as I barrel toward Zurie, ready to bury my claws into her. I'm ready to taste blood and rip her to shreds for everything she did to destroy my life. For all of the ways she tried to kill me and the people I love. For all the ways she controlled me through the years and tried to break me. Tried to sell me. Tried to destroy all the good things in my world.

And I'm so close.

I'm *so* close to justice.

There's a screech, a sort of whistle through the air, and a white dragon dives at me too quickly for me to evade. He barrels into my side, screeching as he knocks me off course. We fall to the trees below, crashing through the canopy.

And as we tumble, I see Zurie fire another shot.

With this one, Eric goes down.

No!

The word echoes in my head, and I want to scream it. Instead, a deafening roar escapes my mouth as the white dragon and I crash across the ground.

Furious, livid, and fueled by bloodlust, I fling the white dragon off of me. He barrels across the ground, his spine cracking against a tree. The trunk splinters, taking the full brunt of his fall, but the bastard still gets to his feet.

He shakes his head, trying to recover from the blow, and trains his piercing eyes on me. His wings spread in challenge, and it takes me a moment to recognize him.

It's been so long since I've seen him in his dragon form that, at first, I thought he was just another dragon in the chaos.

Once he pauses to watch me, however, I recognize that glare.

The greed.

The lust.

It's Guy *fucking* Durand.

I growl, furious and full of fire. It's disgusting to think that this man, of all the people in the world, would be the one to keep me from saving Eric.

That *he* would be the one to keep me from killing Zurie is just *inexcusable*.

I don't enjoy killing, but I won't mind snuffing him out at *all*.

We launch at each other. The moment he charges, he fires a blast of ice toward me. I duck the frosty beam, backhanding him with my claw to throw off his aim. The ice hits a tree behind me instead, freezing it instantly and shattering it to nothing.

Seething with hatred, I dig my teeth into him. My dragon is furious, and she calls on my magic yet again. It burns in my throat, ready to fire.

This exhausted, this bruised, this bloody—I'm having more and more trouble keeping my magic at bay. I don't want to hurt anyone else, but I have no problem hurting Guy Durand. As long as I keep him in my jaws, I should be able to release the magic my dragon is summoning without hurting anyone *important*.

Just him.

He claws at me furiously as the magic builds—as I prepare to release the full brunt of my power into him.

As I prepare to destroy him once and for all.

Panicking, he bites my neck, his teeth digging deep into me, drawing blood and slicing nerves. Despite my training, despite all I've done to learn how to push through pain, I snarl in agony. Impulsively, I release my grip on him as I squirm, trying to throw him off. He soars through the air, downing several trees on the way, and hits the ground with an earthshaking crash.

Guy recovers, teeth bared and bloody as he roars furiously at me.

I snarl, not one to be outdone, and roar far louder in response.

Far *angrier*.

Far more thirsty for blood.

We race toward each other again as an explosion hits the ground between us—a missile neither of us heard in all of our fury and rage.

The force of the explosion throws me back. I sail through the air, crashing through trees that shatter beneath my dragon's body. I roll across the ground and hit something hard, the back of my head smacking against what feels like a rock, or hell, a boulder.

Something cracks from the force of my fall, and I'm not sure if that's the rock or my skull.

I try to stand, but my world is fuzzy. It spins and teeters even as I get to my feet. I spread my wings, trying to balance, trying to recover as the white dragon stalks through the black smoke that lingers after the explosion. He snarls, his wings spreading, but I refuse to let him win.

Unable to keep my balance, I collapse to the ground. My ears ring as I try to recover, but my vision only blurs more with each passing second. The world only spins faster. Darkness bleeds across the edges of my vision as I try and fail to stay conscious.

I can't black out.

Not now.

Not with so much at stake.

CHAPTER THIRTY-SIX

I wake to the sound of clinking chains, my head pounding as I groggily try to come-to.

Something pulls on my wrists, tight and searing, and I wince as I try to move my fingers. My nails scrape against metal, and my heart skips a beat as the memories come flooding back.

The battle.

Zurie.

Guy.

My eyes snap open, and I find myself on my back. I'm not in my dragon form anymore—a loose, white dress covers my body, the fabric stained with dirt and bloodstains.

My blood.

Someone drags me by the metal cuffs around my

wrists, and I arch my back to find Guy Durand dragging me across the forest floor. His bare shoulders glisten with sweat and dirt, his body covered in deep gouges from my claws. He wears only a set of beige shorts, and his bare feet break the twigs along the ground as he steals me away from the battle.

A boom rocks the earth, and I look toward my feet in an effort to get my bearings. Towers of black smoke spiral in the distance, and the flames of the battle recede behind us.

Gods above—how long was I out?

Another explosion rocks the woods around us, the trees trembling from the force. Leaves flutter, shaken from their branches by the boom, but Guy doesn't flinch.

I grimace, fighting the cuffs around my hands, tugging roughly on them as I try to stand. I don't care if I have to strangle him with the chains attached to the cuffs—I'll *kill* him, here and now.

As the chains tense, he drops into a fighting stance and turns on his heels, glaring down at me. With a sharp kick to my side, he laughs bitterly.

I groan as his foot nails my ribs, and I double over in pain.

"Wakey, wakey," he says, sneering as he tugs sharply on the restraints.

"You are *such* an asshole," I say through gritted teeth. I tense, recovering from the blow, and tug sharply on the cuffs.

Just to be difficult.

It throws him slightly off balance, and he yanks hard on the chains to drag me along the ground again. As my body scrapes across the dirt, the rocks and twigs poking me along the way, he pauses now and then to glare at me over his shoulder.

"It didn't have to be this way," he says, disgusted. "I never wanted to work for the *Vaer*. The Darringtons, maybe. Or the Andusk." He spits on the ground in revulsion and continues, dragging me to my doom. "But soon, it'll all be done with. All of it. I hand you over, and voila. New title. New lands. New name."

"Is it like a witness protection program for douchebags?" I snap, tugging fiercely on the chains again out of spite.

He stumbles and wraps the chains around his hand another time, likely to get a better grip.

Idiot.

One more tug, and he's on his ass.

I prepare myself, waiting for the right moment, when a powerful jolt of electricity tears through me.

My jaw clenches shut from the current. My eyes are frozen, and I'm paralyzed as I blankly stare at the

Fairfax traitor. Sneering with wicked delight, he presses his thumb hard against a little black remote I hadn't seen before now.

"Hurts, don't it?" He says, snickering as he nods to the remote in his hand. "Maybe stop being such a little *bitch* and just behave."

He finally releases his hold on the button, and I gasp for breath as the current finally recedes.

That was *horrible.*

I've been buzzed by cuffs like these before, and while it hurt, it was *nothing* like that.

As if reading my mind, Guy Durand waggles the remote at me, smirking like the asshole he is. "Oh, you bet your *ass* we made a custom set of cuffs, just for you, after that run-in you had with Ian." He chuckles. "That dumbass didn't know what he was messing with, Rory, but I do. I know exactly what you are, probably better than you. If you give me absolutely *any* reason to use this, I won't hesitate for even a second—you hear me?"

I wrinkle my nose in disgust, wishing I could just strangle the life out of him right now.

What a *dick.*

Apparently satisfied with being a complete and utter asshole, Guy starts walking again, tugging sharply on the chains. My arms ache as they stretch upward, pulled by the cuffs, and I grimace as my back is dragged once more along the earth.

"We were tricked, you know," he says.

He never did know when to shut the hell up, but I don't mind. If I keep him talking, I can keep him busy.

And he might even give me some useful answers.

"It was Zurie," he continues. "That bitch. Who's laughing now?" he says with a glance over his shoulder at me, chuckling slightly as he talks. "She and I were both after you, and I won."

What a moron.

He doesn't win until we're out of these woods, and Zurie can track him for days even then.

"This was supposed to be a silent infiltration," he admits. "One no one would know about. Zurie said she could get us in, in exchange for you. That's all she wanted, she said. That's all she needed. I hand you over to her, and I get the dojo. I get revenge."

Another boom rocks the forest, I stretch out my fingers inside the iron domes of the cuffs, trying to re-center myself. If I can keep him talking, I can give my body time to recover.

I need to keep him distracted because if I do, I might be able to find a way out of this.

"But let me guess," I say, egging him on. "That was never what you wanted."

"Of course not." He scoffs. "You'd think Zurie would have learned from her first interaction with the Vaer that they don't exactly keep their promises."

An understatement, to say the least.

"I figured it would be easy to kill her," he admits, his voice trailing off as he realizes what a mistake that was. "I figured it would be us against her. I figured that if we had her outnumbered, we could win." He shakes his head, disappointed with himself. "I should have seen it coming."

"You really should have," I agree.

"She just wants to watch everything burn," he says, looking back at the smoldering wreckage of the dojo. "Pitting the Vaer against the Knights. Throwing her Spectres into the mix for good measure. She must really hate you," he adds, looking down at me.

"The feeling's mutual," I say, my eyes narrowing.

As he speaks, my head gradually begins to clear. My world still spins now and then, and the ringing in my ears won't go away. Slowly but and surely, I start to get my bearings.

I reach into my core, searching for my dragon. She's there, but distant. It's like reaching for her through a fog, and my head keeps spinning the longer I try to connect with her.

The more I reach inward, the more of my thoughts

blur. I can taste metal, and I'm not sure why. I shake my head, trying to clear my thoughts, but that only makes the dizziness worse.

"None of it matters," he says, returning his attention to the path in front of him. "All I have to do is get you back to Kinsley. I can't go back without you. Kinsley said so herself, and no one disobeys the Boss."

His shoulders stiffen, and I can practically smell the fear radiating off of him.

A rock digs deep into my back as Guy drags me over it, shooting ripples of stinging pain through me. I grimace as I glare up at Guy. He snickers, and I swear he did that on purpose.

I try to tune him out. I need to focus.

I reach in once again, soothing my dragon. She's in agony, beaten and battered. Bloody and bruised.

There's only one way she and I are going to get out of this.

I reach into the depths of my body, into my core, searching for my magic. I find it instantly, though it feels weak.

Like a dying pulse.

But it's there, and that's all I need.

I tap into it, and my hands sizzle with energy. I can feel sparks dancing between my fingertips. I can sense the magic burning in my veins, dormant and eager to break free.

Weak ribbons of white light filter loosely over my arms, but it's all so distant. I can barely access it, much less control it. Truth be told, I'm not sure if that's the cuffs, the second concussion, or a combination of the two.

A ripple of agonizing pain shoots through me as the cuffs electrocute me once again.

Damn it. He noticed me trying to reach for my magic.

I grit my teeth, my muscles tensing in agony as the current paralyzes every muscle. My heart stutters. My lungs stop. A surge of nausea rises in my throat, and I wonder how I could possibly stay conscious through this pain. Darkness bleeds along the edges of my vision as the electric current threatens to knock me out again.

It stops, and I collapse, my body limp in the dirt as Guy continues to drag me through the forest.

"Stop it," he demands.

He buzzes me again even though I haven't moved, and my back arches in pain. I can't stifle the groan of agony as the electric current burns me. I can barely see, and black spots morph across my vision as I stare up at the canopy.

That's enough.

I won't stand for this.

I won't let him do this to me. Not for one second more.

Seething with hatred, I glare at him. Gritting my teeth through the pain, I use the agony as fuel to push me forward.

As he drags me along the ground, his thumb still pressed against the remote's button, the electric current still burning through my veins, I roll onto my stomach and lift my foot, using a passing rock in the ground to help me stand. I stumble, thrown off balance by the pain and the movement, and instead fall to my knees.

But at least I'm not on the ground anymore.

The chains clink together, and he looks over his shoulder in surprise as I try to get to my feet. He lifts his thumb off the buzzer, almost impulsively, and I suck in a deep breath for what I know is going to be only a moment of relief.

He presses his thumb against the remote, lifting his hand to show it to me, like he wants me to know he controls the source of all my pain. He shakes it a little, his thumb pressed hard against the button as the electric current burns through me, and my shoulders slump.

I'm losing ground.

The current—the pain—it's just too much. I'm starting to lose control of my muscles as the electric current eats away at me.

But the hatred makes me strong.

The adrenaline keeps me going.

I tap again into my magic, using it as fuel to push me forward even though it's distant. Even though it feels so lost within me. The longer I reach for it, the louder it becomes. Slowly at first, growing bit by bit.

But it's there.

It will always be there.

I grit my teeth and struggle to get to my feet, wavering as the pain shakes me. I won't let him take me. I won't let Kinsley dissect me. She wants to do gods know what with me, and I won't allow it.

I'm so broken. So battered.

But I refuse to give up.

I can't.

Irena.

Jace.

Drew.

Levi.

Tucker.

They all need me, and I need them.

As I finally stand, my feet and knees shaking as I

yell through the pain, Guy's expression changes. He doesn't look disgusted anymore, or even annoyed.

He looks frightened.

As he should.

He lifts his thumb off the buzzer, and I let out a slow breath as ribbons of relief weave through me. I figure it's temporary, but his gaze darts behind me.

"She always was a stubborn girl," a woman says, her voice dark and familiar.

A chill shoots through me, and I straighten my back as I look over my shoulder to find Zurie standing in the center of the path behind us.

Guy, thankfully, is distracted enough that he doesn't hit the button again, and that gives me a moment of respite. I manage to stay on my feet as splintering ripples of pain shock me in the aftermath of the electrocution.

Zurie's eyes narrow, her gaze shifting between the two of us, her body tensing as she prepares for what she and I both know will be a true fight to the death.

Unlike Fairfax duels, there will be no surrender tonight.

The Ghost and leader of the Spectre organization, the most feared assassin guild in the world, draws her dagger.

In my periphery, Guy draws a handgun.

With my hands bound, I have no weapons as I face two of the people I hate most in this world.

I can't say I've been in worse situations than this, but I do know one thing. This is not how I die, and it's time for these two to pay for what they've done.

CHAPTER THIRTY-SEVEN

There's a suspended moment in the forest where the three of us simply watch each other, wondering what will happen first.

Who will strike.

Who will die.

I eye the remote on Guy's belt. He's stowed it away to draw his weapon. One hand holds the chains, and his other holds his handgun, a high enough caliber to kill a dragon—but only at close range.

In the moments before all hell breaks loose, with black smoke rising in the background and the billowing flames of a destroyed dojo lighting the sky, I take a brief assessment of my surroundings.

The risks.

The resources.

Zurie is doing the same thing right now.

Though I suspect Guy is trying to do something similar, I truly don't believe he realizes what he's up against.

Time slows as I take it all in.

Zurie wants us dead, both me and Guy.

I want both her and Guy dead.

Guy wants me alive, and he doesn't care about her. To him, she's as good as dead.

There are only a limited number of shots in his handgun, and all three of us know he won't have time to reload it if he empties his clip. Every shot matters right now, and he won't fire unless he's panicking or sure he has a good shot.

He also can't let go of the chains because I'll get away. He has to keep me close, and that keeps his hands full. At some point in this fight, he's going to have to choose— either me or Zurie.

With me in cuffs and her armed, he's probably going to choose Zurie.

I can use him to my advantage. He has no leverage in the situation against me, but I have quite a lot I can use against him.

When I broke Ian's remote what feels like eons ago, it shattered the cuffs and let me free. Guy said the cuffs on my hands were based on the same design.

So, the smash-it-and-run technique will work here, too.

Probably.

As I take a slow breath, knowing that at any moment one of them will attack, I have mere seconds to formulate my plan.

Step one, get the chains out of his hands because it's the closest thing I have right now to a weapon.

Step two, get the remote from him.

Step three, break it.

Step four, kill them both.

Sure. Easy.

I snort derisively.

The tension snaps in the air between us, and we all dive for each other.

Guy lifts his gun and fires at Zurie. The Ghost dodges and rolls, the bullet whizzing by her head and missing her by a hair.

With him distracted, I yank on the chains, pivoting and draping them over my shoulder so that I can use my body to throw him off balance.

It works.

He stumbles, the barrel of his gun pointing toward the ground, and Zurie goes for me.

That was a stupid choice, and I wonder what she's playing at. I'm not the one with the damn *gun*.

With her dagger drawn—the same one she used to stab Irena, its blade still covered in my sister's blood—she swipes at my throat. I lean backward, my shoulders aching as the blade cuts through the air barely an inch above my nose.

Thrown off balance and with very little in the way of leverage, I give into the momentum and fall to the ground. My shoulders take the brunt of the blow, my core tight as I absorb the shock of the fall.

From this new vantage, I kick Zurie hard in the stomach with the edge of my foot. She doubles over, the blade coming down toward my thigh, and I swing my leg to avoid the blade.

It all happens in seconds—barely enough time to breathe.

Zurie stabs furiously at me, barely giving me a second to think, much less move out of the way. Every maneuver I make is an impulsive, purely instinct-driven reaction. At this point, I'm running on my training and muscle memory. The combination drives me and dictates every move I make.

Despite the chaos, I try to keep Guy in my peripheral vision. He fiddles with the gun, reloading it, thinking he has a moment to recover.

Idiot.

He should have used that moment to fire at her.

Yeah, it would have given me a chance to escape. To recover and maybe go on the offense. But he has a clear shot and a distracted target.

And he's *wasting* this chance.

Zurie lifts the blade over her head and brings it down toward my face, probably hoping she can hit me hard enough to kill me with one blow.

With no other options. I block my face with the iron cuffs around my hands. The metal reverberates with a vicious twang as her dagger recoils off the iron. Sparks fly as metal hits metal, and we both grit our teeth, trying to recover after the vicious blow.

The click of a gun cocking interrupts us, and Zurie instinctively rolls backward as Guy fires. This time, however, she grabs my chains and drags me with her, rolling me on top of her and trying to stab me while she uses me as a shield.

Damn, I hate this woman.

She digs the blade into my shoulder, and I grimace in agony as the pain ripples down my arm. She was probably aiming for my neck, but missed in all the chaos.

That's a good sign. If she's missing, she's not on her game. And if she's not on her game, I have a better chance of killing her.

Guy hesitates, not willing to kill me just yet as he

tries to aim his gun towards Zurie in the brief moments when her head appears over my shoulder. I grimace as she pulls the dagger out of my shoulder, no doubt ready to stab me again.

Even though I have limited movement with my hands bound in front of me, I do my best to wrap the chains around Zurie's wrists. She impulsively pulls back, but it's too late. The metal links are already wound around her right hand.

As she tries to shake them off, I violently yank my hands away. The bones in her wrists shatter as the metal chains tighten, and she groans in agony.

I only have a moment before she recovers, and I use it well. I press my upper back against her, pinning her to the ground. With all of the strength I have left, I swing the cuffs over my head, knowing that I'm going to hit at least something.

I smack her hard in the skull, and I hear a crack—one that's not the cuffs.

With her face twisted with pain, she shoves me off of her. It's a violent and sudden movement, and with no way to stop my momentum, I roll across the dirt. The chain connected to the iron cuffs on my hands tangles around me as I tumble, momentarily pinning my arms to my sides as I slide across the ground. I wriggle, trying to break free, but for the moment, I'm pinned.

Awesome.

Frantic, I fight the chain wrapped around my arms. If I can just stand, I can slide these off.

Guy and Zurie face each other. He lifts the gun and fires off a shot as she ducks behind a tree. He hesitates, the barrel raised as he waits for an opening. Zurie, meanwhile, pauses on the other side of the trunk to recover. She holds her hand to her forehead, wincing, and it looks like my hit was better than I thought.

Step two is still in effect. I eye the remote on Guy's belt as his finger hovers over the trigger.

Zurie is clearly dazed, but she's been in worse scrapes than this. She lowers to the ground, preparing herself for the fight.

I won't have long to grab that remote.

No doubt eager to get Guy's weapon from him, Zurie flings a fistful of dirt into the air—right into Guy's face. He winces, cursing under his breath.

"I can't see!" he shouts, the gun wildly waving in the air.

She charges him and knocks him to the ground, the two of them wrestling as she reaches time and time again for the handgun in his palm.

That only makes me wriggle harder, knowing I absolutely must get free of these chains. Zurie *cannot* get that gun. That would make everything worse. It's loaded, and even one shot from that can kill me.

I grit my teeth, the ringing in my ears getting worse the more I move. I'm running on empty and should have seen a doctor over an hour ago, maybe more depending on how long I was out while Guy dragged me through the forest.

Even when I get these cuffs off, I know I'll be running on fumes. I'm not at full power, which is very bad given who my opponent is.

Zurie— the best assassin in the world.

Zurie—the woman who taught me everything I know.

Even at full strength, this would be a difficult battle. I have no idea how I'm going to pull this off as dazed and wounded as I am now, but I have no choice.

There is no facing Zurie again. Whether it's her or me, one of us is dying tonight.

I finally break free of the chains wrapped around me.

Thank the *gods*.

The two of them still wrestle for the gun. Zurie bleeds from her head, her right wrist shattered. That doesn't faze her, though, and she wields her dagger just as easily with the left. She stabs Guy in the fore-arm, and he impulsively drops the gun. Her eyes go wide with excitement, even as he punches her in the temple with his other hand. She takes the blow, barely staggering, and stabs him in the shoulder.

Good. Her aim is still off. That means the blow I gave her was far more devastating than I thought.

As I get to my feet, I wait for an opening—for any chance to grab the remote. Guy kicks Zurie hard in the stomach, and she grimaces, falling to the ground.

With me back on my feet, they seem to realize I've joined the fight again. For a moment, the three of us face off against each other, each getting our bearings as we try to figure out who to kill first.

Zurie wants to kill me, but she probably needs Guy's gun to do it.

Guy wants to kill Zurie, but he knows I'm dangerously close to becoming a real threat.

I want to kill Zurie, but I need to go after Guy. I need that remote.

Everyone tenses, waiting to see who will strike first.

Fine. I'll start this party.

I launch at Guy, and he turns the gun on me, probably on impulse. I know he won't use it. At worst case, he shoots me in the shoulder or leg to try to slow me down.

I'll survive.

Zurie joins the attack, and I realize she was waiting to see if she could use the battle to her advantage. For a brief second, it's two-on-one as she and I gang up against the Fairfax traitor.

He pivots, aiming the gun at her, but she knocks it aside as I wrap the chains around his neck. He grimaces, his fingers digging into the chains as I choke him. I can't keep my footing long, unfortunately, and he manages to flip me over his head.

I sail through the air and fall hard on my back, my head recoiling as it hits the ground hard. I can't contain the pained groan that escapes me as my brain rattles.

Damn, that *hurt*.

Zurie scrambles for the gun, but Guy grabs her arm and twists, forcing her to her knees as he punches her in the temple. She falls toward me, her dagger swinging, and I realized that she probably took the hit intentionally to give her a bit of extra momentum.

I roll, and her blade digs into the grass where my head was seconds ago.

My leg swings around, and I manage to kick her hard in the face as Guys scrambles just ten feet away for the gun. I aim another kick at Zurie's throat, but she manages to duck it. As she recovers, she puts some distance between us.

Good.

This is my chance.

I swing the chains at Guy, aiming for his gut. Instead, they smack against his knee, and it throws him off balance.

Damn.

To my delight, the remote shakes at his hip, and I realize it's about to fall.

Things didn't go as planned, but I can use this to my advantage.

Gritting my teeth, using whatever strength I have left, I do it again. The chains sail through the air, and I hit the remote just as he grabs the gun. The remote flies into the air and skids along the dirt only ten or so feet away from me.

I lean forward, trying to get onto my feet and run for the remote.

But Zurie is just a hair faster.

Her dagger comes again toward my face, and as I lean backward to avoid it, the blade slices my cheek. My face stings, but I have worse things to deal with right now.

Guy stands, the gun once more in his palm as he raises it towards Zurie. She stands, leaning on the balls of her feet as she tries to figure out which way she needs to roll to avoid the bullet.

With Zurie occupied, I scramble toward the remote. A gunshot echoes through the air as he fires. The idiot should have waited to get a better shot. As I get closer to the remote, I peek over my shoulder to find Zurie holding her arm.

He just got her bicep. That's not going to slow her down.

As I rush across the forest floor, Zurie looks at me. An expression of dread washes over her face as she realizes what I'm doing.

Ha.

Took her long enough to figure out my plan.

"The remote!" she shouts.

"Yeah, I'm not falling for that," Guy says, his finger on the trigger as he aims again for her face.

Zurie scoffs in annoyance, like he's a bothersome insect and not a brutal murderer currently holding a gun to her face. "Idiot. Don't let her—"

I get to my feet, running the last stretch of the way toward the remote. I lift the cuffs above my head as I near it and slide on my knees, the little black rectangle finally in my reach.

"No!" they both scream in unison, and I hear them scrambling over the dirt behind me.

Too late.

I bring the cuffs down hard on the remote, shattering it.

The iron orbs hiss and pop apart, and I breathe a sigh of relief as tension lifts from my shoulders, my chest—from everything.

The restraints are off, and even though I'm not at full power, I won't be bound any longer.

I glare at Guy and Zurie over my shoulder, smirking with magic and energy as white light dances over my skin. I don't even try to control it. This close to death, after this many close calls, I need all the fuel I can get. I'm seconds from passing out again, and I won't let anything hold me back.

Not now.

In the past, I would have taken them both on by myself, mostly out of pride. But I'm not alone anymore.

Though I don't have much energy to my name, I fire a thin ray of white light into the sky.

A beacon.

My men will come.

I notice something shift in Guy's expression. I can't quite pinpoint it—something between determination and fear. His back arching defiantly, he crushes the gun in his hand.

Without warning, he shifts. His body blurs and buzzes as his white dragon takes over. The brilliant creature snarls at me, and I figure Guy realized he has a better chance against me as his dragon than as his human self.

It's a smart call actually,

If Zurie notices the subtle shift in Guy, she doesn't seem to care. She watches me, furious, heaving and bloody as she stares. Armed with only a dagger, most would think she had already lost.

But I know her better than that.

Guy's no longer important to me. I fire a blast of energy at Zurie, not bothering with him. She rolls out of the way but only just barely. The blast singes her back, tearing a hole in her clothes as little ribbons of smoke billow from her shirt. As she rolls away, I catch a glimpse of the charred skin along her back as she groans in pain.

I grin in victory, but it doesn't last.

A surge of nausea and dizziness washes over me, and I stagger, leaning against a tree. That one blast of magic took a lot out of me—far more than I realized it would.

The ringing in my ears gets worse. It's so deafening, so overpowering, that I almost can't hear anything else. The explosions near the dojo fade, and the edges of my vision blur.

I don't know how much longer I can stay on my feet. Every second counts.

Across from me, the white dragon opens his mouth. Frost spreads across his teeth as he summons ice.

For all intents and purposes, it looks like he's about to shoot me.

But that doesn't make sense. Since I'm in my human form, that's going to kill me. He has to know that.

Oh.

Oh, crap.

He *absolutely* knows that. He just doesn't care anymore.

At this point, he just doesn't want to die.

That's why he had that strange expression on his face. That was the shift I noticed when I broke free of the cuffs. He realized he was never going to be able to bring me back to Kinsley, that it was an impossible task and one that would kill him if he kept trying. He's given up, and at this point, he just wants out.

I suspect killing me would just be a nice bonus.

Damn, there goes the one advantage I had.

He fires an icy blast into the air, and I barely manage to dart out of the way before it hits. Ice instantly freezes the tree that was behind me, and in the sudden intense cold, the trunk shatters just like my body would have if the blast had hit me instead.

After rolling out of the way, I've changed the layout of our battle. Zurie is now standing between me and Guy, and she dives out of the way as I summon another surge of my magic.

But my body has been pushed to its limits, and my magic is slow to come.

Every burst of power I use from this moment on has to be treated like a bullet—finite ammunition I might run out of at any moment

Every shot counts.

Guy begins to summon another blast of ice magic as I try to recover. I debate firing my own blast at him, hoping I'm strong enough right now to overpower his ice.

But honestly, I don't know if I am, and that's not a risk worth taking.

There's a screech through the air like an incoming missile.

Oh, great. This just keeps getting better.

Caught between the Fairfax traitor and the incoming threat, I have no choice but to look briefly away from him.

In the sky, a black shadow appears in the smoky

night. It's getting closer by the second, but Guy seems too focused on me to notice.

As it nears, I recognize the blue glow of my thunderbird.

I can't help myself. I smile.

Jace careens into Guy just as the white dragon breathes an icy blast. With Guy thrown off balance, the ice beam flies harmlessly into the air above me. It flings a dusting of snow over the four of us.

The two dragons break through the trees, toppling oaks as they duel. Last time they met, both men promised to kill the other—and now it would seem they're going to follow through.

But it's Guy against Jace, and I suspect even Guy knows exactly who will win.

And I'm left with Zurie.

In the splinters and rubbles of the fallen trees, Zurie pushes herself to her feet—battered, bruised, and bleeding.

I do the same, teetering slightly as my world briefly spins.

We tense, ready to kill each other, ready for the day we both said was coming.

Zurie spits blood onto the ground. "It's time we end this, *Little Lorelei.*"

The painful twinge of that long-buried memory

rocks through me, but I don't let the pain linger. I square my shoulders, my magic rippling across my skin as my dragon fights to stay conscious.

"Yeah," I say with a small nod. "I think it's time."

CHAPTER THIRTY-EIGHT

As distant explosions rock the ground, Zurie and I study each other.

We're both wounded, both brutal, and both thirsty for blood.

I want to shift. My *dragon* wants to shift. But that stupid ringing in my ears won't go away. My legs wobble slightly from the battle thus far, from the trauma and wounds I've sustained. Blood trickles down my shoulder. My fingertips go numb, tingling from the blood loss.

But I don't have any other choice. It's not like we can pause our battle to go get some gauze and medical tape.

Zurie attacks, her knife glinting in the orange haze that wafts overhead, and I run on instinct to survive. I lift my arm and block her, letting her forearm slide across mine as I elbow her in the face.

Magic burns along my skin, and I ache to let it free. It has to be strategic, though. I need to make this count. I'm almost positive I have only one surge of energy remaining, and whatever I do, I cannot miss. White light shimmers along my forearms, building in momentum.

I just have to make sure I don't die while it builds.

Zurie pivots, her blade swinging at my throat. I lean back and grab her arm, resting a bit of my weight on her while I pivot on the ball of my foot and kick her broken wrist.

She grimaces in pain and drops the dagger. I grab it midair, snatching it before it can even hit the ground.

Without missing a beat, I swing at her. She ducks, the painfully sharp blade slicing off a bit of her hair as she barely avoids a devastating blow.

Again and again, I dive for her.

Swinging.

Jabbing.

Stabbing.

And *missing* every time.

Her dark eyes are focused on me as she pivots and parries the blade. She lifts her arms, blocking my next blow. Her right arm wraps around mine, careful to avoid her broken wrist. Her left hand grabs the wound in my shoulder and squeezes. Hot blood bubbles out of me as she presses her thumb into the injury, and I bite back an agonized scream.

I manage to grip the knife through her attack, but only barely. I almost drop it, and just to spite her, I push through the pain and kick her sharply in the gut.

She doubles over, but Zurie is never out for long. She recovers quickly and kicks my feet out from under me.

I fall with the knife still gripped tightly in my hand, and I nearly land on the blade. I barely twist my body in time to avoid a dagger to the gut.

Unfortunately, that means I lose my hold on it.

She grabs my wrist and kicks me hard in the knee. The shockwave of the blow loosens my grip despite how hard I cling to the hilt, and I fall to the ground. She kicks me hard in the gut, tossing me back across the dirt and leaves.

Damn it, she's armed again.

I grimace, my hands unconsciously holding my stomach as I try to recover. Black and white dots flutter through my vision, threatening to knock me out cold.

That was a hell of a blow.

It's hard to focus on anything but Zurie. She's such

a brilliant fighter that it takes all of my focus to just not die.

I'm mostly aware of the war around us. Of the bloodshed and the men yelling for backup in the distance. The soldiers screaming for anyone who can hear them to help as gunshots patter through the air.

I need to end this. I can't let it go on any longer.

Reaching deep within, I try to shift again. My dragon leans in to me, battered yet willing, but we're both stretched to our limits. We're moving slowly, slower than either of us want to move right now.

The connection starts to build. We start to blur and fuse, but Zurie charges again, and the moment's gone.

My former mentor sneers as she swipes in my face, missing me by barely an inch.

"Look at what you've done," she says, breathing heavily. "Look at all the blood on your hands."

I duck, avoiding three consecutive blows in a row, barely listening even as she tries to goad me.

"Do you know what I've had to do?" she snaps, driving the blade into my bicep.

I grimace, punching her hard in the throat as she pulls the blade out of me to attack again.

She coughs, sputtering, staggering backward as she glares at me and holds her one good hand to her throat as she recovers. "You know the favors I've had to cash in? The money I've spent just to *kill* you?"

"Do I care?" I ask, shaking out my hands, ready for more.

"No, of course not," she says, spitting blood onto the ground as she violently stabs the blade at my face, missing by an inch. "You only ever cared about yourself."

I reach for the blade, and my fingertips brush the hilt a she pivots away from me. "I only cared about escaping you. You were the one who wanted me to be your pet. Your assassin for hire. Your *legacy*," I add with a mocking sneer.

I am so sick of this woman's hypocrisy.

"And look what it got you," she snaps, dragging the blade across my forearm. I wince as blood pools along my skin, dripping down my arm from the gash, but I won't let it stop me.

"I have a *family*," I snap. "A team of people who love me. I'd say it got me pretty far, thanks."

"You think they're safe?" she says, scoffing. "You think they're even alive? You're the only one left, Rory."

I laugh dryly. "You don't know my men."

"I do know your sister," Zurie says, the corner of

her mouth curling into a sinister smile. "She's dead. I saw to that."

"You weren't fast enough. I saved her." I say, circling Zurie as she gauges me, sizing me up, trying to figure out where she's going to attack next.

"Not possible," Zurie says with a confident shake of her head. "No one comes back from a wound like that."

I know she's goading me, but I can't fight the pang of dread and trepidation that she might be right.

I grit my teeth and fight through it, trying to shake the thought from my head so that I can focus. I won't let her distract me, not now, not with everything at stake.

"I have six hit squads in the fray," she says, pausing to wipe my blood from the blade onto her shirtsleeve.

How interesting.

This is a tactic I've seen her use before, albeit not often. Now and then, when she's backed into a corner, she will compile every power move she knows. Wiping my blood onto her clothes is supposed to make me feel insignificant and disposable. Talking about all the ways she's planning to kill me, all of the backup plans she has in place—that's supposed to make me feel hopeless.

I don't think she realizes how much I hate her.

"All six of those hit squads have just one purpose," she continues, her dark eyes narrowing. "To kill the six of you. What are six people against thirty Spectres?" she asks, pausing as we slowly circle each other, as if she expects me to fill in the silence with an answer. "None of you will survive this fight, Rory. Not even if you kill me."

"*When* I kill you," I correct her. "Your squads won't stop us."

"No?" she asks, shaking out her shoulders, her chilling grin never once fading. "Then how about the sleepers? The ones I have in the Knights? All of the Spectres hidden throughout the woods—the ones who have snuck into the dojo, the ones who will strike in your sleep."

Well, shit. I sure hope *that's* a bluff.

She swipes at me again, and I dodge it effortlessly, grabbing her wrist and twisting. I nearly snap it, but she knees me in the back, freeing herself with seconds to spare.

I stumble forward, falling against a tree as my wounds continue to bleed. I really hoped they would have clotted by now, and it's a terrible sign that they haven't.

Come on, baby dragon, I say inwardly. *We need to shift.*

And we really do. I'm running out of energy, and I think at this point only my dragon can save us.

She leans into me again. She's trying.

Really trying.

My magic pools in my fingers, but at this point, I'm not even sure if I can access it. My head spins, the world tilting as Zurie stalks toward me. Darkness bleeds into my vision, clouding the edges and obscuring my periphery.

I try to access my magic anyway. Fueled by my rage. By my anger. By my hatred. By my pain. Fueled by all the ways Zurie has tried to break me.

"There are a half-dozen backup plans strung together to ensure none of the six of you survive this fight," Zurie says as she stalks toward me, slower than I expected but still standing strong despite all her wounds and broken bones. "In fact, here's one of them," she adds, pulling a detonator out of her pocket and lifting it into the air.

She sneers and presses her thumb against the button.

But nothing happens.

I grin. "Oh, were you referring to those explosives down by the water?"

Her smile falls, and she tosses the detonator aside like it's garbage.

Like she's not devastated it didn't work.

Like she wasn't counting on it, when I know she was.

I stand, my shoulders squared. "You don't scare me anymore, Zurie. You used to have so much sway. So much control over me. But I'm stronger than you now. The magic helps, sure, and the dragon, yes, but most of all I'm stronger than you because you have to do everything alone. That's your weakness. Not mine."

"Even if you all kill me, the Spectres will never stop," she snaps. "Diesel hates you just as much as I do."

"It *will* stop," I correct her, balling my hand into a fist. "Because I won't stop with you. I'll annihilate the Spectres. I'll kill Diesel. Everything you've built, I'll destroy."

"I won't let you have the chance," she says, her grip tightening on the blade in her hand.

She attacks me furiously, done talking—and that's fine. She and I have nothing left to say to each other.

We fight, the blade whizzing through the air as we steal it from each other and dodge each other's blows —one after the other after the *other*.

I can feel my dragon burning with hatred within me, aching to kill the woman who has threatened everything we care about and everyone we love.

A surge of adrenaline pumps through me, a second wind of sorts, as I realize I can finally be free of her. I can really do this. I can take down the woman who has tried to cripple me from the start.

Zurie stabs me twice in quick succession, the blade ripping deep into my side.

As pain splinters through me, I yell, fighting through the agony and reaching into the depths of my soul for the last reserves of my energy.

And as I yell, it becomes an ear-splitting roar.

My dragon leans into me, and the two of us finally fuse. I shift, my brilliant scales glimmering in the low light as my hands become talons that press deep into Zurie's chest.

I lean forward, the shift happening too quickly for her to move out of the way.

As I roar into her face, magic burns in my throat, powerful and deadly—an unstoppable force.

My former mentor looks up at me, and in that moment, I see her resign herself to death. I see the fire and fight leave her eyes, and it's strange. I've never seen her calm before. I've never seen her surrender.

She knows the fight is done.

The magic is too powerful to contain, even if I wanted to. I let loose the fearsome blast aimed right at her, not even giving her a chance to even breathe one last breath before she dies.

Blinding white light decimates the forest around me, illuminating everything for a few breathless moments. I can't even see anything but the brilliant white, and when the light does finally fade, only a charred black crater remains beneath me.

Nothing of Zurie is left. Even the blade is gone, just like her legacy.

There's nothing to remember her by but my scars, and I'm fine with that.

Panting, I teeter, my head still spinning. My body bleeds, even as a dragon.

As I regain my balance, I stare at the charred earth beneath me. Part of me mourns the woman who raised me. But she came here to kill everything I love, and that's not something I could ever forgive.

But she's gone.

Zurie is finally gone.

I roar into the sky, partially in victory and relief, partially from all of the pain rattling across my body and, just the tiniest part of me, in grief.

CHAPTER THIRTY-NINE

Even with Zurie dead, I can't linger here.

It doesn't matter how wounded I am. How battered. How bruised. My men and my sister are still in danger.

Exhausted and struggling to stay conscious, I take to the sky. I beat my wings on the air, my claws digging into trees as I pass, doing anything I can to get airborne.

Once I'm in the sky, flying low over the canopy, I carry myself back toward Jace, listening to the pulse of him in my heart. The sensation leads me to him and lets me know he's still alive.

It gets stronger the closer I get.

As I fly, a blast of electricity cuts through the air, laced with a brilliant blue glow.

Jace's magic.

Afterward, the forest goes eerily silent.

Too silent.

As I approach the source of the blast, I land, taking down a tree as I skid across the ground, not really caring about grace or elegance as long as I can get to Jace.

As long as I can help.

Through gaps in the trees, I spot my thunderbird in a clearing. He stands over a white dragon's body, his chest and wings heaving as he breathes heavily, gasping for air.

I charge through, taking down another couple of trees on my way. They splinter and snap, falling to the ground, and he looks at me over his shoulder with murder in his eyes.

But this is Jace.

My Jace.

He would never hurt me.

I limp toward him and, as I reach him, lean my head against his. It's an act of comfort, of soothing. For a moment, he's stiff and still, but as I lean into him, he nuzzles back. His wing wraps around me as our connection opens, and blurred emotions of bloodlust and concern for me bleed through.

I sigh, giving in, and I don't even try to mask the

relief that bubbles deep within me— the relief I know he can feel.

We're both so tired, so pushed to our limits, that we can't even form words.

I look down at Guy, his body stiff and still, his wings draped over his stomach as his head cranes back at an unnatural angle. His body smokes slightly, and from here, I can see the hole cut clear through his stomach from Jace's blow.

He's dead.

I snort, white sparks fizzling from my nose as I glare at the asshole.

Serves him right.

Even though I can barely stand up, a gnawing worry eats at my gut. I nudge Jace and nod back to the dojo. *Where are the others?*

Under heavy fire, he admits, chest still heaving as he leans into me for support. *I barely made it out. Took a lot of blows and it hurt like hell, but I had to.* He growls possessively, wrapping his wing around me. *We need to get back to help them.*

Even as I hold Jace, trying to recover in this brief moment of respite, I snarl at the idea that anyone would dare hurt my men.

Time for those bastards to die.

Together, Jace and I take to the sky. Dawn cuts

along the horizon, bleeding red and yellow into the dark blue night as the sun chases away the stars.

As we fly, I survey the ground below us. Most of the fires are now smoldering ruins, nothing but towers of black smoke as the last bits of kindling burn away.

Though the sky had been full of dragons, it's now clear. Instead, dragon corpses lay across the ground, still as death. With every body I pass, all I can think is the same thing over and over.

Zurie did this.

Zurie did this.

We soar toward the dojo ruins, and calling the rubble a ruin is honestly being a bit generous. Half of it is destroyed, nothing but piles of cracked rock. An orange glow fills dozens of the windows as fires continue to rage inside, and the roof collapses as we fly closer. Black smoke billows into the air as uncontrolled flames lick the timbers.

Dojo soldiers circle the center courtyard and the south fields, and it would seem that Harper's arrival did in fact change the tides of the battle.

Russell is *never* going to live that down.

Men kneel in even lines across the field and courtyard, their hands on their heads as they surrender. Several jet-black Vaer dragons snarl as dojo dragons roar back at them, trying to get them to cooperate. One particularly feisty Vaer gets a clubbed tail straight to his skull. He snarls, shaking his head in pain but shifts to his human form and kneels with his hands on this neck.

One by one, the Vaer and the Knights surrender.

I do not, however, see any Spectres.

Black trucks rumble up the roads, bypassing the debris and downed dragons, and I figure those must be prison trucks here to take the captives of war away, since the dojo lays in ruin.

There's no sign of Drew, Tucker, or Levi. I snarl anxiously.

I spot Harper patrolling the south fields, her soft lilac scales impossible to ignore. But Jace banks toward the center courtyard instead, and I follow.

As we near, the same lines of surrendering prisoners fill the courtyard, and dojo dragons circle above or stand guard on the walls. Jace angles downward, and I brace myself for impact.

There isn't much space for me to land, and I do my best as my claws drag along the black stone. I wobble a little from inexperience and exhaustion, but no one seems to notice or care. I scan the prisoners as they glare at me, most of them peeking up even as their hands remain glued to the back of their heads, and I wonder what will happen to them. I wonder if they'll comply or if, as Russell said, they'll resist.

A familiar golden thunderbird circles overhead, the yellow glow of his magic still bright even as the sun dawns. He angles toward us, barreling into the courtyard at breakneck speed.

Toward me.

Jace instinctively steps in front of me, his wings spread in defense and warning.

Not to be outdone, Russell snarls, warning Jace to step aside without uttering a single word.

I growl, the sound fierce and unafraid as I snap at the air, not really in the mood for either of them.

Russell lands, the ground shuddering as his claws dig into the black rock. He snorts in anger, a surge of yellow light shooting from his nose.

He forcefully presses his forehead against mine, and as the connection opens, I push back. A flurry of anger surges from him into me.

I told you not to fight, he says, furious.

I snort, sparks and magic curling on my breath as I'm pushed to my limit, to the depths of how much I'm willing to put up with.

Almost too exhausted for words, I spread my wings and stomp my claw into the ground. The rock cracks under the force, and a burst of energy radiates in every direction. Sparks fly on the ripple of magic. It knocks over several pillars nearby, the rocks tumbling to the ground from the sheer force.

I am not in the mood, I warn.

In my periphery, Jace stands a little taller, his wings tucked to the side as he watches me proudly.

Russell stiffens, and I figure he's trying to figure out if that's a challenge to his authority. In the end, he wisely lets it go.

Did you find any Spectres? I ask through the connection, eager to get on with this and change the topic.

He leans back, breaking the connection and watching me from the side of his eye. For a moment, he doesn't answer, and I wonder if he even will. But after a pause, he simply nods.

I let out a sigh of relief. Thank goodness.

He brushes my wing with the tip of his to open the connection again in a less threatening way this time.

They're taken care of, he says simply.

Good, I say, nodding. *Irena—*

Is with the nurses, recovering, he interrupts, looking around and surveying the damage surrounding us as he speaks. *She will limp for a while, but she will be fine.*

And Eric? I press.

Russell growls angrily, his lip curling as he snarls. A flood of grief comes through the connection in the moments before he snaps his wing away to break our link. He surveys the sky, unable to talk. I suspect he's trying to hide the raw emotion, but I already felt it.

I hang my head, my heart shattering.

He's... he's dead.

I pinch my eyes shut in grief. For him. For the dojo. For Russell. For Jace.

But mostly for Irena.

Eric is dead—the one man she started to open up to. The one man I could see her really falling for.

Dead.

I snarl in anger, my rage and hatred burning again in my throat. I want to burn the energy off, but I can't yet. We're not done.

Not caring for protocol or courtesy or good manners, I brush my wing against Russell's to once more open the connection. *Zurie said she had sleepers in here within the Knights and—*

We found them, he interrupts, his gaze shifting toward me as his eyes narrow.

I lift my chin, not quite believing him, but Russell has surprised me before. I simply nod. *Good.*

Movement in the corner of my vision catches my attention, and I look over as Tucker runs toward me from the open front doors of the destroyed building.

Drew and Levi fly over the burning roof toward us as well, landing with thuds and nuzzling me in gratitude.

All at once, the connections open. I'm flooded with relief. Affection.

Love.

In the past, I would have shied away from it, the sensation too intense to really consider or indulge. But right now, after everything we've endured...

I send love right back.

With Jace, Drew, and Levi around me, Tucker has to elbow his way through.

"Yeah, I'm not a big, fat dragon, but geez, give me a bit of space, will you?" he says, nudging Levi playfully in the shoulder.

I laugh, the hot air rolling through my nose as I brush my forehead against his, just grateful they're all alive.

"Let go of me!" someone shouts.

I look over my shoulder to find a Knight being brought in across the bridge, his hands bound behind his back as he fights the dojo soldier carrying him toward Russell.

The dojo soldier is in human form, wearing loose shorts and nothing else as he pushes the man to his knees in front of Russell.

Tucker stiffens, stepping in front of me and squaring his shoulders. "Brett."

"Tucker," Brett says, sneering.

Ah, this is Brett Clarke—the General's new favorite.

"You're wasting time," Brett says to Russell, scowling. "Just kill me. The General won't negotiate with the likes of you, and he won't take me back. He will think I've been compromised," he adds with a hate-filled glare at Tucker.

I figure the policy on accepting prisoners of war back into the Knights has changed since Tucker sided with me.

Tucker scoffs. "Dragons aren't that cruel, Brett."

"What, you think they're going to put me up in a nice hotel? I'm a dead man, Tucker. Don't delude yourself to help you sleep better at night."

"I sleep fine, thanks," Tucker snaps. "They're not going to kill you just because of what you are. You're a prisoner, yeah, but as long as you comply, you don't die. Don't do anything stupid, and you won't go to your maker." Tucker pauses, giving Brett a once-over. "Yet."

Russell huffs impatiently, a not-so-subtle order for everyone to shut the hell up.

He takes a few steps toward Brett, lowering his

head and baring his teeth as Brett lifts his chin defiantly, glaring at the dojo master.

The shifter he's been sent to kill.

The two watch each other for a moment, two leaders facing off, with one of them as the clear victor.

I suspect that's all Russell wanted—to remind Brett that he lost. To remind the Knights who's in control.

Russell lifts his gaze to the dojo soldier behind Brett and briefly nods, turning his back on the Knight as if he's not a risk. As if he's nothing to be concerned with any longer.

Of everything in this interaction, I would say that simple movement—that simple act of turning his back on the enemy—was the most wounding of all.

For all his fire and fight, Brett is left utterly speechless. Two dojo soldiers grab him by the arms and lift him to his feet, yanking him backward over the bridge and toward the prison trucks.

As Brett is shoved into the nearest truck, he looks over his shoulder one more time. I expect him to glare at Tucker or Russell, but he watches me instead with a strange expression. It's a blend of curiosity and confusion, with maybe a bit of hope.

Jace growls behind me, interrupting my thoughts. Drew and Levi follow suit, the three of them curling their necks and leaning against me again, growling in victory and relief as our connections reopen. Tucker joins in, wrapping his arms around my head as he holds me close.

These men—they're going to make me blush, giving me all this attention.

Ah, who am I kidding? I love it.

In all this chaos, I was deeply worried I might lose them. With Zurie after us, I feared she would take one of them from me.

But we won, and she failed.

In the flurry of joy and love that blurs through the connection we share in this moment, I allow myself to simply enjoy them. To celebrate.

To give in to these men who changed me.

CHAPTER FORTY

Exhausted, bruised and bloody, I let the nurses patch me. There's not enough room in the infirmary to house all the injured and all those on death's door. So, after I'm suitably bandaged, I'm sent up to my room.

I want to help, but since I can barely see straight, much less dress a wound, I'm ushered out fairly quickly. There's morphine and lots of sleep involved, and I wake as the last rays of sun appear over the mountains beyond the dojo.

Dressed, bandaged and still slightly drugged with just enough medication to cut through a bulk of the pain, I wander through the halls in the medic ward once again, this time looking for Irena. I peek into her room, but to my surprise, it's empty.

I frown, my intuition flaring. The bed is unkempt, but the bathroom is empty.

She's gone.

I stiffen, a surge of adrenaline shooting through me as I wonder if a Spectre slipped past Russell and got in here. I draw the gun at my waist, ready to kill someone, ready to break down doors and kick some ass.

But then I notice the note on her pillow. I grab it, unfolding the paper with one hand as I holster my gun.

Irena's handwriting scrolls across the page, and for a moment, I simply stare at it. The two little words written across the sheet carry so much weight to them.

I can't, it says.

She can't handle the pain.

She can't handle being in the space where she met Eric.

She can't handle being this raw.

She can't handle the grief.

So, she's running away from it all, running instead toward her perceived purpose—her mission to destroy the Spectres.

And she's doing it alone.

I crumple up the note in my hand, furious that she

would leave. Livid that she would go injured into battle right after we just came out of one.

The anger burns in my chest, simmering and smoldering, and my body buzzes with a sudden need to shift—the sudden need to burn off this energy in any way I can.

I suck in a deep breath through my nose, rooting my feet to the ground and shaking my head as I try to soothe myself. To calm down.

The surge of fury fades, and I once again look at the crumpled note in my hand.

Irena touched this. Wrote on it. Left it as her final message for me. In many ways, it's the last thing I have of her.

I smooth it out against the bed, doing my best to ease all the creases in the page. I lean my hands on either side of the paper, my palms resting against the mattress as I just stare at the two simple words.

I can't.

With a deep sigh, I fold it neatly and tuck it gently into my pocket.

My brain buzzes with disbelief as I walk through the hallways, feeling like a lone ship in the ocean of chaos as the world buzzes around me. I retreat within, a little aimless as I walk outside, surveying the wreckage of this once-beautiful embassy yet again.

The piles of rock. The hole in the roof. The streaks of soot along almost every window, the stone charred from the flames.

In the center of the courtyard, I pause, turning in a slow circle as I take it all in.

Up on a nearby hill, I see a familiar blonde sitting on a boulder, the wind kicking up her hair as she stares out over the dojo wreckage as well.

Harper.

I take my time climbing the small mountain, and after about twenty minutes, I join her on the overlook. We stand there together in silence and mourning as we watch the soldiers try to reclaim and recover what they can.

Without saying a word, I set my hand on her shoulder in comfort. In solidarity.

She and I—we're in this together.

For a moment, she doesn't move, and I wonder what she must be feeling. What she must be going through.

A second later, she sets her hand on mine and looks over her shoulder at me. Her face is numb, her eyes dazed and distant.

"This means war," she says calmly, as if it's the only thing she's thought about since the battle faded. "War with the Vaer. It changes everything."

"Apparently, it was supposed to be a silent snatch-and-grab," I say. "All they wanted was me, and it went horribly wrong."

"That it did," she says sadly.

"Harper, listen," I say trailing off, trying to find the words. "I'm sorry. This—"

"No, it's not your damn fault!" she snaps, her eyes narrowing in annoyance. "They came for me, too."

I shake my head. "If I'd left—"

"I wouldn't have let you," Harper interrupts again. "And neither would Russell."

"That's true," I admit, more than a little grateful for my friends. "Well, if this war is really coming, Harper, you have at least one ally."

A small and grateful smile breaks across her numb expression, and she looks back out over the ruins of the dojo.

"We're not staying here," I say, crossing my arms.

"Well, yeah, it's in ruins," she says with a shrug. "You'll stay at the capital."

"No," I say simply.

She glares at me over her shoulder. "What are you talking about?"

"We've put enough pressure on you," I say, knowing she will take the hint. "We'll leave."

"It's not safe, and we won't let you."

"You're not *my* Boss," I say with a smirk.

Her nose wrinkles slightly in annoyance. "I don't care. Let me help you, Rory."

"If you want to help me, then help me find Ashgrave," I counter.

"Ah." Her expression shifts, and after another moment, she nods in understanding.

She gets it.

The two of us survey the damage in silence, and the more I take in, the more it fuels the smoldering rage that has become a constant in my core. Even Zurie didn't realize how dangerous this war is that she started.

I don't care. I'm going to finish it, one way or another. For Harper. For Jace. For the dojo dragons who risked their lives for us. For all of the dragons I adore.

The sad fact is that this world doesn't want me in it. I tried too long to make them leave me alone.

That doesn't work, and it never will.

It's time for me to fight back and carve a place for myself on a planet that's actively trying to kill me.

There's no more shadows, not for me. No more hiding. There's just the sun and the sky.

And the furious dragon-fire raging in my core.

CHAPTER FORTY-ONE

A week after the battle for the dojo, I lean my head back into the steaming water raining down from the massive showerhead in the ceiling of an ornate mansion. The walls around me are covered in granite with flecks of gold leaf embedded in the stone, and it's almost hard for me to believe such an opulent mansion is ours for the taking.

Drew secured this safehouse for us, and we'll use this as home base for the time being.

Until his dad finds it, of course, but we have a little while before that happens.

I run my hands through my wet hair, relishing the hot water as it rolls over my skin. Beyond the dojo walls, I'm exposed. Every move has to be careful and calculated out here.

That's why it's all the more important that we find Ashgrave.

In the bedroom beyond this lavish master bath, the mattress creaks. It's the slightest hint of a sound, but I pause, listening as my senses tune to the world outside the shower.

Someone's there.

I turn off the water and wrap a towel around me, trailing little puddles of water as I step into the bedroom.

Drew is stretched out across the bed, one leg propped as he leans his head on his fist. His eyes rove over me, a ravenous expression on his face.

"I know you just got clean, but do you want to get dirty again?" he asks, a devilish grin on his face.

I laugh, and just to mess with him, I drop the towel to the floor.

His eyebrows shoot up his forehead, and I'm sure he thinks he's about to get lucky. I lean across the mattress, pressing my palms into the blanket as I gently walk my hands across the sheets—only to grab my shirt and the jeans lying in a pile beside him.

I wink and retreat, starting to get dressed as I throw the shirt over my head.

"Mean," he says, his voice a dark growl.

"You like it," I say, grinning.

"I really do." His eyes rove over me again as I tug on some fresh underwear.

He pushes off the bed and comes over, kissing my shoulders as his hands weave their way down my waist. He fights with my grip on the jeans, trying to block me from buttoning my pants.

I laugh, smacking his hands away, and he groans in disappointment as I zip them up.

We walk into the hallway and out into the sunken living room in the luxurious center of the house. The vaulted ceilings climb almost two stories in the air and end in a glass atrium that lets in the brilliant sun above us.

Levi and Tucker look over their shoulders as they sit on the couch watching TV, both of them grinning in welcome as we approach.

I scan the room, wondering where my thunderbird is. "Where's—"

Soft footsteps interrupt me, and I turn around just as Jace wraps a possessive arm over my shoulders and kisses my hair roughly.

"Present and accounted for." He grins, looking at Drew, and less than subtly drags me away. "Dibs."

Drew snorts and grabs my waist, throwing me over his shoulder as he carries me away from the former dojo master. "Nope."

I laugh, wriggling out of Drew's grip and sitting instead in an overstuffed chair nearby, smiling as they joke like brothers.

My men. I love them.

It's nice to see them relaxed, if only for a time. With the world after us, dragon and human alike, we won't get much peace in the near future.

But for now, for this moment, I can enjoy what we have.

Each other.

That's more than enough.

Rory, Levi, Tucker, Drew, and Jace will return in *Fall of Dragons*, coming soon.

Join the exclusive, fans-only Facebook group to get release news & updates.

Read on for a special note from the author.

AUTHOR NOTES

Hey, babe!

I love this book with a ferocious passion.

There was so much to say. So much to tell you. So much growth and change in all of our characters. I fell even more in love with Rory. With Tucker. With Levi. With Drew. And, yes, with Jace—his growth and change in this book was probably my favorite.

This book has filled my heart, and I'm so grateful I got to share it with you.

Rory has opened her heart in so many ways, and we really got to see that change firsthand. There were so many times when we got to see her react in a way that's stronger and more emotionally powerful than who she was at the beginning of book one.

I mean, Rory was always a badass. Don't get me wrong. But in this book, we get to see her be not just a badass, but a strong woman who is stepping into her own.

After all, she's stepping out of the shadows—and carving a place in the world for herself and her loved ones. No more trying to hide.

In *Reign of Dragons,* for the first time in her life, she defied her master.

In *Fate of Dragons,* she learned how to give up a bit of control. How to compromise.

In *Blood of Dragons,* she learned what it means to have family. To trust, to let down her guard to her inner circle, and grow as a person.

And in *Age of Dragons,* Rory has finally accepted who she is: a dragon, a warrior, and someone worthy of being loved.

All while remaining her beautiful badass self, of course.

Tucker was such a badass hottie in this book. I mean, he always is, but I loved watching him play with so many guns. Especially while shirtless. He had to deal with the reality that his father wants his woman dead, and we saw him open up to Rory emotionally, too. It's always a treat to peel back the goofball exterior Tucker always shows to reveal the complicated, intricate man inside.

Drew is a powerhouse and always will be, but in this book we also got to see a bit of his vulnerability. His priorities shifted. He realized that protecting Milo wasn't worth it anymore—not that Milo was ever grateful for it.

Levi learned to open up and trust, even going so far as to ask Jace for help reconnecting with his dragon. He's opening up to others, speaking his mind, and showing up as the brilliant strategist he is. In a world that tried to break him, Levi remained his endearing, good-hearted self.

And Jace.

Oh, *Jace.*

Swoon.

The former dojo master finally realized that Rory truly is his equal, in a powerful moment she didn't even register at first. She saved his life when he missed the Spectre hiding in the shadows, and she just shrugged afterward. Now they're partners in crime, together to the end. I love their new dynamic!

As for the universe of the Dragon Dojo Brotherhood? I have absolutely loved diving into and expanding it. There's so much here—so much lore, so many new mysteries to explore, so much to uncover.

In the next few books, we're going to learn about Rory's magic—where it comes from, what her limits are, and if she is, in fact, a god.

Of course, I couldn't play in this world so much if you didn't love reading it.

So, from the bottom of my heart, *thank you.* Thank you a million times over. If I ever get to meet you in person, I'm going to give you *such a big hug.*

You truly are such a gift to me!

I know you're probably chomping at the bit to learn what happens next. To figure out where Irena went, and how her leaving will affect Rory. To learn about Ashgrave, and find out what's left of it—if anything. To learn more about that strange crystal that sucked away Rory's power, and the scream that followed. We both know that wasn't Zurie—so who was it?

With Zurie dead, Diesel is the Ghost. We know he hates Rory and has a soft spot for Irena, but he's a brutal man with ulterior motives. What will happen with the Spectres now?

The Knights are still at large, and the General has to be even angrier now that his joint-force attack on the dojo failed.

The Bosses were quiet in this book, but come on—we know they won't be silent for much longer. They've all been trying to apply political pressure on Harper to get her to give Rory up, but now that Rory is in neutral territory, she's fair game.

And Kinsley Vaer—the Boss of the Vaer family—is through playing games. Guy made it clear that Kinsley wants Rory. Zurie claimed to have tricked the Vaer into declaring war on the Fairfax, but Kinsley is a crafty woman. Are we sure this isn't what she wanted?

My goodness, Rory has a ton of enemies.

Lucky she and her men are such brilliant fighters. They won't let anything come between them. Whatever lies ahead, they're ready.

Are you?

The next book will be available in two short months. Make sure you **join the exclusive, fans-only Facebook group to get the latest release news & updates.**

Until next time, babe!
Keep on being your beautiful, badass self.
-Olivia

PS. Amazon won't tell you when the next **Dragon Dojo Brotherhood book will come out, but there are several ways you can stay informed.**

1) **Soar on over to the Facebook group, Olivia's secret club for cool ladies,** so we can hang out! I designed it *especially* for badass babes like you. Consider this as your invite! We talk about kickass heroines, gorgeous men, our favorite fantasy romances, and... did I mention pictures of *gorgeous men?*

2) **Follow me directly on Amazon**. To do this, **head to my profile** and click the Follow button beneath my picture. That will prompt Amazon to notify you when I release a new book. You'll just need to check your emails.

3) **You can join my mailing list by going to** https://wispvine.com/newsletter/olivia-ash-email-signup/. This lets me slide into your inbox and basically means we become best friends. Yep, I'm pretty sure that's how it works.

Doing one of these or **all three** (for best results) is the best way to make sure you get an update every time a new volume of the *Dragon Dojo Brotherhood* series is released. Talk to you soon!

The Nighthelm Guardian Series

City of the Sleeping Gods

City of Fractured Souls

City of the Enchanted Queen

Demon Queen Saga

Princes of the Underworld

Wars of the Underworld

Sentinel Saga

By Dahlia Leigh and Olivia Ash

The Shadow Shifter

ABOUT THE AUTHOR

OLIVIA ASH

Olivia Ash spends her time dreaming up the perfect men to challenge, love, and protect her strong heroines (who actually don't need protecting at all). Her stories are meant to take you on a journey into the world of the characters and make you want to stay there.

Reviews are the best way to show Olivia that you care about her stories and want other people discover them. If you enjoyed this novel, please consider leaving a review at Amazon. Every review helps the author and she appreciates the time you take to write them.